DATE DUE

A SUMMER IN THE TWENTIES

A Summer in the Twenties

Peter Dickinson

PANTHEON BOOKS
NEW YORK

Library of Congress Cataloging in Publication Data

Dickinson, Peter, 1927-
A summer in the twenties.

I. Title.
PR6054.I35S9   923'.914   80-8652
ISBN 0-394-75186-8 (pbk.)

Manufactured in the United States of America
First American Paperback Edition

Contents

Note for railway enthusiasts

The author is aware that historically the Hull & Barnsley Line (referred to in this book as the Wold Line) crossed the N.E.R. line by a bridge at Eastrington, and that there was no junction.

1

Hendaye, 6th April, 1926

'Everything's changing so fast,' she said. 'Isn't it stunning to wake up every morning and feel that the whole world's brand-new again, a present waiting for you to unwrap it?'

For emphasis she stabbed her foot-long cigarette holder towards the Pyrenees, to declare them part of the present, with the snow-glitter along the peaks a little tinsel to add glamour to the gift.

'It's all yours,' he said, generously including in his gesture not only the mountains but the nearer landscape, and the cubist spillage of roofs down the slope below the terrace and the two crones in black creaking up a cobbled alley, and nearer still the elderly three-piece band nobly attempting a Charleston while their souls still pined for the Vienna Woods, and even the braying group of young French rich, already into their third cocktail at half past three.

She threw back her head and laughed like a boy. Her teeth flashed like the sudden glimpse of brilliance along the wing-front of a White Admiral when it snaps its wings open and shut again. He felt woozy with love for her. Three days ago, when he had first met her, she had seemed to be just the kind of pretty flibber-tigibbet you would expect Bertie Panhard to fill his villa with for Easter. Then chance had paired them in the foursomes against the great Joyce Mallahide and Bertie himself—Mrs. Mallahide ageing now but implacably steady, and Bertie wild with his drives but deadly with his putter. Incredibly the match had gone to the twentieth, with side-bets accumulating which would bite deep into next quarter's allowance. Then she had sliced her drive into the rough, leaving him a foul lie, but he had swung with a sudden exhilarated ferocity as though past and future were pivoting around the instant when the niblick shaft whipped between the coarse tussocks, and he had watched the ball climb endlessly into the blue, curve, fall, bounce twice on the green and trickle over the far lip. She had nodded approval, pursed her lips a little when they found the ball bunkered, but without fuss put him within nine inches of the hole. And at the same time laid Bertie a perfect stymie.

From that moment she had been Artemis, even when her hunting-spears—the golf-clubs—were put away and she had only her cigarette holder to brandish like a ritual dart. And now here they were, the impetus of celebration having lasted through the hours of sleep and whirled them up in her rowdy Frazer-Nash to see the famous sunset, alone together all afternoon apart from the waiters and the band and the braying French.

'But I'm serious,' she said. 'About things changing, I mean. Don't you feel it—since the War, I suppose—how old were you when it ended?'

'Fourteen.'

It seemed another measure of their intimacy that he could answer without stiffness or shame at the introduction of this half-tabu subject, which so permeated the ideas and talk of Father's generation, and his brother Gerald's too, but was so deliberately ignored by his own.

'I was twelve,' she said.

'You don't think people our age have always felt the world was changing, even when it wasn't?'

'Of course they have. But really they knew what was going to happen next week, next year, next . . . what's the word for ten years?'

'Decade.'

'I never went to school, you know. Yes, they knew what was going to happen next decade, who they were going to marry, which house they were going to live in, how they were going to die, even. We don't.'

'I don't care. Now's enough.'

(Oh, the talks with Father over the cigars, and the mapped future, and the painstaking staff-work to ensure that the long campaign of a career should trundle victoriously forward, and produce and rear a fresh generation of Hankeys to inhabit Sillerby and maintain it!)

'That's what I mean,' she said, 'That's what's so stunning. If there's no point in worrying about tomorrow, then you've got to squeeze everything you can get out of today. Thou shalt not waste one instant—that's the first commandment. I bet you hadn't guessed Daddy's a parson.'

'Great Scott!'

'Mummy inherited a shipping line, luckily for me. It'll be mine one day I suppose, and I shall have to start grinding the faces of the workers, except that I'll copy Mummy and pay people to do it for me.'

'But that's tomorrow.'

'Exactly. As a matter of fact I do know who I'm supposed to marry, and where I'm supposed to be going to live, but I bet I don't. So now I'm not even going to think as far forward as the sunset. What shall we do *now*? What would you do, supposing you were alone up here?'

'Climb further up the hill and look for butterflies.'

'All right. I don't know anything about them. You'll have to tell me.'

There were clouds of them in the warmth of the western slopes. The fine spring must have brought on the hatchings. They flickered among the scrub and over the slants of shale like flakes of light. He told her their names—only the common sorts, various blues and coppers and some early orange-tips and painted ladies, and a surprising number of pearl-bordered fritill-aries—nothing that was needed for the Collection. Suppose there had been . . . he had his net and bottle in his satchel and could have taken specimens, and so far he had done only one afternoon's hunting since coming to France. But he sensed her mood, that the butterflies were a part of the whole ecstasy of living in the instant, and that to touch or kill one would have blurred its purity. For once the notion did not seem to him senti-mental.

They wandered to and fro along goat-tracks, then sat on a bank of nibbled grass to watch the sunset. It performed for them as promised, like some grand old actor dying on his sword for the thousandth time in bronze and blood. Then they climbed back down the hill and drove towards the sea down steep white tracks. The air still prickled with the aftersense of heat, but dusk and nightfall drew out fresh scents of growth from the barren-seeming hillsides. Twice she pulled him into caves of shadow under pine trees so they could kiss and fondle for a while, lightly, skimming above the surface of their sensuality like martins fly-catching along a river-reach. They timed it all well and got back to the villa as the gong was sounding.

'That you, Tom?' called Bertie from his "study" at the foot of the stair.

'Hope we're not late. That was only the first gong?'

'Simply stunning sunset,' she added. 'We had to see it all, really we did.'

Bertie lounged out into the hall, already dressed for dinner in the purple jacket which added a characteristic note of near-cad-dishness to his persona, a conscious assertion that he could afford to take the risk, thus making it no risk at all. Despite his taste for rather loud clothes Bertie always looked preternaturally neat and clean, especially when he had changed for dinner. Snub-nosed, large-mouthed, black hair slicked back, skin so smooth and creamy that it might have been painted, he had the perky look of a ventriloquist's dummy or the hero's asinine friend in a comedy thriller.

'Wire for you, Tom,' he said, his grin somehow incorporating both malice and benevolence.

The envelope refused to tear tidily. Minutes seemed to pass before he could scrumple the message free and unfold it.

CAN YOU PLEASE COME HOME STOP SORRY STOP FATHER

He stared at it, quite dazed, so that he was not conscious of having handed it across to her. Bertie craned, unabashed.

'Oh,' she said tonelessly.

'That's a bit rough,' said Bertie. 'Rows with the parents must be hell—we orphans have all the luck. What about it? Going to do what Daddy tells you?'

'Asks, not tells,' she murmured.

(Cyril dead at Polygon Wood, Gerald still quite unpredictable eight years after the Armistice.)

10

''Fraid I must,' he said.

'Right-oh,' said Bertie. 'Too late to book a sleeper, but there's no point—you'll only be two hours later at Dover if Fletcher drives you in to the 6.20 tomorrow morning. I'll fix that now.'

'Thanks,' he said, and went up to dress, not daring to look at her.

He lay in the dark, rotating excuse after excuse to send home, but knowing he would have to go. It had not crossed his mind, even as a wish, let alone a hope or possibility, that she should come to his room, but she did.

2

Sillerby, 8th April, 1926

'Morning, Master Tom,' said Stevens, holding the front door.
'Don't you bother about your traps. Pennycuick and me'll get
that lot in.'

'Thanks. Where's the General?'

'In the Collection Room. We got your wire yesterday, so he'll
be expecting you. Good journey, Master Tom?'

'Fine, thanks.'

In fact in the undiminishing daze of love Tom had barely
noticed the battering French trains, or the crossing, or the
somehow less heavy-breathing English engines. The only part of
the last two days that had been free of the unreality of dream had
been the evening in the Smoking Room at the United
University, spent writing a nine-page letter to Judy. He didn't
go in at once but stood under the portico looking round. Even
Sillerby was less solid than usual. The first faint bloom of weeds
was beginning to show in the sickly rose-beds that ringed the
turning-circle of gravel. The paint was flaking on the billiard-
room window. Usually these dilapidations, and the difficulty of
getting them all attended to with Sillerby's diminished and
increasingly arthritic staff, oppressed him; but in this glittering
noon they became part of his mood, symbols of growth and of
transience, of the need to snatch the instant.

'Any news of Master Gerald?' he said casually.

'Not that I have heard, Master Tom. Still with Miss Nan, I
believe, and doing well as can be hoped.'

'Oh ... Right, I'll go and find the General. That middle-
size case is all laundry so it might as well go straight out to Mrs.

Bird. And I've torn my green plus-fours, so don't hang 'em up.'

'I have a suit of the General's to go to London. I'll send the plus-fours with them.'

'Right oh.'

Climbing the stairs Tom began to realise a mild unease, almost shock, at the news that Gerald was 'doing well'. This was the family euphemism for his not having broken out into some drunken uproar to offend yet another unwilling host, and perhaps even get into the local papers, but being still with his sister Nan in the isolation of her Scottish island. Tom had assumed all through the last two days that the message from Father meant that Gerald had got loose, but now he saw that his reasons for this belief were concerned not with its probability but with the level of family duty involved. It had to be a need of that order to make the parting from Judy tolerable, reasonable, inevitable. As he stood and held the handle of the great mahogany door a weird horror flowed through him—he had been sent for for no reason at all, other than to separate him from happiness. He shook the nightmare from him and pushed the door open.

Like an enormous egg perched on an intricate brass stand, Father's bald and freckled cranium floated above his microscope, exactly as Tom knew from experience he would find him. Lieutenant-General Lord Milford, CB, DSO, at work on his Collection.

'Tom? Be with you in a brace of shakes.'

Nothing seemed changed. Sillerby continued to drag itself out of the dream-world, to assert its absolute and independent reality, by presenting Tom with objects and facets he had known and accepted as the one reality since childhood. Father's tone was exactly what it always was, very level and soft. The Collection Room too had its usual air of permanence. It was a Long Gallery with black linenfold panelling and diamond-paned windows and the portraits of ancestors staring, heavy-eyed with brooding ennui, from beneath obscuring layers of varnish and candle-smoke; but before Tom had been born the collection cabinets had been moved in, fifteen blocks of pale mahogany running down either side of the gallery beneath the portraits, each containing its eighteen glass-topped drawers, four feet wide. Sixteen thousand dead butterflies had taken over from the dead ancestors as the primary occupants of the room.

'Well?' said Father, straightening from the microscope. 'Any luck?'

'Not much, sir. The hatchings were early, but . . .'

'So were you. Quite quite. Nothing at all, then?'

'*Zerynthia rumina*—two very nice ones.'

'A bit out of their range, weren't you?'

'That's what I mean, sir. I was surprised to find them over there at all. And I'm not sure there isn't something a little unusual about the dots on the hind wing.'

'Ah.'

Father was a very old-fashioned collector, displaying only perfunctory interest in matters such as the range and habits of specimens, but any hint of a variation—which might indeed be associated with an unusual locality, was the breath of life to him.

'And I took half a dozen of the spring form of *Pontia daplidice*,' said Tom. 'Isn't one of ours a bit rummy?'

'Yes, I believe you're right. Let's see . . .'

Father moved a few paces down the gallery, did a full knees bend by Cabinet H and pulled out a drawer.

'I think it's the one below, sir.'

'Of course, of course, I'm getting old. Yes, you're right, Tom. One little beggar here's thoroughly strafed. A good 'un would make the set. Excellent!'

He was genuinely pleased—pleased as much at Tom knowing the Collection so well as at this new specimen—but he was also play-acting. If he had nothing on his mind it would be inconceivable that he should pick the wrong drawer. Of course there had been an element of play-acting about the whole expedition—it wasn't a sensible season for bug-hunting in the Pyrenees, but Tom's allowance wouldn't have stretched to the trip, and it was understood that he didn't ask for anything extra. So Father had saved face by forking out from the Collection fund and pretending that Bertie's invitation fitted in neatly with his needs, though they both knew the money was really a reward for Tom's success at Oxford, giving him a chance of a brief holiday before the Finals term. Still, that bit of play-acting was over. There was something else in Father's manner as he brooded for a little at the *Pontias*, then rose, reflexively sliding the drawer shut with his knee.

'Bit early, of course,' he said. 'A lot of 'em won't be hatching for a month. Nothing else?'

'Nothing much, sir. I was planning to wait for a few more days before I started in earnest, but . . .'

'Yes. Sorry about that. Having a good time of it?'

'Oh yes, sir. Very.'

'Ah . . . Met someone?'

('The trouble with Father,' Gerald had once said, 'Is that you keep forgetting how bloody sharp he is. Most of the time you chat away and he's a harmless old buffer who's mad on bugs, and then he lets something slip and you realise he knows exactly what you're thinking about, and like as not every damn thing you've done since he last saw you. We all ought to go down on our knees at night and thank God for putting bugs into the world. If Father had been as interested in us as he is in them we'd be living our lives in glass cases with pins through our abdomens.')

'Well . . . as a matter of fact, yes,' said Tom.

'Care to tell me her name?'

'Judy Tarrant.'

'Of course. Pretty little piece, eh?'

'You know her!'

'Went to her christening. Parents set on having a boy, I remember, but they were issued with a girl. Some reason or other they knew they couldn't produce another one, so they made the best of a bad job by calling her Julyan, with a Y—show she was almost a boy but not quite. Don't know who had the wit to start calling her Judy.'

'She did. She insisted when she was four, she told me.'

'Lot of will-power there—on the mother's side, of course—the father's a holy worm.'

'Judy seems quite fond of him.'

'Of course, of course. Shouldn't have said that. Probably a much more interesting fellow than meets the eye. Often happens when one of a couple makes all the running, you know—turns out the other one's much more worth study.'

'It's extraordinary you should know them, sir.'

'Not as rum as you think. Admittedly that's a cut-off bit of

country down in the Wolds, but it's still no more than the next
Riding. If your mother had been alive you'd have been meeting
young Judy at dances these last couple of years at least. My fault
you don't go to that many, I suppose.'

(There was something unspoken here. It had been Gerald's
behaviour, far more than Mother's death, that had caused dance
invitations to the youngest Hankey to be less than automatic.)

'But still . . .' said Tom.

'Staying with young Panhard, weren't you? First ran into him
at one of Belford's shoots, eh?'

'That's right. I knew him by sight at Eton, but he must have
been three years ahead of me.'

'Well, Panhard's land marches with Rokesley, so it's natural
he should be at the shoot. And Belford's some kind of cousin of
the Tarrants, I seem to remember, and they live only a dozen
miles further on, so it all hangs together. Things mostly do . . .
Tell me, what do you make of Panhard?'

'He's all right.'

'Brains?'

'I don't know. He pretends to be a bit of a silly ass, but he isn't.
Not like Woffles Belford, I mean. He often says quite sharp
things, but usually he sounds surprised about it, as if he'd said
them by accident.'

'Interesting you should say that. Try watching him when
other people are talking . . . In my opinion he's got more than his
share of brains. Not your kind, Tom. He'd never be in line for a
Double First—not the application, but . . . pity in a way he came
into all that money so early.'

'He's very decent about it, sir. Generous, I mean, and he
doesn't put on side at all.'

'Glad to hear it, but that's not what I meant. Hardly know the
fellow, of course, but the couple of times we've met it's struck me
that he's got ambition—more than his share—and nothing to
grind it on. He's not the sort to make a go of politics. Wilming-
ton collared me last year to meet him in York. Idea was to sound
him out about standing as Member for Weighton, but Panhard
turned us down. Gave very good reasons, no hard feelings,
made out he was very flattered and not up to the job and so
on—but my guess is his real motive was he wasn't prepared to

start as low down the ladder as an ordinary County Member. Supposing he'd needed to make his own way a bit more from the beginning . . . see what I'm driving at?'

'You may be right, sir.'

As the words hung in the air Tom realised that he had allowed a note of detachment to infect them. Father of course perceived it at once.

'Don't like me putting your cronies under the lens, Tom?' he said, his voice softer than ever.

'It's all right, sir. We're used to it—and there's no way of stopping you.'

(And better you should be sectioning Bertie's character than Judy's.)

Father loosed the sudden, direct blaze of his stare—a mannerism that often startled strangers—then smiled and glanced down at the twinkling tubes of the microscope. There was no telling whether the smile was an acceptance of Tom's mild impertinence or an intuition of the thought about Judy. Tom waited. Interviews with Father did not normally end in the air.

Behind Father's left shoulder a window opened onto the familiar but always to Tom heart-tightening view of the Home Farm, the line of willow and alder which showed where the river twisted along the valley, the rising fields of Gatting Farm and Hatchers (so disastrously sold by Grandfather) and beyond them the sharp-edged moor. One evening, when Gerald was fresh out of hospital for the first time, Tom—only fourteen then—had found him standing at this window in the dusk with an empty tumbler in his hand.

'Tom? Glad to see you. You'll be able to help me down. Got to get back to bed before Birdie brings my tray up and finds I'm missing.'

'You shouldn't have come up . . .'

'Tosh. What I shouldn't have done is brought the brandy with me. Thought I'd need it. I've been saying good-bye.'

Tom had followed the half-gesture and seen the decanter on Case F.

'I thought you were staying for weeks, Ger.'

'Good-bye for old Cyril. That's what he died for, you know. You don't die for England. You die for a few fields and a slice of hillside. Less, much less. There were chaps in my company who died for one of those bloody little strips of back garden, all dahlias and cabbages, you see from the railway. Question is, can I even stand without something to lean on? No. Put the glass down—don't forget to come back for it or Stevens will lose his rag. And the decanter, of course. Now, if you can get me to the banisters I'll go down the stair on my bum . . .'

To Tom at the time the scene had been mainly embarrassing. He had cringed partly at having to cope with Gerald half-drunk, and partly at hearing speech about the unspeakable. Now the shyness was gone, overwhelmed by the knowledge of tragedy— Gerald's even more than Cyril's—and the tragedy had been given its Sophoclean dimension by the slow discovery that this view—farms, river and moor, represented the England that he too would die for, if the moment came.

'When are you planning to go up?' said Father suddenly.

'Full term starts on the twenty-fifth. I'd meant to settle in on Monday—that's the nineteenth—until . . .'

'Until you met young Miss Tarrant. Sorry about that, Tom. If I'd known, of course, I wouldn't have wired. Any good if I called it off and you went straight back?'

'No, sir. She's got to drive across and join her parents at Marseilles the day after tomorrow. They're on a cruise.'

'Ah well, there it is. She'll be in London for the season, presumably, and then she'll be coming up to Yorkshire I should think. You ought to be able to see quite a bit of her one way and another when you're through your Finals. Meanwhile, if you still go up on the nineteenth that gives us a bit over a week, eh?'

'Yes, sir. What do you want me to do?'

'I want you to learn to drive a train.'

Tom managed to keep his mouth from gaping but he felt his eyes widen. Father looked up, rubbing his hands like a pawn-broker as if to emphasise the profit in his scheme.

'Been reading the papers?' he asked.

'Hardly at all, sir.'

'Coal,' he prompted.

'Oh, I know about the row between the owners and the miners. Didn't the Government hold a Commission or something and get them to agree?'

'Yes and no. Herbert Samuel made some recommendations which the miners would have accepted, but the owners dug their heels in. The whole industry's a bloody great potmess, with a lot of ramshackle old mines which can only keep going if they pay the men starvation wages, and those owners are the ones who've got the whip hand. The Government bought a bit of time with a subsidy to keep them going, but Samuel's plan would have meant closures and amalgamations. I met Ducky Gowling in the Club last week and he told me the owners aren't going to budge, and the subsidy's due to run out at the end of the month.'

'So there'll be a strike.'

Tom was used to Father's precise knowledge of the shifting currents of politics and business, though he appeared to sail those waters hardly at all. It was as though influential men, burdened with secrets, tried to bury some of their hoard in the mind of the eccentric old bug-hunter, knowing that he would not bother to spend it. So Lord Gowling would have told Father what the owners planned, and furthermore Father would have judged correctly whether Lord Gowling was right, and whether the owners would stick to their guns without their nerve breaking.

'Not a strike, a lock-out,' said Father. 'The owners want the men to work longer hours for less pay, and if they refuse they're going to close the mines. That's important, because it's where the trains come in. Last year the Trades Unions got together and passed a resolution that if the miners were locked out the railways wouldn't move any coal. I think they'll stick to that—in fact I think they'll go a good deal further and there'll be a General Strike and nothing will move at all. Steed Maitland tells me that a lot of the Cabinet are spoiling for a fight—Churchill and Hicks, of course, and half a dozen of the others longing to strafe the Bolshie. They'll tie Baldwin hand and foot, so that he can't come on with his famous man-of-peace turn, and that'll force the unions into an all-out strike. I've got a bit of sympathy for the miners and not much for the owners —after all, I know quite a pack of them—but if we let the unions close the country down and keep it closed for a month, we're done for.'

'Bad as that, sir?'

19

'I think so. On the other hand, I don't think they'll last a month, not once they see the strike isn't working. They've got to be shown we can get along without them. It doesn't matter so much what happens in the factories—takes a long time for people to realise how that kind of strike is affecting them—but if a fellow can look up from his allotment and see the six-twenty steaming through . . . you follow me?'

'Yes, sir.'

'This is your chance, Tom.'

The words were almost inaudibly soft, but carried compressed layers of meaning. Cyril was dead, Gerald ruined. The entail by which Gerald would inherit Sillerby would cost too much to break, but it was accepted by all the family, Gerald included, that he would have no children and the male line would continue through Tom. Tom was untested. He had been too young for the war. His achievements—the scholarship to Trinity, the Blue for boxing, the First in Mods—were not the same thing. Father's argument was on the face of it absurd. Tom knew that one or two chaps at Oxford had volunteered last year for some kind of training scheme in case there was a General Strike, but his impression was that it had been what Father would call a pot-mess. So unless ten thousand fathers were having similar talks with their sons this week only a train here and there would be able to run when the railwaymen withdrew their labour. The banner of civilisation would not be the smoke of the six-twenty as it thundered past the allotments but a few rare-seen puffs half way across the county. Still, the emotional logic was too strong for reason. Your Country Needs You. The foreshortened index finger pointed straight at Tom's heart.

'Right oh,' he said, 'I'll drive a train. When's my first tutorial?'

Father rubbed his hands again. Clearly he had it all worked out, and even arranged. Grandfather had spent twenty years on the board of the N.E.R., and Father, though having no official connection, still retained a good deal of family 'pull'. In partic- ular the Shed Manager at Middlesbrough was a chap called Douting, whose sister Rose had been in service at Sillerby until she went into munitions in 'sixteen . . .

Tom divided his mind, as he often did in the duller type of lecture. He was able to absorb what he was told and recall it when he needed to, but at the same time he could think remoter thoughts, thoughts that had the wandering quality of dream.

He remembered Rose, a fierce and dumpy girl who cleaned the first-floor bedrooms and carried on a niggling war with Mother's own maid, the famously neurotic Dora, who had eventually taken one of Father's guns and tried to shoot the butcher's boy at Diggleton for not joining up . . . His eye was caught by an April cloud-shadow swooping along the rampart of the moor. In August he would take Judy up there on the pretext of walking up grouse (they were still too scarce to be worth beating). They might even get a few—she was certain to be a corking shot—she could use Mother's twenty-bore Purdy . . .

'Douting says you're going to have to be a bit canny,' Father was saying. 'He'll pick a fellow who's not that keen on striking to give you a ride or two on the footplate. You won't have to lie, not if you manage it properly. Just don't give your reasons. People don't expect reasons, you know. Much happier without them.'

There was a pause as though the interview had ended and was only waiting for its closing formality—some remark about the weather, or the Collection, or Stevens's latest fit of temper. It came, but in an unexpected form.

'Packet of money there,' said Father broodingly. 'Just the girl, and it's all coming to her.'

3

Market Weighton, 16th April, 1926

'I'm so glad you could come,' she said, separating the words a little as though speaking to a foreigner. 'I was afraid you might have gone up to Oxford already.'

Her postcard throbbed in his breast pocket. His whole urge was to pick her up, to hold her close, to feel their bodies seeming to melt into a unit, but she had taken precautions against such a move. He was ten minutes earlier than she had suggested, but he could see from her half-emptied tea-cup and the subsided centre of the untouched buttered toast that she had already been here some time, and had moreover chosen a place in the almost empty tea-room at which he could only sit opposite her, with the stodgy black oak of the table between them. There was nothing for it but to fall in with her mood. He touched the back of the empty chair.

'May I?' he said.

There was relief as well as formal permission in her smile. As he sat down and looked at her—looked at something other than her eyes and face—he perceived that she was dressed and made up in a deliberately subdued and old-fashioned style. Without quite knowing where the differences of fashion lay he was aware that these were last year's modes, or even the year's before. No doubt some of the cause lay in her having driven over from home; her mother sounded the sort to have intransigent views on how the modern girl should dress; but still she wore the clothes, and was now taking a stubby cigarette holder out of a plain crocodile handbag, in a deliberate manner, as though they were aspects of a role she had herself chosen.

'And what have you been doing?' she said brightly.

22

'Learning to drive a train.'

That made the mask slip, but before he could explain the waitress was at his side.

'Er . . . tea and toast, please. Would you like some fresh tea, Judy?'

She was in profile now, staring through the window at a lorry stuck and throbbing while a drove of sheep from the market surged round it. She shook her head.

'No tea-cakes, sir? Baked on the premises—very naice indeed.'

'No thank you.'

'You ought to have a nice cake, Tom,' said Judy, still looking out of the window. 'I want you to.'

'Oh . . . right oh. I'll have a squint at the cake-tray, please.'

The waitress withdrew.

'Father wouldn't have sent that wire if he'd realised I might be doing anything . . . except collecting butterflies for him,' he said in a low voice.

She swung round from the window and faced him, recovered now, but a little mocking.

'When she's brought your naice cake,' she said. 'we'll talk about that then. Tell me about the trains. Which ones were you driving?'

'Usually the ten-twenty-three from Middlesbrough to Scarborough and the three-oh-nine back. You weren't one of our passengers, were you?'

'That would be one of Worsdell's oh-six-ohs, with Tubby Drake or old Hackby driving,' she said.

'Harry Hackby . . . How on earth . . .?'

'Daddy's loony about railways. All the parsons I've met are loony about something. You couldn't have known. He's got his own locomotive—an incredibly ancient Whitby Bogey four-four-oh built by Fletcher—you're supposed to say Great Scott!'

'Great Scott! Why?'

'It's the last one left. It should have gone to the breakers years ago. It's had about three new boilers.'

'Does it still go?'

'Oh yes. There's a private spur line in the valley which used to serve an old gravel pit. He keeps it in the shed there and drives it up and down the spur. The choirs in our churches come for outings and he takes them for rides, but what he really loves is a dock strike, because then there aren't any goods trains running on the main line between the midnight mail and the milk train, and he goes for what he calls night runs, all the way up to Selby.'

'They let him?'

'It's a wangle. Mummy's got a lot of shares, you see. She'd be on the board if she was a man. Daddy pulls a van with some instruments in it and pretends he's testing the track, but I don't think they pay any attention, really, when he sends the reports in. Anyway, that's how I know about trains. You see, he always rides on the footplate of any train he catches if the drivers will let him, and they usually do, even the London expresses. He used to take me on the local stoppers when I was little. He loves your line—all that reversing at Guisborough and Whitby, and the bell on the Staithes Viaduct. That's where I met old Hackby.'

'I see.'

It seemed incredible that she should have ridden on the same juddering footplate. He wasn't at all sure that the coincidence was a good omen. It seemed such a world away from the hill above Hendaye, and the butterflies.

'Did you do any shunting?' she said.

'I watched it being done. I didn't do much driving, as a matter of fact—I couldn't afford to seem too anxious. I think I could take a train out now along a fairly straightforward line, but shunting looks tricky.'

'Yes, it is. Daddy does it, down in the docks, of course, where the tracks belong to us and they can't really stop him.'

'He must be good.'

'Oh, yes, he's good at *that*. Of course, that's why they both wanted me to be a boy, Mummy because of the ships, and Daddy because of the railway engines.'

The waitress came back with a pot of tea, a plate of steaming toast sliced into triangles, and a wickerwork tray of fancy cakes for Tom to choose from. Without thought he reached for the least fanciful, a plain rock cake knobbed with a few charred raisins.

'No,' said Judy. 'They're quite good but ordinary. Is there one of those yellow ones with a twirl of cream and a nut on top. Yes, there! Have that one, Tom. They're special.'

'Why don't you have it?'

'I daren't any more. It's so unfair. When I was fourteen I could have eaten six of them and not got any fatter, but now . . . I ordered toast because I knew I wouldn't want to eat it. It doesn't seem fair just to order tea. No, really I won't.'

She smiled with such friendliness at the waitress that she conjured an answering smile from the drawn and listless face. The girl poured a cup of tea for Tom and moved away, going out through the shadowy door beyond a rank of gleaming brass bedwarmers that ornamented the inner wall.

'That's a good omen about the cakes,' she said. 'I was worried because the waitress is different, but the cakes are still the same. I haven't been here for . . . what's fourteen from twenty-six?'

'Twelve.'

'Twelve years then. A bit less than that, I suppose, because the War had just begun so it must have been autumn. I had a new Nanny who'd come to us from a family near Haughton. Mummy would never let any of my Nannies stay for more than a couple of years in case I got too fond of them. This one was young and pretty, and once a week when she was supposed to be taking me for a walk a car would be waiting at the bend of the road where it couldn't be seen from the Lodge gates and we'd get in and the man would drive us down here and he and Nanny would hold hands and whisper while I ate as many cakes as I could stuff into myself. I sort of half understood, but not really. I knew he wasn't a servant, or anything like that. In fact he was the father of the family she'd come from—she'd had to leave because his wife had found out about them and made him sack Nanny and promise never to see her again, but he'd managed to find her this job near enough for him to drive over once a week. It didn't last, of course. His wife found out again. She must have been a silly woman because she forced him to choose and he chose Nanny. He was going to marry her, but he got killed somewhere before he could. That's how I know it must have been just when the war was beginning. The wife had written to Mummy of course, so Nanny had left us by then. I don't know what happened to her. She was only with us a few months, but . . . I'm telling you this, Tom, because I want you to understand. This is a between place for me.'

25

'Between?'

'There are places where you do your living, where things happen that belong together and add up in a way you can't get away from. Most places are like that. But there are a few between places, which aren't part of that sum at all. Do you see?'

'I half see, I think. I'm not sure I live my life quite like that.'

'But you understand that I do? It's important, Tom.'

'I understand that it's important. But you'll have to explain a bit more. For instance, was Bertie's . . .'

'Oh no! If you thought that you wouldn't understand at all! Hendaye wasn't, even before . . . They aren't like that, you see. They're small and secret and either nobody knows you're there or nobody knows who you are. You can't make them up. You can't say "This is going to be a between place from now on." You can only find them by accident and realise what they are. This one . . . perhaps it was because it mattered so much to Nanny Brice and the man, it can't matter to anyone else . . .'

'Yes, I see. But I know who you are. Why did you ask me to meet you here? Hasn't that got to be part of the sum?'

'I don't know—I haven't tried this before—using one, I mean —taking it out of between . . . oh, Tom, I wanted to talk to you, but it had to be outside anything that's happened, or anything that's going to happen.'

'Do you want to tell me you made a mistake?'

'Oh, no! But Tom, I want . . . I want to change the rules of the game. I know that's cheating when we've already started, but . . . you do see, don't you?'

'What are the new rules?'

'Well . . . we met at Bertie's. We won the foursome. We drove up into the hills and watched the sunset. We canoodled a bit in the car coming back. Perhaps we'd have fallen properly in love in a few more days, but you got a wire from your father and had to come home. That's all. They're quite easy rules.'

'Easy to understand. Difficult to play.'

She did not answer. He looked at her, but though she met his gaze directly he could read nothing in her eyes, nothing but candour, colourless as air. Her brow was perfectly smooth— what he could see of it under the dark brown cloche—and her lips were a little open, but not to speak or smile. His own mouth, though empty, seemed coated with greasy pulp, and as he looked away he saw that he had been absently munching at the toast the waitress had brought him. One triangle was gone, and the next was in his hand with a moon-shaped bite chewed from it. He put the fragment back on his plate and fretted the tips of his fingers together to rub the melted butter away. Beside that plate was the cake she had made him choose. The crinkled paper cake-cup held a little turret of amazingly yellow sponge, roofed with a baroque twirl of cream with a filbert for finial. It seemed to bulk very large in his vision, though at the same time he was seeing it from a distance as remote as lies between mountains. A hand, his own, moved into the patch of vision, picked up a knife and neatly cut the cake in two. Normal seeing and feeling came back to him as he pushed the plate across to her and raised his eyebrows.

'I think Nanny Brice's dead friend would like you to have some,' he said.

'That's not fair, bringing him in! . . . But all right. You can keep the nut. It's the way the cream goes with the sponge that matters.'

They ate their halves in silence. The sponge was flavoured with orange and with something else he couldn't put a name to, and was extraordinarily light. Without the cream it would have been textureless. She tilted her head to one side as she ate her last mouthful, waiting for his judgment.

'I'd never have guessed to look at it,' he said.

'You haven't eaten the nut.'

'No. If you don't, I don't.'

'All right.'

They were silent again. She began to smile in what he was learning was a characteristic way, self-pleased but oddly mocking—so characteristic, indeed, that it was hard to tell whether it was a signal of some inward thought or a meaningless mannerism. He guessed that the main purpose of their meeting was over, that the 'rules' had been amended and agreed, and that to ask or even to hint at asking whether what the rules governed was no more than a game would be to break those rules. This did not seem to him unfair. If Father had not sent that wire, forcing her hand . . .

'Why trains?' she said, suddenly.

He felt his eyes widen.

'Oh, you mustn't think I'm loony about trains too,' she said. 'In fact I think they're rather a bore. I just know about them because I can't help it, Daddy being Daddy. It seems a funny thing to come home for. I suppose it's so you can help when they have this strike Mummy keeps talking about.'

'That's right. That's why I had to make out to Harry Hackby and the others that I wanted to ride on footplates for the thrill of it. I don't think Harry believed me, but he's not that keen on a strike so the pretence was enough.'

She nodded.

'How soon is all this going to happen?' she asked.

'Next month, if it happens at all.'

'You'll have to come back from Oxford.'

'I don't know. I might find something useful to do down there. I must say, I hope it doesn't happen. With a bit of luck I'm in line for a First and I want to try and make sure of it. Time's awfully short, and I'd planned to use every minute of it, working like blazes.'

'But you'll get it easily, won't you? You're the cleverest person I've ever met!'

She was staring at him, almost amazed. Her reaction seemed wholly straightforward, with none of the play-acting the 'rules' had seemed to demand. For the first time he realised that despite the glamour of her life—travel, and the smartest dances in the season, and familiarity with a dozen night-clubs in London and Paris, and clothes that would have cost him a whole year's allowance—her world was in other ways extremely limited. He did not think of himself as specially clever. In his first year at Eton he had been sent up to the Lower Master for Good Work. He could remember now the long pale face under the mortar-board scanning in a few seconds down his carefully re-copied set of elegiacs, and the rather automatic nod of approval. 'Boys are learning-machines, and you seem to be an efficient one,' the Lower Master had said. Tom still thought it a fair summary, if brusque. When he considered the brilliant men he met every day at Oxford . . .

'That can't be true,' he said, laughing because the idea was too absurd even to be embarrassing. 'You've met Bertie Panhard, for instance.'

'*He's* not clever!'

'He only pretends not to be, and I must say he took me in. But Father said something and since then I've been thinking . . . Bertie's a good bit cleverer than I am in a lot of ways.

'Will your father drive a train?' he asked. 'If there's a strike, I mean?'

Evidently she did not like the idea. She frowned, poured herself another cup of tea, tasted it, made a move, put the cup down.

'Oh no. He might do some shunting down inside the docks, but he wouldn't dream of doing anything to upset the N.E.R. drivers. They really hate strike-breakers, even the men who didn't want to go on the strike in the first place. I'm afraid old Hackby won't speak to you afterwards if he learns you've been a black-leg.'

'I'm not going to let on I drove his line, so with luck I won't get sent there. You know a lot about the working classes, Judy.'

'Oh, I have to. It's the docks, you see. We've got a real gang of Bolshies down there, and a lot of rows between union men and the others. They'll go on strike about anything, and what's more their women will back them up. There's an extraordinary girl called Kate Barnes who's as red as red can be. She goes to the mass meetings and climbs onto the platform and yells at the men to fight the bosses, and they cheer her like a football crowd. She's only a few years older than me, too. I've never been to a meeting, but I admire her like anything. Mummy won't let us mention her name at home, you know.'

While she was speaking she pushed her crockery a little to one side, stubbed out her cigarette in the ash-tray and put the holder away.

'Shall I see you?' he said.

'This is a between place, Tom. You don't make plans here.'

'Let's go outside.'

'Remember we've changed the rules. A chap in your position would probably write to a girl he'd met and ask her to a Commem Ball, don't you think? I went to the House last year—it was fun.'

'What would the girl do?'

'She might say yes at once. But if she's got any sense she'll wait a couple of weeks and see what other invitations she gets.'

'Not very sporting.'

'Very sporting indeed. For all the chap knows she may have had some invitations already.'

Her eyes flickered a little to one side. He turned and saw that the waitress was hovering by the bed-warmers. At his nod she came over with the bills.

Outside on the pavement the afternoon was bright and warm, the air still faintly scented with the passage of the sheep.

'I didn't spot the Frazer-Nash,' he said.

'Oh, I leave that in France. It's such a bother taking it to and fro. That's mine. It's a bit staid, because sometimes I have to take Mummy for drives.'

She pointed to a silver limousine parked in the shadow of the church—a Lagonda two-litre, he thought, the rectangular propriety of windscreen and roof at odds with the dashing length of bonnet.

'Where are you?' she asked.

'Over there.'

Suddenly and for the first time with her ill at ease about such matters, he pointed at the Daimler.

'Heavens!' she said. 'That! I thought somebody must have come with a choir outing!'

'Choir outings seem to play a big part in your life.'

'Of course they do. We've got four churches in Hull, as well as Brantingham. Did it get you here all right, Tom? It looks antediluvian!'

'Oh, it purrs along—Pennycuick looks after it beautifully, and really it's not all that old—Father bought it just before the war. I don't have a car of my own. My grandfather made a complete mess of things, so now there isn't all that money to spare.'

'What rotten luck . . . That could make things a little bit dicey, Tom.'

4

Oxford, 27th April, 1926

'More fizz, Tom?'

'No thanks. I've got a tute at eleven.'

'Is that some kind of medical treatment?' said Bertie, still proffering the bottle.

'It is a very old-fashioned cure for the disease of ignorance,' said Dick Standish. 'Primitive homeopathy, you might say. Tom has to read an essay to his tutor at eleven, for which purpose he requires to remain elevated, but not sozzled.'

'Better stick to coffee then,' said Bertie, swapping the jug for the bottle. 'What about you, Woffles? Don't imagine you've got an essay to read.'

'Wrong there,' said Woffles Belford, a little over-dignified with drink. 'I've got a top-hole essay and I'm going to read it to my tutor tonight. Can't remember what it's about at the moment—I've found a brainy little blighter in Wadham who's got exactly the hang of what I want—last fellow used to put in a lot of names I couldn't pronounce.'

'What's the going rate?' asked Bertie.

'I pay this new fellow a fiver a time.'

'Going to ask him to take a cut in wages?' asked Dick. 'It seems to be the patriotic thing these days.'

'You'll get a strike of swots,' said Woffles. 'This blighter I've got now couldn't afford to stay up if it wasn't for fellows like me.'

'Not a penny off the pay, not a word on the es*say*,' said Dick. 'Woffles is being industrially naïf. If he manages things right he might be able to force the dons out in sympathy.'

'Is that a paradox?' said Bertie. 'I thought Oxford had given

31

up being paradoxical twenty years ago. They were frightened by what happened to Oscar Wilde, I expect.'

Dick ran his fingers through the black lock of hair that tended to flop down over his pale forehead—perhaps he cultivated it for the sake of the finger-running gesture. Tom realised that Bertie, without seeming to, had made a perceptive point. There was something out-of-date about Dick's aestheticism. Although he was in most of his friends' minds part of the essential spirit of Oxford, to the extent of having had his rooms twice broken up by hearties, he still in a mysterious way didn't quite belong. It was not, Tom now saw, that he was out of place, but out of time. If you had met him in London you might have perceived at once that he evoked a period twenty or more years earlier, but the curious gauzy quality of Oxford life, the sense of veil behind veil of past undergraduate generations still floating around one, tended to conceal the dislocation. Indeed it might have been the dislocation itself that made Dick seem so imbued with the essences of Oxford—and it might also explain why nobody had seen him quite sober during the past eight months and why his final results were going to seem a come-down after his top closed scholarship to New College.

'. . . not a paradox at all,' Dick was saying. 'Merely the fruits of my upbringing as a mine-owner's son. The whole art is to play one set of workers off against another. Now, I admit I have a low opinion of the intellect of dons, but I have no amount of respect for their capacity to look after themselves. They'd certainly go on strike rather than listen to the sort of tosh they'd have to if Woffles wrote his own essays.'

Woffles nodded agreement, though his slightly wrinkled brow showed that he might not have understood the argument. It was hard to tell. As Dick had once said, the mode for the silly-ass look made it difficult to tell where one was with a genuine silly-ass like Woffles. He was a large young man, played rugger for his college and would have been in line for a Blue if he'd been prepared to train at all. Tom had once seen him running from the Bulldogs, and had been amazed by his turn of speed until he had collided with a lamp-post and laid himself out. He was, of course, on opposite sides from Dick in the fashionable, but to Tom thoroughly tedious, skirmishes between the hearties and the

32

aesthetes, but being old Yorkshire friends the pair got along very well in private. As they were both in their fourth year—Dick, like Tom, to read Greats, and Woffles in theory to make one more attempt to pass at least one examination but really to run the Drag—most of their Oxford friends had gone down and they now saw a good deal of Tom and each other. Woffle's face, flattish, square, still tanned from late-season skiing, bore a look of puzzlement even in repose, though his pale blue eyes always gleamed with interest, as though eager to confront life's next mystery.

'You must not tease Woffles,' said Bertie. 'He's been reading a book.'

'Who now can claim that Oxford has ceased to be a seat of learning?' said Dick.

'What's more, the book has given him an idea,' said Bertie. 'That's why I've asked you fellows to breakfast. Shall I explain, Woffles, or will you?'

'I'll start and you can take over when I get stuck. It's an awfully good book. I've read it again and again, and I bet you have too. It's *The Black Gang*. Do you remember, there's this fellow Drummond who gets a few of his pals together and they put on masks and go round bashing up Bolshies? I thought we might try a spot of that.'

He looked round the table, full of puppyish good-will, as though he had brought his lead and was asking to be taken for a walk. Tom managed to stop himself from laughing aloud and at the same time remembered to look and see how Bertie was taking this lunatic proposal—a proposal which, apparently, he had already heard and to discuss which he had driven down to Oxford and given this champagne breakfast. For once Bertie seemed unaware that he was being observed, because he was himself watching Dick Standish. His face was the usual mask of indolence, but for the moment the eyes were clearly those of a personality behind the mask.

'First catch your hare,' said Dick. 'How many Bolshies do you know, Woffles?'

'Don't move in that sort of circle,' said Woffles. 'But look here, there's a lot of them around. Everybody says so. Toby Callivant was telling me only the other day about some don at

Balliol who got squiffy and started singing "The Red Flag" at High Table. And there's that fellow Russell, had the divorce, brother's some sort of earl—he went to Moscow, didn't he?'

'So your proposal is that we should pay a call on Bertrand Russell and soften him up with rubber truncheons. Would we have to wear morning suits with our masks, do you think? I'm a great respecter of the peerage.'

'No problem about the Balliol man,' said Tom. 'Spread the word in Trinity and we'd be over the wall in a jiffy.'

'Tar and feather the whole High Table,' said Dick. 'Be sure of getting the right man.'

'I wish you'd take this seriously,' said Woffles. 'Bertie's come down from London to back me up. *We* don't have to know who the Bolshies are—we can pay some blighter to find out.'

'Advertise for a traitor in *The Weekly Worker?*' asked Dick.

'Oh, dash it!' said Woffles.

'I think he's stuck, Bertie,' said Tom.

'I'm glad you weren't around when the fellow invented the wheel, Dick.' said Bertie. 'Woffles has got a sound notion—it just needs a few of the details filling in. For instance, has the rumour penetrated this seat of learning that there is about to be a General Strike?'

'I saw a cartoon about it in *Punch*, I think,' said Dick, taking care to yawn as he spoke. 'Aren't we supposed all to rally round in benighted areas like Clapham and get the trams going?'

'Exactly,' said Bertie. 'And what do you think the tram-drivers will be doing then?'

'Running a book on where the trams end up,' said Dick. 'Woffles driving a tram would be a better laugh than *Kid Boots*. Have you seen that, Bertie? Rather dreary, really . . .'

'Stick to the point,' said Bertie. 'You're wrong about the tram-drivers. They'll be down at Clapham too, seeing that the trams never get out of the sheds. There are going to be some ugly scenes, chaps.'

'Surely the police . . .' Tom began.

'Not enough to go round. No, what we want is a posse of fellows to show up at spots like that and keep order—see that the trams get out and so on. I'm only using trams as an example, mind you. Same applies to trains, buses, unloading at the docks, coal depots and so forth. Even that's only a start, and we haven't got time to get it organised. Organisation's the key, and not just on our side. You don't think the men will turn up at the sheds to stop the trains running without a bit of organisation, do you? Take that organisation away and the problem's at least half solved. This is where Woffles' notion comes in. I propose to form a secret flying squadron to see that the Bolshies don't do any organisation, and I want you three in on it.'

This was an unfamiliar Bertie. He was tilting his chair back from the table and his fingers twirled the stem of his half-empty glass so that the wine climbed almost to the rim. His voice was light as ever, but the habitual note of facetiousness was missing. He was still looking directly at Dick.

'I follow your drift,' said Dick. 'But why me? Woffles is a thug, and Tom spends his spare time knocking people around in a boxing-ring—I can see they would be useful. But where is the lolling contemplative going to fit into this squadron of yours? I'd be happy to design the uniform, of course. Masks purple, with a touch of gold braid?'

'Wouldn't plain purple be enough?' said Woffles.

'Shut up, Dick,' said Bertie. 'I don't want Tom for his boxing —though of course it might come in handy. I want him because of who his father is, and even more I want you because of who your father is. Listen. We can't organise the whole country. There isn't time. We haven't got the people. We couldn't even manage one county. My idea is that we should try the thing out this time on a small scale in the area we know, and make it work. *Then* . . . you realise there's going to be a next time, chaps, and another after that, and so on? This strike next month looks serious, but it'll be nothing more than a side-show compared with what we'll be seeing by nineteen-thirty. And by then we will be able to cover the whole country. We'll have an army! But this time we'll concentrate on our home ground. Tom's father is very thick with Lord Foxhaven—in fact he's your godfather, isn't he, Tom?—and Foxhaven's Lord Lieutenant. We've got to have some pull with the police. That's vital.'

'Get them to arrest us with trick handcuffs so that we can slip away as soon as we're round the corner?' asked Dick. 'I'm sure Lord Foxhaven will be delighted to arrange for that.'

'Do shut up, Dick. The police are vital because they know a lot of things they can't act on. Time and again in an affair like this they're perfectly well aware of who's causing all the trouble, but they can't do anything about it because the blighter's taken care to stay the right side of the law. There's nothing the police would like better than to know someone who they could pass a quiet word to, and next thing the trouble-maker would break a leg, or find his office broken into and all his files gone, or simply disappear into thin air. That's why I want Tom. And I want you even more, Dick, because your father's Deputy Chairman of the Yorkshire Federation of Coal Owners . . .'

'Is he now?' said Dick. 'I knew he was something—but why is he only Deputy Chairman? I must have a word with him about that. Can't have the older generation slacking, you know.'

'Fernyhough's Chairman, but he doesn't count for anything. Your father's the man. The strike's about coal, you see? The other unions are striking to try and stop the mine-owners locking the miners out, but I bet their hearts aren't in it. The railwaymen won't do anything to help get the trains going, but they won't do much to stop them either. That'll be the miners, and they won't manage much without organising. Your father, Dick, is in a position to find out who's behind any trouble that's going to break out. When Woffles explained his idea you said "First catch your hare," and you were right. That's the difficulty, but with your father's help and Tom's I think we can get a good idea of where the hares are lurking. After that I can find any number of sturdy young fellows like Woffles to do the actual jugging.'

Bertie was tilting his chair a shade further, to a point where it looked as though it was already off balance, but somehow he didn't tumble. Tom had been absorbed in watching him, in perceiving clearly for the first time the energy and ambition Father had guessed were there, and so had barely wondered what he thought of the plan as far as it affected him. Bertie was wrong about the railwaymen of course. Even one week's riding on footplates had been enough to make Tom sure that though they were not anxious to strike, once they had struck they wouldn't be half-hearted . . .

'To judge by the tone of your *re*-marks,' said Bertie, 'you don't seem all that keen to plunge into the world of action, Dick.

Tell me one thing before you make up your mind—what sort of a future do you see for yourself in this vale of tears?'

'Only the past has any interest for a man of my temperament. The future, frankly, is a bore.'

'You will find it even more of a bore if you haven't any money to soften its rigours,' said Bertie. 'You don't imagine, when the Bolshies take over, they'll want to keep you in the manner to which you've been accustomed? When they've nationalised the mines and redistributed the land into farming co-operatives, there's not going to be much left of the Standish fortune. You'll be wise to come in with me, Dick.'

'You haven't considered the alternative,' said Dick.

'What might that be?'

'To go in with them.'

'Oh, come,' said Woffles.

Slowly, enjoying the luxury of surprise, Dick took his wallet from his breast-pocket and drew out a rectangle of card which he flipped across the table. It curved in flight and fell in front of Woffles, who picked it up and read it aloud.

'Communist Party of Great Britain! My dear old Dick!'

'I know a few Bolshies, you see,' drawled Dick. 'I move in that kind of circle. It's all right, Bertie—I'm not going to peach on you. I've been thinking of resigning from the Comrades since that row last term.'

'What was that?'

'Don't you remember? The police raided Party Headquarters and took a lot of papers away. One of the things they found out was the names of a couple of undergraduates—not me, thank heavens. Birkenhead tried to get them sent down, though what the Secretary of State for India . . .'

'Don't resign,' interrupted Bertie, evidently as uninterested in the past as Dick claimed to be in the future.

'Perhaps I won't,' said Dick. 'My real reason for joining was to rag the guv'nor, but when it began to boil over last term I saw it mightn't be such a rag after all. I am an example, you see, of what the Comrades quite rightly refer to as dilettantism. It was quite amusing for a bit, but the rigours of the Marxist prose style are a terrible thing for a dilettante to endure . . .'

'Don't resign,' said Bertie again.

'I don't know that it'll be all that useful to you, Bertie. The Comrades who know what's going on are terribly secretive, even with other Comrades. I think I might be able to get something out of the guv'nor—but I want more of a hand than you've dealt me. I don't know about you fellows, but I've found myself wondering more and more what it would have been like if I'd been old enough for the War. Would I have been any good at that sort of thing? Since the apples of the tree of knowledge—at least the Oxford branch of that tree—have turned to Dead Sea fruit in my mouth, the question has been troubling me quite surprisingly. It seems to me that you are offering us the chance to find out.'

'I wouldn't have been the slightest good in the trenches,' said Woffles. 'I'd have been in a blue funk every time a shell came near me.'

'You'd have been a top-notch regimental officer,' said Bertie. 'But God help your men if you'd ever got beyond half-colonel. Right, Dick. I'll take you on those terms. What about you, Tom? Are you on?'

'Fraid not.'

'Oh.'

'Look, for a start you're wrong about Father. The last way to get anything out of him is to send me along. You'd much better talk to him yourself. I've no notion what he'll say, but I know he's taking this strike just as seriously as you are. He thinks it's going to happen, and if it lasts more than a few weeks we're done for. But I promise you the last way to get him to help you is through the family. He probably wouldn't even see you if you tried that. But go and talk to him straight and tell him what you want and he'll at least listen. Don't put on your lazy-bounder act, by the way. He's seen through that. In fact he thinks there's a bit more to you than meets the eye, so you've a good chance.'

'Thanks, old man. I take it you're planning to stay up and get your First. Can't say I blame you.'

'No, I'm . . . you remember that wire Father sent me while I was staying with you at Hendaye?'

'Never forget it. Didn't know a fellow's jaw could drop that far.'

'He wanted me to come home and learn how to drive a train. That's what I was doing the week before last. It seems a pity to waste it, supposing this strike comes off.'

For the first time that morning Bertie seemed actually taken aback—far more than he had been by Dick's disclosure of his membership of the Communist Party. Perhaps he didn't care for the notion that somebody besides himself had been making plans —even thinking along roughly the same lines. At any rate he let his chair tilt upright, then took his pipe out of his side-pocket and frowned at the recesses of its bowl while he answered.

'Yes. Yes I suppose so,' he said. 'Pity . . .'

'How long is this going to last, d'you think?' said Dick. 'According to my guv'nor, the miners are ready to stick it out all summer.'

'So I hear,' said Bertie. 'But the question is how long the other unions will back the miners up. Their leaders are little men, mostly. My bet is they've only got to get frightened and they'll be looking for an excuse . . . When are your Finals, Dick?'

'End of May. I don't know . . . some ways I wouldn't mind if it dragged on—give me an excuse for disappointing the guv'nor. He wasn't what he insists on calling a 'varsity man, so he's rather set store by me doing well . . . Next thing he'll be buying a job lot of ancestors to hang on the walls at Throcking. You don't have any to spare, do you, Tom? You know, people are strangely down on families making their way up the social ladder, but they don't seem to have any idea what a trouble and worry it can be.'

'Probably even worse coming down,' said Bertie.

The words sounded entirely casual, with no perceptible shade of emphasis in them and no aim at any particular person in the room, but for the last few minutes Tom felt as though he had acquired an extra category of perception, or shed a hitherto unperceived layer of deafness where Bertie was concerned. Any remark now seemed to carry little probing tentacles of meaning.

'Dragged on?' said Woffles, half a lap behind in the conversation. 'That won't do. Can't have it running into Commem. Week, I've asked little Judy Tarrant up for the House Ball. Awfully jolly girl—I'm supposed to be marrying her some day— she's my second cousin, you know, and her mamma and mine fixed it up when we were both still in our cradles, almost.'

'Time you were making a move, Woffles,' said Bertie, 'or you'll have some Johnny-come-lately running off with her under your nose.'

There was a minute pause. Bertie had not even glanced at Tom, but his remark had ended on a note of vague interrogation, as though it were somebody else's turn to join the talk.

'Which day's the House Ball?' said Tom. 'I've asked her to Trinity. I hope you don't mind. We're Wednesday.'

'We're Tuesday,' said Woffles, 'so that's all right. I didn't know you knew her, Tom.'

'I met her at Bertie's, in France. Bertie had cunningly fixed to play the foursomes with Joyce Mallahide, but Judy and I beat them on the twentieth.'

'I wonder what she's doing Thursday,' said Dick. 'On the principle of draining life to the dregs, I suppose one ought to attend at least one Commem. Ball during one's sojourn here.'

'You'll be too late, old boy,' said Woffles. 'She'll have fixed herself up weeks ago. And she'll have been to all those beanos they hold at Cambridge the week before.'

'How too sordid,' said Dick.

'She likes to play the field, little Judy,' explained Woffles. 'Good thing, I say, before she settles down.'

It was interesting, Tom thought, that Bertie had refrained from dropping any hint about what had happened at Hendaye— you'd have expected him to derive a vaguely malicious amusement from the rivalry of two of his friends. Instead, without seeming to make any special move of dismissal, he somehow signalled that the meeting was over. All four got to their feet, Woffles stretching hugely, like a waking hound.

'Right, chaps,' said Bertie. 'I'm going north this evening. I'll drop you a line—Dick, you'd better be in touch with your pater, sounding him out. Careful what you say, specially in writing. Which way are you going, Tom?'

'Back to College.'

'I've left my bus in Holywell, so I'll come with you. Hang on, will you, while I settle up?'

It was almost ten, so the Broad was as usual full of men on their way to lecture rooms, their short gowns flapping in the late April gusts. Tom would have been among them, going to hear whether old Atherton had anything new to say about the pre-Socratics this year, but contact with his few remaining fourth-year friends had seemed more worth while and he had not wished to rub Dick Standish up the wrong way by arriving with a gown over his arm, symbol of hard work and high hopes.

'It's a pity about the trains, Tom,' said Bertie. 'I see your father's point, but . . .'

'Do you think this notion of Woffles' is really a runner?'

'Between you and me, no. That's to say I'm not taking it seriously, not in the way Woffles thinks I am. As far as I'm concerned it's a way of getting him and a few chaps like him into an organisation. You can't expect them to make much of the serious side of politics, but give them something that's a bit of a lark and they're on. Then, when the organisation is in existence, I can start moving it in the direction I want. That's why I particularly want you in, Tom. I came to Oxford for you. I know I talked more to Dick, because he likes attention, but it was you I was after.'

'There's plenty of other men . . .'

'Of course there are, but I've got to get them. And with most chaps it's going to depend on who I've got already. If I can tell them So-and-so's joined, and so has Thingummajig, and they're well known to be solid fellows, that'll do more than any amount of argument to rope in the rest.'

'You've got Dick and Woffles.'

'I wouldn't call Dick solid, would you? And Woffles . . .'

He managed to make the name hang in the air in such a way that they both laughed together at the solidity of Woffles.

'But you're just the ticket,' Bertie went on. 'First class brain, famous name, Blue for boxing and all that. People know about you, even if they don't know you personally. You see what I'm getting at?'

'It doesn't necessarily follow . . .'

(Gerald, for instance. A better brain, Mr. Goodhart had said. Keeper of School Field, Captain of the Boats; heir to Sillerby and the title after Cyril's death; the same apparent advantages as Tom, and more.)

'Of course not,' said Bertie a little impatiently. 'It isn't what you are that matters—it's what people think you are. My mistake, I see now, has been letting people think I'm either a bit of an ass or a bit of a cad, or both. Now I'm going to show them

they're wrong . . . Great Scott! Who's the darkie? I thought you
didn't let them into Trinity—I thought that was Balliol.'

Prince Anakitakola of Goodra, late as ever, came scurrying
out of the College gateway, clutching the pile of books that he
would not actually need at any lecture but always took along to
boost his own picture of himself as a potentially learned scholar.
He simpered at Tom as he passed. Two books fell but he did not
stop for them. A moment later Dudu, the Prince's ever-silent
white-robed servant, who had a special dispensation from the
Dean to sleep across the door of his master's room, strode out
into the Broad. He already had one book under his arm, and he
moved along the pavement picking up the others as he came to
them, like a tracker following a blazed trail.

'Friend of mine,' said Tom, more stiffly than he wished. 'His
name's too long to remember We all call him Annie. His father
owns most of India. He's a good egg, all the same.'

'Sure he is,' said Bertie placatingly. 'It was just the way he
shot out that startled me. Can I tell people you're in, Tom?'

'I don't know . . . You see, Bertie, I've rather made friends
with some of the railwaymen . . .'

'Of course you have. Most of the people in this country are absolutely sound. All I want to do is take a few rotten apples out of
the basket.'

'I'll have to think about it.'

'Don't take too long—I'm in a hurry . . . Tom?'

'Yes.'

'Judy Tarrant. Nice child.'

'Certainly.'

'You may need a bit of a hand there, you know. Helen Tarrant
—well, she's not a dragon, exactly, but she's pretty formidable,
and Woffles is quite right about the understanding between her
and Lady Belford. It'll take a lot to make her change her mind.'

'One can but hope.'

'One can do a bit more than that, old boy. It happens that
Helen and I get along surprisingly well, and what's more this
scheme of mine is just the sort of thing she'd approve of. First
thing when I get home I'm going to get her to put a bit of money
into it—not because I need the cash but because I want to spread
the backing around as much as I can. Now, I promise you,

Helen Tarrant will look a lot more favourably on a chap who comes in with me than on one who doesn't.'

Although Tom felt, suddenly, very angry indeed, he did not find it difficult to smile. The rules he had agreed with Judy in the tea-room at Market Weighton were by now part of his habits of thought, and had already proved their use that morning when Woffles had made his revelation about his own plans for matrimony.

'I thought you were going to show people they were wrong, Bertie.'

'About what?'

'About thinking you might be a bit of a cad.'

5

Leeds, Selby, Hull, 5th May, 1926

Gingerly Tom eased the regulator over. The start from Leeds
Central, though not actually a disaster, had been almost farci-
cally inept, with a mess of sparks and black smoke roaring up
into the girderwork and the big drive-wheels spinning uselessly
on the track while a line of picketing railwaymen jeered inaudibly from beyond the railings. Determined not to have that
happen again, Tom had edged away from Marsh Lane so slowly
that the sturdy old 4-4-0 might have been hauling twenty
coaches instead of four. Even so he had managed better than
yesterday.

Now, with increasing confidence, he let his arm feel rather
than his mind judge the relationship between the steam in the
cylinders, the mass of his load and the friction of the track. The
pistons sighed, shoved, blew with a deep note of satisfaction.
The platform began to edge backwards. He felt a hint of slither at
the end of the fourth piston-stroke, but caught it before the
wheels began to spin. Now they were travelling at a walking-
pace, and the gaps that seemed to separate the pulses of power at
low speeds were joining, ready to build up into the familiar
juddering rush. He peered forward along the cutting. The signal
arms were down, but his instructions were to ignore all signals
and only pay attention to red flags waving from windows. This
was his third journey along this line, and only his second in this
direction, but already he regarded the moment of leaving Cross
Gates as the point at which the preliminaries were over and the
run began in earnest. It was not simply that till now he had had
to ease his train round the tight curves and over a whole series of

racketing points as the line wound out of Leeds. It was the almost magical moment of change that lay just ahead.

Cross Gates Station stood at the mouth of a cutting. On either side a complex of slate roofs sloped down, then rose to further ridges, crowned with yet more houses and here and there a church spire blackened all down one side by soot blown on the prevailing wind. Then, as the train moved forward from the platforms the cutting closed around, shutting out the view. A branch line snaked away north. Just beyond the junction a bridge spanned both lines. Beyond the bridge the cutting would continue for a couple of hundred yards and then they would surge out into the open and Leeds would be gone, vanished, and all around would lie open fields, a wood or two to the north, one large house and a wandering line of trees that showed the course of a stream. Yesterday it had been a total surprise, a transformation scene from the alien and menacing gloom of urban industry to the England Tom felt at home in. Today was another pearly May morning and he was anxious not to miss the moment.

'How's the fire, Horace?' he shouted.

Horace Smith, crouched double as he shovelled coal into the firebox, probably didn't even hear through the gathering racket, but his attitude somehow combined contentment with eagerness. Tom could feel against his right calf the orange-gold glow from the firebox door, and could see that the plume of smoke from the stack was a good clean white, so he guessed that Horace had learnt yesterday's lesson and was not overdoing the firing. He eased the regulator back as they approached the junction-points—with the signal-boxes largely unmanned there was always the uncomfortable possibility of their being set for the other line—but with a judder and clack they were over. The bridge loomed. He fed more steam to the cylinders and craned for his transformation scene.

Momentarily the bridge closed their own smoke round them, and before it cleared the methodical bang and clank of engine and wheels were punctuated by a new loud noise, a wrong note, only partly metallic. He looked rapidly round the cab for some shattered component, but suddenly his eye was caught by a movement further off, a man, silhouetted against blueness at the top of the cutting wall, his whole body poised statue-like to aim and hurl. The statue moved.

'Down!' yelled Tom, ducking into the shelter of the cab-side. With a crash the thick glass of the forward window shattered in a shower of splinters and coal fragments. Tom reached forward, grabbed Horace by the scruff of his jacket and pulled him against the cab wall, booting the fire-door shut as he did so. Either that movement or some unregistered impulse caused him to shove the regulator, and the good old engine responded with a loud wuffle and an immediate change in wheel-rhythm.

'What's up?' yelled Horace.

'Throwing coal at us,' Tom shouted back. 'Fire do?'

'Think so.'

Now, above the engine noises Tom could hear the taunting shouts of men's voices, a smashing of more glass, the scream of a woman. Looking back under the arch of the cab roof he could see a line of men ranged along the embankment wall, all stooping to pick up coal or in the act of hurling it at the coaches. They were black against blue, their faces undistinguishable, not individuals at all, but embodiments of rage and destruction, a frieze of devils. More coal thudded against the cab, but now Tom hardly cared about what happened to his section of the train. Violence against the locomotive and the men driving it seemed almost legitimate compared to the senseless attack on his passengers. He rose from his crouch, pulled his goggles down over his eyes and peered into the rush of air that came through his shattered window. The end of the cutting widened in a wedge of brightness. There was no obstruction on the line—thank God they had not gone that far, forcing him by their bombardment to duck out of sight and then letting him run full steam into an obstacle. Behind him his coaches continued to run the gauntlet, while on either side the sunlit fields of England opened around him, ruined.

'Je-hoshophat!' shouted Horace. 'All over? Can I get back to my fire?'

'Think so. Little and often, Horace. Just burning through. Banked into the corners.'

'Righty-ho.'

Tom stared ahead, desperately trying to remember details of

the line that yesterday had not seemed to affect him. There was a cutting in about a mile, just before Garforth Station. No level crossings for a while. Bridges might be dangerous—but there were innumerable methods of stopping a train, for anybody bent on more than symbolic malice. At least bridges and crossings meant roads, and that might mean police . . .

The cutting neared, dead straight, a notch in the forward horizon. It seemed unguarded. He dared not rush through, or he would overshoot the station beyond. Anxiously he eased the regulator back and began to apply the brakes. No trouble at all.

There were several passengers waiting at Garforth, and at once they were joined on the platform by knots of others from the train. Several began to argue and gesticulate, or crane around for official reassurance. A young man in the most extravagant plus-fours Tom had ever seen was standing aloof, with two signal flags under his arm. When passengers approached him he shook his head and grinned.

'Nip back down the coaches,' said Tom. 'Tell everyone I'll give a series of short blasts on the whistle if I see trouble coming. They'd better stand on the seats then—get above the flying glass.'

'Righty-ho,' said Horace, climbing eagerly down.

'Don't forget to tell Dampier,' shouted Tom.

Horace waved and trotted away. He was a very puppyish young man, not an undergraduate but a trainee clerk in a Reading insurance office, who had been positively instructed by his employer to join the volunteers. Horace had shown considerable initiative in travelling to Oxford to do so, on the grounds that it would be 'more fun to be with the 'varsity fellows,' and had been rewarded, apparently beyond dreams, by being driven north in a Rolls-Royce otherwise crammed with Magdalen men and with a crate of champagne in the dickie, and now was helping take a train through romantic perils with the Honourable Thomas Hankey beside him in the cab. If Tom had been told a week before that it was possible to like and respect a man who took blatant delight in matters like these, and who moreover said 'Righty-ho' almost every other sentence, he would have laughed in a slightly embarrassed way—and would, he now saw, have been mistaken.

The passengers gathered round Horace, clearing the way for the young man in plus-fours to stroll forward without risking contact with them.

'You look as if you'd been strafed a bit,' he said.

'This end of Cross Gate cutting,' said Tom. 'Line of men chucking coal. Get on the blower, will you, and see if the police can't stop them?'

'Right you are. Nice to have something to do. I was beginning to think I was wasting my time. You're my first train through. If things don't jolly up a bit I'm not coming back tomorrow.'

'You can't . . .'

'Oh yes I can. Yesterday there were a gang of chaps out mending track up at Horsforth. We're all sleeping in the same school, you know. One of them showed me his hands, all covered with blisters, said it was the most boring day he'd spent in his whole life. They're none of them going back tomorrow—they're going down to the tram depot, see if anyone will let them drive a few trams.'

'If the junctions aren't manned the trains can't go through,' said Tom. 'It won't be safe.'

'Doesn't look all that safe as it is. Ready to go?'

'Just waiting for my fireman. Here he is.'

Horace came trotting up the platform, grinning as he ran.

'All right?' said Tom.

'Fine. One or two old pussies wanted to get off, but I bundled them back on. We've lost about a dozen windows—quite a lot of compartments weren't touched at all, they must have been rotten shots. I say, there's a bookie in the second coach taking bets on how far we're going to get. I put a couple of bob on us making it the whole way. D'you think I'm safe?'

'I'll do my best,' said Tom.

After that they steamed the twelve miles to Selby without incident. Most of it, once they were down out of the hills, was straight track, without gradients or even cuttings and embankments. Several level-crossings might have stopped them, but most were only farm-tracks and stood open. Only the last one crossed a proper road, forcing Tom to stop, start and stop while Horace and Dampier (a serious middle-aged businessman, quite unlike most of the volunteers, who was acting as guard) worked the gate-routine they had evolved yesterday. Waiting for Horace to come running up the track while Dampier closed the gates, Tom thought about him again. He was really rather bright; he had immeasurably improved his firing technique since yesterday, and was not constantly fiddling with the injectors or peering at the gauges as he had done then, but had worked out what was necessary and was doing that without fuss. Perhaps even the episode with the Rolls and the champagne had not been pure luck—Horace was the type not simply to take his chances but also to make them. One day, if all went well for him, he might be a very rich man. Indeed, *mutatis mutandis*, the founding Hankey could have been a chap rather like Horace. Suppose all went other than well for Tom himself, and Sillerby had to be sold, why, Horace—Sir Horace by then—might buy it and found a new line . . .

'It looks as if you're going to get your two bob back,' said Tom.

They were waiting for the flag at Selby. Horace straightened from stoking for the move-off.

'Hope so,' he said. 'Mr. Thwaites gave me a fiver for expenses, but . . .'

He sounded genuinely bothered at the thought of losing his florin. Once again Tom felt the mild shock that comes from a change of perspective about something taken for granted. His own poverty, or rather the family poverty, had always been measured in pounds or even fivers, in the fact that Stevens ought to have retired on a pension three years ago, and that Pennycuick mowed the lawns as well as driving Father and caring for the cars.

'Oughtn't to be any problem,' said Tom. 'Only those beastly crossings.'

(There were ten between Selby and Hull, but some were at stations where they would have to stop anyway.)

At last the crates of hens were loaded and the stationmaster—a grey-haired and strained-looking railway employee who had not joined the strike—gave Dampier the signal. Dampier produced a long blast on his whistle, waved his flag and scampered for the van. Tom pushed the regulator.

He was answered by a prodigious belch of smoke and a wild rush of useless power from the cylinders. It was Leeds all over again, but worse. Even with the lowest possible steam the wheels spun and the connecting-rods threshed round. The train itself barely moved. Tom leaned from the cab till he could see the near rail. It gleamed with something duller than the polish of use.

'What's up?' shouted Horace.

'Some blighter's greased the rails, I think.'

'Better than chucking coal.'

'I'll try the sand-boxes.'

'What's that?'

'These levers here. You do your side. Shove it right up. Fine. They dribble sand onto the track in front of the drive wheels. Don't let me forget to close them once we're going.'

Harry Hackby had told Tom a famous railway chestnut about a driver who had brought the London express up with his sand-boxes open all the way, and arrived at York with his wheels so worn that they had flanges on both sides. Really any fool could drive a train when all went well, but it was in the nature of railways that all did not go well, and immeasurable layers of skill and experience might still not be enough. Determined at least to show that he was not any fool, Tom tried again. The wheels spun, half-bit, spun again, held, and they were moving.

'Well done,' yelled Horace. 'Don't look so peeved. This is fun!'

'It was those men throwing coal,' Tom shouted back.

'I don't know. I was thinking—next time there's a strike I might have a go at that. I bet it was a real lark for them!'

Clearly Horace was only teasing, but Tom didn't answer. There was a sharp curve out of Selby after the clanging Ouse bridge, which needed all his attention, and then two junctions close together. The points on the second one had yesterday seemed to him unnervingly rough. After that the track ran almost due east, straight as a Roman road along the meadow-levels of the Ouse. He increased speed, producing a rush and clatter which made discussion impossible. Horace was right, in a sense, he thought. The idea of greasing the rails (a well-known engine-shed prank, according to Harry) had certainly been a lark; and no doubt the men on the Cross Gate embankment had enjoyed their shying, as if at a glorified fun-fair, the prize being the crash of glass. But the episode had changed Tom's attitude to what he was doing. Yesterday he had been driving this train because it was what Father wanted him to do, because it was the sort of thing that was expected of him. Today he was driving it in order to defeat an enemy, an enemy symbolised by the devils of destruction silhouetted at the top of that embankment wall against an English sky. Victory, for the moment, consisted in getting the train through to Hull Paragon.

But there was almost a sense of deflation as the victory began to near. On this stretch the only conceivable difficulties were the tedious stops and starts of the level-crossings. Perhaps on the outskirts of Hull itself there might be further trouble. Meanwhile Cliffe Halt, Wressle and Howden North came and went, with a few passengers boarding and alighting at each as though all were perfectly normal except that the train was running some forty minutes late.

'You'd better keep your eyes skinned in case your bookie friend welshes before we're there,' called Tom as he fed the steam to let them chunter smoothly out of Howden.

'Righty-ho. Aren't you going to push her along a bit? We're beastly late.'

'Junction coming up. After that . . . Hello! What's this?'

In the distance, almost a mile out of Howden, a bridge crossed the line, and on its parapet pranced an extraordinary figure, semaphoring wildly. Horace craned from the cab, peering forward. Tom began to close the regulator.

'Red flag,' said Horace, drawing back into the cab.

'That's what I thought.'

Tom let the engine slow and got ready to brake.

'Where's he gone?' he shouted.

'Coming down the bank, I think,' said Horace.

'Only one of him?'

'Far as I can make out. But get ready to move, eh?'

There did not seem to be anywhere, except the parapet of the bridge itself, for an ambush to hide, and from a distance the man with the flag appeared to be wearing the standard strike-breaker's uniform of plus-fours, cap and scarf. Even so Tom took the train clear through the bridge before bringing it to a

halt. No attack came. He waited for the signaller to come panting along the track.

Close to, the man—little more than a boy, really—was just as
odd as he had appeared when first seen. He was so pink-faced
with his run that he looked as though somebody had put his head
in a bucket and scrubbed him. He wore a tweed cap, too large for
him, and a strip of pink cloth which might once have been a
college scarf but seemed to have been used more recently for
cleaning purposes. He wore a waistcoat but no jacket. His
striped shirt was buttoned at the sleeves, and his dark flannel
trousers were tucked into thick grey socks and then tugged down
in imitation of plus-fours. His boots were heavy and workman-
like.

'They've took up the track!' he shouted. 'They've took up the
track!'

'It was all right yesterday,' said Tom.

'In the night. See there!'

He pointed along the line. Tom stared ahead. The rails ran
straight as a ruler, diminishing into a single gleaming line somewhere beyond Eastrington village, but their monotony was
interrupted first by the points of a junction where a branch line
curved away north, and then a quarter of a mile beyond that
where a gang of about five men were working. Even at this dis-
ance it was possible to make out a gap in the right-hand rail.

'You must take the old H and B,' said the man. 'Buggers
never thought on that! We've set the points.'

His eyes, blue and candid, flashed with excitement as he gestured towards the tracks that branched away north-eastwards at
the junction.

'But I'm supposed to be going to Hull!' said Tom. 'How long
will it take them to mend the track?'

'Five hours, maybe. They're not that skilled in it. But see
there, the H and B goes to Hull, long way round, coming in
through the Wolds.'

'I've got passengers for Brough and Ferriby and places.'

'Then you must take them into Paragon and there'll be a
push-and-pull running out back to Eastrington.'

'I see. Do you know what this track's like? Are you sure it's
clear?'

'Clear all the way through.'

'What are the gradients like?'

'One-fifty up from Newport through Drewton Tunnel. Sharper nor that down to Springbank. But nowt worse than a hundred. You'll pull it easy, only four coaches.'

Tom withdrew into the cab.

'What do you think, Horace?'

'Rummy little bounder . . . and why's he dressed like that, and talking like that?'

'That's just Yorkshire. But he seems to know a lot about railways.'

'That's what I thought. What's a push-and-pull?'

'No idea. Hang on a tick.'

Tom leaned from the cab again.

'Do you work on the railways?' he called.

'Nay. Me Dad does, and he's agin the strike, but he dursn't black-leg. Heard the blokes saying as they were taking up the track, so he sent a message through to Paragon and they sent a gang out. I come up to stop the trains, see there. My Mum dressed me up this gate to look the same like one on you.'

He grinned all over his face at the joke of it. Once more Tom and Horace withdrew into the privacy of the quietly hissing cab.

'What do you think?' said Horace.

'It sounds possible. I think they told me about this line yesterday, but there was so much to take in. I seem to remember they said it went to Hull too. Look. I want to get this train through.'

'Oh, so do I. I've got two bob on it.'

'Well, we aren't going to make it down the main line. If this chap's having us on, we shan't make it this way either; but if he's telling the truth we'll get through.'

'Done!'

'All right. I'll take the rap if it doesn't work out. You'll have to do a bit more firing than we bargained for—one-fifty gradients take a lot of steam.'

'Righty-ho.'

Once more Tom pushed the regulator across, but kept the speed right down until the train had clunked through the points and taken the branch line. Horace slung coal into the firebox with eager vigour. Tom opened the regulator further and stared anxiously along the strange track, glancing from time to time southwards to where the Hull main line, a dark streak across green, ran towards the houses of Eastrington. The tracks diverged but were still close enough for Tom to see that the workmen were actually levering a length of rail up onto the sleepers. The men stood up and waved, then bent to their work again. Slightly relieved he returned to peering along the line, which now ran level and steady towards the green rampart of the Wolds. Horace tapped his shoulder.

'Bit of trouble back there,' he shouted, gesturing with his thumb.

Tom leaned from the cab and looked back down the line of coaches. Its regularity of paintwork and windows and brass door-handles was interrupted by a number of heads, and even some half-torsos, leaning out. Mouths yelled, arms signalled. Tom tried to make reassuring signals in return, then withdrew into the cab.

'I'll stop at the next station,' he shouted. 'You can run back and tell them what's up.'

'Righty-ho.'

The place was called Sandholme. There was, not surprisingly, no staff at all at the station. A canal—it must be the one from Market Weighton—ran north through flat fields, but it too seemed strike-stilled. Indeed the whole landscape, apart from the hissing engine and Horace surrounded by a scrum of passengers twenty yards down the platform, seemed to have obeyed the call to inertia. The hills were unchanging, and no breeze stirred any leaf or flecked the glassy stillness of the canal. All lay gripped by peace.

Tom felt he could do with a bit of peace. Neither of his tutors had been at all enthusiastic about his volunteering, and had only supported his request for leave of absence under heavy pressure from the Dean, who had been a most ferocious recruiter. Tom had had to promise to get through a full stint of reading every day, come what might, and to return with one full-length essay on the use of the arts to support or attack the concept of the imperium in the post-Augustan era, and another on the ontological argument in the light of the Hegelian categories. He had the *Pharsalia* in his pocket today. Late though they were running, the turn-round at Hull would still take a good three hours, which should be enough to skim through it.

The group round Horace broke up. Two old women with parcels stayed on the platform but the rest of the passengers climbed back into the train. A farmer in gaiters hauled a sack out of the guards-van and joined the women. Horace trotted back up the train, closing two doors as he passed them. Dampier walked more slowly back to the van.

'Those three are walking home across the fields,' said Horace. 'The farmer'll send a pony for the sack. I say, Tom, Dampier thinks that fellow at the junction was having us on.'

'He may have been,' said Tom. 'But we've got nothing to lose —it's a secular version of Pascal's bet, I suppose.'

Horace grinned, bright-eyed. Presumably he had no idea what Tom was talking about, but his manner was perfectly designed to conceal the fact. A whistle shrilled. Leaning from the cab Tom observed that Dampier was contriving to wave his green flag in a manner that signalled total foreboding.

The line curved gently, twice, until it was running almost due east. A gradient notice glimmered, became readable and was gone. One-fifty. The landscape still ran almost level towards the Wold escarpment, with straight dykes slicing it into rectangles, but already the line was rising onto a long embankment. The note of the cylinders deepened from easy puffs to soughs of effort, despite more steam. He slowed for a station—the signboard said it was North Cave—but there was no point in stopping; no one was waiting on the platform, nor was there any sign of staff. The embankment became a cutting, but still the line climbed.

As they swung out of the cutting along the contour of a rounded hill Tom realised that he was enjoying the adventure, the sense of exploration through unknown lands. Moreover— unlike the clanging levels of the Ouse meadows—the country was beautiful, a clean chalk upland, quartered by abruptly plunging valleys. The line must have been crazily expensive to build through such gradients, but the result was splendidly dramatic. They steamed, climbing all the while, into another cutting, steep-sided and rimmed with woodland to the north. A bridge spanned the cleft and beyond it the mouth of the first tunnel loomed. Tom signalled to Horace to open the fire-box door. The tunnel was quite short so that as they approached its blackened brickwork he could see the inner arch of whiteness at the further end, but even so he instinctively slowed to meet the darkness, like a man groping along an unlit corridor and ducking from imagined door-sills. They churned into the reeking and clanging dark, with the cab lit by the hot glow from the firebox, then out into a brief patch of day and into dark again. Horace hunched, choking, against the cab wall. Tom grabbed for his handkerchief and held it across his face—Harry Hackby always carried a few bits of wet sacking for tunnels—but he too was starting to cough when there was a second or two of the golden fog turning silver and they were in sunlight, churning up the gradient at about twenty miles an hour. Tom gulped the lovely air that streamed in at the broken window. He peered through his goggles for the next tunnel.

They were in a long cutting, wooded to the north above its steep white bank, but curving to the right so that the far end was out of view. A lone signal-box stood at the crown of the curve. About a hundred yards this side of it the line was blocked by a fair-sized tree.

'Hold tight!' he shouted, hoicking the regulator shut and with his left hand loosing the vacuum that would close the brakes. With a roaring sigh they bit. The jar of deceleration flung him forward so that he had to clutch at the safety-bar to stop himself from being thrown against his controls.

'Oi!' yelled Horace. 'Mind what you're at! You damned near chucked me in the fire!'

He had been bending to consider whether he needed to stoke again, and was quite naturally furious with fright.

'Sorry—tree on the line!' answered Tom.

'How'd it fall that far?'

Now that they were stopped the mild wind was blowing their smoke forward up the cutting. The tree, thanks to the gradient and their slow approach, was still some eighty yards away. A flaw in the grain of the wind suddenly whisked the smoke aside and for the first time Tom saw the obstacle clearly.

'Hi!' yelled Horace. 'It's been cut! the rotters!'

There was a moment in which the stillness and secrecy of the long cutting seemed to overwhelm even the impatient hissings of

the engine, a short dull time in which peace grew ominous. Tom
started to spin the tiller-like wheel that would reverse the drive
from the cylinders, leaning from the cab as he did so to look back
along the line of the coaches. The last wisps of smoke were still
streaming up from the tunnel mouth. Passengers were craning
from windows, partly obscuring the track beyond. But something was happening there. Leafage, another tree, men. A harsh
and excited cheer.

Now men were running towards him alongside the track.

'The rotters!' said Horace again.

All along the northern rim of the cutting men had emerged
from the trees. Some had large lumps of chalk in their hands,
half-poised for throwing. Others held club-like lengths of
branch, and one or two had mattocks. They stood for a moment,
and then without any apparent signal came leaping down the
bank.

Horace snatched up his shovel and held it like an assegai,
ready to repel boarders.

'Mind that side!' he shouted.

On the southern side the men who had hauled the tree across
the track were almost at the footplate step, and more of the
attackers from the wood were surging round the front of the
engine to join them. One or two were climbing the nearest
coach. In a few seconds they would be up in the tender, with
several tons of coal to use for missiles. Defence was hopeless.

'We'll have to go quietly, Horace,' said Tom over his shoulder.

'Not on your life!'

The rush of men stopped. There were not in fact all that many
of them on Tom's side, less than twenty, jostling in a half-circle a
yard or two clear of the tracks, waiting for the threat from the
tender to put an end to resistance. A man pushed through the
front rank, very short, almost a dwarf, but with a disproportion-
ately large head. He held his fists in a sparring position as if
about to punch the engine itself and pranced from foot to foot,
shouting 'Come down and fight! Come down and fight, then!'
His shabby cap tipped off backwards as he glared up at Tom with
very pale blue eyes and grinned with victorious rage. Looked at
from this angle he seemed to have no body at all, to be just that

furious egg-shaped head with a pair of prancing boots attached at the neck and big fists jiggling near the chin. The men round him laughed and cheered.

'Give it him then, Billy!' they called.

So encouraged the little man jerked about like a puppet. He was obviously some kind of idiot, a gang mascot, cared for by his mates but laughed at more than with. His presence transformed a scene which Tom had hitherto found merely frightening into something that was also repellent. Anything to put an end to it. Without thought he swung his left leg forward as if about to descend. Instantly silence gripped the men beneath him.

'All right,' he said. 'I'll fight. Who are you putting up?'

Murmurs swelled to a cheer. Heads twisted and craned. Somebody shouted 'Where's Tinker?'

'Back other side!'

'Eeya, Tinker, round here!'

'Tinker!'

Several men broke from the line to scamper round the front of the engine but were met by a surge of others from the far side. The crowd re-formed now three and four deep, eddying where a man was being pushed to the front. Tom climbed down onto the step.

'You'll let us through if I win?' he said.

There was a growl of contented laughter.

'*Iffun* you win,' said a voice, mock-solemn.

'And a silver coop, by pooblic subscription . . .' cackled someone else.

More laughter.

'Don't let's worry about the cup,' said Tom.

He had to turn his back on them to reach the ground, then lost his footing on the slope of ballast beyond the sleepers, and half-staggered. A hand like an armoured glove gripped him by the elbow, steadied him and at the same time swung him round.

He found himself face to face with the man who, it was instantly clear, was to be his opponent—roughly Tom's height but half again as broad; remote, dark, speculative eyes under brows white with scar-tissue; a much-broken nose, thick and unsmiling lips, a broad but stubby jaw. But for the intelligence of the eyes this was a face which Tom knew well, from gyms where the pro-

fessional sparring partners waited for one of the young gentlemen to fee them for a bout.

'Mr Tinker?' he said, holding out his hand.

The harsh fist gripped it briefly.

'Tinker Donovan,' said the man. 'And who may you be?'

'Tom Hankey.'

'Fought afore?'

'Yes. Quite a bit. Not without gloves, though.'

'It'll have to be bandages. Three minutes the round?'

'Suits me. How many?'

'Till one on us stays flat.'

'Oh . . . all right? Where? I don't fancy fighting on the track.
What's the ground like out of the cutting?'

Slowly and with obvious confidence Mr. Donovan turned and
spoke to the men beside him.

'Stack of sleeper up by signal box,' he said. 'Lay us a stage
across the tracks, willa?'

At once almost the whole crowd marched off up the line,
leaving only three or four by the engine.

'Ay,' said one of these. 'Better down in the cutting, then us
can watch from off of the wall, like.'

The others grunted agreement. Apart from the prospect of
fighting this formidable man, things seemed to be turning out remarkably well. At least it looked as though no one except Tom
was likely to get hurt. The better humour the men were in . . . a
thought struck him and he turned to see Horace craning,
worried but thrilled, from the footplate.

'Is your bookie friend still on the train?' he asked.

'Think so. He had a ticket to Hull.'

'Fetch him along. Tell the passengers what's up. Some of 'em
may want to watch too.'

'Righty-ho.'

'Think any on the lads will be backing *thee*?' said one of the
men.

'I suppose not. Perhaps they can bet on how many rounds I
go.'

'Aye.'

Mr. Donovan was already striding away along the track. Tom
and the others followed. He was conscious of more movement

behind him—passengers helping each other down the four-foot drop to the ground—but did not look back. The men walking just in front of him did not speak much to each other, but their mood seemed now entirely benevolent. Horace had been right, Tom realised. The ambush of the train, like the attack by the coal-throwers outside Leeds, had been only partly an act of war; it had also been a lark, a break, a longed-for defiance of authority. Given a different reception by the train-crew the war element would have prevailed and the episode have become an unpleasant skirmish; as it was, more by luck than design, the lark had for the moment come out on top. The ambush had worked as planned, and now there was going to be the bonus of a fist-fight to watch. Tom thought it possible that if he did well enough the men might let the train through after all.

The southern bank of the cutting rose steadily higher. From the crown of the curve Tom could see that the line ahead ran, still climbing, along an impressive chalk canyon. The effect was almost gothic—certainly romantic, as if he and his passengers had been ambushed by bandits in some remote Albanian pass, which they had been tricked into taking instead of the drab, safe levels of the Humber plain. Here the men were working systematically, unbuilding a stack of sleepers and laying them between the tracks; another layer, laid across these and the rails themselves, would make an adequate platform for the fight. It would clearly take some time before they were ready, so Tom walked past them, climbed the northern wall of the cutting, and sat down. He could see very little more from here than he had been able to from the tracks. The wood behind him rose steeply, blanking out all the northern landscape; so, for the most part, did the cutting wall to the south. Only to his right Tom could see a stretch of steep hillside, close-nibbled, crossed with sheep-tracks and sparsely dotted with thorn-bushes. Close to one of these, but on the skyline from where Tom sat, stood a man, presumably a look-out. There seemed to be absolutely no possibility of intervention from the outside world. If you were going to ambush a train you could not have chosen a safer or more secret place. Undisturbed by the bustle in the cutting a few Small and Holly Blues sunned themselves on the bank beneath him, while a pair of Speckled Woods danced up and down through the leaf-shadow. He wondered what Judy was doing. He had a card from her in his pocket, accepting his invitation to the Trinity Commem. and saying that she was staying at Brantingham to help with the strike, but not what that help would be. For a moment he imagined himself and her, walking hand in hand through the silence of this place, quite alone, watching the butterflies as they had at Hendaye. He was glad she wasn't here now—he was fairly sure he was going to be hurt quite badly. Donovan looked immensely strong and hard, and though his movements were slow one couldn't be sure that this would remain part of his fighting style or whether it was a deliberate restraint which he would put aside in the ring. He was older than Tom, but still young enough to be quick. Even bandaged, his fists would be a great deal more painful than any glove. On the other hand the scar-tissue above his eyes . . .

A man picked his way slantwise up the cutting wall.

'Can I take your shirt, sir, to cut the bandages?'

Tom nodded, rose and began to strip.

'I thought as you'd run,' said the man, 'till I saw you squatting up here.'

He took the shirt and stood inspecting Tom's torso.

'You've some meat on you,' he said. 'More 'n I'd guess. Think you can go three with him?'

He sounded genuinely interested. Tom looked down into the cutting to see what Donovan was doing but couldn't for the moment spot him. A knot of men surrounded one of the passengers, a stout old man in the traditional loud tweed of the bookmaker.

'It depends if he catches me with a couple of good ones, doesn't it? He looks as if he could punch.'

'Ay. Would have been Northern Champ, Tinker, but for having his fights stopped. Cuts bloody awful.'

'Can you find me a second?'

'We reckoned as your fireman . . .'

'I'd rather have somebody who knew his stuff.'

'Ay. I'll ask.'

'Thanks.'

Now Tom saw Donovan. He was pacing to and fro on the nearly completed platform, prodding here and there at the baulks with his feet. Tom put his jacket over his bare shoulders, slithered down the bank and went to join him. Somebody had found a length of thin cable and the men were using this to lash the top layer of sleepers to the rails. When they had done it would all be firm enough, though nothing like as smooth-surfaced as a proper ring. It would be dangerously easy to catch one's heel at a place where one sleeper projected a quarter inch above its neighbour, or on the wires themselves. The platform was small, too, about fifteen feet square, with a fair drop at either end and a shorter one where it crossed the tracks.

'That's not bad,' said Tom. 'I suppose we can't do anything about ropes.'

'I've fought on worse,' said Donovan. 'The lads 'll keep the ring. Ready?'

'If you are.'

A thin man with a long grey face came up, shook hands with Tom and said that his name was Percy Garner and he would be Tom's second. Other men had been elected time-keeper and referee, and they too came and shook hands with Tom, as if anxious to demonstrate to him that the fight was going to be fairly fought and judged. Mr. Garner took from one of the other men a series of two-inch-wide strips of Tom's shirt and started to bandage Tom's hands. He at once gave the impression that he knew what he was doing. In the middle of this Horace came bustling up.

'I say,' he said. 'You should have let me be your second!'

'Mr. Garner's done it before, you see,' said Tom. 'But he'll need some help. He'll tell you what to do. I hope you haven't bet on me.'

'Yes, of course I have. I got twenty to one.'

'I'll do my best. Are you sure that's tight enough, Mr. Garner?'

'Close tha fist, sir.'

With his hand flat the bandages had felt distinctly loose, but as Tom bent his fingers the cloth tightened, making a taut pad several layers thick from the back of his hand to the first knuckle. He tried the feel of it against his cheek while Mr. Garner started on the other hand. It seemed, if anything, harder than a bare fist might have been—in fact the function of the bandages was clearly to protect the hand rather than the target.

When Mr. Garner had finished bandaging the other hand Tom began to jig a little, loosening up his leg-muscles. It felt strange to be doing this in boots. He was still getting used to the sensation when the time-keeper blew a long blast on Dampier's whistle and the crowd in the cutting began to climb the banks, looking for ledges and footholds on the steep slopes. Tom went to his corner. There were no stools, so he stood and waited until the referee waved him to the centre of the ring. Tom and Donovan and the referee closed together into that strange, almost conspiratorial, instant of peace that precedes any fight. The referee said the usual brisk formula, solemn as any official at a regular championship. On his way back to his corner Tom saw that five men stood along each side of the ring, ready to prevent the fighters from falling through where the ropes should have been. He handed his jacket to Horace. The whistle blew.

Tom had been expecting an immediate rush from Donovan after the first ritual touch of fists and was on his toes to cope with it, but Donovan simply moved to the centre of the ring and stayed there, firm-footed in the classic pose with his chin tucked down as he watched Tom from under heavy brows. Tom tried a tentative lead and Donovan knocked it away. The men on the banks gave a yapping cheer at the contact and fell silent, apart from individual shouts of encouragement to their fighter. The closeness of the cutting picked out every sound, but to Tom, concentrated into his task, the shouts were as irrelevant and remote as birdsong. Stripped, Donovan was very impressive, a bit over-muscled but without the beer-induced suet common in gymnasium pugs. Tom led to the body and landed a sound punch, but it was like beating a tree-trunk. The jar of his own gloveless fist into hard flesh was shocking but exhilarating. Donovan had barely altered his guard to meet the blow, had simply allowed it to land. Clearly he was going to cover his face at all costs.

At least the punch stimulated him to attack. He came forward, suddenly and much more nimbly than Tom had expected, with a smart double-jab. Tom swayed inside it, ducked out of an incipient clinch and circled away. There was barely room for such work. His heel must have come within inches of the drop before firm hands met his shoulder-blades where the rope would have been. To discourage Donovan from a series of such rushes he jabbed hard for the face, swayed clear of the predictable counter and got in a right to the body with all his weight behind it. Though it seemed to him that his fist rebounded like a ball from brickwork, he saw the brooding eyes flicker with the impact.

By the time the whistle blew for the end of the round the pattern seemed clear. Donovan was a competent, orthodox fighter who relied on sheer strength to wear his opponent down. He could be held more easily by a threat to his head than an actual blow to his body. No doubt the ungloved fists and his known tendency to cut contributed to that. He knew that Tom was having to spend twice the energy he himself was, because he could hold the middle of the tiny ring and merely turn while Tom had to circle round him. He had not yet landed a true punch—indeed on orthodox scoring Tom had won the round by several clear points—but he had effectively established dominance.

Tom rested after the whistle with head bowed and shoulders hunched, systematically heaving in the clean hill air. Horace fanned him with his own jacket while Mr. Garner whispered pleadingly as he adjusted the bandages.

'He's playing with thee, man. Tha must go for his head. Forget about the body. Never been stopped, Tinker, but by punching to the head. And watch for his right. He'll be coming at thee with a one-two and tha'll be thinking he's done, when he'll fetch another right at thee. Won fight after fight that gate, Tinker.'

'Thanks.'

'Eeya, man, but tha's quick! Happen he don't catch thee with his right and tha'll last three rounds yet!'

Tom nodded and looked at him. The grey, gaunt face was fanatic for the cause, Tom's cause, loyalty to one's own corner. The strike and the ambush were swept away by the flood of the fight.

'Hope so,' said Tom. 'Wish I was in better training.'

Early in the next round he misjudged the speed of Donovan's left. It caught the side of his head, at an angle only, but he felt as if he'd banged into an oak beam. A flurry or two later it became clear that Donovan had changed his tempo, was coming forward more and faster, and was now prepared to risk a counter-attack to the head. The round was running to a new pattern, its rhythm quickening towards a climax. Donovan was still only using his left, but with each attack his right hung a little lower, a little further withdrawn. A full-blooded left walloped into Tom's guard, and deliberately he let the impact throw him back against the waiting hands so that Donovan's right had to reach too far for its target. As it went back for the second stroke Mr. Garner had foretold Tom loosed his own right, looping high to the temple. His bandaged knuckles seemed to crack with the impact and the bones of wrist and arm to jar to the shoulder-joint. Donovan stood back two paces and nodded, not as though clearing his head but as if accepting a new fact. Tom became conscious of the pain in his hand and wondered if he'd broken a bone. The yells of the men filled the cutting.

And then there was a change. The intensity of focus, the sense of all the universe peering down into the cutting through a lens of sky, blurred. Tom first became aware of it at the edge of his vision, in the background to the fight. It was as though cloud-shadow had lifted from the watchers on the steep southern bank, though the light on the ring had not changed at all. At the same time the shouting faltered, then swelled on a quite different note. All this he was only vaguely conscious of. But now Donovan frowned, backed two clear paces away and held up a hand, palm forward. He was looking not at Tom but over his shoulder. Tom saw that the alteration in the texture of the crowd was caused by the same thing—they were no longer watching the fight, but the bank behind him. He dropped his guard and swung round, panting.

There was some sort of a disturbance in the crowd here. At first it seemed merely that some of the ones at the top had lost their footing and, falling, brought down the watchers below them in a series of slithering tumbles. Then it became clear that those who remained on the rim of the bank were not part of the crowd, but newcomers, deliberately spaced a few yards apart. They wore sporting clothes and carried shotguns and rifles held half-raised. They might have been an out-of-season shooting party, except that their heads were covered by dark and shape-less hoods.

One of them tilted his gun skywards, without lifting it to his shoulder. A sharp explosion filled the cutting, followed by silence.

'Don't anybody move,' said a voice. 'These guns are all load-ed and we won't hesitate to shoot.'

The men who had fallen from the bank picked themselves up. Whispers and mutters began to spread.

'Eeya!' called a voice from the southern bank. 'Wunnit be the close season?'

'Not for vermin,' answered one of the hooded men towards the end of the line.

The man who had fired the shot raised his gun slightly, imposing silence.

'Passengers back in the train,' he said. 'Who's the driver?'

Tom raised his hand. The speaker was clearly Bertie Panhard, not only from his voice, but also from the characteristic tweeds of his suit, which would have looked more at home on Horace's bookmaker friend. The man who had made the remark about vermin had been Dick Standish. They were pretending not to recognise Tom, and he was relieved. He wanted, he now saw, absolutely no part in Bertie's schemes. Indeed, for an instant when he had first realised that the newcomers were not part of the crowd he had thought that they were the coalthrowers from the cutting outside Leeds, returned for a fresh onslaught; and now, though he knew them to be in other contexts his own friends, they retained for him a sense of the same horror and revulsion. These armed and hooded intruders were wrong, alien, both to him and to his idea of England, whereas the fight with Donovan, for all its absurdity, had been acceptable, a meeting-ground. Ignoring the men with the guns he turned to his opponent and held out his hand.

'Sorry about that,' he said. 'I think you'd have done me in the next couple of rounds.'

'Aye,' said Donovan, unsmiling.

At once his glance returned to the line of armed men.

'The buggers,' he said. 'Who'd have thought it?'

'Let's hope it doesn't get any worse.'

'Aye.'

'Get moving!' called Bertie. 'Passengers and crew back in the train, I say. You men, start taking those sleepers off the line. Number eight, you take a dozen of them and clear the treetrunks. I want to see that train moving in ten minutes.'

Tom hesitated, then began to push his way through the crowd who stood below the northern bank. He climbed slantwise up the steep chalk until he stood a little below Bertie.

'What are you going to do with them?' he asked.

'Teach them a lesson.'

'You must let them go as soon as we're through.'

'I'm in charge here.'

'If you don't, I'll let on who you are.'

A brief pause.

'We'll let them go,' said Bertie drily.

'Fine.'

'Aren't you going to say thank-you?'

'No.'

Tom turned and let himself tumble down the bank in a controlled rush. Horace came towards him holding his jacket. Tom put it round his shoulders and walked across to Donovan, who was now standing at the edge of the ring talking in a low voice to one of his friends.

'I think it'll be all right,' he said. 'Provided you do what they say. Nobody'll get hurt.'

Donovan glanced at him and nodded. Tom started to walk along the track with Horace beside him. Only now, as the last urgencies of the fight seeped away from his muscles and mind, did he take it into his head to be amazed that Bertie and his army had arrived on the scene at all.

'I say,' Horace kept repeating. 'I dashed well say.'

By mid afternoon Tom's fingers were so fat with bruising that he found it difficult to turn the pages, but at least no bones seemed broken. His whole body ached, seemingly less from the fight itself than from the juddering rush down to Hull, and then the weary business of backing up along unfamiliar urban tracks, stopping at every lot of points to make sure of their setting, until they had worked their way round the outskirts of Hull to Paragon Station, two and a half hours late. The buzzing remains of unused adrenalin still trembled through his body. Lucan seemed weary stuff, each call to heroism before action wholly unreal. You never knew what action was going to be like until you were in it. But afterwards . . . Tom's inherited rules of conduct, the deprecation of one's achievement, the embarrassed acceptance of praise, seemed very unsatisfying. The body itself demanded something more—something like Beowulf's ritual boasting—to lay the demons of battle back to sleep. Tom was conscious of having managed things well in the cutting, thus making up for his idiocy in letting the lad at the junction deceive him. Father would certainly have approved, but how was Father ever to know? Tom himself could hardly tell him.

'I say, Tom . . .'

Horace's voice was hushed and urgent. Tom, sitting on the footplate of his engine, in the smutty sunshine of the sidings between the Hessle Road and the river, looked up from his book. The air smelt vaguely of the sea, but more of smoke and coke.

'Sorry to interrupt,' said Horace. 'I know you want to swot. But there's something rummy happening back there, where they're loading. Dampier sent me.'

For the return journey Tom was to take two goods trucks back to Bradford, tacked onto his four coaches.

'What is it?' said Tom.

'Four fellows have just turned up with a lot of boxes. Their papers are in order, Dampier says, but they don't look like our chaps at all. They're so deuced sullen. I can't get a word out of them. They look like dockers to me, but aren't all the dockers supposed to be on strike? I wish you'd come and take a squint at them.'

'All right.'

As they walked back beside the coaches Tom said 'Horace, that business in the cutting this morning . . .'

'Yes?'

'You won't tell anyone about that, will you?'

'Oh. Why? But it's such a spiffing yarn!'

'I don't want any of those chaps to get into trouble. Blocking the track, you know—they could be sent to prison. I don't want that.'

'Oh but . . .'

'Did your bookie pay up?'

'Sure thing.'

'Well then?'

'I suppose so. If that's what *you* want . . . Look, there. The other two are in the truck. One of them looks the most frightful Bolshie. You wait till you see him.'

Tom stopped half way up the ramp of the loading platform and pretended to be studying the coupling of the first goods truck to the guard's van. Up on the platform two men were heaving a series of small crates off a hand-trolley. The crates were obviously pretty heavy.

'Dampier thinks it might be guns,' whispered Horace. 'Or explosives.'

'He'd better look and see, then, as soon as he gets the chance.'

'He's not allowed to. But if I say *you* said so, Tom . . .'

At that moment the two men on the platform heaved the last of the cases in and straightened up. One of them noticed Tom, and spoke to the other, who turned and came striding forward. He looked the very opposite of 'deuced sullen', a small man, quite elderly, the round face pink and pop-eyed under the flat cap, the mouth smiling and eager, the whole head cocked sideways like a robin's.

'You're the lad fought Tinker Donovan?' he said.

'That's right, but . . .'

'What's your name, sir?'

'Tom Hankey.'

'I'll shake your hand, then. Eh, but you haven't the weight of Tinker. I've known the lad fifteen years, and he's a fine boxer still. I'd have thought he must have been playing with you.'

'No, I don't think so. He was a bit cautious because of the way he cuts, but when he hit me it hurt all right. He'd have nailed me in another couple of rounds. How did you hear about it? It was only this morning.'

'One of the women was on that train, she told her man and he told me. Any sort of match, they know I like to hear.'

'Oh. Look, I really don't want it talked about. I don't want anyone to get into trouble, you see?'

'Aye, there's that. Was it true how it ended? Men with masks on and guns.'

'I'm afraid so.'

The man shook his head, half disbelief and half disgust.

'Aren't you on strike too?' said Tom.

A reserved air crept into the man's hitherto straightforward glance. At the same time the men who had been stacking the boxes inside the truck stepped out onto the platform. One of them—a tall man, gaunt-faced and with a shock of jet-black hair —saw Tom, took a pace or two along the platform, then stopped.

'Give us a hand with the side-gate, Ned,' he called in the mildest of voices.

The little man smiled and nodded at Tom, then turned away.

Momentarily routine resumed. The train became the normal 4.00 pm from Hull to Bradford. No doubt by the time it reached Leeds, and perhaps even earlier, it would need a new description, but now it waited under the handsome wide girderwork of Paragon Station for the last hurrying passengers. Tom leaned from the cab and saw Horace coming down the platform. He had something tucked secretively under his jacket, but looked a little down-cast.

'Not revolvers or bombs, then?' said Tom.

'Only beastly Bolshie pamphlets.'

Horace drew his prize forth and handed it to Tom. It was crudely printed, some twelve pages long. On the cover were the words 'THE SICKLE', and a coarsely-drawn cartoon of a scythe labelled 'Revolution' sweeping through a crowd of fat men in top-hats and women in long dresses.

'We could stop and sling them in the river at Selby,' said Horace.

'Better not. Tell Dampier to take a note of the name and address of the consignee and report it. Mind if I keep this one as a souvenir?'

A whistle blew. The green flag waved. He moved the regulator to begin another journey.

6

Oxford, 16th and 17th June, 1926

'Woffles says he saved your life in the strike.'

'He's exaggerating a bit. What else did he say?'

'He was awfully mysterious. Woffles being mysterious is like
. . . I don't know what it's like . . .'

'A hippopotamus hiding behind a lamp-post?'

'Sort of. No, not really . . . What happened, Tom? Do tell.'

He laughed. It was too late now. There had been a time, just
after the event, when he had felt that he would have given anything to spend an hour with her, just that she should know what
he had done. Though for weeks after the strike was over the
papers and magazines had been full of trivial anecdotes about
the doings of the volunteers, there had been nothing about his
adventure. A police inspector had interviewed him, very gingerly, in his digs in Bradford, but had seemed relieved when Tom
had said he could not name any names and was unlikely to recognise even the man he had fought, though in other districts
charges were being pressed against men who had caused far less
serious interruptions of train services. On his return to Oxford
he had found Dick Standish hostile and Woffles surly, but this
had not really worried him while he submerged himself in the
flood of Finals. After a while it had only seemed important that
Judy should know.

And now even that longing was gone. He realised that the episode in the cutting had become remote and unreal. It felt like a
school play in which he had suddenly been asked to take a leading role because of the illness of one of the other actors, and had
stumbled through the part without making a fool of himself—

71

had even inwardly relished the posturing and braggadocio—but within a week of the last performance had forgotten all his lines. If he'd been asked to play the part again it would have been a nightmare. Certainly it now had only the quality of dream.

But then so in a sense did the present moment, strolling with Judy on the crunching gravel paths of the President's Garden with her arm through his and the night at last a true soft summer after weeks of wet, a night for moths with the white syringa reeking of June and the dance-band wailing and thumping in the marquee beyond the high brick wall.

'Go on,' she said. 'I do want to know.'

'I was driving a train . . .' he began.

'Where? Don't leave anything out.'

'It was supposed to be the stopping train from Bradford to Hull via Leeds and Selby, but . . .'

'That goes right past our front door, almost!'

'Yes, I know. I used to look up at the hills and wonder what you were doing.'

'Go on.'

'Well, that morning some strikers tricked us into diverting onto a branch line at a place called Eastrington . . .'

'That's the Wold Line! Don't tell me . . . Oh, Daddy will be positively emerald with jealousy! He's never been allowed to, though he's wangled and wangled. Go on.'

'They ambushed us in a place called Drewton Cutting . . .'

'Terribly romantic. A great gorge. What did they do?'

'Blocked the line with a tree and trapped us. Then somehow or other we made a bargain that if I boxed one of their chaps and won they'd let us through. But we'd hardly begun when Woffles and some of his friends turned up with guns and made them let us through anyway.'

'Oh . . . You make it so . . . At least Woffles was mysterious about it. Why did he say he'd saved your life? Wouldn't you have beaten the man hollow?'

'He was pretty good, and much stronger than me. I think he'd have nailed me.'

'But for Woffles. And that's another thing. How did he . . . In my experience Woffles has a genius for turning up at the wrong moment.'

'He's probably lurking in those bushes.'

'Don't!'

She giggled like a shop-girl. Her finger-tips, slightly cold, caressed the back of his hand. Suddenly he longed to suggest that one of the shadowy nooks in the garden might be what she called a 'between-place'—though they'd be lucky to find one, as all such corners were already full of whispers and laughs and the paths held several more strolling couples, no doubt each man with a thought like his in mind. So far this evening he and Judy had been playing her 'rules' with care, in fact with a skill that had made them enjoyable. There had been five other couples in their dinner-party at the Randolph, besides Lady Fitzpeter whose presence in Oxford provided a token chaperonage to appease absent mothers. In the early part of the night he had done his duty dances with all five girls, behaving as though Judy were merely his official partner for the evening; but now, with frightening suddenness, her slight and chill caress loosed energies inside him that raged without any outlet. His throat tightened, and the muscles of his arm ached with the effort to hold it still, merely supporting hers and not dragging her body crushingly against his own. He and she were not strangers. They had lain sleepless together in one bed, all through a sighing, whispering, tingling night. And now they had to walk on gravel paths and talk about Woffles. He particularly didn't want to do that, as Bertie had sent a request, by way of Dick, asking him not to tell anyone more than that his rescuers were out rabbit-shooting, had heard the noise in the cutting, and had come down through the woods to see what it meant. (In fact during their single uncomfortable interview in Tom's rooms Dick had claimed that the rescue had been almost as fluky as that—the ambush had been planned in Leeds by a hot-head group of strikers meeting in the back room of a pub; the landlord's son had listened at the door and passed the news on to his scoutmaster, who had told a friend of Dick's—not, as Dick had rather shiftly admitted, a very reliable chain of communication.) His frustration erupted into a futile snort, which he half-contrived to convert into a laugh.

'What was that about?' she said.

'Nothing. You haven't told me what *you* did in the great strike.'

'Oh, we had colossal fun. You know Mummy owns this ship-ping line—well, she doesn't exactly own it but she's the main shareholder and anyway all the other directors are too scared to argue with her—well, we filled the house up with lots of chaps from Cambridge and they drove down to the docks every day and loaded and unloaded things and then the cars came back for us and we went to the docks too and became canteen girls and gave them luncheon on the quay and then we came home and made ourselves into ladies again and I bought an extra gramo-phone and a pile of new records so we could dance all night.'

'I wouldn't have thought they'd have been much good for the loading and unloading next day.'

'Oh, we made them work shifts—at the dancing, I mean. When your partner fell asleep in your arms you'd push him off to bed and go and wake up a fresh one. There were about forty of them, you see, and only seven of us. The cars would come round to the front for them at the crack of dawn and we'd stagger off and sleep until it was time to become canteen girls again.'

'Good training for Commem. week, by the sound of it. What did your parents think?'

'That was interesting—you'd have expected Mummy to be absolutely horrified, but . . . I suppose it was a bit like war-time for her . . . everybody relaxes their standards a bit . . . we were keeping the troops happy, sort of . . . Of course Daddy hardly noticed.'

'Too busy going for night runs?'

'Oh no, there wasn't any of that, not with you amateurs barg-ing up and down the line—it would have been incredibly dangerous, and he's absolutely mad on safety. He always rings up the crossing-keeper at Broomfleet to tell him to pass the message along to the other keepers and signalmen. That's why it's got to be a dock strike, not a rail strike. No, he went down to the docks and did a lot of shunting, so he was perfectly happy. But you must get him to take you on a night run when you come to stay.'

'Oh. When's that?'

'We always have a house party for the York races—I expect you do too.'

'We used to until my mother died. Father doesn't care for

racing.'

'I hate it—it's the most boring way of losing money anybody ever invented. Would I like your father, Tom?'

'Why don't you come and see? He's always complaining that I don't bring any pretty girls to Sillerby.'

'I could drive over. I'd love to see the house, anyway. Oh, it's absolute ages till York, and I've got to go to Scotland before that —tell you what, I'll try to wangle Mummy into having a house party next month. Shall we go back and dance?'

'If you like . . . Or would you like to see the river by moon-light? I managed to get a punt hidden away, in case . . .'

'The chap who asked me to the May Ball at the other Trinity took me out in a punt. He was one of our volunteer dockers. He'd behaved awfully well while he was with us, but I'm afraid he got a bit tiddly at Cambridge and tried to sing gondolier songs while he was punting and then he fell in and left me floating away in the punt. Somebody rescued me, of course, and David swam ashore, but he couldn't understand why nobody wanted to dance with him any more. He hadn't got anything to change into. It would have been like waltzing with a drowned man. He just sat in one corner grinning like a fool and smelling like sheep in the rain.'

'Poor blighter. I promise not to fall in. Or sing.'

'Let's dance for a bit. You're pretty good, Tom, especially at waltzes. You're full of surprises, really.'

'You didn't notice at Hendaye?'

'Hendaye was different.'

There was no special emphasis on the words, but yes, Hendaye had been different—trying to dance on the pink-and-white marble of Bertie's tiny terrace, with Bertie the only one who could tango to a decent standard and so insisting on playing nothing but tango records.

'I absolutely loathed my dancing lessons,' he said. 'Penny-cuick used to drive me over to York. I suppose I was about four-teen—I know all the other boys were younger than me but the girls were all ages . . .'

'I bet they fought to dance with you!'

'A bit. That made it worse, because they'd lose their rag if I got it wrong, and Miss Owlish would tonk away at the piano and

suddenly leap up—she'd go on singing the music for the others
—and snatch you from your partner and push you round the
floor, still singing—*da* doodle, *da* doodle, *da* doodle, like that—
but breaking off to yell at the others because they weren't swaying enough—she was a terrific swayer, a bit like our old
Daimler, really, almost made you car-sick and smelt like the
Daimler too, sort of leathery—and then she'd toss you back to
your partner and tonk away again . . .'

She laughed her clear laugh and stood still.

'Listen, they've started a waltz!' she said. 'Let's go and
sway!'

Gripping his fingers between hers she dragged him towards
the music.

Under the lights in the marquee she glistened with youth and
freshness. It was impossible to believe that she had danced till
dawn at the House last night, and then slept less than three
hours. They swung among the twirling couples. Her eyes shone
with almost hysterical delight as she chanted to the swing of the
band.

'*Da*-doodle, *da*-doodle, *da*-doodle . . . am I swaying enough?
. . . *da*-doodle . . .'

A tall dark girl in a remarkably short apple-green dress called
over her shoulder at them 'Somebody's been to Miss Owlish's.'

'Not me! Tom!' shouted Judy, slipping from his hold, somehow detaching the tall girl's partner (a puffy-faced, pink young
man with black hair slicked hard down) and swirling away with
him, crying 'Don't forget to sway!'

Tom and the tall girl laughed. She shrugged, mock-rueful.

'May I?' he said.

'Was that Judy Tarrant?' she said as she took his hand.

'Do you know her?'

'Not to talk to, but she's rather famous.'

'What for?'

'Oh . . . this sort of thing, I suppose.'

There was no way of enquiring further. They danced the rest
of the waltz together. The girl's name was Janet Stott and she
came from a village near Tadcaster, the other side of York from
Sillerby. They had a few friends in common but did not seem to

have overlapped at Miss Owlish's. Conversation was jerky as half Miss Stott's attention was concentrated on watching her real partner's progress, as if to make sure Judy didn't spirit him clear away. When the dance was over they both almost plunged through the chattering couples towards where the other two had last been seen. Judy came towards him looking a little nervous, or pretending to.

'I say, Tom, I've done something . . . I hope you won't think it's a bit off. Was the girl all right?'

'Perfectly pleasant, but not the same thing.'

'I should think not! I'm afraid Guy—that's his name—was a bit shirty at first. He's terribly in love with her. He made me feel guilty at stealing her, even for only three minutes, so to make up, you see—I do hope you don't mind—I said they could borrow your punt.'

'All right.'

'I'd much rather dance now. I'm in the mood. Perhaps we could have the punt back to look at the sunrise.'

'Provided they're not so much in love that . . . Come in, Number Eight—your time's up. Hang on here a tick while I go and explain where it is. If you don't hide 'em they get snaffled.'

'Oh, Tom, you are an angel. You're sure you don't mind?'

'No reason why a sunrise shouldn't be as enjoyable as a sunset.'

'No . . . I suppose not.'

Sunrises, too, turned out to be different from the sunsets supplied at Hendaye. This one was beautiful in a still, chill English fashion, and their kisses had much in common with it. In fact her hand-clasp as he walked with her back to the Randolph had seemed more intimate than their modest embraces on the river. It was as if her fingers acknowledged the reality that lay beneath the rules, while her lips pretended not to.

Even so, as Tom stood on the doorstep of Mrs. Godber's and fished in his waistcoat pocket for his key, he felt an astonishing after-tow of exhilaration. For one thing, he knew he had moved the game on a stage—not a large one but more, he guessed, than Judy had intended. But there was more too it than that. He wondered whether she had somehow sensed his sudden uprush of anger and frustration in the President's Garden and had deliberately set herself to be marvellous company, walking with heedless poise along the dangerous edge between laughter and hysteria. Janet Stott's strange remark had nagged for a little, but then been absorbed into the mood of the long dawn.

As he climbed the narrow familiar stair and smelt Mrs. Godber's peculiarly pungent lino-polish, Tom realised that he did not even wish to fantasise that Judy had somehow flitted from her hotel room and found his window and was waiting for him here. That would be too drastic an alteration of rhythm. He would actually prefer to find his bed empty.

It was not to be. A tousled head lay almost face down on his pillow. A bulk, too large for a woman, hummocked his blankets. Craning amazed over the sleeping form he saw that it was Gerald. By no means a welcome visitor, but not one either who could be tumbled out of bed and booted downstairs. Forbearance with Gerald, the family had proved in a series of unhappy experiments, caused less trouble in the end. With a sigh Tom straightened and went to the sideboard. The gin bottle was empty, but had been nearly so last night. The sherry seemed untouched. He took the decanter out into the corridor and tucked it behind the spare towels in Mrs. Godber's linen-cupboard. It was bad luck the house was full; though some of Mrs. Godber's lodgers had gone down, she had let their rooms for Commem. week. All Tom could do was take a couple of blankets back to his room, change into his pyjamas and curl himself up on the slithery leather of his sofa.

'Sorry about taking your bed, old man.'

'That's all right, Ger. I wasn't using it. How did you get past Mrs. Godber?'

'Told her who I was and turned on the old charm. I can still do it if I have to, you know.'

It was hard to believe. Gerald looked terrible. If you had seen him coming towards you as a stranger in the street you would have been certain that he was about to beg the price of a packet of fags off you and tell you a story about not having eaten for five days. His eyes were sunken, his face grey-yellow, his whole body constantly trembling. It was difficult to guess whether he hadn't

78

shaved for a week or had shaved incompetently three days ago. When he moved it was with a slouched, whipped-hound mien. He had woken Tom by clattering the doors of the sideboard, presumably looking for the sherry.

'Let's hope the charm hasn't worn off,' said Tom. 'I'll go and ask her for breakfast. Could you eat an egg?'

'I'll have a go. Where's the rears, old man?'

'Next landing up. I'll show you.'

This too was family habit. You could not start Gerald on however short a journey and trust him to reach his destination; you had to watch and see that he got there. The only thing about his presence in Oxford that Tom felt fairly sure of was that he was supposed to be somewhere else. On his way down from the lavatory Tom took the decanter from the linen-cupboard and carried it on to the kitchen.

'Morning, Mrs. Godber.'

'*Good* morning, Mr. Hankey,' she answered, taking the decanter from him and putting it on a shelf of the dresser. 'Was it all right letting the gentleman in?'

'Yes, thank you very much. He's my brother.'

'Oh, I saw the likeness, so I believed him.'

'Very good of you. I'm afraid he's . . .'

'You needn't tell *me*, Mr. Hankey. It's sad how many gentlemen I see like that. Ones who lodged with me, oh, thirty years back turning up on my doorstep looking like something the dog sicked up. In vacations only, that's natural, isn't it? They can't face the colleges and besides they know all my rooms would be full.'

'And you let them in?'

'Depends how I feel. First time, usually, I let them have a bed and a meal—but I make sure they understand it's no use coming back again. Now you'll be wanting breakfast for two. You'll see that the gentleman eats as much as he can, won't you? And I expect you don't feel that bright yourself. At least I hope the young lady was nice to you.'

'Charming, thank you. I got in about six, but I'm not too bad. And I think you're an absolute marvel, Mrs. Godber.'

The wizened head nodded on the crooked neck. Tom had never seen Mrs. Godber smile but he had learnt to know when she was pleased.

When he turned into the corridor towards his room he found Gerald rummaging in the back of the linen-cupboard and felt ashamed for both of them.

'I expect I could find you something if you want it,' he said.

'Eh? No, oh no. Glad, really . . . Do you know, old man, *it's not there at all*?'

'I took it down to the kitchen as a matter of fact.'

'Not there either. Complete illusion. Only think it's there because of the sin of Adam, that's what they say, though I can't quite swallow all that yet. Got a razor I can borrow?'

'What were you saying about illusion?' asked Tom.

It seemed important to discover quite how far-gone Gerald had become. Previously, however drunk or hung-over he had been, his speech had retained an uncanny coherence, but the mumblings outside the linen-cupboard suggested that this was no longer the case. Shaved and washed he looked several degrees less appalling, but still not an acquaintance any fastidious person would be glad of. He had started to eat with a grimace that had made Tom think he was about to vomit, but quite soon he had evidently rediscovered the meaning of hunger.

'Illusion, eh? Oh yes, it's all illusion,' he said, waving an egg-dripping spoon at Mrs. Godber's orange wallpaper, but implying all Oxford in the gesture and the round world beyond it.

'Don't tell me you've become a Platonist, Ger.'

'Eh? Oh, no, I don't think so—though he was half way there, of course—shadows in the cave, all that . . . I want your advice, Tom. That's why I came to see you. Minnie got your address out of Nan.'

He tore a piece of toast in half and buttered it in silence. Tom, perhaps light-headed with lack of sleep, experienced a sudden tremor of apprehension, something more than the mild shock at discovering that Gerald had arrived in Oxford, in however ramshackle a state, on purpose.

'*My* advice?'

'Not quite like that . . . your thoughts, more like . . . tell me, Tom—how would you feel if I pulled myself together?'

'I would think it was the best thing that ever happened.'

'You're a good chap, Tom. What's more, I believe you'd still have been a good chap if you'd been half blasted to bits in the trenches, like me . . . I knew you'd say that, but you haven't really thought about it.'

'I don't need to think about it. It's obvious.'

Gerald began to speak very slowly, separating the words so that Tom could hear the blur round each of them, like the stain spreading round a drop of ink on blotting-paper.

'When I say "Pull myself together" I mean come back to Sillerby, manage one of the farms, shoot a bit, fit into the county, give Father a hand—it won't be long before he needs it—take over when he dies. All the things you were expecting to do, Tom.'

'I still think it would be the best thing that ever happened.'

If the sherry had been illusion, this was illusion of illusion, a typical sad, vague fantasy of reform. Tom was certain that his own voice rang with insincerity. Perhaps Gerald heard the note, for he actually laughed.

'Had a bit of a lapse on my way through London,' he said. 'Forgot they'd turfed me out of the club after that business with the piano. If only there'd been a train straight from Paddington . . . but you see it was ninety minutes till the next one and there was the bar right there by the platform. That must have been yesterday. No, the day before, at least. I did get on a train somewhere. Wales, probably. I seem to remember the accent. They wouldn't stop rolling milk-churns . . . Pulling yourself together isn't all that easy, Tom. Fact, it's a bit like when they stitched me together in the hospital. After a bit you think you can get out of bed and stand without help but as soon a you try it you keel straight over. But listen, Tom. Do you know what I've been doing these last six weeks? You'll never guess. I've been staying in people's houses, walking moors—I actually caught two sea-trout one morning—and in the evenings I've been sitting over the port and listening to the usual chat about ghillies and poachers and the way the crofters are all melting away to Glasgow, and I've been joining in, too. I didn't even smash one chair. I only fell asleep once—and I wasn't the only one because Potty Caithness wouldn't stop talking about his scheme for importing reindeer . . . I don't expect you've heard him, Tom. He's better than any insomnia pills I've ever taken . . .'

'You've been staying at Auchtermochty!'

'I have. Five days.'

'That's marvellous, Ger!'

Tom had never met Lord Caithness, but of course had heard of his notorious shortness of temper, especially where guests were concerned. It was still disputed how accidental had been the shooting of a car-load of London acquaintances whose self-invitation to Auchtermochty Lady Caithness had weakly accepted. If Gerald had lasted five days there . . .

'I've had help, you see Tom. That's why I'm here. Minnie thought the time had arrived when I'd better come and warn you things might change.'

'You'll have to explain about Minnie.'

'Minnie Heusen. She's a Scientist.'

Tom felt that he was becoming more light-headed than ever. He had a dream-like vision of a severe woman in a white coat and steel-rimmed glasses standing by Gerald's bedside manipulating retorts and glass tubing full of bubbling green liquids.

'A Christian Scientist,' said Gerald.

'Good Lord! How did you get a hold of her on Malinsay?'

'She just came to stay. One of Nan's old school chums wrote to say she was doing the Western Isles with an American friend and would Nan put them up for a few days. I must say, Tom, Nan's been pretty good to me but it's been Ian whose been the real brick. It can't be much fun having a wreck of a brother-in-law doddering round your castle for several years, and keeping all your whisky padlocked the whole time . . . Where was I? Yes, last August it was, these two females turned up. I don't think I even knew they were there—I was having a bad patch—but apparently Nan and Minnie hit it off and Minnie persuaded Nan to try something out on me. First I knew of it, Nan came into my room one morning—September, I suppose—I was feeling ghastly—I get a sort of rheumatic fever which makes it agony even to turn over, so I hadn't slept in spite of taking dozens of my pills—and when Nan announced she'd brought a visitor to see me I told her I was damned if I'd see anyone at all. She just smiled and slipped out, and I heard a whisper or two and then in came this fellow—I knew he was some kind of Holy Joe as soon as I clapped eyes on him—short grey hair, a long grey face like a horse, a bloody great bony nose and a collar three sizes too small for him. He pulled a chair up beside my bed and stared out over me like a dying duck in a thunderstorm, and said 'All is Mind.' He had an American accent like a circular saw. 'By God,' I said to myself, 'the bugger's potty.' He didn't say anything else for a couple of minutes and I was damned if I was going to help him, then it came again—'All. Is. Mind.' Like that. He said it half a dozen times. He wasn't talking to me, or to himself—fact, I got the idea he was somehow talking to the universe. I was all set to have hysterics, only I didn't dare because it would have hurt so much . . . and then, Tom, the most amazing thing, I realised I could have hysterics if I wanted to. I mean, the pain would still have happened, only it wouldn't have been part of me, anything to do with me myself, only something that was happening to a lot of shot-to-blazes meat lying on my bed . . .

'The American—his name's Scott Warren and he's the most amazing man, been going round Scotland all last summer talking to fellows like me and literally jerking them out of their beds and putting them back on their feet—he knew I'd got past the first barrier and then he started to talk, a lot of guff about mind and matter, with bits out of the Bible. Honestly, I thought it was the most awful rubbish. But that's only what I thought. It wasn't what I felt. I simply wanted him to stay with me and go on talking, because suddenly I was beginning to feel like the real me. First time in years, except when I've been half cut. That's why you drink, you know. There's a sort of self which you know ought to be living inside your body but somehow it's strayed away and got lost, and a couple of drinks give you the illusion that it's somewhere quite close, just out there in the darkness, longing to come home . . . so you have a couple more, and then of course . . .

'I still can't accept the logic of it, Tom. I'd like to, but I can't. The meanings they read into the Bible, for instance. The fall of Adam consisted of the creation of the material universe, you know . . .'

'William Blake said something like that, I think. And don't the Swedenborgians . . .'

'Oh, it goes right back to the Gnostics. But it doesn't really matter, old man. All that matters is that they've got hold of something, and I'm here, on my feet, to prove it. The women seem to take all the Bible stuff in their stride. I'd better warn you Nan's become a fervent Scientist, and it's causing a bit of a rift between her and Ian. Old Scott only stayed a couple of nights till the next ferry, then he pushed off and Minnie Heusen came and took over. Took me over. She's a wonder, too. I'm going to marry her.'

'That's marvellous, Ger! Congratulations!'

Gerald mumbled his thanks without really noticing and went on with his story. His voice was still slurred but he had stopped shaking and looked either at the table-cloth or earnestly into Tom's eyes. Very likely this was the first time he had had a chance to explain the events of the last six months to anyone outside them, and so, in a sense it was the first time he had explained them to himself.

'She's older than me—thirty-five. Very neat and quiet and small. Not at all my idea of an American. She's read everything, and thought about it. Been everywhere too—mention a country and she's stayed there and looked at the temples and met the Minister of the Interior and inspected the gaols—she takes a little typewriter everywhere she goes and before anyone else is awake she gets up and taps away for a couple of hours, sending off reports to all the organisations she belongs to about all sorts of things . . . Minnie's all energy, and yet somehow she finds time to sit all morning with a neurotic old soak like me, or go bird-watching with Ian—he approves of her no end, spite of what she's done to Nan—she isn't any kind of fanatic, you see, although she believes absolutely implicitly . . .

'Anyway, when she's around I feel I can manage. And it's true, Tom. She stayed on Malinsay for a month and then Nan got in touch with a few friends on the mainland and asked if Minnie and I could come and stay. They were pretty chary, you can imagine. After all, some of the things I've done when I was cut are pretty well folklore by now in the West Highlands, but for Ian's sake and Nan's they said yes, mostly. And it turned out all right. Honestly, you'd have laughed to see their faces changing the first evening when they realised they weren't going to have to get the chauffeurs in to hold me down. And of course they adored Minnie. You should have heard Potty Caithness grunting away at her when we were saying good-bye, asking when she was coming again . . . And I can keep it up, Tom. I'm getting better all the time. What happened at Paddington was the first real splurge for months . . .'

'Are you going to tell Miss Heusen about that?'

'Yes, of course. You can't shock her. She won't even make me feel ashamed. She's Mrs. Heusen by the by. She was born Minnie Gassaway, of all things, but when she was nineteen she married this fellow, old enough to be her grandfather but she seems to have been very fond of him. He passed on five years ago. There weren't any children, but she's not too old to have them, and she wants to.'

'You seem to have fallen on your feet at last. I can't tell you how glad I am. Have you said anything to Father?'

'I've funked that so far. Minnie made me come down to talk to the family, but I thought I'd better clear the ground with you first. Of course once I set Minnie on Father she'll have him eating out of her hand. How's the old devil keeping these days?'

'Just the same. Butterflies and regimental history and county skulduggery, varied by the odd crazy scheme. He made me learn to drive a train for the General Strike. I had quite an interesting time of it . . . One thing, though, Ger—he talks about money more than he used to. It's preying on his mind a bit. You mayn't find he's all that set on taking you on if you aren't bringing anything in.'

Gerald laughed, an outpouring of good humour, an almost painful echo of times spent larking around Sillerby when Tom had been a small boy trailing in the wake of his hero-brothers.

'He can stop worrying if I marry Minnie, Tom. Old Heusen owned a chain of shoe-factories and left her the whole lot. Our idea is that we should buy back Gattings and Hatchers and do up one of the farm houses and live there until Father goes. Minnie could do all that, and put Tapwith and Home Farm in order too, and re-lead the roof at Sillerby, and not even notice she's spent the money.'

For the first time Tom felt a curious pang, not exactly of jealousy but of pointlessly wasted stress and penny-pinching all his growing years.

'If it's illusion anyway,' he said.

'Eh?'

'Money.'

'Uh . . . that's a rum thing, Tom. Scientists, you know—
they've done wonders for me, and their healers really can heal,
and the rest are good, quiet, serious, admirable people. But
practically all the ones I've met are absolutely rolling.'

'Perhaps you've just met the ones who are rich enough to travel.'

'I don't know . . . I ought to send Minnie a wire, I suppose.
And Father. Have you got a Bradshaw? I'd like to get straight up
to Sillerby, if I can. You've been a great help, Tom, and I'm
ever so grateful to you.'

Tom told Judy about the visitation while they were sitting
under a willow in a meadow below Cumnor Ridge. Her silver
Lagonda blazed in the sun where she had pulled it off the road by
the old stone bridge. A swan and five half-grown cygnets drifted
just below the arches, maintaining their position with apparently magical indifference to the rush of the stream; one had to make
a deliberate effort to envisage the rubber-black legs paddling
steadily below the still bodies.

'You're glad?' she said.

'Of course. It solves such a lot of problems—Gerald, Sillerby,
me too. It makes me free.'

The sun went in behind one of the lolloping silver-and-dark
clouds that the wind was trundling in from Wales. Judy smiled
and ate another of the strawberries, acid from a feeble summer,
which they had bought in Abingdon. They were supposed to be
having luncheon at the Randolph, so that Lady Fitzpeter could
see that she still had all her charges undamaged, but Judy had
telephoned the hotel from Abingdon with a totally false story
about the Lagonda's carburettor; then they had bought their
picnic and found this meadow.

They threw twigs in the river, drank white wine scarcely less
acid than the strawberries, and discussed the permutations of
pairing that had taken place in Lady Fitzpeter's party between
dinner and dawn; the other men were strangers or half-strangers
to Tom, but Judy seemed to know all the girls. They analysed
these transient amours a little patronisingly, as if looking down
on shifting dunes from the stable platform of their own love.

Touch and even glance might be subject to Judy's rules, but there seemed to be quite large areas of the relationship to which they did not apply.

Tom discovered another such area, much less comfortable, when he was holding the door of the Lagonda for her an hour later. They had been driven from their idyll by the appearance of the cob-swan, who came at them up the bank, neck held low, hissing, wings half-spread. The clouds too, had massed into a rain-impending darkness. Judy paused on the running-board, turned and put her hands on his shoulders. Her eyes were level with his and she looked at him for quite a long time with a strange, cold, speculative stare, like a farmer considering whether one of his beasts is ready for slaughter.

'You're going to have to be particularly nice to Mummy now,' she said.

Before he could answer she pulled him close and began to kiss him, angrily, so that both their mouths hurt.

7

Brantingham Manor, 6th July, 1926

Mrs. Tarrant caressed the rump of a cast-iron chamois.

'Of course it's perfectly ridiculous,' she said, 'but I am used to it. In fact I'm rather fond of it, which is just as well. You have only two choices with a thing like this, Mr. Hankey. Either you keep it in good order or you get rid of it.'

She was by no means the leathery, vinegary dragon-priestess Tom had expected. Her face under her wide straw hat was creamy and rounded, with a softly elastic look, as of marshmallow. Her eyes were a strange pale brown, wide set, and her figure, though plump, was not at all stodgy. She moved in an aura of relaxed self-certainty which made it difficult to tell whether anything she said (and so far Tom had only exchanged with her a series of commonplaces about the weather and a few shared acquaintances) was sensibly reserved, or ironic, or (as it appeared when one thought about it afterwards) weirdly imperceptive.

'You'd have a job getting rid of it, wouldn't you?' he said.

It was a fifty-foot model of the Jungfrau, made of rocks set into concrete, adorned with knee-high metal fauna, and planted with even more out-of-scale alpines.

'It is hollow, of course,' she said, stamping her flat-heeled shoe as though she expected the mountain to boom.

'Do you keep anything in it?'

'Only mowers and things. Cyprian has always wanted to keep his steam engine here, but we found that laying the track up these slopes would be ridiculously expensive.'

'I'd love to see his engine.'

'No doubt Cyprian will show it you,' she said, turning away as if more interested in the view than in railway engines.

The view was admirable in a vaguely oppressive way. Far to the south-east lay the green undulations of Lincolnshire vanishing into mist beyond which lay the North Sea. Nearer, but still three or four miles away, the Humber estuary stretched in gleaming stillness. Belts of woodland hid the industrial villages of the nearer shore, and sooty Hull was out of sight to the left, behind Welton Wold. Half way up the escarpment this strange foreign-seeming garden had been planted, the site deliberately chosen and enhanced so that its owners could gaze out at a huge tract of the England they were prepared to acknowledge and not see any of the England they preferred to ignore. The house itself —dark granite, sprawling, spired and turreted, both harsh and fanciful—was hidden by the crescent of Wellingtonias that had been planted to shelter the miniature mountain from the north and east. Tom tried to imagine Judy, four years old, trundling her wooden wheelbarrow across the slope of lawn below them. It must have been fun for a child having a private mountain to scramble over.

'Do the chamois have names?' he asked.

Mrs. Tarrant turned back to him with a very odd look, as though he had said something which it was not his place to say.

'They did once,' she answered. 'It is strange you should ask that. I haven't thought about it for years, but a few nights ago I dreamed I was climbing up these paths trying to remember the names of the animals, and I couldn't. When I was a little girl, Mr. Hankey, I'm afraid I was very difficult. My parents thought there was something wrong with me because I refused to walk or talk, though I was quite capable of doing so. The only person I would talk to was my Nanny. I could make her do whatever I wanted, you see. I used to make her push my perambulator out here and put it by that tree, and I would lie there and look at the mountain all morning. Doctors came to Brantingham to see me, specialists from London and Vienna, but it was no use. Either I paid no attention to them or I screamed until they went away. When I was six Papa had an old Swiss botanist to stay. Papa had met him at Interlaken when he was plant-collecting and the Swiss gentleman would not believe everything Papa told him

about the plants he managed to grow here, so far north. Papa
forced him to come and see. We are a strong-willed family, Mr.
Hankey. While he was here he wandered out one morning to
look at the rockery and found me lying in my pram. He was the
kind of tiresome old gentleman who tries to strike up friendships
with strange children. I do not remember anything about the
episode, but apparently he told me that he lived near the
mountain. Because his English was not good I believed he was
saying he lived *in* the mountain. I got out of my pram and took
him round all the paths and introduced him to the iron animals.
That broke the spell. Do you understand?'

'After that you walked and talked like anyone else?'

'Not merely that, Mr. Hankey. I became a sensible and
obedient child. I made my parents send Nanny away. I must
make it clear that I do not approve at all of the way I behaved until then, and I would never have allowed it to happen to my own
daughter.'

Mrs. Tarrant nodded decisively. There was a sense of closing.
She became like one of those remote, white Mediterranean
houses, extraordinarily secret-seeming despite being so clearly
visible amidst its vineyards. A moment before there had been a
glimpse of lives being lived—a child crouched at the gate, a
woman calling from a window—but now the shutters were blank
and the place might not be inhabited at all. He wondered why
she had told him about the episode. Perhaps it was because the
dream had disturbed her, an uncontrolled upwelling of a spirit
which she thought long since bound fast in one of her inmost
caves. Tom's chance remark had allowed her to bring the
creature out into open day, inspect it, renew its gyves and send it
back into the depths. So far he had been unable to perceive in
either of Judy's parents any kind of likeness to her, physical or
habitual, but Mrs. Tarrant's picture of the silent, wilful child,
screaming at one specialist and ignoring the next, had something
in it that related to Judy's curiously scheming impulsiveness—
will embodied in action, the action apparently random but the
will directed to a goal. And at least he could guess now why
Judy's Nannies had never been allowed to stay long enough to
acquire a hold over her.

Tom was out on the rockery this morning as a result of another apparently random action. Mrs. Tarrant had a formidable notion of the role of a hostess at a house party. As breakfast was ending she produced a list from her bag and held up her hand for silence, then read out her orders of the day, assigning each guest to some officially recognised pleasure for a precise number of hours. Tom had been cheered that first morning to find himself down to play golf in the same foursome as Judy, but just as he had been getting ready to come down and join the others in the hall a maid had brought a note to his room saying that he was now booked to help Mrs. Tarrant on the rockery. 'My daughter has thoughtlessly made some arrangement with a neighbour' was all the explanation the note had contained, and Mrs. Tarrant had told him no more. He had become that unwanted creature, an extra man, and something had to be found for him to do. Normally, he assumed, one of the half-dozen gardeners would have helped Mrs. Tarrant.

He had not been pleased. Gardening was an activity he had hitherto viewed from a distance and without interest. There were of course gardens of a sort at Sillerby—the melon-ground, between whose worn brick walls Plaice grew his regimented vegetables; the rose garden with its geometrical beds of always ailing Ophelia and Etoile; dark banks of reverted rhododendrons; the little West Garden, with its sundial and curlicue beds edged with lobelia and carrying in unvarying succession through each year wallflowers, then tulips, then geraniums. For Tom one had gardens round a house in the same way that one had wallpaper in a room, and that was all.

Gardening with Mrs. Tarrant turned out to be more interesting than he had expected. At least it had the fascination of watching an expert at work.

'Can you tell one plant from another, Mr. Hankey?'

'I know my wild flowers pretty well.'

'That will not do. You can fetch and carry for me, if you would be so kind. It is quite hard work but you look a strong young man. Really it is less nerve-racking for me to work with somebody who does not claim to be a gardener—quite sensible-seeming people still pull the wrong things out. I never let any of my own men do anything but fetch and carry up here. Now, if you will start by bringing me a bucket of peat and another of granite chips—the peat is the second mound along and the chips are at the end . . .'

She knelt, took a crooked little tool from the pocket of her apron and began to fossick briskly but deftly through the soil round a tuft of gentians. Tom spent his morning running up and down the Jungfrau with a bucket in each hand. Every little pocket of soil seemed to require a slightly different cocktail of ingredients, and there was a surprising amount of rubbish to ferry down—weeds, and the dead-heads of spring-flowered plants, and thinnings from drifts of seedlings, and sometimes perfectly healthy-seeming clumps which Mrs. Tarrant rooted ruthlessly out, declaring that she used to like them but was bored with them now. Between each journey, while he waited for his next task, a stint of conversation took place. These were rather like the pockets of soil on the mountain, each apparently unrelated to the next, unpredictable in shape and content, but (he came to the conclusion) solemnly planned. He got the impression that while he was away Mrs. Tarrant selected not only the subject of the next exchange, but the course it must take, and if one of his answers diverged along some other channel she ignored it as completely as if he had not spoken. Certainly there was no question of his initiating a subject, however uncontroversial or trivial. He discovered this on his first return, when he arrived with the peat and chips and remarked that this was the sort of training of which the coach at the gym would approve.

'Put them there,' said Mrs. Tarrant. 'I'm not quite ready yet. Does your father let all the Sillerby farms, Mr. Hankey, or does he have some of them managed?'

Tom explained. Her further questions, though well within the proprieties of inquisitiveness, were clearly designed to elicit evidence of the solidity of the Sillerby finances, but though the subject was far from fully explored by the time she sent him off on his next errand, she did not return to it. Instead she talked about a seaman's charity of which she was president and expanded from there to the running of 'our' churches. He remembered that Judy had used the same phrase in the tea-shop at Market Weighton. 'Our' churches did not include Brantingham, of which Mr. Tarrant was Rector. They were in fact one church and three chapels built in the dock area by Mrs. Tarrant's grandfather, and remained as foci for all the intricate politics of alms. Next time she asked Tom what he had done in the strike, and he was able to point out the run of the line on the plain below, along which he had taken his train seventeen times in nine days. She had evidently not heard of the fight in the cutting (strange that the place should be only a few miles over the wold behind them) so he said nothing about it. For one thing the adventure seemed even more absurd now than it had when he had told Judy about it in the President's Garden; for another thing, though she evidently approved of his driving a train in the strike, he sensed that the anarchic, improvised nature of that particular adventure would not, in her eyes, do.

'I will certainly suggest that Cyprian gets his engine out for you tomorrow,' she said. 'He will enjoy showing it off to somebody who knows about trains. And it will make a change from choir-outings. The engine is always a great success with the boys in our choirs, of course, though they do tend to become boisterous. Now will you please bring me half a bucket of larch-mould and some more of the coarse grit?'

The summer had taken a turn for the better. As the morning passed, heat-haze engulfed Lincolnshire, turning the distance into an amorphous green dimness. At the same time Tom found that the nature of his nervousness was altering. It had begun as a tight knot of apprehension near the centre of his being—the importance of hitting it off with Mrs. Tarrant and the obvious difficulty of doing so made him feel mentally gawky. Now, helped by the growing heat and the physical exercise, the knot seemed to loosen itself, but its elements did not vanish. Instead they travelled, as it were, outwards to the frontiers of his consciousness, manifesting themselves as bouts of awareness both about himself and about this place, which seemed to be also discoveries about a whole series of possible selves and places.

There was a lull in the talk while Mrs. Tarrant concentrated on extricating from a clump of trailing flowers small sections which had rooted themselves, and replanting them in the tray of damp, peaty soil he had brought her. The plant had a lush, clover-like leaf, but bright blue pea-shaped flowers on stiff little stems.

'That one's lovely,' he said. 'I haven't seen it before.'

She seemed not to have heard him but when she had finished

and given him the tray to carry down she suddenly said '*Parochetus Communis*. It's too early to do this, but I shall be away in September. Yes, it's pretty, isn't it? Don't drop them.'

Picking his way down precipitous and irregular steps he discovered that that abrupt exchange had quite altered his perception of her. She was still an obstacle, but no longer a demon or goddess who had to be placated by a ritual of acceptable behaviour. She was certainly difficult to cope with, but he rather admired her, in the way that one might find one admired a particular building in a style which one had hitherto thought unsympathetic. It was even conceivable that he would one day come to like her. As he was proposing to make her his mother-in-law, this was perhaps just as well.

At once a long stretch of time displayed itself before him, invisible in detail like the fields beyond the Humber, but still unavoidably there. The discovery made him stop half way down the mountain, as one might to look at a view; in fact he stood gazing at the tray of plants in his hand, their leaves already floppy from shock, and without any effort of imagination perceived himself (knee-joints beginning to creak, straw hat on balding brow) carrying this tray and these plants down this path when Mrs. Tarrant was dead and gone. Since his acceptance of the possibility that Gerald's Christian Scientist might get him on the rails enough to take over at Sillerby, Tom's own future had consisted (insofar as he had thought of it at all) of images of Arcadian freedom, shared with Judy. Suddenly, as if in some elaborately staged play with huge slabs of moving scenery, a definite vista of the future opened before him, but at the same time other alterations took place, walls sliding close on either side, silently eliminating the unnumbered possible lives and homes which had been there, however vaguely, five minutes before. If Mrs. Tarrant was to become his mother-in-law, then eventually he and Judy would live here, at Brantingham Manor. Their children would scramble over the mountain and devise names for the iron chamois.

He shook his head and finished his descent. At the lead trough beneath the Wellingtonias he lowered his tray onto the rack where its soil could suck up water from below and settle comfortingly round the startled rootlets. The plants did not look at all happy. No doubt Mrs. Tarrant knew what she was doing, but even she had said that it was too early for such a disturbance. He climbed back to her empty-handed.

'I believe you are a friend of Bertie Panhard, Mr. Hankey.'

'Well, I don't see all that much of him, but . . .'

'You stayed with him in France.'

'That's where I met Judy.'

'Of course.'

A tacky little pause. Evidently Tom's acquaintanceship with Judy was not the subject of this exchange.

'Bertie,' he said. 'Well, he just asked me. We were at one of those Christmas dances and we were talking about how we were going to spend the spring vacation, and I said I'd probably go butterfly-collecting for my father. That was when he asked me to stay. The western end of the Pyrenees hasn't been very thoroughly collected, you know.'

She did not, and did not wish to.

'Was that the first time you had met him?'

'Oh no. I think the first time was at Rokesley. Woffles Belford and I were at school together, you see, and Woffles . . .'

'I much prefer to hear him called James.'

The remark was little more than a murmur, but somehow manifested the so-far semi-mythical Mrs. Tarrant of whom both Father and Judy had spoken, that embodiment of pure will who even as a child had contrived to force her world into the shape she chose.

'I'll try and think of him as James,' said Tom. 'You'll have to forgive me if I slip up, because I've known him as Woffles so long. I think he brought the name to Eton from his prep-school, even.'

'Exactly,' she said.

'Anyway, James usually asks me over to Rokesley for the partridges, even though we don't see as much of each other at Oxford as we used to at Eton. I think the year before last was the first time Bertie was there too.'

'You are a good shot?'

'Fair. About the same standard as James, though he gets more practice of course. Bertie's first class.'

'So I understand. He's a very interesting young man, Mr.

Hankey.'

'My father thinks so too.'

Mrs. Tarrant turned back to her work with a quite definite air of rejection. For a moment this was hard to understand. Had she perceived that Tom had deliberately introduced Father into the conversation? Was she simply not interested in any judgments other than her own? Did she actively disapprove of Father, as sections of the county certainly did? There was no way of knowing. Watching her snip the dead heads off a cluster of straggling, rush-like plants it struck Tom that she seemed in no way impressed by pedigree. This was a mild surprise. Even as apparently sophisticated a friend as Dick Standish could be sensed to acknowledge the fact that the Hankey fortunes, however dwindled, sprang originally from the plunder of monasteries and that this gave them a mystical precedence over larger collections of money that came from mere nineteenth-century coal. To Tom, having to live within the Hankey income, the precedence was illusory and tiresome. He knew quite well that if the family's finances were reduced to the point where Sillerby had to be sold the Hankeys would within a generation find themselves a long way down the social ladder, but he was aware that for the time being many quite sensible people thought the distinction real and serious. Mrs. Tarrant, though on almost exactly the same social footing as the Standishes, evidently did not.

'Bertie is trying to do something very important,' she said without looking up. 'I think you are aware of that.'

'Yes. In fact he asked me to help him during the strike, but . . .'

'You were needed on the railways. I think you were quite right, Mr. Hankey. Bertie's plans during the strike came to absolutely nothing.

'He got me out of a bit of a jam, as a matter of fact.'

Silence again. She moved up the steps to another group of plants, motioning to Tom to pick her snippings out from among the spiky leaves. It was clear now that despite her alliance with Bertie he had indeed told her nothing about the fight in the cutting. On the other hand it was beginning to look more and more as though this whole episode on the rockery had been planned, not by Judy but by Mrs. Tarrant herself—or perhaps Mrs. Tarrant had taken advantage of a scheme of Judy's for her own ends. So

Bertie had asked her to talk to him. Had he told her about Tom and Judy? Probably not. Bertie was a miser with secrets . . .

'What are your plans for the rest of the vacation, Mr. Hankey?'

'Well, it's not really a vacation. I've finished with Oxford. I'm going to take the Civil Service exam in January, and I'll have to do a bit of work for that . . .'

'Not the Foreign Office?'

'My father's getting on. I don't want to be out of the country for long periods.'

'I thought you had an elder brother.'

'Gerald's not been well since the war.'

Did she really not know? Were there corners of the county into which the legends had not penetrated? Or perhaps she simply chose not to know, her will-power being sufficient to enforce ignorance of the most notorious misdeeds. The tone of her response supported the idea.

'How sad.'

'Yes . . . yes, very. Anyway, I'm going to start cramming for these exams in September. 'Till then I haven't any real plans.'

(Except to be, as far as possible, wherever Judy is—an aim as unpredictable as the pursuit of some erratic-flighted specimen across gusty uplands.)

'I think, Mr. Hankey, you ought to talk to Bertie again. I agree that in normal times a young man deserves a holiday after coming down from university, but these are not normal times.'

'Won't he be in France now?'

'He is spending only three weeks there this summer. The rest of the time he will be staying here in Yorkshire.'

'Good Lord.'

'He realises that we must all make sacrifices.'

They had hardly looked at each other during this exchange, each crouched on the path and concentrated on their work. Now Mrs. Tarrant rose and came down the steps holding a trug loaded with debris for him to take from her. Her plucked and arching brows expressed no kind of question. She was not in fact asking one. She was making a statement about what he must do.

'All right,' he said. 'I'll give Bertie a tinkle. Perhaps Judy could run me over.'

'Certainly.'

8

Holme on the Wold, 8th July, 1926

'Ah,' sighed Bertie, leafing with fastidious fingertips through Tom's copy of *The Sickle*, rather as if he had been a surgeon who had traced a difficult disease to its source in one of the muckier regions of the social anatomy. He began to read the lurid and inflammatory prose, giving little grunts of satisfaction as he did so.

Hitherto the interview had not gone well. It was Tom's first visit to Holme Lodge, and he had not been quite prepared for the effect, had perhaps subconsciously been expecting an English version of Bertie's style at Hendaye, the relaxing comforts of affable wealth. The Lodge, though it lay at the end of a mile of drive through deer-stocked parkland, was not aggressively large, a symmetrical white regency house with little onion-domes at the end of either wing and a larger, flatter one at the centre. It was clearly kept in perfect trim, and in any kind of decent weather would have sparkled on its hill-side, but on this drenching morning had the snug, smug look of a pretty woman walking well weatherproofed in a shower.

'Doesn't he like you to smell the money?' whispered Judy as she braked the Lagonda beneath the pillared porte-cochere.

Both leaves of the front door opened before Tom could pull the bell-knob. Two footmen—black coats and trousers, yellow satin waistcoats—produced slight, unsmiling bows.

'Miss Tarrant and Mr. Hankey?' said one. 'Miss Tarrant is to wait in the drawing room. Mr. Panhard will see Mr. Hankey in the library.'

It was a manner of speaking, for at first Bertie seemed deliberately not to see Tom, merely gesturing towards a chair with an index finger while he dictated into a machine what sounded like a political speech, the orotund phrases contrasting with the brisk, flat tones. It ended with a mystical-sounding passage about the coming age, when the new men had done their work and cleansed and purged the social fabric, and England would be England made all glorious once more. Tom was struck by the difference between Bertie's vision of England and his own. Bertie's desk was the largest he had ever seen, but most of its acreage seemed used, with reference books, files, piles of papers, stacks of pamphlets, all in their allocated spots, and all looking as though they had a reason for being there. By contrast the uniform editions of books in the library shelves stood so crisply in their ranks that it was hard to believe that any single volume had ever been taken down. Its absence would have left too glaring a gap.

At last Bertie had put the mouthpiece down, clicked a switch and turned to gaze at Tom with piercing and unfriendly eyes.

'Strong stuff,' said Tom, nodding towards the dictating machine.

Still Bertie did not smile.

'I think you owe me an explanation,' he said.

'If you'll tell me what needs explaining.'

'Your behaviour in Drewton Cutting.'

'Oh?'

'I was set to teach those fellows a real lesson. You stopped me. And in front of my own men.'

'Sorry about that. It was on the spur of the moment, of course.'

'Of course. You imply that you would have acted differently if you had had time to think.'

Tom hesitated, already aware that the interview was moving in an unsatisfactory direction. He guessed now that Bertie had asked Mrs. Tarrant to try and manoeuvre him into making this visit, and that that had been the main purpose of the morning on the rockery. If they were working in such collusion, it might be more important than he had realised to appease Bertie . . . On the other hand, it was no use building a temple of peace on a totally false foundation . . .

'No,' he said. 'I think I'd have done the same.'

'Oh?'

'You couldn't know what had been happening before. We'd reached an arrangement . . .'

'You were fighting.'

'According to the rules. It was absolutely fair. They all could see it was fair. I didn't mind you stopping the fight so much . . .'

'You weren't going to win.'

'No . . . but I think they might have decided to let the train through after all. That's not the point. Don't you see, after we'd come to a fair agreement, I had to do my best to stop you doing something outside the agreement—what you call teaching them a lesson?'

'What would you have done if I'd gone ahead? Let on who I was?'

'I don't know.'

'That's what you said at the time.'

'Yes, but . . . I'd have tried to think of something else.'

'Why?'

'Because you'd told me that in confidence, I suppose. It was all I could think of at the time.'

'Not wholly lost to decency, then?'

'Not wholly.'

Bertie continued to stare at Tom as if he were Mowgli demonstrating his power to dominate the lesser beasts by gaze alone. It was obvious that he resented the interference with his plans not for the sake of the plans but because they were his. That phrase about 'in front of my own men' was rather revealing. Tom's hitherto vague determination not to become one of those men grew sharper and more purposeful. And yet some kind of co-operation was necessary, to prevent Bertie telephoning Mrs. Tarrant and declaring Tom an enemy, even perhaps telling her what he had guessed about Tom and Judy. Tom took his copy of *The Sickle* from his jacket pocket and pushed it across the desk.

'I did find something which might be useful to you,' he said. 'When I knew I was coming over I rang home and asked them to send it. It came this morning.'

Bertie continued to stare at him for several seconds before withdrawing his gaze and picking up the pamphlet. His mouth bunched into a pout of rejection, relaxed, opened, released its sigh. It was at this point that the mood in the room changed—so suddenly that for a moment Tom thought it must have stopped raining outside and the sun be trying to emerge. But the steady drizzle continued to shroud the Vale of York as it had done all morning.

Tom was thinking about Judy, deliberately composing in his mind a back view of her at another of these tall windows in her typical tom-boy stance with one hand on her hip gazing at the same grey view and thinking perhaps about him, when Bertie slapped the pamphlet down onto the desk.

'How did you get hold of this rag?' he barked. The bullying tone was still there but did not quite mask the excitement. Tom explained the episode at the Hull goods sidings. Bertie continued to stare, but now his eyes, which so far he had kept cold as stones, glittered with such frenzy that Tom felt the need to close on a deprecatory note.

'There must have been several thousand in the batch,' he said. 'Some of them must have got into the hands of the police, I should think.'

'You didn't think of taking this along?'

'I believe Dampier took some but they sent him away with a flea in his ear. They were pretty stretched, remember.'

'Yes, of course, but . . . You kept the addresses, Tom?'

'On the back page. Only one address, for notification. The boxes were marked to be collected.'

'I see. We'll have to look into that, but it's not the main thing. As you say, the police have pretty certainly got copies up in Bradford. It's the Hull end that interests me, and we've got something there the police haven't.'

'Oh?'

'Has it struck you at all, Tom, that your story didn't get into the newspapers, considering how they went grubbing around for weeks looking for idiot little episodes to show how well the volunteers ran things?'

'Well, as a matter of fact, yes. I tried to keep it quiet, asked all the passengers I could catch not to talk about it, but the chap I met in Hull knew that afternoon. Did you have something to do with it not getting out?'

'I had everything to do with it. I killed that story in three separate newspapers. Not for your sweet sake, my dear Tom, of course, but . . .'

'How on earth?'

'You never met my grandfather, I imagine. No, you'd have been about ten when he died.'

'My father sometimes speaks of him.'

'No doubt. A notoriously unpleasant old man. But a genius, Tom, a prophet, after his fashion. He not only saw the war coming, he saw what kind of war it was going to be. He was still buying and selling shares on his deathbed. That's a fact. I have a copy of a transfer he signed on the morning of May the Fifth, Nineteen Ten. He was dead by supper-time, and it wasn't a sudden death. He knew it was coming.'

'Good Lord.'

'I don't know. There's something admirable about dying as you've lived. I hope I bring it off. Be that as it may, he left my trustees very little discretion to buy and sell, so that when I got my hands on things there was quite a bit to be done, and other things I wanted to do. I have my own purposes, you know. I've deliberately taken losses that must be making the old brute turn in his grave, but the result is I and my nominees have controlling interests in quite a number of very useful enterprises. I don't actually sit on boards if I can help it, but I can make things happen the way I want.'

'I see,' said Tom.

It was a little surprising to hear Bertie talking in this vein. Usually the most he would acknowledge about his own past was some harshly flippant reference to his parents' divorce—once, even, a dismissive remark about his father's subsequent suicide —but always as though the past was no more real than some novel —the latest D. H. Lawrence, say—which he had read in order to be in the swim but hadn't much enjoyed. One might have thought that his grandfather, that ogrish miser and litigant, would have provided Bertie with a fund of freakish anecdotes, but apparently the old man was too closely involved with Bertie's own wealth and ambitions to be exploited in such a fashion.

'What's more,' he added, 'I can find things out. You know that. When you were in that mess in Drewton Cutting . . .'

Tom almost laughed. Bertie responded with an icy glare but

replaced it almost at once with his most charming and self-mocking grin.

'Oh well,' he said. 'But my lines of communication are usually a cut above the Boy Scout movement. People really want to do me favours, and it doesn't take them long to learn I like to know what's going on. Hull, for instance—there's something happening there, and this ties in.'

He tapped the pamphlet with a pecking forefinger. His smile was thin and knowing. Tom made the expected questioning grunt.

'Have you thought about Hull, Tom? Big timber trade. Main port for the Baltic. Ships in and out of Russia itself. If the Bolshies want to set up a bridgehead, apart from London, they could hardly do better.'

'I suppose so.'

'I'm pretty sure so. This rag confirms it.'

'Hull might be only a staging-post. Suppose they printed it in Russia and smuggled it in. It looks somehow foreign to me.'

'I'll check that. But you're wrong, Tom. I've heard enough about the Bolshies in Hull to know they're more than a staging-post. They're something really quite serious. I want you to find them for me.'

'Oh, well . . .'

'Do you care about England, Tom?'

'Of course I do.'

'You don't want to see red revolution coming here, then?'

'That's not the point. What chance have *I* got of finding these blighters for you? You've just been telling me how good your sources of information are. Well, if you can't do it, what hope have I got with no sources at all?'

'A very good chance, Tom, because you've seen 'em. You've talked to one of 'em. My problem is this—there's a barrier beyond which my probes can't reach. I know there's a Bolshie group in Hull not because anybody has seen them at work—that happens beyond the barrier. It's the effects of the work which emerge on this side, such as this rag here, which allow us to deduce the existence of the group. But by a pure fluke you've got through, you've made contact on the other side . . .'

'Look, even if I could find the chap I met I can't simply say to him "Right oh, I'll talk to you about boxing if you'll talk to me about Bolshevism." '

Bertie sighed.

'Of course you can't. Let's just think this out . . .'

He rose and paced to and fro behind the desk, head bent, hands clasped behind his back, as if he had been the captain of a man-o'-war calculating the chances of some perilous engagement. Suddenly he swung and leaned eagerly forward, resting his knuckles on the desk.

'I've got it,' he said. 'By Jove, you know, I think things might work out remarkably well! Even that business in the cutting—it's going to be a godsend I didn't take it any further. You go and find this chap and tell him you want to finish the fight with Donovan and he's got to arrange it for you . . .'

'Surely I'd go to Donovan for that.'

'You've been to Donovan.'

'Uh?'

'You've tried that, I mean. When you made enquiries about him you were told he was in bed with flu the whole week of the strike. I happen to know that's what you *would* be told if you *did* make enquiries.'

Tom nodded. It struck him that he had never told anyone Donovan's name. He guessed that Bertie, baulked of his plan to teach the strikers a lesson, had resorted to some indirect revenge —told the police something about the ambush perhaps and thus learnt that Donovan had equipped himself with an alibi. No doubt Bertie would not even perceive that this was a breach of their agreement in the cutting—his morality, as well as his ambitions, had a Napoleonic tinge.

'So you've decided to approach things from the other end,' said Bertie. 'You're looking for someone who can persuade Donovan to trust you, someone of his own kind. It shouldn't be difficult.'

'A needle in a haystack, I'd have thought.'

'You're wrong. The chap you met is a fantastic. He'll be well known. You've only got to ask a dozen men, I bet you, before one of them will know who you're talking about. And I tell you what—I'll give you a start. Soon as you're gone I'll give Helen Tarrant a tinkle and ask her to get her chap

Hutton out to talk to you.'

'Who's he?'

'Wharf Manager. Very bright young man indeed. Going far. Knows the docks like the back of his hand. If she gets him to Brantingham tomorrow you could start next week.'

'Fraid not.'

'Oh?'

'I have to be at Sillerby next week. My brother is bringing his fiance to meet the family.'

'You don't say! Gerald? I thought . . .'

Bertie grinned. His eyes sparkled, no longer the blazing glare of the autocrat but the flicker of social calculation.

'Well, that's news!' he said. 'What does Helen Tarrant think?'

'It hasn't been announced. In any case, it hardly concerns her as yet.'

'You mean she isn't aware that it might concern her. But it will, Tom. I know her pretty well, and I can tell you it will concern her very deeply. Well, well, well . . . but let's get back to our muttons. You can't manage next week, but you sound as if you didn't want to take this on at all.'

'I must admit I'm not that keen. It sounds a bit of a wild goose chase to me.'

'It is very far from that, Tom. I assure you that it is of the utmost importance. These people are there. They are truly dangerous. If they can be found, they must. You have a very good chance of finding them. I should be extremely disappointed to see you turn it down.'

Tom was surprised by the genuine appeal of Bertie's speech. He hadn't realised that he was capable of harnessing the apparently scattered energies of his personality and applying them with such effective pressure. For the first time that morning Tom considered the possibility that Bertie might actually be right about the Bolsheviks and Hull. If so, he was also right about Tom's duty to try and make use of the scrap of knowledge that had come his way. Moreover Hull was a great deal nearer Brantingham than was Sillerby. Bertie seemed to guess his thought.

'Helen Tarrant will let you have a bed, of course,' he said with an almost leering smile. 'Look, I'm not asking you to spend all summer messing around in dockland. I'm asking you to give me a week—one week of genuine effort. In exchange for that I'll do everything I can to smooth your path in other directions. Is your brother coming back to Sillerby?'

'He may do.'

'Well, remember what I was telling you earlier. I have quite a bit of pull here and there. If you're . . .'

'I think I can manage a week.'

'Good man. When?'

'Um. Gerald's coming next week, and my sister Nan the week after. That's not so important, but I don't see all that much of her . . .'

'Monday fortnight, then?'

'Right oh.'

'Give me time to get a few things organised for you and see what I can gather about the Bradford end. I'll set Dick onto that. I've got to go over to Paris that week, and I'll be taking the chance to drop in at Hendaye for a few days. I want to be back for Woffles' beano on the fourth. You coming to that?'

'Indeed yes.'

'See you there, then. Now let's go and find out what mischief young Judy's been up to. By the by, I see you got your First. Congratters and all that. No doubt you're in the mood for a glass of bubbly.'

'Always.'

'Come on, then.'

Bertie seemed to have relaxed completely into his normal manner. At the library door he paused and glanced sideways at Tom.

'I've just had a thought,' he whispered. 'Suppose this chap swallows your story and actually fixes you up a fight with Donovan, what'll you do?'

'Fight him, of course. I'd like to.'

'Good Lord.'

They found Judy not in Tom's imagined pose but sitting on the carpet with her legs tucked under her and talking to a red setter. She made it seem a quite unaffected thing to be conversing with a dog. The dog itself lay full length with its head on her lap and gazed up into her face with adoring incomprehension. Several feet away its large tail thumped rhythmically to and fro across the carpet. The room, though Bertie had less obvious use for it than he did for his library, seemed considerably more human. Somebody had arranged large displays of flowers in several places. The lilies filled the long room with a pungent, almost meaty odour. The chairs and sofas looked extremely comfortable.

'Beastly sentimental bitch,' said Bertie.

For a moment Tom thought he detected the note he had heard earlier, when Bertie had complained of being humiliated in front of his own men. Not even a dog was permitted to show affection for anyone but her own master. But Bertie laughed with apparently real enjoyment when Judy looked up at him, clowning affront. One of the footmen ghosted into the room.

'Bollinger, I think, John,' said Bertie. 'And some chocs for Duchess.'

'Very good, sir.'

9

Hull, 23rd July, 1926

At the lowest ebb he could remember since the meaningless despairs of childhood, Tom stood in the darkness of the chapel porch and watched the men stream home from work. It had been a hot afternoon and the air was sour with the city-pervading reek from the Fish Dock, a quarter of a mile west. The chapel—a grimy brick barn—stood half way down one of the streets that ran in a monotonous grid through the area behind the main docks. The builders had crammed the site to an incredible degree with squat brick houses. Each street was in fact a street of lesser streets. Instead of the houses running in a single terrace along the pavements, they stood for the most part at right-angles to it, a block of a dozen houses facing a similar block across two gardens the size of a kitchen table and a narrow flagged path between. At the back of each block there was only the path, a yard-wide canyon, with the back of yet another block on its other side.

The men seemed animated, even boisterous, perhaps because Friday was pay-day. Some of them bicycled but most walked in small knots, habitual partners for the journey home, like children loosed from school. Occasionally a man would break from his companions with a grunt of farewell and move off up one of the paths between the gardens and into the house behind it. As certain bicyclists came up the road their progress was marked by calls from the pedestrians, a greeting or perhaps a question. These were evidently popular or influential figures, for they seemed to ride past barely acknowledging the shouts, but pedalling stolidly on, often at little more than walking speed, as if taking part in a ritual procession which had to be performed with funereal dignity. At first Tom had been unable to understand any of the shouts, blurred with dialect and street-echoes, but by the time the current of men had dwindled to a few single pedestrians, hurrying now, he had heard one exchange so often that he knew what was being said. 'Tha'll be coming back for the meeting?' 'Aye.' 'Don't let tha woman talk thee out on it.' From where he was lurking he could see the faces more clearly than he could hear the words. None of the several hundred men who had gone by had been among the four who had loaded the Bolshevik pamphlets onto his train in the goods sidings.

Another blank day, the fifth of a blank week. Tom was oppressed not merely by failure, though this was tedious enough. He did not think it likely that either Bertie or Mrs. Tarrant would accept that he had genuinely tried, and so earned his release from any obligation to be incorporated among Bertie's henchmen. In his own mind he had promised a week and was giving a week, but their minds were not his.

The looming weekend offered no reprieve. No doubt the men, off work from Saturday noon, would be more accessible. He planned to join them at the football match, rub shoulders, try yet again to get into a conversation, but from his last five days' experience he knew quite well he would get nowhere. And meanwhile Judy would be away from Brantingham, staying with cousins for a dance up near Northallerton before going on to Scotland. Woffles was to be one of that house-party.

Tom found that he was shocked by spasms of jealousy, recurring like an intermittent toothache. Hitherto he had accepted that Judy's 'rules' were simply her way of having her cake and eating it; though committed to him by events at Hendaye, she still wanted to relish the intricacies of a longer courtship. Now he was nagged by the memory of Janet Stott, waltzing in his arms at Trinity but glancing all the time around the floor to check on her ravished partner. 'Is that Judy Tarrant? . . . She's famous for this sort of thing.' The willed impulse, disruptive as a motor accident, tearing lives apart. Had Hendaye after all been merely an extreme version of 'this sort of thing'? Were Judy's rules in fact an attempt to will the accident out of existence? Perhaps Woffles would take the chance at Northallerton to propose . . . Perhaps Judy . . . Tom was angry and ashamed with himself for entertaining what he had always imagined, considering it from the outside, to be a thoroughly mean emotion, but the ache would not go away.

He was tempted to run, to go and hide his sorrows in the lair of home, but he knew that that would for once offer him little relief. Sillerby too had changed. Minnie Heusen and Gerald would not in fact be there this weekend. But although not one cup in the china cabinets, not one pillow-case in the linen-cupboards, was in anyway altered from what it always had been, the air of Sillerby had become mysteriously unfamiliar. A combination of hope and apprehension seemed to Tom to tinge the servants' voices, the sound of Pennycuick's mower, the unceasing leaden knock of the ram that drove the water from the bowling-green spring to the attic cistern. Could it be true that the mortar was crumbling less grimly from between the worn old bricks of the melon-ground, as if the forces of decay now despaired of bringing them down before the Heusen money had them re-pointed? Certainly Father had changed. At his last visit Tom had spent a whole day re-labelling the *Hesperiidae*, and Father had not once put his nose into the Collection Room; he had apparently spent the morning sorting out papers in his study and the afternoon walking round the farms with Gerald and Minnie. But most changed of all had been Tom. His future life, which a few months ago had seemed so fixed that it had the nature almost of an historical fact, apart from being in the future, now was dissolved—the decades of employing his intelligence and strength to keep Sillerby in being and the Hankey line flourishing within its walls, gone. He did not even know what would happen to the Collection. Would it go to a museum? Would the Heusen money run to employing a Keeper for it? The future of those dead butterflies, which all his life had seemed twined into his own fixed future, was now separate and just as vague. He was dismal with the discovery that he did not much care.

These separate discontents should all in their own ways have been endurable. He was, after all, full to the skin with the sense of his own being and relishing his glorious luck in love, quite enough to dispel the little imps of ennui and a week's frustration. The trouble lay elsewhere. It was like a dank fog off the moors which had crept imperceptibly down, blotting out his homely landscape, chilling all his pleasant places. His failure consisted not in having failed Bertie or Mrs. Tarrant, or even himself, but something larger and vaguer. It really mattered that he should find the man he was looking for, mattered in the same way that it had mattered that Cyril and Gerald should have gone to France and died or been ruined there ten years ago. He believed this not because of Bertie's rhetorical appeal, but because of what Mr. Hutton had said, and not said, in the smoking room at Brantingham, especially about a man called Ricardo.

They had met on the afternoon of the visit to Holme on the Wold. The same drear rain dripped from the Wellingtonias and wiped the Humber estuary from the view. As Bertie had implied, Mrs. Tarrant's Wharf Manager was surprisingly young, less than thirty, but pale-faced and not far from going bald. His dress was that of an office-worker in a west-end comedy, the collar a little too high and a little too tight, the dark cloth of his suit harsh and gracelessly cut, the black boots mirror-bright. The first two fingers of his left hand were orange with nicotine. All the same his personality, which ought to have been harassed, eager and inept, was quite the opposite. He was perfectly confident and, as far as the suit permitted, relaxed, and throughout the interview his pale eyes watched Tom as if judging his worth for quite other purposes.

'I want no part of this, Mr. Hankey,' he said as soon as Mrs. Tarrant had left the room. 'I cannot tell her to her face, but you'll be better without me and I'll be better without you.'

His voice was so soft that Tom had to strain to be sure of the words. There was a faint hint of the whinnying Hull accent, almost overlaid by education.

'Oh,' said Tom.

'I cannot think what she's at,' said Mr. Hutton. 'Three generations her family have been owners, but they will not learn, any more than they will forget.'

'Learn what?'

'How to deal with the men.'

Mr. Hutton spoke without vocal emphasis, letting the gleam in his pale eyes give weight to the words.

'Are dockers so different from other trades?'

'A different world, Mr. Hankey. They're a law to themselves. It comes of being in work one week, laid off the next. Even when the work's there, a man can't be sure he'll be picked for it—and that's been the way for generations. Now only a dockie knows what it's like to be a dockie.'

'You sound as though you had a good idea yourself.'

'My grandfather was a dockie all his life, and my father started as one. Then he began a little business and was lucky with it—so you could say my family's changed sides. I've cousins still who are dockies, and sometimes we meet at a family funeral or the like, but anything to do with the docks they'd no more think of doing me a favour than I would them. There is a chasm between us you can scarcely get your voice across, let be going yourself.'

'You are telling me that I've no hope of making contact with the man I want.'

'I understand from Mrs. Tarrant that you are looking for a group of Reds, Mr. Hankey.'

'That's right.'

'You'll meet a brick wall. Try to get past it and there's a fair chance you'll be found floating in the river.'

'Seriously?'

Mr. Hutton barely nodded, but continued to gaze at Tom as if speculating what quality of corpse he would make.

'Are there a lot of Bolshies among the men?'

'It depends what you mean by the word. With the coming and going of ships to the Baltic there's plenty of opportunity for dealings with Moscow, but I doubt there's more than a score of Communist Party members. I cannot tell you who they are—they'd get no work on my wharf if I knew their names. Then there's very likely a hundred or more who are good as members, apart from paying their subscriptions and such. And so on, working outwards. Larger numbers, weaker sympathies. But I can tell you, Mr. Hankey, that if you try to come to them through me, every man jack you talk to might as well be taking his orders from Moscow, for all the help you'll get from him.'

'I see. You'd rather I didn't go at all?'

'To be blunt, Mr. Hankey, much rather. I cannot imagine what Mrs. Tarrant thinks she's up to, setting you in there at a time like this. She knows, for I've told her often enough, what the mood is like along the waterfront. Hull is a hot town at the best of times, and the docks are the hottest part of it. We had trams burnt during the General Strike, which is worse than you can say of most of the towns in England. A lot of the men remember nineteen eleven, when there was rioting and arson, and warships in the Humber with their guns loaded. Now the men are still bitter from May—their leaders were all for staying out with the miners, and it was touch and go whether they went back. Trade's bad, with no coal going out and a lot of the other firms not really recovered from the General Strike. The shipowners have been losing profits all summer, and Monday week they'll be announcing a cut in the men's rates. There'd be trouble about that at the best of times. But now, with some of the men's leaders arguing for blocking the coal imports . . .'

'These leaders—they won't be the men I'm looking for?'

'One or two, maybe. There's leaders and leaders. Hull's not like other ports—the Unions haven't the hold here, not since the owners broke them in 'ninety-three. There's a lot of little organisations, and a tangle of loyalties and feuds. Suppose one were to pluck the leaders out from among them all of a sudden, just when trouble came to a head . . .'

For the first time Mr. Hutton made a gesture, lifting his right hand and removing with precise fingers an imaginary particle from the air in front of him. He smiled rather pleasantly at Tom, as if apologising for the touch of melodrama, and returned his hand to his knee.

'I understand,' said Tom. 'You don't want me putting anyone on their guard, or making them nervier than they are already.'

'No.'

'Well I don't propose to. I wasn't going to go about it that way at all. I happen to be interested in boxing, and I believe one of the chaps I'm looking for may be too. I thought I'd start there.'

Briefly he explained about Donovan. Mr. Hutton appeared to lose interest, scarcely in fact to be listening. When Tom finished he sighed.

'What do you think?' prompted Tom.

'I think you'll do no harm. I doubt you'll do much good. But

Mrs. Tarrant must have her way—I understand that.'

The interview had seemed to be at an end, a waste of both their times. Mr. Hutton had got to his feet and was looking at the rain with a grim kind of pleasure as if it would suit his mood to trudge home to Hull through it instead of being chauffeured back in one of the Brantingham cars.

'Do you think these men are dangerous?' asked Tom.

'Dangerous?'

Mr. Hutton did not turn, and the word was almost too soft to hear.

'I don't mean in the sense that one might get knocked on the head,' said Tom. 'I suppose I mean are they worth finding? Are they really dangerous to society at large? No doubt they think of themselves as doing great things, but do they actually make much difference—I mean beyond stirring up a bit of trouble in the docks, making the odd strike a little more bitter than it might have been and so on? Mightn't one do more harm by trying to get rid of them than by leaving them alone?'

Slowly Mr. Hutton turned and looked at Tom, for the first time, it seemed, as though he might have something of interest to say. He drew his mouth together so that the lips disappeared and the little moustache marked where it ought to be. He took some time to answer.

'That's a good question,' he said. 'The answer to it is yes. They are dangerous. They are worth finding. If somebody could come in, like I was saying about the strike leaders, and pluck them away, he would have done the country a service.'

'Couldn't the police do that, supposing it was known who they were?'

Mr. Hutton shook his head—a gesture typical of him, somehow both slight and emphatic.

'There's very few of them the police could hold,' he said. 'They're too careful for that. Myself, I'm a strong believer in the law, but there comes a time when the law can't act, and then somebody outside the law must act for it.'

(No wonder, thought Tom, Bertie found Mr. Hutton impressive. It would be interesting to know whether they had ever talked about this sort of thing, or whether their understanding was intuitive. At least it was almost as though Mr. Hutton had guessed that Bertie's private army, or something very like it, might exist.)

'Well, that's a great help,' said Tom, rising. 'It certainly sounds as though I ought to have a go.'

Mr. Hutton stood where he was, still gazing at Tom, indeed now clearly studying him from head to toe, as if sizing him up and making a mental comparison with himself. When at last he moved it was not towards the door but back to the window.

'I'll tell you one thing more,' he said. 'I hadn't meant to, but I will. There's a man they call Ricardo.'

'A foreigner?'

'I don't think so. More of a *nom de guerre*. Don't you breathe his name. Don't you go even hinting that you might have heard he exists. I wouldn't care to have it on my conscience that you were fished out of the river with your head split open because of something I told you. Don't even mention it to your own friends, or Mrs. Tarrant, or the police, in case it gets back. I'm putting my own life in your hands telling you this. But that's the man you're after. Not the fellow you met who's interested in boxing, but the one who's at the heart of all the trouble.'

Mr. Hutton didn't look at Tom as he spoke but gazed at the rain, as though as far as possible dissociating himself from the secret he was passing on. The effect was remarkably powerful. Ricardo at that moment sprang into Tom's mind not as a vaguely rumoured bogey-man, but as a quite definite and serious adversary, capable of doing all that Mr. Hutton implied.

'How did you hear of him?' he asked.

'I can't tell you that. I can risk my own safety on your good sense, but not anybody else's.'

'Right oh. I'll stick to my boxing and see where I get.'

The answer had been nowhere. The only glimmer of light had come on the very first day, when an old bruiser at the Hull Sporting Club had said he had heard of the man Tom was after but didn't know his name. Tom gave him half a crown and he promised to make enquiries. But next morning the bruiser, very surly, returned the coin and said that the man he'd been thinking of had died last year. He knew of nobody else who could help and would make no suggestions. After that, to Tom's increasing sur-

prise and desperation, he achieved nothing. It proved impossible to get into conversation with any of the dock-workers. He
would not have believed that there was a part of England in
which a remark about the weather would not evoke a response of
some kind from a stranger in a pub, but the best he got was a
grunt, and more often than that a swearword or a blank look as
though he had not spoken at all. One evening he heard a man ask
a friend the closing score in the Leeds Test Match, but when
Tom supplied the information the pair of them simply turned
away. He began by Wednesday to feel that the men had actually
received orders not to speak to him, though it seemed impossible
that there could be any mechanism by which they could know his
purpose—unless they had a spy among the Brantingham servants. Or could the silent John who had brought Bertie his Bollinger have spent the previous twenty minutes listening at the library door? By Friday evening he could think of nothing better to
do than lurk in this chapel porch and peer at faces.

The last stranger strode by and there was nothing to see but
the blank side-walls of Rosemount Close and Paradise Close,
with beyond them the corner of a bigger block, the Seaman's
Hostel—very likely the same one that Mrs. Tarrant had spoken
of on the rockery. So very likely too the porch in which he was
hiding belonged to one of 'our' churches. The thought widened
the chasm. There seemed an immeasurable gulf between this
sooty, hulking, dismal edifice and the neat little stone church
beneath the woods at Brantingham, where Tom had attended
Mattins last Sunday and listened to his host, the Reverend Cyprian Tarrant, fluting his way through a sermon on the symbolic
meaning of the two stones on the shoulders of the ephod
described in *Exodus* 28, xii. Tom had been in the pew behind
Judy, but she had been wearing one of those hats with an almost
blinker-like brim framing the face, so he had had to make do with
a view of a few square inches of neck for his only chance during
the five days of the house-party to watch her without seeming to
stare.

With an exploding sigh of frustration he turned and opened
the door of this chapel. It was not like Brantingham. That too
was Victorian, but very plain and cool, with a clear country light
behind the stained glass windows and the stones of arch and

pillar cut from some open hill. This was brick, with plaster painted to look like marble; the pews were dark pine, the carpets and hangings a monotonous dull maroon, the windows dingy with exterior soot. The occasional sparkle of polished brass emphasised the gloom, and the air smelt stale and dusty. If one closed one's eyes one might have been in a warehouse.

Tom mooned around as one does in such places, reading the black-lettered brass plaques to the memory of dead aldermen, and the names of men killed in the war. For once there were more ships listed than regiments. To waste time thus seemed no more pointless than roaming the streets looking for his quarry until he had to catch the train to Brough. When at last he returned to the door his hand was on the handle before he realised that there were voices just outside—undistinguishable beyond belonging to a man and a woman, and arguing. He stepped back, assuming that they were about to enter as soon as they had composed themselves into chapel manners. The next words came clear, the woman saying 'Ah, get off, you stupid git!' The man's answer was indistinct, but had the banal rhythm of swearing for emphasis. The woman's reply was cut short. Tom hesitated. He had little desire to intervene, but less to stand there listening and embarrassed, and miss his train to boot. He opened the door.

They were in the dark-shadowed corner where he had lurked ten minutes ago. The woman was almost hidden, but clearly struggling. The man had her pinned against the wall with his arm round her shoulders and was trying to force his mouth against hers while she wriggled her head away. Neither had noticed the movement of the door. Tom felt an utter fool. He could quite well have slipped past and left them to solve their own problems, but this seemed to be, so to speak, culturally impossible. If his training had had any purpose, surely that purpose included the moment when he would need to ask some lady whether some gentleman was annoying her. He stepped forward and tapped the man on the shoulder.

The struggle stilled. The man grabbed the woman's arm and turned slowly round, giving Tom time to retreat a pace before their eyes met. For a moment the man stood there with his left arm twisted behind his back, still gripping his prey; his large oval face was flushed with struggle, his thick lips were moist and his eyes a furious blue. The woman, still invisible, was making a curious noise which Tom assumed to be sobbing, but before he could embark on the inane ritual of chivalry the man let go of her and rushed at him. Tom sprang back, caught his heel on the doorstep and sprawled into the aisle; even as he was falling he had seen the man's rush converting itself into a kick. He twisted to one side. The heavy boot scraped painfully but not harmfully along his ham and buttock. Without thought he grabbed at the swinging ankle and heaved. The man flew on beyond him, yelling as he fell.

They got to their feet together, three paces apart. At once the man lurched in, his right arm flailing back for an enormous punch. Tom slipped inside it and closed, driving his left hard into the man's stomach, then stepped back to give himself room for his right. All the week-long waste compressed itself into the stabbing uppercut that caught the descending head full on the chin. Even the blaze of pain round Tom's knuckles was like a shout of triumph. The man straightened. His head went up and sideways like an El Greco saint in prayer. The straightening movement continued and he went arcing over, landing on his back with a single huge thud. He did not move.

Alarmed Tom knelt by his side and felt for his pulse with his left hand. A voice behind him said 'Don't you trouble, mister. He was three parts soused, and drunks fall easy.'

Tom looked over his shoulder. The woman was standing under the arch of the doorway, her face as pink with effort as the man's had been. But she wasn't sobbing, she was laughing.

'When he comes round and finds himself in chapel!' she whispered.

'I can't just leave him . . . his pulse is OK . . . breathing . . .'

'Sleeping like a babe,' she said, coming nearer to gaze down at the man. 'Tell you what, I'll drop by Mrs. Pollock and get her to send one of the bairns round to his missus, tell her where to find him . . . Oi! I know who you are!'

Tom had risen while she was speaking but stood where he was, uneasily studying the unconscious man. Startled by the change in her voice he turned. Her mouth was open, as if she'd started to blurt something out and stopped herself just in time, but he'd barely glimpsed the look when amazement became amusement.

'You're the one who fought Donovan!' she said, and laughed aloud.

She was no beauty—a square-set body in a shabby dark suit with a skirt six inches longer than anything Judy would have dreamed of wearing. Her face was squarish too, its features large, eyes dark but lively. Her hair was a golliwog tangle of jet-black curls which stuck out stiff as wire all round her head.

'That's right,' he said. 'Er . . . can I see you anywhere?'

It seemed an absurd offer, almost as out of place as his intervention in the porch, but she accepted it with a decisive nod.

'If you please,' she said, turning to the door.

He held it for her and closed it behind them. In the porch she bent and picked up from the corner a shiny black straw hat. She patted her hair about, without as far as Tom could see having any effect on its intransigent stiffness, and settled the hat on top. Then she slipped her arm through Tom's and stepped into the street.

'My name's Tom Hankey,' he said, feeling that this sudden intimacy demanded some kind of introduction, however belated.

'I'm Catherine Barnes.'

'Oh. The, er . . .'

'Say it.'

'Agitator—I suppose it should be agitatrix, really.'

'What a lovely word! Aye, that's me, Red Kate Barnes.'

'Are you going to the meeting?'

'Aye, but how did you hear of it?'

'Some of the men were shouting about it just now, on their way home.'

'It's my Uncle Ned, you see. According to him I've got to have a man along of me. He says it's in case I have trouble with some of the Company men, but really he's just set in his ideas about women.'

From the first he had noticed an oddity in her voice. Now he saw that although she used the same vowels and rhythms as a workman she was actually an educated woman. She chose to speak as she did, but need not.

'That chap in the church,' he said. 'He was supposed to be

your escort?'

'Harry Struther? He's all right. There wasn't any work for him today so he spent his dinner boozing. He'll be crawling with shame tomorrow, poor lad . . . if he remembers what happened at all. I'll tell Mrs. Struther he passed out with the beer and we put him in the church.'

'He'll have a bruise on his jaw.'

'Fell against a pew end . . .My, that was a peach of a punch, Mr. Hankey!'

Embarrassed Tom flexed his hand. It seemed tender all down to the wrist.

'Oh well . . .' he said. 'Tell me, how did you hear about the Donovan business?'

'Uncle Ned was full of it. Scuse me.'

They had walked down the street with the chapel in it, round the corner that led to the docks, but then up the next street and so back in the direction they had come from. Now she slipped her arm from his and strode down the path between two of the facing sets of glum little houses. In the garden of the third one along two urchins were fighting while a fourteen-year-old girl, large-eyed and hollow-cheeked, leaned against the doorpost and watched them apathetically. She smiled at Miss Barnes, who spoke to her briefly and then screeched through the door towards the innards of the house. A vague croak answered her and she came back grinning. Tom realised that he had been wrong about her being no beauty.

She had none of the assets of beauty, apart from a complexion of rustic-seeming pink and white, but even that was coarse-grained in a way that suggested that in a very few years it would begin to raddle. Her beauty lay in the energy that seemed to flow from her, not merely from her quick and brilliant glance, but energy—intellectual, moral, sensual—borne in an aura round her. Despite her square shoulders, apparent physical strength and stumping stride she was not at all mannish—much less so than Judy could in some moods be, for instance. It struck him that he knew now why Harry Hackby and his friends referred to their engines as 'she'. With them, too, the beauty lay in energy and in the mode of its expression.

'What are you laughing at?' she said as she took his arm again and motioned to return the way they had come.

'Oh, nothing. But I'd like to meet your Uncle Ned. He's keen on boxing?'

'Why, he can tell you fights, round by round, that happened before his father was born. He was cursing his luck not being there when you fought Donovan.'

'He sounds the very chap I'm looking for!'

'That's as may be. Tell me what you're doing down in dockland, Mr. Hankey. We don't see many of your sort.'

'It's a bit difficult to explain without sounding stupid. Did you hear how the fight stopped?'

'I did.'

'I didn't like it either.'

'Do you know who those men in the hoods were?'

'I've a pretty good idea about one or two of them, as a matter of fact.'

'Will you tell me the names?'

'No.'

She nodded, as though that was a perfectly satisfactory answer —the one she had hoped for, even.

'Go on about the fight then,' she said.

'As I say, I didn't want it to end like that. It wasn't . . . *Fair*'s a silly word but it's roughly what I mean. I was glad to get my train through, of course. You knew I was driving the train?'

'To think of me, Red Kate Barnes, walking arm in arm with a blackleg!'

Teasingly she pulled him a little closer, as if contact with so strange a monster gave her an exotic thrill. It was clear that she considered him a complete joke.

'You have to learn what's right and wrong by doing it, sometimes. I think I'd do that again, but not quite in the same spirit . . . Anyway, I thought I'd like to finish the fight with Donovan, in a proper ring with gloves . . .'

'He's not a Hull man.'

'Yes, I know. I started on the railways, of course, but they're all scared stiff. They took up a rail, you see, and blocked the other line with trees. They could go to prison for that. The railwaymen I've talked to swore Donovan was in bed all that week, and I bet they'll have the same sort of story about the chap who was my second. I didn't get anywhere with them, so I thought I'd come and look for the man I met in the Hull goods yard, because he said he knew Donovan and sounded interested enough to help me. All I knew about him was that his name was Ned. I just guessed he must be a docker.'

'Not much chance looking for Uncle Ned in Chapel! He's a through-and-through atheist.'

'Oh, I just went in to have a look round. I was getting pretty depressed. It wasn't just not finding your uncle—it was the way no one would even talk to me.'

'Aye,' she said. 'We're close with strangers, close as a coal-shed door, sometimes.'

She had slipped back into dialect. For the past few minutes her voice—quiet and low but not throaty—had been modulating itself into more neutral tones, without any affectation of gentility. By now they had reached the Hedon Road and were moving east, with the high wall of the Alexandra Dock on their right and on their left irregular blocks of old warehouses and shipping offices, a pub or two, very few shops and no houses. Rails crossed the cobbled road at frequent intervals, and sometimes ran along it for a while before swinging between huge gates— closed now—in the blank wall of the dock. They had not been alone for some time. Groups of men were moving with them, very likely the same men that Tom had spied on earlier, now walking in the other direction, silent and earnest. The setting sun gave the backs of their coats a goldish tinge, and all the dusty urban air was still and golden too. One could smell but not see the muddy Humber beyond the wall.

'Tell me, Mr. Hankey,' said Miss Barnes suddenly. 'Do you know anything about our lives? You can't have lived like us, I know, but have you, for instance heard of Karl Marx?'

'I'm trying to read *Das Kapital*, as a matter of fact.'

'Are you now! And what do you mean, *trying*?'

'Well, I had a look at a couple of English translations and they seemed to me pretty awful, so I'm giving it a go in German. I learnt German to do Kant and Hegel, but it's still fairly heavy going. As a matter of fact Marx's German is a lot livelier than either of theirs, but that doesn't mean I can read it any faster.'

She loosened her hold on his arm and moved a pace away.

'You've been deceiving me, Mr. Hankey,' she said in tones so prim that they parodied their own note of woman betrayed.

He laughed, perfectly understanding what she meant. Though she seemed several years older than him, about twenty-seven, perhaps, he felt as though he were back at Oxford and walking to a lecture with some friend exactly in tune with his own mental processes.

'Oh well,' he said. 'I admit what I've been doing in Hull sounds pretty idiotic, but I'm not brainless all through. I don't think anybody is. But quite brainy people can be pretty stupid, and other people—ones who are useless by any academic standards—can still be full of good sense.'

'You should meet my Aunt Tess,' she said.

'I'd like to.'

'I must look in my etiquette book,' she said. ' "Say hello to Mr. Hankey, Auntie. I met him punching of Harry Struther in t' Chapel." '

'Will your Uncle Ned be at the meeting?'

'Aye. You want to stay for the meeting?'

'I'd be very interested. But I particularly want to meet your uncle.'

She looked at him half sideways for several seconds, her lips puckering as if she was having difficulty keeping a straight face, but all she said was 'I'll have to ask.' Then she fell silent.

Tom became aware that the men they walked among, more of them now, glanced at him from time to time. He saw a newcomer from one of the side-streets fall into step with a group and almost at once give a querying jerk of the head in Tom's direction; he was answered by shrugs and murmurs. Miss Barnes paid no attention, indeed she seemed to have fallen into some kind of trance, striding along unaware of the crowd, and Tom, and the bronzy reeking air. Her broad lips moved in silent mutters and some of the colour seemed to have gone out of her cheeks. Tom did not deceive himself that by being in the crowd and moving with it he had in any way become accepted as part of it, but for the first time all week he felt as though it might actually become possible to make the necessary contact. He had not enjoyed lying to Miss Barnes, but the necessity had not much troubled him.

The dock wall curved away towards the river. A patch of open ground appeared on the right, crossed by a few railway tracks. It was a dreary flatland of several acres, through which the old Holderness Drain oozed from the north between steep straight banks. Two signal boxes and a number of other sheds punctuated the expanse, but mostly it was waste, covered with ragwort and willow-herb and tufted grass, their growth and sappiness already coarsening with the weariness of summer. Some of the sheds were in disrepair, and brambles twined through discarded parts of what might once have been cranes. A long ridge of scrap-iron still blocked out the river to the south, and further along the bank rose the wall of the new King George Dock.

This wasteland was fenced from the road, but the wires had parted in a number of places, and through these the men pushed. Once inside they did not gather to a centre but stood around in inward-turned groups talking in low voices but with jerky and emphatic gestures. There were only a hundred or so of them there when Tom arrived but they continued to pour through the fence and either to join themselves to the existing groups or form fresh ones. Miss Barnes went up to a man who was standing near one of the gaps, watching the rest stream in. He stared at Tom and said something. She answered briefly and asked a question. He gestured with his head towards the middle of the arena. She came back and led Tom in that direction, past groups some of whom called cheerfully to her. She waved back or answered with a grin. Most of the men glanced at Tom, then quickly away.

'Wait here,' said Miss Barnes. 'If anyone tries to throw you out, say you're with me.'

She strode on and joined herself to a group some thirty yards away. Newcomers wandered past in increasing numbers, but between the moving men Tom caught glimpses of her, clearly involved in an argument and putting her case with passion. The man she was mainly talking to was turned away from him, but from his stance and the wild black hair Tom was fairly sure it was the one who had been in charge when the pamphlets were loaded —conceivably therefore the mysterious Ricardo. Something was settled. Next time he could see her she had moved a little apart from the group and was peering in his direction. He waved an arm, but still she seemed not to notice. For a moment he lurched back into the half-mad sense of actually not existing in these other people's world, but then a small man on the left of the group answered his wave and came across at a pace so eager that it was almost a trot. Still the taller man did not look round, but moved away taking Miss Barnes with him.

The small man was older than most of the rest, and his head under its cloth cap was cocked in bird-like interest. If Tom had not been concentrating on his Ricardo-suspect he would have recognised him at once. Where had he been all these five days? As soon as he was near enough the man started making little signals of greeting. Tom held out his hand.

'How do you do,' he said. 'Nice to meet you again. Are you Miss Barnes's Uncle Ned?'

'Aye, Ned Barnes. And you're the Honourable Thomas Hankey.'

'Tom Hankey.'

'I like to get things straight first.'

Before releasing Tom's hand Mr. Barnes turned it sideways and inspected the knuckles. He nodded.

'You've been looking for me, I hear tell,' he said.

'That's right. Am I allowed to stay for the meeting?'

'Aye, you may. Others didn't like it, but our Kate talked them over. It's difficult, don't you see, more than half the men not being in the unions. The companies will always try and sneak some of their own men in, to mess a meeting up, like, see as we don't reach a clear-cut democratic decision. So you'll pardon us being suspicious of strangers.'

'Of course.'

'What come to Harry Struther, Mr. Hankey?'

'The chap who was supposed to bring Miss Barnes to the meeting? I'm afraid he'd been drinking, and he passed out. Miss . . .'

'That's not how Kate told it us.'

'It's what she's going to tell Mrs. Struther, though.'

'You've been fighting again, Mr. Hankey.'

It was neither a question nor an accusation. The words were spoken with a slow, meditative satisfaction, while the brown, lop-sided face peered up at Tom, pale eyes bulging with eager joy. Tom realised that he was dealing with an obsession, comparable in a way with Father's. Mr. Barnes collected boxers.

'I don't think you can count it,' said Tom. 'It wasn't under rules for a start, and if it had been we'd both have been disqualified in round one.'

Mr. Barnes nodded, accepting the argument but not amused by it.

'Where did you learn to fight, Mr. Hankey?'

'Oh, school, and then Oxford. Really it was a way of getting out of playing football. I kept it up because I got into the school team, and so on.'

'Eton College, that would be?'

'Yes. How did you . . .'

'Day you fought Donovan, we met, remember. You shook my hand and told me your name. I like to get things straight in my mind I tell you, so while you've been asking about me, I've been doing the same for you.'

'People seem to have been more willing to answer your questions than they were mine.'

'Aye . . . Did you ever see Pat O'Keefe fight, Mr. Hankey?'

'Only photographs.'

'You've a look of him, if you don't mind me saying. Now, I saw Pat fight Billy Wells at Bradford, nineteen thirteen, when he was nobbut starting. There was a fight, now. A young 'un and quick against an old 'un and crafty. Wells weighed in . . .'

Mr. Barnes recounted the preliminaries of the fight with a scholarly aridity that would have done credit to old Atherton, but as soon as the actual encounter started he changed his style, acting the bout as much as telling it, becoming each fighter in turn and differentiating clearly between them. In fact he moved remarkably little, adopting a pose and staying rigid as a sculptor's model, freezing the flow of instants until he sprang into the next pose. His must have been a well-known and well-liked performance, because about twenty men detached themselves from the discussion groups all round and formed a ring to watch, silent and absorbed. The imaginary fight was interrupted in the middle of round four by a noise from across the wasteland, a curious, rhythmic, throaty whooping from many mouths. Mr. Barnes dropped his posture of defence and smiled with sudden shyness, as if apologising for having been carried away. The other men were already moving towards the noise and adding their

own voices to it, close enough for Tom to hear that they were repeating two words over and over, like a war-cry. 'Git gangun.
Git gangun. Git gangun.' Even Mr. Barnes had joined the
chorus.

'What does it mean?' asked Tom.

Mr. Barnes, moving now with the rest of the crowd, repeated
the phrase three or four times more before breaking off to explain.

'Ah, just our way of calling the lads together, like. There was
an old fellow before the war, Sammy Dudlow, always impatient
for the meetings to begin, used to go round among the men
shouting like that, and of course we took it up, to chivvy him,
like. Then he fell off Number Two Quay in the Alexandra, nineteen twelve it would have been, and the tender swung in and
crushed him against the quay. That's how Sammy Dudlow died.
Next meeting some of the lads started the cry and the rest of us
took it up, out of respect to old Sam, and that's how we've done it
ever since. In the old days we rang a bell to start the proceedings,
only now we ring it to stop the shouting. Git gangun. Git
gangun . . .'

The explanation was logical and even pleasing, in that it
seemed to emphasise how a gathering such as this, organised by
Bolsheviks with the ultimate aim of destroying all accepted
codes, could still be affected by the curious tendency of the English to invent customs and keep them going. Tom could imagine
a group of Lower Boys, waiting in November drizzle for a Field
Game to begin out on one of the remote grounds beyond Agar's
Plough, setting up some such chant because their predecessors
had done so. That was not an Eton custom, but it easily might
have been.

The calling did not last for more than a minute or two. As soon
as a solid nucleus had formed in the crowd, and while the other
fringes were still gathering towards it, a man climbed onto some
kind of platform and swung a handbell vigorously to and fro
above his head. The shouting stopped at once. The man climbed
down and another took his place, elderly and grey-faced, wearing not the normal cloth cap but a bowler of ancient design. The
men cheered.

'Charlie Pottinger,' muttered Mr. Barnes. 'Transport and
General. Don't want a strike, but don't want to lose his

members either. He'll blow hot and cold.'

Mr. Pottinger had taken off his hat, revealing a curiously pointed bald head. Over this he slipped a strange apparatus. For a moment Tom thought he was taking nip from a metal flask, but when he lowered his hands there was a small speaking trumpet attached to his face by a couple of straps round the back of his head. He put his hat back on and raised his arms for silence.

'Brothers,' he began, 'the first thing I have to say is this. Let's have a nice orderly meeting. Let's not have any of the papers saying . . .'

'Who owns the bloody papers?' shouted a voice from the crowd.

'We all know who owns the newspapers,' answered the speaker. 'So let's not have them saying *we* gave any cause for trouble. If there's company men here . . .'

He paused, evidently expecting a growl from the crowd, and got it.

'If there's company men here, let them take note this is a peaceful meeting. Our friends the police . . .'

This time the growl seemed unexpected, but came.

'Our friends the police have been informed of the meeting, so let's have no trouble, brothers. Let's show the world we can make decisions with our minds. Let's show the world we do not need our fists. Let's . . .'

The emphatic rhetoric was ruined by the voice, nasal, whining, thin. He would hardly have been heard without his speaking trumpet, but unfortunately what it added in power it lost in spread. He tried to remedy this by swinging from one part of his audience to another, spraying his words over the crowd like a child hosing a flower-bed. The first half of a sentence might be clear, and even cogent, but then he twisted away and the rest was lost in mutter. He attempted to overcome this further problem by repeating individual phrases in successive sentences, and also by using his arms a great deal for emphasis, wagging his forefinger, counting off points, shaking a clenched fist or slamming it into the other palm, or raising both arms in world-accepting gestures of embrace. As far as Tom could make out he was telling his hearers that the shipowners had failed to keep some agreement which his union had negotiated in 1923, and had even tried to use it as an instrument of oppression beyond whatever oppression had existed before. He finished in a frenzy of barely audible rhetoric.

'. . . all over again? Will . . . never learn? Will the owners . . . ting is on the wall. They have made no official . . . firm for your rights. Stand firm for your . . . a living wage, brothers. It is not even a dying . . .'

He was cheered at the end with great enthusiasm by men who, Tom thought, had been thoroughly bored by the whole performance. How could you take decisions on the basis of incomprehensible and mainly inaudible jargon? Mr. Pottinger climbed down and was replaced by a younger man with a round, suety and complacent face.

'Sam Pragg,' explained Mr. Barnes. 'Gas Workers and Allied. Won't like what Charlie's been saying, but won't show it. That was a *joint* agreement, twenty-three.'

Mr. Pragg had a clear enough voice, but so heavy as to sound listless. Moreover he read his speech from a large green notebook. This was no doubt necessary as it consisted mainly of a great many dates and figures, apparently to do with the piece-work rates for different grades of dockers. The men seemed to be listening with care and even grunting assent now and then, affirming Mr. Pragg's veracity over a detail, but it meant very little to Tom. His eye was caught by a movement among the three or four men who stood just behind the platform, presumably on some kind of lower step, because their heads and shoulders rose clear of the audience. The movement was little more than a stare by one of them, a shared mutter, more stares and a nod or two. Carefully Tom turned to see what they had been looking at.

Being a few inches taller than the average docker he was able to see over the massed heads to the edge of the wasteland. A group of men, dark-uniformed, were crossing the footbridge that spanned the Holderness Drain at its southern end, and along the fence by the Hedon Road two similar groups had appeared. These were clearly policemen, some thirty of them, simply standing and waiting. There seemed to be something a little different about the men crossing the footbridge, but he was too far off to make sure.

Tom's attention returned to Mr. Pragg, who had closed his notebook and was embarking on his peroration, which was strangely impressive. He was able to speak in quiet, almost fatherly tones but still be heard.

'The companies have let us down,' he said. 'It is not through incompetence, though Lord knows they have their share of incompetents on the boards. Sometimes I think they breed incompetents deliberate to put on the boards. No, lads, this time they have let us down because they wanted to let us down. They wanted to show us who's master. A crack of the whip and we'll come to heel, they thought. And will we so come to heel? Eh, lads, will we?'

'No,' bayed the crowd, and broke into cheering. Mr. Pragg nodded at them like a master whose class has given the right answer to a school inspector and smiled for the first time.

There was a brief pause while he climbed down, and Tom was about to ask Mr. Barnes what on earth gas workers had to do with a dispute in the docks when somebody yelled 'Where's Kate?'

'What have ye done with Kate?' called someone else.

'Married her off to the boss's son,' chanted several voices to the tune of *Nuts in May*.

'Boss's son, Boss's son,' sang several hundred men, out of both time and tune. 'Married her off to the boss's son on Christmas Day in the morning.'

This was evidently an old joke and popular, another element of half-ritualised horseplay which Tom found comforting, though he could see that Mr. Barnes didn't much care for it. Then Miss Barnes herself climbed or was lifted onto the platform, looking flustered but cheerful.

'I'm still here,' she called, as the applause died away. 'I told him to ask me again some time.'

'When, Kate, when?'

'When his father pays the workers a living wage.'

This evidently ancient riposte was answered by another baying cheer, during which Miss Barnes made meaningless adjustments to the position of her hat on her shock of hair. Then she lowered her hands and held them waist-high, arms half spread, a signal answered by almost immediate silence. She launched herself into her speech with absolute confidence, in a clear carrying voice that could afford to start at a seemingly quiet level and still leave plenty of room for crescendi.

'My father died in the Alexandra,' she said. 'A derrick slewed and crushed him. The company paid my mother twenty-five pounds compensation. Twenty-five pounds for a man in his prime. That was the going rate, then. And it would still be the going rate if the Companies had their way. If you men had not fought year after year and generation after generation for better wages and better conditions.

'Your committee have asked me to speak to you, but if they hadn't, I would still have the right. And what gives me the right? Not my father who died for twenty-five pounds in the Alexandra. Not my grandfather, who worked the Victoria, when there *was* work, for twenty two shillings a week. Not my great-grandfather who came to Hull to dig the St Andrews Extension. No. It is my mother, and my grandmothers, and my great-grandmothers. Women of Hull who generation after generation have had to feed their men and raise their children on a wage that would not keep one of Mrs. Tarrant's lap-dogs in chicken for a week. Generation after generation you men have fought to raise that wage. You have squeezed a penny here and a penny there to feed your women and your bairns from men who have let you have it as though each farthing was their own hearts' blood. And these were the men, these were the men, who thought nothing of buying gold horseshoes to bury their favourite hunter!

'And now what, comrades? Now what? These self-same men are trying to take those farthings back! They are trying to take those farthings back at a time when prices are rising. You know that the tobacco in your pipe costs more this year than it did last year. You ask your woman, and she'll tell you that the meat in your dish and the clothes on the backs of your bairns and even the soap she scrubs her front step with all cost more! And where is that extra money going? Is it going to provide better wages for your comrades who stitch those clothes and your comrades who boil that soap? No it is not. It is going straight into the pockets of the shareholders.

'And who are these shareholders? Why, they are the very men and women who sit on the boards of the shipping companies.

This is the great capitalist conspiracy. The self-same men who are sending out the notices next Monday, the notices informing you of a cut in your rates, these men are going back to their clubs to lunch off lobster and champagne and pay for it with money that you have given them when you buy shirts for the backs of your bairns. This very Monday you will get the notices. It is all very well for Charlie Pottinger to say that the Companies have made no statement. Nor have they. Nor will they. They will just give each of you a notice when you come to work on Monday.

'How do I know? I know because I have seen that notice. I know because I have a copy of it here . . .'

Her hand plunged into the side-pocket of her jacket and pulled out a buff-coloured sheet of paper which she unfolded and brandished in the air. A solid roar arose from the crowd, nothing like the jocular crowing that had greeted her when she began, but a deep, angry bellow. Objectively Miss Barnes's style was extremely effective. The short sentences, the repetitions, the slow delivery that ensured that not a word was lost but at the same time never dragged thanks to the sustained energy of her personality—these could not have been better done. Earlier Tom had thought for a moment that she had something of the appeal of a steam locomotive, and now he saw that he had been right. In action she had just that impression of blunt unmitigated power driving with all its energy towards its distant purpose. Her wild hair, her flushed and passionate face, transcended categories of human beauty and made her something other— Bellona, Tom's schoolmasters would have said, breathing rage into the minds of men. The classic image was quite inappropriate. Though she had appealed to the past at the beginning of her speech she seemed to Tom a new and very dangerous phenomenon.

For, though impressed, he was also deeply shocked, not so much by what she said as by the fact that it was her saying it. It seemed to him that her performance was an act, put on to deceive unsophisticated listeners, and that the real Miss Barnes was the pleasant, quiet, amused and intelligent woman who had walked with him down the Hedon Road. That woman had been much too perceptive and subtle to believe the misleading simplicities she was mouthing. He noticed that she had not started calling her listeners 'Comrades' until she was sure that she had them hooked. And the details she chose to illustrate her argument, though dramatic and effective, were coarsely out of alignment with the truth. Yes, Mrs. Tarrant did keep two yapping and neurotic dachshunds, but she was unlikely to feed them on chicken. It would be one of Mrs. Tarrant's many certainties that dogs should eat dog-food. And yes, Lord Belford, Woffles's grandfather, had buried his favourite mare in golden horseshoes, but the gold had been paper thin, and Belford had never turned a labourer off any of his farms because the man was too old or ill to work, but had kept them all and their widows on pensions in their own cottages, rent free, even when it meant building new houses for the men who replaced them on the farms. The world Tom knew was other than what Miss Barnes declared it to be.

As he watched her hold her sheet of paper aloft like a fiery cross he felt ashamed for her, and was beginning to wish he had not stayed for the meeting. Then, in the middle of the cheering, something altered. There was a moment of uncertainty in her movements. A small dark object flashed past her head, and the next instant another struck her shoulder and burst apart, manifesting itself to have been a clod of earth. The volume of shouting faltered, changed, rose. More clods flew. Miss Barnes did not flinch, but held up her arms for silence, peering at the same time in the direction of the attack with a vague and craning stare that made Tom realise suddenly that she was extremely short-sighted. Several more missiles flew, but only one hit her. They must appear to her to be coming at her from out of a misty sea of faces, though Tom thought there were only two, or possibly three, groups of assailants, one quite close to him. He turned and saw an upheaval in the crowd, a definite centre of scuffling. The men round him were pressing in that direction, yelling with anger. Tom moved with them without thought until a hand tugged at his elbow.

'You better stay out on this,' shouted Mr. Barnes.

Tom nodded and began to work his way sideways, clear of the press of men. It was thus that he saw what happened next.

The fight was taking place right on the edge of the crowd. Three, or perhaps four men, were defending themselyes against the rest. Despite the numerical odds they had a momentary advantage because they had armed themselves with rough clubs of driftwood, picked up presumably on the wasteland before the fighting started; but the crowd was closing round them like an amoeba digesting a particle and in a few seconds they would be overwhelmed. Just before the crisis of the fight a man who had been standing a little clear of the crowd drew something from his jacket pocket, pulled his cap down to cover his eyes and barged into the melee. His arm rose. The thing in his hand was a revolver, which he pointed at the sky. Before the shock of the explosion was over his arm was withdrawn and he was barging his way out of the crowd again. With rapid, rehearsed movements he snatched his cap from his head, stuffed it into his pocket and knotted a red scarf round his neck.

The shot produced only a brief shock-wave of silence before fresh roars began, but the man who had fired it turned almost jauntily and began to thread his way clear. Tom was about to follow him when he saw Mr. Barnes jammed between two larger men who were struggling to close with the men with the clubs. Tom took him by the shoulder and heaved him clear.

'I saw the chap with the gun,' he shouted. 'He wasn't one of you.'

'Where?'

'There! Red scarf!'

At once Mr. Barnes dashed after the man and seized him by the sleeve. The man swung round, his fist doubled for a blow. Mr. Barnes flung up an arm and warded it off. Tom was rushing to help when a swirl of men hurtled against him from the flank. His legs caught against each other and he fell to his knees, but rose at once and shoved his way towards where Mr. Barnes was still gripping the man's sleeve and with his other arm protecting his own head. Before he could reach them another rush of men, dark uniformed, closed round them. Truncheons rose and fell and Tom saw Mr. Barnes stagger to one side with blood streaming down his cheek. The man with the scarf was slipping away between two policemen. Tom ran forward and caught Mr. Barnes by the shoulders, shouting 'No! No!' and holding up his free arm to cover the old man's head from the next blow. The shock of it numbed his fore-arm, and in almost the same instant something crashed against his own head. There was pain and a dark red roaring, another shock of pain and darkness.

Consciousness came in waves, first as mere pain in the head, followed by more blackness. Then, added to the pain, there was knowledge of being face down on harsh earth with a huge weight on his shoulders, his right arm twisted behind him, and sour vomit in his mouth, mixed with the softer taste of blood. Next time he could hear the yelling and the sharp bark of orders, and knew where he was, lying on a patch of waste by the Hull docks while a man knelt on his back and locked his arm behind him. Around him the police were breaking up the strike meeting. When he tried to protest and ease his position the man on his back swore and twisted his arm still further. The pain slid him back into darkness.

But now through the darkness he could still feel pain, and hear the shouts and fighting, and a new roaring, the engines of large vehicles like lorries, throbbing erratically closer as their drivers eased them across the hummocky ground. They ceased. The shouts moved further away and the voices of command became less urgent. 'Right, Ted, we'll have your one now,' said someone. The weight left Tom's shoulders. Hands seized his arms and dragged him up, then thrust him, staggering through red-gold glare, towards a dark bulk. All edges were blurred and double. His shin bashed a sharp barrier. 'Step *up*, you silly bugger.' Obediently he pawed for the step with a foot, found nothing, was heaved from the ground and thrown forward, sprawling.

Men caught him half fallen and passed him, crouched and staggering sideways, easing him onto a harsh bench, close against someone's shoulder. Almost at once, with new noises of stumbling and scrabbling, a body thudded onto the bench on his far side, propping him upright. He moved his head to and fro trying to clear the darkness, but then perceived that it lay outside his mind, that he was sitting in a dark tunnel lit only by an upright slit through which several more men—blurred forms still—stumbled or were propelled.

The slit closed with a bang. Locks rattled. The throbbing engine roared and the darkness began to jolt and sway. Men clutched at each other, swore, groaned. Somebody vomited. Tom's head hurt too much for him to think or consider anything at all, or do more than accept without noticing the easing of the jolts and change of gears when the truck reached a road surface and could move faster and more smoothly.

When the drive stopped and the door was thrown open he found that despite the continued pain his vision was improving. He could see that he had been sitting in a large, metal-walled space with benches down either side on which two rows of men faced each other, tight packed, many with bloody faces, and all looking sick, or at least stunned. A voice barked 'Let's have you, then! One at a time!' A large policeman climbed into the space and moved down the centre gangway, peeling the men from the benches by snatching at a shoulder and as the sitter rose giving him a shove towards the door. Tom emerged to find the fading daylight darkened by the walls of a small courtyard across which the file of men from the truck was being hustled between two ranks of policemen. The prisoner in front of him paused in his shambling trot and turned as if to make some sort of protest but before he had begun the policeman behind him seized his elbow and propelled him on, maintaining the momentum of sub-jection. Tom was in no state to think out a course of action, but instinct and schooling told him that there was no point in protest-ing to underlings. These policemen were simply the cogs and rollers of a conveyor belt; somewhere somebody controlled a switch.

There was a short, dank, stone-flagged corridor, a half-flight of steps down to another corridor lit by yellow-green gas, a door on one side through which the men ahead of Tom vanished, a heavy clang of metal and a shove in the chest, forcing him to jostle back against the men behind, another door unlocked and a counter-shove on his shoulder-blade forcing him on and through into a small bare cell lit by a heavy-barred window a foot square. Men followed him. The door clanged. Its lock snicked. All the men in the cell let out their breath in a long, communal sigh. Somebody said 'It's a bugger, eh?' Nobody demurred. 'Our friends the police,' said someone else. 'Half on 'em sodding dock rozzers.' Grunts of assent. Another sigh. 'Az onyonyeonyonye?' Cigarettes were passed round. Tom shook his head when one was pushed at him, but the man said 'Best have one now, mate. They'll be taking them off of us.' Tom accepted the wizened object, bent to the last half-inch of a shared match and sucked the smoke in. It was as rank as cow-manure but its very pungency seemed to clear his brain. The men smoked in silence, venting little mutters of outrage and disbelief, calming their shock like a sleeper woken from a nightmare who attempts to restore his confidence in the solid world with small twitches and movements, only gradually loosening the residual stillness of dread.

The window became quite dark. About two hours passed. There had been movements and voices outside the cell, the sharp clink of keys, footsteps, orders, the heavy jar of doors. Tom refused any more cigarettes. He had given up his pipe during his second year at Oxford, and now smoked only the occasional after-dinner cigar. This tobacco was far too strong for him and he had no wish to add his vomit to the already reeking cell. The other men smoked steadily until they had no tobacco left.

Quite early there had been a muttered argument in the far corner, and then somebody had asked him why he had been at the meeting. He'd said that Mr. Struther had been ill so Miss Barnes had asked him to go with her. That had apparently settled the argument, but he became more and more aware that they would have talked differently, more easily, if he had not been there. When one man began to ask who had fired the shot the others shut him up. Tom decided they believed him to be a reporter from a local newspaper—judging by Mr. Pottinger's remarks at the start of the meeting that would account for their obvious suspicion.

When at last keys rattled at the door of the cell he woke from a chill doze where he had been sitting wedged into the further corner. He felt sick and feeble, and his headache, which had begun as a beam of pain running from temple to temple, had dulled but now infected his whole head and neck.

'Youanyouanyouanyou,' said the policeman at the door, picking out the nearest four men. They rose and went without a murmur. The door closed and was locked, but ten minutes later it was opened again and the policeman called the rest of them out. He directed them further down the corridor, up steps, across a hallway and into a fair-sized office with high barred windows. The air had the dry, almost peppery smell of that special dust which collects where paperwork lies in piles and is endlessly sorted and re-sorted. The centre of the room was lit by a low-hanging gas-mantle, under which a sergeant sat at a large desk with open ledgers before him. A constable sat beside him and another stood behind his shoulder. In the shadows around the central pool of light vaguer presences loomed.

The prisoners were lined up behind the desk, Tom hindmost. At once the constable who had escorted them rifled through the pockets of the first prisoner, laying the contents on the desk and enumerating them in a low voice to the seated constable. At the same time the sergeant asked a brisk series of questions and wrote the answers in his ledger. The belongings of each prisoner were slid into an envelope, which he signed across the flap. The whole process took about two minutes a man.

'Name?'

'Hankey.'

Hands, quick and unfumbling, were already going through Tom's pockets.

'Christian names?'

'The Honourable Thomas Paul Dettinger.'

'. . . pocket-knife, matches, leather wallet containing . . .'

The constable's voice faltered to count the notes, but the sergeant's pen had already stopped writing. He looked round, over his shoulder. A man came heavily forward.

'What is it, sergeant?'

The sergeant's finger tapped, almost gingerly, at the name he had half written. The constable put the wallet back on the table and pushed it a little away, as though it might be infected with some disease.

'What is your address?' said the man from the shadows.

'Sillerby, Sill, North Riding.'

There was a short pause, unconvincingly concluded by a cough.

'Ahem. Well now . . . there has evidently . . . would you step in here for a few minutes, sir?'

'You haven't finished listing my possessions.'

'If you'll take them back for the time being . . .'

'What about these other men?'

'Sir?'

A shuffle, the movement of a door, footsteps—the next batch for questioning being led in.

'If you're going to list theirs you must list mine.'

A sigh.

'If you *would* mind stepping . . .'

'I want my possessions listed.'

'Very well. Carry on, then, sergeant.'

'. . . leather wallet containing, er, nineteen pounds. Seven shillings and fourpence change. Wristwatch . . . is that gold, please?'

'Yes.'

'Gold wristwatch. You keep the handkerchief, er, sir.'

Tom bent and signed the envelope flap, then followed the man from the shadows through a door. All through the previous exchange he had kept his head bent, obsessed by the lit rectangle of the desk and the need to go through the same machinery as the other prisoners. This had been the only plan he had been able to make during the wait in the cell, that the authorities should have no doubt who he was, and should understand that he refused to be differently treated from the other men they had so violently and outrageously arrested. Even to put it like that was to make his reaction sound far more willed and rational than it truly was. It was literally a reaction, a slow but still involuntary, almost physical process, like the blink of an eye to a threatened blow, an assertion of his oneness with the fabric of England.

Now, raising his head, he saw a small drab office, also lit by gas but fully lit, so that there could be no unseen presence in shadows. The man who had brought him here turned out to be a rather ordinary middle-aged police officer, clearly very tired and equally clearly troubled.

'If you'd take a seat, sir,' said this man, sitting himself at the roll-top desk and pointing to an upright chair beside it.

Tom hesitated, dragged the chair out and sat.

'What's your name?' he asked.

'I'm Chief Inspector Whitehorn.'

'Are you in charge of all this?'

'If you will please let me ask the questions. Now, sir, how did you come to be at the scene of the riot?'

'Riot?'

'Of the events on Marfleet Strand?'

'A lady asked me to accompany her to the meeting. I stayed to watch, out of interest.'

'A lady? That would be the woman Barnes.'

'Miss Kate Barnes.'

'And what would be your connection with, uh, Miss Barnes?'

'I have no connection with Miss Barnes other than having accompanied her to the meeting.'

'Come now, sir . . .'

'Did *you* see what happened at Marfleet Strand, Chief Inspector?'

'If you will please let . . .'

'I'll tell you what happened. There was a perfectly peaceful meeting. Two male speakers addressed it. There was no trouble. When Miss Barnes began to speak a few men started to throw clods of earth at her. These men were clearly attempting to provoke the meeting, which was why they had waited for Miss Barnes, who is very popular with the men, to speak. Naturally some scuffles broke out. The men who had been throwing things were obviously expecting this, as they had armed themselves with clubs. I saw another man who had taken no part in the fighting draw a revolver from his pocket, push into the crowd and fire a shot into the air. He immediately left the fight, took off a cap and put on a red scarf. I could see that he had planned to do this —in fact the whole episode so far was planned. I told Mr. Ned Barnes what I had seen, and he followed the man and quite properly tried to detain him. The man fought back. Before I could come to his help a group of policemen arrived and hit Mr. Barnes with truncheons. They made no attempt to hit or arrest the man who had fired the shot—in fact I saw him slipping away, evidently with their connivance. I didn't see any more because I was trying to protect Mr. Barnes when somebody knocked me unconscious.'

'I see, sir.'

'Now the first thing I want to know is whether all the policemen on Marfleet Strand were under your command?'

'If you'll . . .'

'As soon as I am free I shall write to the Lord Lieutenant and ask him to set up an enquiry. I know him personally, and I am quite sure he will believe what I tell him.'

'An enquiry will want to know what you were doing in Hull, and how you came to accompany a known Bolshevik agitator to a docker's meeting.'

'I suggest you telephone Mrs. Tarrant at Brantingham Manor and ask her that question.'

Chief Inspector Whitehorn sighed and studied the papers on his desk. Tom waited. He felt no embarrassment at all at spending the currency his birth and upbringing had endowed him with. What was it for, if not to use in a matter like this?

'Chief Inspector,' he said, 'I must make it clear that I do not believe all the police at Marfleet Strand were under your command or your control. In fact I have reason to think that the initial assault on the crowd was made by dock police, who had been expecting a shot to be fired so that they could intervene. I am sure that you are as shocked as I am by the course of events.'

Tom was aware that his speech during the interview had become steadily more stilted. He was speaking the language of authority as if it were the dialect of his tribe—a dialect he had never really needed to use, but which now that the need arose came readily to his lips. Chief Inspector Whitehorn opened his mouth as if to repeat the sacred formula about who should ask the questions, then closed it again. He looked worse than merely tired. His face was as grey as concrete and his lips almost blue. Tom wondered whether he was about to have some kind of seizure, but the convulsion that had appeared to signal it became a weary rising to his feet, followed by a long frowning hesitation and a sigh.

'If you would wait here a few minutes, sir . . .'

He paused at the door, visibly reassuming the carapace of authority, and left.

Time went by. At first Tom sat with his head in his hands and his elbows on his knees, fingering the bruise on the side of his head. The pain inside his skull throbbed in slow waves. During one of its lulls he picked up the paper the Chief Inspector had studied and began to read it. It was a list of names with symbols opposite them—ticks, double ticks, the occasional cross or query. High on the list came Barnes, E. and Barnes, Miss K.

Barnes, E. had a tick and a query, Barnes, Miss K. was in brackets with a cross beside it. There were about thirty names in all, but Ricardo was not one of them. The last entry, in a different hand from the rest, was not a name but a dash, followed by the words 'with KB' and a query.

Without shame he reached for the further stack of papers, but these seemed solely concerned with routine police administration. He re-read the list, but as soon as he made any effort to memorise the names his headache leaped back at him. He put the paper where he had found it and waited.

Chief Inspector Whitehorn was already speaking as he came through the door, evidently having found fresh resources of energy somewhere. He looked and sounded distinctly angry.

'Well, sir, I have been able to check the account you give of yourself and you are free to go.'

'What about the others?'

'They are being released pending a decision.'

'A decision about what?'

'I must tell you that I have also begun to make enquiries about the events surrounding the firing of the shot. May I take it that you would recognise the man you say was responsible?'

'Yes, I'm pretty sure of that.'

'And the individual officers who you allege struck Mr. Barnes?'

'No. No, I don't think so. I might, but . . .'

'Very well. Now sir, I accept that there is evidence of, uh, excessive zeal on the part of some of the dock police who were working in collaboration with the regular force under my command. If this evidence can be corroborated an enquiry will be held. Meanwhile I would advise you, sir, not to prejudice its findings by speaking to anyone about the matter.'

'But . . . oh, very well, I'll see what happens. But now we can all go home?'

'I have your personal belongings here. If you would be good enough to sign this receipt . . .'

Tom signed before he took the envelope. As he slotted its contents back into familiar pockets he became aware of an odd sense of restoring parts of his living self that had been amputated by their removal, though he had not noticed this at the time.

In the larger room a rhythmic murmuring had begun, interrupted by the occasional calling of a name. When Tom came through the door he found the place thronged with the men who had been arrested, waiting their turns to go to the desk and check their belongings. Their behaviour, though still subdued and shocked, was different from what it had been earlier, suffused now with a sort of puzzled interest. One or two glanced at Tom and nudged neighbours. As he passed behind the desk he saw that the policemen working there had also changed, subtly, both in posture and tone. What was clearly an angry argument was being whispered between two of the figures in the further shadows, but these voices stilled as he went by. In the hallway a policeman pointed him without a word towards where two of the released men were disappearing through another door. Beyond it was a large room divided by a mahogany counter. Two more doors and he was standing on the front steps of the police station, breathing the musky soft air of a summer night.

He looked at his watch. Ten to eleven. There might still be a train on the Leeds line, but the ancient taxi would long since have ceased to haunt Brough Station, and Brantingham Manor would be locked for the night. In any case coping with Mrs. Tarrant tomorrow, let alone trying to explain his night's adventure to her, was beyond contemplation. It would have to be an hotel.

More men came out of the police station and at once attached themselves to the large group, both men and women, who were waiting on the far pavement. The newcomers immediately began to explain with jerky gestures and reiterated swearings what had happened to them. The crowd was fairly quiet but an air of jubilation and excitement hung round them as they looked eagerly at the doors for each new arrival. Tom loitered to one side until he realised that he was doing so in the unconscious hope of being at least thanked by someone, and that this was not going to happen. He was moving away when he heard a step behind him and a hand touched his elbow. It was Mr. Barnes.

'Mr. Hankey, sir.'

'Hello. Are you all right?'

'I'd like to shake you by the hand, sir.'

Very pleased Tom took the grainy fist and shook it warmly.

Mr. Barnes had lost his cap. Dried blood smeared the side of his face and he had a huge swelling above his left eye, but seemed bird-bright still.

'You fetched us all out of there, Mr. Hankey.'

'Oh, I don't know. They couldn't have kept you. Obviously the whole thing had got out of hand.'

'It had that. Did you hear the policeman in there, swearing to make the devil blush at what the dockie police had landed on them? Aye, but it would have been a night in the cells for all on us, and charges in front of the magistrates and fines, and prison for some of the lads. Did you hear the dockie police Inspector in the back room, raging into the telephone about us being let go?'

'I heard a bit of a row between two men but I couldn't make out what it was about.'

'Ay, that. That was who must take the blame over arresting Mr. Hankey. Once you were clear of the room they started yelling at each other. And where will you be going now, sir?'

'I've missed the last train. I'll see if I can find an hotel.'

'They lock up timely in Hull, like. It's not London, is it?'

'I suppose not.'

'There's a sofy in our front parlour, Mr. Hankey. It's not that long nor broad, but it'll be better nor nowt.'

'Well that's very kind of you, but what will Mrs. Barnes . . .'

'If she says a word I'll wallop her!'

(It took Tom several weeks' more acquaintance to discover that this was Mr. Barnes's favourite joke, made straight-faced always, and always providing him with vast inward satisfaction.)

'Well, thank you very much.'

'Come and meet the lads, Mr. Hankey. They'll be honoured to shake your hand.'

In fact when Mr. Barnes led him back to join the crowd on the pavement several of the men came and shook his hand and thanked him, but he was aware that some of them did it more for Mr. Barnes's sake than his, and that others preferred to retain their aloofness. Friendly or not, his presence constrained their ease among themselves, so he was glad when the last of the arrested men came down the steps and the crowd broke into smaller groups and they all began to walk, leaden-legged, from pool to pool of gas-light along the cobbled streets.

10

Rokesley Hall, 4th August, 1926

Bertie Panhard shook his head, making the side-pieces of his wig flap like a spaniel's ears. His face was far too short and square for Charles II, but the heavy-lidded eyes and the little greasepaint moustache gave it the right look of melancholy and dangerous humour, and he had adopted all, and more than all, the lounging affability the role demanded. He was sitting in a corner of the library at Rokesley, converted to the supper room for Woffles's party as the Great Hall was being used to dance in. Behind him, on shelves intricately carved in the style of a Gothic rood-screen, climbed rank on rank of leather-bound books, probably none of them once opened during three generations of Belfords.

'Egad, Master Thomas,' he said. 'You seem to have made an unconscionable mess of matters in our city of Kingston upon Hull. Good Mistress Tarrant has been—what's the word I want? "Irked" doesn't sound quite in period.'

'Sorry about that,' said Tom. 'She wasn't pleased. I still don't see what else I could have done, but I couldn't make her understand.'

'I hear she turned you out of the house,' said Dick, who had come to the dance as a Bolshevik but was making no serious effort to play the part beyond brandishing a round object with a short piece of cord attached to the top. The thing was labelled "Bomb", but from time to time he unscrewed the fuse and took a swig from its contents. He was already fairly tight, and beginning to look convincingly haggard and wild-eyed.

'No, she didn't,' said Tom. 'I was leaving in any case, but she was perfectly polite and said I could stay on if I wanted to, but she let me see that she was extremely angry.'

'Would that we had been present to witness the interview,' said Bertie. 'Both for the sight of Mistress Tarrant enraged, and for the hearing of Master Thomas endeavouring to expound a moral principle to her. Mistress Tarrant is a woman of many virtues, but the Creator in His wisdom omitted from her gifts all capacity for abstract speculation. Oh, dash it, I can't go on like this. I spend so much time thinking how to say things that I don't get anything said, and I've got the next dance down with that wench of Teddy's. Tell me your version of what happened, Tom. I must say, I wish you'd sent me a wire—I'd have come beetling back. Start at the beginning. Last I know was asking you to nose around in Hull and see if you could find one of the fellows you'd seen loading that Bolshie rag onto your train. Off I go to France, conscious that the future of the nation is now in steady hands, and the next thing I hear is a letter from Helen Tarrant saying that you have been siding with a mob of Bolshie-led strikers and impeding the police in the course of their duty—and worse than all that, infuriating little Judy's Mama. Tom, Tom, is there more in this than meets the eye?'

'Less, I think,' said Tom, only just restraining himself from tugging at his collar. The uniform in which Grandfather had sat with Lord Raglan on the ridge and watched the Balaclava charge was a great stand-by for fancy dress and fitted Tom perfectly, but by this stage in the evening it tended to feel as though it had been deliberately cut to allow the wearer as little movement as possible. How Grandfather had saluted, let alone brandished his sabre, was a military mystery.

'I don't think there's time to tell you all the details,' he said. 'I'll just give you the outline. I wasn't getting anywhere with looking for the men I'd seen, but I managed to get into the first big strike-meeting. The ship owners were planning to reduce some of the men's rates because of their losses from the coal strike, and the other dockers were going to strike to prevent it. The meeting was quite peaceful until some men who had been planted in the crowd started throwing earth at one of the speakers. Naturally scuffling broke out, and a man fired a shot, giving the police an excuse to charge in and arrest the strike-leaders. I just happened . . .'

'Half a mo,' said Bertie. 'You are implying that all this was arranged for the benefit of the ship-owners. Why should they want to do that?'

'Two things. The most important is that the dock-workers at Hull are only about half union men, and there are several unions. That makes it very difficult to keep a strike solid, especially when it's only for the benefit of one section of the men, the ones who handle the coal. If you can break up the leadership by arresting them and getting some of them sent to prison, you increase your chances that the strike won't hold. I only worked this out afterwards, of course. I was absolutely bewildered by what happened. The other point is that strikes aren't all that popular with the general public just now, and the owners would have much more sympathy on their side if they could show that this one began with a violent riot.'

'Do you know,' said Dick in a mock-shocked voice, 'even *Punch* had a go at the mine-owners last week. I felt as though I'd been stabbed in the back by the parish magazine!'

The interruption steadied Tom. He caught a flash of the peculiar glint in Bertie's eyes even as Charles II let himself erupt in regal laughter. He remembered to think of Bertie's ease and friendliness as external, almost in the same style as his wig and ruffles. In fact Tom had been as angry with Mrs. Tarrant as she with him, startled and finally furious at her moral intransigence. If he could use Bertie to appease her a little, that would at least make Judy's life easier.

'I see,' said Bertie. 'Your argument is coherent, Tom, but not utterly convincing. One thing I've been learning about our Bolshie friends is that they are in favour of mayhem of any kind, provided it helps them set the workers against the bosses. What is there to show that they didn't lay the whole fracas on with that in mind? Get a shot fired, start a riot, blame it on the bosses and inflame the strikers to violence?'

'Oh, they're capable of it,' said Tom. 'Some of them, anyway. But I happened to be near the man who fired the shot. I saw the dock police actually help him get away when one of the dockers tried to detain him. Then I got laid out and arrested, and when I told the regular Chief Superintendent what I'd seen he pretty well admitted that it was the dock police who had really started things.'

'That still doesn't explain why Mrs. Tarrant is so shirty with you.'

'Well, I insisted on his letting all the men he'd arrested go. I told him that I was going to write to the Lord Lieutenant and tell him what I'd seen and ask for a fully enquiry.'

'Dear Uncle Nobby, some of your policemen have been perfectly horrid to me.'

Bertie's tone was so light that it took Tom a second to register that Bertie not only remembered Lord Foxhaven was his godfather, but also knew the family name for him.

'A little more formal,' said Tom. 'In fact I haven't written. It was a sort of understanding that if they let the men go . . . At first they simply wanted me to slink away while they charged all the others. That's what I found so difficult to get Mrs. Tarrant to understand.'

'Honest Master Tom,' said Bertie. 'You really are a creature out of the past, you know, but that uniform's too effete for you. It struck me when we found you engaging in fisticuffs in Drewton Cutting, you know. It was like a chapter in one of those awful novels. *In which our hero stakes life and honour upon an encounter with a notorious pugilist,* and so on. Am I doomed to go on rescuing you from imbroglios in which your old-fashioned honesty has landed you? I suppose you expect me to appease Helen Tarrant, whom you have affronted by your overweening honesty.'

'Well . . .'

'You must fight against these impulses, young man. Every time you feel an honest urge rising within you, you must say to yourself, "I am above that sort of thing." '

'Seriously, Bertie . . .'

'Seriously, Tom, I will do what I can. Tell me, what did your friends the dockers think of your efforts on their behalf?'

'They don't say much, actually, but they've begun to behave as though I wasn't quite the man from Mars they thought I was at first.'

'Do I take it that your efforts have extended beyond the week you originally said you'd do?'

'Well, yes.'

'That's very gratifying. So you've changed your mind?'

'I suppose so. Mr. Hutton started it really. He agrees with you that the Reds in Hull are a genuine menace, and it's worth trying to find them. Since I'd made a start, I thought I might as well carry on.'

Bertie nodded, watching him half sideways under the beetling wig. Tom would have liked to tell him about the mysterious Ricardo, but had promised not to. On the other hand, there would have been no point in attempting to explain the attraction of his new relationship with the strikers. Bertie would take that either for soft-headedness or outright treachery—just as would take the pleasure of Kate's companionship for something other than Tom felt it to be. It was best to hurry on.

'I've taken a room behind the docks,' he said. 'I stay there a couple of nights a week and help an old fellow I met run a make-shift gym.'

'Do you now? That's rather ingenious. The fellow who was supposed to be fixing you up the fight with Whatsisname?'

'Donovan. He won't play. But yes, that's the man.'

'So you are getting somewhere in the hunt for our Red pamphleteers?'

Tom felt an honest urge rising within him but took Bertie's advice and fought it down.

'I'm making progress of a sort,' he said, 'but not quite like that. I have to be pretty careful because as soon as I start asking questions they shut right up. But I happened to have been reading Karl Marx and I said so to one of them, and last week at a meeting a chap I didn't know came up and started talking about alienation. I got the impression it was a try-out.'

'They let you come to the meetings?'

'Oh yes. I'm a sort of mascot, I suppose, but in theory they put up with me because they think the police will be more careful if I'm around.'

'And is that the case?'

'Things have been pretty peaceful, really. I did get attacked on my way home from the gym one evening.'

'Oh come. You aren't saying Helen Tarrant and her colleagues . . .'

'Of course not. Things aren't like that. What you get is a group of roughs brought in by the companies as strike-breakers.

It isn't a vast conspiracy. These men act pretty much on their own initiative—they're much less organised than the strikers. In fact I doubt if any of the company officials actually knew what was planned at the original strike meeting—I expect the roughs and some of the dock police fixed it up among themselves.'

'Not very intelligent.'

'There's not a lot of intelligence around.'

'No. Did you get hurt when you were attacked?'

'Not at all. They'd chosen a stupid place, not fifty yards from the gym. My boys came out before it had really begun and came legging along to help me and the men had to run for their lives. They caught one of them and threw him in the river.'

'Lucky old Tom,' said Dick, bored and disdainful.

'True word,' said Bertie. 'I'm a great believer in luck. In spite of appearances you seem to be getting on extremely well, Tom. And you've learnt quite a bit, by the sound of it.'

'I suppose so.'

'How long will this strike last, do you think?'

'I don't know. The mood's getting pretty grim, really. The dockers believe that the board are determined to break them, and they're determined not to be broken . . . Hull has been a militant town for years. During the General Strike they burnt trams.'

Suddenly Dick straightened from his slouch and made a sweeping gesture with his bomb.

'You pierce my soul!' he cried. 'What poetry! What insight! What stark realism in those three syllables! They burnt trams! The flaming omnibus! That is the symbol of the future! Why didn't Woffles throw a tram-burning party instead of this effete bourgeois frippery?'

He reached over and tugged at the nearest locks of Bertie's wig, as if at a bell-pull. The wig and the wide plumed hat came clean away, leaving that square puritanical head protruding from the finery of lace and braid. With the black unreal moustache and the shiny black hair slicked back so hard that it looked like the painted locks of Shem in a Noah's Ark set, the effect was theatrically sudden and revealing—as though Bertie had carelessly allowed his real self to protrude inside the camouflage of fancy dress and Dick's ambush had trapped it there before he had time to withdraw it inside the familiar disguise of skin. The revelation lasted only a second, and then Bertie was shrugging tolerantly as Dick paraded off between the supper tables, preaching bloody revolution to Pierrot and Columbine, to Zulu warrior and Little Bo-Peep, brandishing his bomb in one hand and his royal scalp in the other.

'I mean what I say about luck,' said Bertie very quietly. 'I believe in it. I have a feeling that you are my luck, so I'm not going to let you down. I'll have a word with Helen Tarrant—I'm seeing her next Monday. I'll tell her you've saved her bacon. If those men had been charged and sentenced, Bolshies or not, she'd have been put publicly in the wrong. That's not the sort of thing you can keep quiet for ever. And what you've been up to since then has been spot right . . . I take it you aren't planning to spend the rest of your days in Hull, though?'

'Not really. I can spare another month or so. Then . . .'

'Right. Now I want you to carry on as you've been doing, but I also want you start looking for a different kind of chap, somebody who'll play for us.'

'That won't be easy.'

'When I say "Play for us" I am talking about a professional.'

'You're proposing to pay this man?'

'Quite well, so he must like money. That's a prime consideration. Reasonably intelligent, of course, and young, so that it won't look rummy if he suddenly takes it into his head to become a Bolshie. One of the lads who comes to your gym, eh? Give him time to grow into the part. I mightn't want to make use of him for several years, so by then he'll have had time to work his way up the organisation. You follow?'

'You want me to find you a spy.'

'A secret agent. It sounds less brutal, don't you think?'

'I'll see what I can do.'

'Excellent. I will continue to trust in your luck, young Tom. I have a feeling that you will go far. I shall take care to tell Helen Tarrant that you have a great future before you . . .'

'Poppycock,' said Dick.

Tom looked over his shoulder and saw him swaying, outlined against the intricate plaster nodules of the library ceiling.

'Tom won't go anywhere,' said Dick, his high spirits now

transmuted into aggression. 'He has a tiny future before him. Poor Tom. Handsome, brainy, grand old family, but . . . You know, we had a house don at Winchester who took pleasure in flogging small boys. He liked it best when they blubbed, because then he could produce his bon mot. ''You'll never be Prime Minister, boy,'' he'd say. ''Ambition should be made with tougher . . .'' '

Before he could finish Bertie had risen to his feet and tried to snatch his hat and wig back. Tom got the impression that at the same moment some kind of minor violence, a kick on the shin or a stamp on the toes, had taken place around floor-level. As if to underline the drama of the instant there came from somewhere beyond the Library door a great, cymbal-like clash, the tinkle of glass, and feminine cries of mingled excitement and alarm. Dick, with the amazed look of a drunk who has not noticed how drunk he is until he walks into a door-post, stepped back from the apparent onslaught, a movement which took the hat and wig out of Bertie's reach. Bertie reached further, grabbed and tugged. Dick resisted teasingly, but something gave and Dick was left holding only the curling ostrich plume. Bertie laughed with no geniality at all, clapped Tom on the shoulder and strolled away.

'What was that about?' said Dick.

'Bertie was at a beating house,' said Tom. 'I believe they almost killed a boy once, but that was before I got to Eton. I don't know, but I wouldn't be surprised if Bertie had a pretty bad time of it when he was a fag.'

Dick appeared not to have heard. He was studying the objects he held with rapt amazement, like a stage mime drawing attention to his props. Carefully he put his bomb on the table, opened its top and stuck the feather in it, then sat heavily into Bertie's chair and reached for one of the menu cards.

'The world is coming to an end,' he said sombrely. 'I shall now make my will, and I advise you to do the same.'

He took the plume from the bomb and made writing motions on the card, apparently absorbed. Tom rose and headed for the ballroom. A dance had just ended and a stream of couples were coming into the Library for supper, so he had to thread his way against the current.

Suddenly he felt peculiarly sour. Until Bertie had collared him for what he called a palaver, all Tom's evening had been concerned with Judy's game, and he had thoroughly enjoyed the process of working from an apparently hopeless position to one of real promise. During his occasional brief encounters with her he had sensed that she was playing the game along the same lines. She was looking marvellous, in theory dressed as a male Chicago gangster but in fact, and despite the wide Fedora, producing an effect much more like a Paris gamine. The chief obstacles in the game arose from the fact that Judy was one of the party actually staying at Rokesley, whereas Tom had been assigned to dine and come over with the notorious five-daughter Gorringes, a likeable brood of large weather-beaten girls who made no bones about hating dances but whose mother insisted on their going and therefore on partners being supplied for them. They had come in perfunctory peasant dress, which in fact suited their style much better than more elaborate costumes might have, and dancing with them had turned out to be less of a penance than Tom had imagined. They took their dances as no doubt they took their fences, with dash if nothing else. Steering one of them round the floor had something in common with driving a train—you had masses of power at your command but had as far as possible to move in straight lines and allow a lot of space for braking. He danced with all five of them and then, mysteriously, they disappeared. They were perhaps missed from the dance-floor, but not regretted.

Their Cinderella-style vanishing left Tom free, provided he avoided Lady Belford's vigilant concern to attach spare males to lonely and neglected females. His two dances with Judy were booked for late in the night. (She had made a great show of finding space on her card and crossing off some other man's name, but it had probably been mere tease.) He had been lurking, ready to see if he could detach her from her party when the next dance ended, when Bertie had insisted on the palaver. Until that moment he had experienced a growing enjoyment, a promise of exhilaration.

Now all that had gone flat. As soon as Bertie had described the 'spy' he wanted Tom to find a particular face had flashed into mind—eager, lively, slightly pocked with acne, snub nose, heavy dark brows, and eyes—eyes that seemed to belong to a quite different face, withdrawn behind a layer of apparent dullness, but occasionally glancing sideways and then seeming not dull at all—Ernie Doyle, Uncle Ned's prize welterweight. Bertie might almost have been thinking of him as he spoke.

And why not? More than ever now, since he had crossed the chasm and begun to move among the people of the dockland, Tom was convinced that the Bolshevik group in Hull existed and was a menace which should be destroyed. Its individual members might be, as Kate surely was, intelligent and serious people, but collectively they were a disease, and at their centre . . . Not once since Mr. Hutton had whispered it in the smoking-room at Brantingham had Tom heard the name Ricardo, but from certain silences, changes of conversation, reluctances to take some particular decision, particularly on Kate's part, he thought he could induce the existence of such a figure. In much the same way Wyatt was said to have discovered the Priest's Hole in the old part of Rokesley from the measurement of other rooms. And if Ricardo really existed, though so far as no more than a solider darkness amid other shadows, he must be found and fought—as Mr. Hutton had said, by Bertie's methods if no others could be had. Suppose it were possible to explain all this to Ernie Doyle, he might even of his own unbought will agree to join the fight . . .

But the image of Ernie's face brought with it other images: Mrs. Barnes—Kate's Aunt Tess—on her knees blacking her stove as if she were worshipping at her private shrine; Harry Struther—the man Tom had fought in the chapel—coming round in his Sunday best to apologise and despite being almost tongue-tied conducting the interview with dignity; Mr. Barnes hauling up from the allotments a spare sheet of corrugated iron he had found to patch a leak in the roof of his 'gym'; Kate herself striding through the grid of streets swinging a handbell—the one they used to start the strike meeting—while children streamed from the side-alleys because it was the day of the Withernsee Picnic and the bitterest strike was not enough to interfere with that (indeed the money to pay for the charabancs came from a fund controlled by 'our' churches); Kate again, sitting on a drifted tree-trunk on the reeking foreshore with ripples of light playing across her face where the muddy Humber reflected the evening sun; or shaking off one of her fits of depression with a toss of her golliwog head and burst of self-mocking laughter; or wild as a Maenad, drunk with argument . . . And less personal things: five or six men on a pavement, gathered in theory to compare the merits of two racing pigeons but so infected by the inertia of the strike that not one of them moved or spoke for what seemed like minutes on end, a motionlessness that imbued them with the unreal quality of art; a similar group of women by the window of the corner shop (its scant shelf-space already two-thirds empty) nodding their heads to the inaudible chorus—*Aye, it was hard*. And *Aye, it would be harder come next week*.

Who was Tom to feel squeamish at the prospect of buying a spy for Bertie? Had he not, at least in part, been bought himself by Bertie's promise of help in appeasing Mrs. Tarrant? Of course there was a difference, in that he would be asking Ernie Doyle to betray a world to which he genuinely belonged, whereas it was a sentimental delusion to believe that even Mr. Barnes thought of Tom as anything more than a friendly alien. But though he did not belong to that world Tom had begun to feel that in a mysterious way it had begun to belong to him. If, as Gerald had claimed, Cyril had died for an England which consisted of the few acres you could see from the windows of the Collection Room, Tom's own version of that view had stealthily enlarged so that now he was almost startled to find that it included—mistily, as if in a mirage—the crammed habitations between the Holderness Road and the brown Humber. It was as if, striding in dreams through the clean moor air, he could smell all the time the reek from the Fish Dock.

The dining-room at Rokesley, where the dancing was taking place, was always called the Hall, and had indeed been the Great Hall of the old manor-house round which Wyatt had added the vast romantic flummery of Gothico-Tudorbethan. Tom edged round the floor and climbed the twisting stair to the Minstrels' Gallery where he joined the three or four couples already leaning on the parapet watching the dancers below. One would have thought that Judy's pearl fedora would flash among the swirling motley like a signal lamp, but it wasn't there, and though there was no good reason why Judy should not be doing something other than dancing at this moment its absence added to his unease and depression. He saw Lady Belford—very grand

155

indeed though decidedly out of character as Catherine the Great
—inspecting the throng from the further door through a hand-
held eye-glass which gave her something of the air of Nelson not
seeing the signal at Copenhagen. Tom was edging towards the
cover of the central pilaster when a hard object poked into his
ribs and a voice hissed 'Just don't move, mister!'

He raised his arms and turned slowly. She held a toy pistol
and had the brim of her hat pulled so far down that he could
barely see her chin.

'Is that thing loaded?' he said.

'Only with champagne. It doesn't squirt as well as water.
Look.'

She aimed out over the parapet and shot a jet into space. It
dispersed into mist as it fell so that none of the dancers seemed to
notice.

'It's the bubbles, I think,' she said, as if announcing a
scientific hypothesis that awaited further experiment.

There was no one with her.

'How have you been getting on?' he said. 'All my Gorringes
have melted into thin air.'

'Oh, yes. That's what they do.'

'Magic?'

'No. Daisy smuggles a jigsaw in under her skirt and when
they've done their duty dances they sneak off somewhere and
put it together until they can decently go home.'

'Lucky it didn't burst while I was dancing with her. She was
pretty vigorous. I wonder where they've got to.'

'Woffles's old nursery, I should think.'

'Clever of them to find it.'

'Oh, I told Puffy where it was.'

'That was friendly of you.'

'Yes. Shall we go and see how they're getting on?'

'You wouldn't rather dance? If you're free?'

'I'm not free, so I wouldn't rather,' she said with a sly glance
over the parapet.

'We'll still have to cross the floor.'

'Don't forget Woffles is my cousin. I wasn't quite born at
Rokesley, but . . .'

She moved down the gallery and pulled aside one of those unsittable gaunt chairs one finds in such places. Behind it was what looked like a cupboard door in the panelling, but when she opened it he saw a flight of stone stairs spiralling up. Tom tapped the nearest man on the shoulder.

'Put the chair back, will you?' he said, then followed her up.

The stair emerged after less than one full turn into a quite ordinary passage smelling strongly of floor-polish and more faintly of bath-soap and the fluffy scents that linger where women have dressed for evening parties. The central strip of red carpet and the row of bedroom doors down either side were typical of an upper floor in any large country house; only the vista stretched into such distance, under a series of ogive arches, that at first Tom thought he must be seeing part of the view reflected in a large mirror. Though he had visited Rokesley several times, he had never been upstairs.

'Gosh, it's vast,' he said.

'Isn't it? Uncle Duff used to organise a special sort of bicycle race down here in wet weather, with handicaps like having to push a golf ball along the floor with a croquet mallet. Sh, now. I want to sneak up on them.'

She stopped at a door that seemed like any of the others, turned the handle and opened it very gently. Beyond her Tom saw a ring of light under which the circle of girls sat, like peasants round a fire, absorbed in their game. Behind them, just visible in the shadowy fringes of the lit space, were the up-curving rockers of a proper rocking-horse, identical with the one at Sillerby. Judy motioned him out of sight then stepped into the room.

'This is a stick-up,' she said.

The murmur of welcome mingled with shushing noises, changed by the hiss of Judy's pistol into a squeak of protest and more shushing.

'It's all right,' she said. 'There's no one around. I just wanted to make sure you'd found the way and tell you not to be too clever at the jig-saw.'

More murmurs. She came out and closed the door, but instead of turning back up the corridor led the way on.

'Do you think they'll ever grow up?' said Tom.

'Oh, they're very grown up in their own way—much more than most of us.'

'Jig-saws . . . and running away like that? Who on earth's going to marry any of them?'

She shook her head as if agreeing that that was a problem, but stopped after a few more paces and laid her gloved hand on his arm.

'Tom, if I tell you something, will you keep it an absolute secret? Not tell anyone?'

'Yes, of course. But you don't have to. I mean, if it's a secret . . .'

'No. You see you're wrong about the Gorringes and Puffy's my best friend so I want you to understand.'

'All right.'

'Well, Susan is married and Daisy's engaged.'

'But . . . I had dinner at Wiverham. There wasn't anybody . . .'

'Of course not. Susan's husband is the head groom. He's a widower, about fifty-five. She had a baby last Christmas.'

'Great Scott!' Does Sir Oswald know? And Lady Gorringe?'

'Of course they do. Uncle Ozzy absolutely dotes on the baby. Of course they weren't very keen at first, but Uncle Ozzy didn't want to lose Trenchard which he'd certainly have done if he'd kicked up a row because Susan would have run off with him, but they've got used to it now. They're quite pleased about Daisy's fiance. He's the son of one of their tenant farmers. It wouldn't work, bringing him to something like this, though.'

'But keeping it all so quiet.'

By now she had moved on and they had reached the top of a precipitous stair going down into dimness. The smells had changed—floor-polish still, but soap of a different kind, the coarse yellow bar used to scrub stone flooring. Somewhere below must lie the service areas of the house, beyond even the kitchens —sculleries, larders, bottle-rooms, laundry and such. Judy pattered down the flights, her feet apparently so familiar with them that she could talk over her shoulder as she did so.

'They're an extraordinary family,' she said.

'So it seems.'

'Oh, I don't mean that. They never seem to need to discuss anything. They know what they're all thinking, so they just agree without talking about it. Like twins. Anyway, they decided that if the county found out about Susan and Trenchard it would ruin the other four's chances, so they're going to pretend it hasn't happened until Babs is twenty-one.'

'So if a rich and dashing duke picks up Puffy he won't find he's got a stable-hand for a brother-in-law until he's signed the marriage lines.'

'Oh, tosh. Of course they'd tell him before that. But you know what I mean.'

Tom did. From childhood he had been aware that certain families were classed as 'odd'. Even now he seldom knew in all cases what the 'oddness' consisted in. But there were degrees, and these did not necessarily correlate with the apparently similar gradient from eccentricity to rabidly anti-social behaviour. Indeed the Hankeys themselves were mildly 'odd', and more because of Father than because of Gerald; quite likely Gerald's difficulties were traced back to Father's 'oddness' by the county experts in this field. The Gorringes would occupy about the same place in the spectrum as the Hankeys, as things stood; but if they were to make any kind of parade of Susan's marriage, or even let it become widely known (no doubt Judy wasn't the only outsider in the secret) then they would be moved many notches down the scale and the younger girls' selection of possible husbands (if you took 'possible' not to include head grooms and the sons of tenants), which were already fairly restricted by their behaviour, would dwindle to almost nothing.

Two floors down Judy turned left. The stairs continued into darkness, and presumably cellars, but this corridor was lit by dim and wide-spaced bulbs under white enamel shades. Its floor was stone slabs, irregularly yellow and grey and worn into hummocks and hollows by passing generations of servants. Though it seemed already to be the very back of the back regions of Rokesley it too reached on into dwindling distance, but half way along it Judy stopped and studied a large board hung with innumerable keys on wooden pegs. The nearest light was well beyond her and she stood outlined against its yellowish stingy glow, posed in her double-breasted black jacket, flared trousers and ridiculous hat. The effect was piercingly feminine, so that memory made an almost startled contrast with her boyish look in the frock she had worn in the hills above Hendaye. Tom's gloom was gone, but had left as it were an aftertaste. He was tingling with the exhilaration of her company and yet there was an edge of danger to the excitement, as though things might still go badly wrong. She had moved the game on another stage by telling him about Susan Gorringe's marriage—acknowledging that he and not anyone else was close enough to her to know—but at the same time it seemed a curious move, in that she had made it before extracting all the amusement that was still to be had in the state of the game as it had stood.

'I think that's the one,' she said, taking down a large, intricate iron key. 'Bother, there used to be a torch on the shelf here.'

'Are we going outside? There's little lamps in glass pots all across the courtyard.'

'That'll do. This door here. No, it won't be locked.'

He had been standing waiting for her to give him the key she had taken, but apparently that was for something else. He pulled the heavy door open and the night air came lazily through, an odour of summer woods and gardens laced faintly with petrol. They came out into the wide cobbled courtyard round which Rokesley was built. There was no moon, so the contorted chimneys and pinnacles of Wyatt's roofline stood very black against innumerable stars. A double line of small lamps, green, orange and violet according to the colour of the glass, marked the path from the back entrance of the main house to the archway beyond which most of the cars were parked. Judy led him across to this and picked up one of the lamps, but instead of turning along the path she slanted off towards the further side of the courtyard, which he remembered consisted mainly of old coach-houses, converted to garages, with the stables at the western end. (Generations of Belfords had treated horses at least as companionably as humans.) Judy led the way to a pair of doors higher and wider than any of the others.

'Hold the light, pal,' she said in her utterly unconvincing gangster accent. 'This is a break-in. Oh, Tom, do you know, I used to have to bring a stool to stand on and I needed both hands to turn the key! There. Mind the bottom bit.'

He followed her through the dark slot she had opened, a human-sized wicket set in the enormous doors.

'Just pull it to,' she said. 'Ah . . . doesn't it smell marvellous!'

Tom closed out the far noises of the dance and sniffed. It seemed to him a quite ordinary set of smells for such a place, cold stone and old leather and wormy timber. The only difference from the coach house at Sillerby was that there Pennycuick used it to store the mowers, so there was an extra smell of machine oil and cheesy rotting grass which was missing here. He held the lamp high, and though its minimal light penetrated only a few feet into the darkness he was aware that the space around them was larger even than a normal coach-house. At floor-level the shafts of a pony trap projected into the circle of light.

As he followed Judy down the gap between two such traps larger shapes started to loom beyond them, landaus and other old conveyances. He felt oddly disturbed. All this seemed too obvious. Though half an hour ago he had been wondering whether to explore the house for some secluded niche where they could be alone together for a while, he found he now didn't want it to happen like this, in a series of planned manoeuvres with the luck-God given no chance to add his blessing. Why, Judy must even have organised that he should be Gorringe-fodder, because she had known that they were going to do their Cinderella trick at midnight. She had actually helped them vanish. The realisation came so suddenly that he snorted.

'Yes, it's a surprise, isn't it?' said Judy.

He stared at her, then saw that she was looking not at him but at a curving arc of bright yellow with spokes running off towards a dim-seen hub, a great iron-rimmed wheel, bearing a contraption twice the size of any they had passed. The body seemed to sag beyond it, glossy brown paint picked out in red. She ran her fingers along it, lovingly, as she moved down its length. Now he could see that it was a huge old family coach. She stopped at its door, on which was the Belford rebus, the bell in the river.

'Good Lord!' said Tom, 'I never thought I'd see one of those except in the movies. I suppose they used it to go to London before the railways were built.'

'Oh, much longer than that. Uncle Duff's father had a row with one of the companies. They got an act through Parliament letting them buy a bit off one of his farms where hounds had ended a famous run, and he'd promised his father he'd never sell. Until he died he never allowed any of his family or any of the servants to travel on a railway.'

'I see. That's why it's in such good condition.'

'Yes.'

She lingered on the syllable, nudging it towards being a question.

'There's something else,' he guessed. 'Is it one of your between-places?'

'The very first,' she whispered.

(. . . *you wouldn't understand at all . . . they aren't like that . . . They're small and secret and nobody knows you're there.*) Some of Tom's unease lifted.

'Ah, I see,' he said.

She climbed onto the high step to reach the handle and deftly swung herself round the door as it opened, then turned on the step.

'What do you see, Tom?'

'Oh well . . . it's just . . . I'm afraid I thought you were pushing the game on a bit fast, and it worried me . . . arranging for me to come in the Gorringes' party and so on.'

Her eyes widened like a child's caught out in mid-deception, then she gave him a mock-sweet smile and vanished into the darkness of the coach. Her grey-gloved hand fluttered in the doorway like a moth, a gesture of farewell, a challenge to follow.

The interior reeked of mothballs. The lamp gave too little light to show how dusty it all was, but it had the feel of having been regularly looked after. The body was wide enough to take four large people a side and Judy had settled into the furthest corner, shrunk into it as if for refuge. Tom put the lamp on the floor, hiding all but her legs in the upward shadow cast by the seat. When he sat, half way along and on the same side, the whole body of the coach swayed on its ten-foot springs, and the leather of the seat crackled with age.

'It's funny,' she said in a dreamy voice. 'I was an unhappy little girl. Now she seems a quite different person. I don't often think of her as me. She used to spend a lot of time alone in the dark here, hiding.'

'Your mother told me *she* had been a pretty rum little girl.'

'Did she? Why did she tell *you*? She never talks about that sort of thing—at least I've never heard her.'

'Something started her off—a dream she'd had, and then

something I said which reminded her of it. I don't think she really wanted to tell me. It just came out.'

'What have you done to upset her, Tom? I can't ask. She'd guess at once why I wanted to know.'

He told her, taking much longer over it than he had with Bertie, trying to explain his feelings as well as the events around them. This turned out to be almost bafflingly difficult. At the time he had done what seemed to him the only possible thing, but when he came to analyse why this should have been so reason was very little help, the hindsight a positive barrier. He had been moving according to laws of emotional logic in which the categories of Aristotle or Hegel, though they might describe parallel phenomena belonging to the world of reason, could not make adequate connections. He was not at all sure how much Judy understood. She said nothing until he came to the meeting with Kate Barnes.

'Oh, was it really her? What's she like? I should love to meet her—though I suppose she'd think I was a complete fribble.'

'I don't know. She certainly thought I was a silly ass of the first water—I think she's changed her mind now—but she was very jolly about it. She laughs a lot, you know. Shall I try and fix a meeting?'

'Oh, yes, do, please. We mustn't tell Mummy. Go on.'

When he had finished she sat silent for a while, and then said something which seemed to have nothing to do with his story, though her tone showed that she thought it relevant.

'Guess who I met in Scotland?'

'No idea. Mr. Baldwin?'

'Doesn't he go to Aix or somewhere? I was staying with the Dunnerys.'

'Don't know them. Friends of my sister Nan's, I think. Oh, I know—Gerald!'

'That's right.'

'Good Lord . . . I suppose it's not as surprising as all that. He told me he was going the rounds of all those loopy Highland earls. Did he have Mrs. Heusen with him?'

'Did he not!'

'What did you make of her?'

'Terrifying. Small and quiet and hard as teak.'

163

'Gerald said . . .'

'Oh, I don't mean she's wicked or anything. Fact, one of the ways she's terrifying is being terrifyingly good. But it's her and your brother . . . You know Mummy's horrid little dogs? They're actually pretty sporting. Mummy isn't much of a one for walks, but when Mr. Binns comes—did you meet him? He's Daddy's curate—he takes them up the Wold and lets them chase rabbits. So whenever he's in the room they just sit and watch him, waiting for him to snap his fingers at them to show he's ready to go. Your brother watches Mrs. Heusen like that, all the time.'

'He's been in a pretty bad way, you know. If he's able to stay with Lord Dunnery and not get slung out in forty-eight hours, it's all because of her.'

'He's very sweet. I got him to myself one afternoon and we spent it all talking about you. He thinks you're the bee's knees, but he's worried about you, Tom.'

'About him taking over Sillerby?'

'About Mrs. Heusen taking over Sillerby. That's what's really going to happen, and he knows it. She's quite like Mummy underneath.'

The link between Gerald and the episode on Marfleet Strand suddenly became obvious.

'I rather like your mother, you know,' he said. 'She may not like me, but . . .'

'Oh, but she does! She told me. That's the real reason she was so furious. She couldn't understand how somebody she wanted to have on her side turned out to be an enemy.'

'I don't think I'm an enemy.'

'But I'm glad you like her. I do . . . especially when she's not there.'

Tom laughed and stretched.

'But she's terrifying too, isn't she?' said Judy. 'I know she can't *do* anything to me except stop giving me money and anyway I'll have some of my own when I'm twenty-five, but . . . You know, I sometimes truly think she's a sort of witch. I've got a witch-mother. She has this power over me which isn't anything to do with the ordinary world . . .'

She was absolutely serious. He could hear her voice shaking.

'Sometimes you can undo that sort of spell with a kiss,' he said.

There was a brief pause.

'All right,' she said, and before he could move flung herself along the seat and into his arms. The touch of her lips, stiff, chill and rubbery, confirmed her tension and showed no sign of relaxing. Grandfather had been notorious for his gallantries, but surely not with the help of this uniform when it came to the actual encounter.

'Something's missing,' he said, letting her ease free so that her head lay on his shoulder. 'Eye of newt, do you suppose?'

'I've told Woffles I'm never going to marry him.'

'Poor old Woffles. He can't have everything.'

'I told him I didn't see how he could expect me to marry a man who gave a stunning fancy-dress party and then came to it dressed as a carrot.'

'Did he actually propose?'

'Not exactly, but he wanted the last six dances. I tried to tell him about not really wanting to spend half the night with a prize vegetable, and we had a row, and it worked up to that.'

'How did he take it?'

'It's difficult to show your feelings when you're a carrot. He knocked over a tray of champagne glasses.'

'I heard the crash.'

Her hand roved among the braid of his chest, tracing the stiff intricacies.

'Woffles tells Aunt Ivy absolutely everything,' she whispered. 'I'm surprised they don't call each other ''Dearest''.'

'She'll tell your mother?'

'Yes.'

He felt her body soften, relaxing in the slight release of fear that comes from the mere admission that fear exists.

'I think I want to stop playing the game, Tom. It's been fun. I was planning to spin it out for months. I had my eye on a chap I was going to make you desperately jealous of this Christmas, but now . . . I'm frightened, Tom. I want to get it over.'

'Tell your mother, you mean?'

'Everything's gone so wrong. First I thought because you were going to have Sillerby she wouldn't mind so much about

Woffles and Rokesley—it's Rokesley more than Woffles, you know. She's supposed to be best friends with Aunt Ivy, and she is, but she's envious all the same . . . then Mrs. Heusen got hold of your brother and she's going to get hold of Sillerby too and I was a bit frightened, but you met Mummy and she really fell for you, and Daddy adores you anyway because you know a bit about steam engines and the Early Fathers, so I thought it might be all right even without Sillerby. Somebody's got to live at Brantingham, after all . . . Would you like to, Tom?'

'I think so.'

'It's hideous, isn't it?'

'I rather fell for the rockery. I'm going to read up about Alpines this winter.'

'Did you know that's where the soul of Brantingham is? Not in the house at all—in the rockery.'

'I'm not surprised.'

'Where's the soul of Sillerby?'

'I'm not sure. I think it used to be in the stuffed deer in the billiard room, but Father's moved it up to the Collection Room.'

'He shouldn't have done that. It doesn't work. Of course the soul of Rokesley is *here*.'

She patted the crackled leather of the seat.

'I suppose it is.'

'Oh I do love you, Tom! It's amazing, isn't it? You're so clever and I'm so stupid and we still think the same way.'

'You're not stupid, and I'm only good at my books, which is a very minor sort of cleverness.'

'Tosh. Shall I tell Mummy? I don't know what will happen, I really don't. She thinks you're an enemy.'

'I'm a neutral.'

'Mummy hates newts much worse than enemies. You should have heard her during the war . . . Oh, Tom! You were right! Eye of newt! Did you say that on purpose?'

'The first words of a lover after . . .'

This time her kiss had that startling ferocity of which she was capable and it took him some time to make her gentle. She slid her cheek along his and whispered in his ear.

'Now say something. Don't think about it, just say it.'

'I'm a different species of newt.'

'What does that mean?'

'I suppose I'm trying to fight both sides—some of Kate's friends, who want rifles and barricades in the streets, and decent landlords hanged at their own gates. And Bertie too . . .'

'You've got to be careful about Bertie. Mummy . . .'

'I know. Listen, you don't have to tell her for a bit. Bertie's going to talk to her about what happened at Marfleet Strand and try and persuade her I was right.'

'Why? I thought he . . .'

'It rather depends what I find out. I'll make up my mind then.'

'Are you really fighting Kate Barnes? You sounded—I'm not jealous, honestly, but you did sound a bit enthusiastic about her.'

'She's an extraordinary woman. I like her, personally, very much. I suppose this is always one of the problems—a lot of your allies are stupid stodges, and a lot of your enemies seem much more amusing. Anyway, I've been thinking about her quite a lot, and her uncle and aunt and some of the others, and I still don't know the answer. What Kate wants in the end sounds fine. It's the way she thinks she's got to go to get there . . . somehow she doesn't see—doesn't *feel*—what it's going to mean to the people who have to live through it. I don't mean her enemies, I mean the people she thinks she's working for . . .'

She slid her head back, let her lips brush his as they passed and then settled against his shoulder.

'What does it mean to *us*, Tom?'

His hand caressed her small hip. Above the belt-line of the trousers one layer of sliding silk intervened between his palm and her skin. He was aware of the poised instant of choice. All the tension now lay in the carapace of his uniform. He had only to take her hand, move it up and show it the little brass hooks that fastened his collar, and then her fingers would begin to undo them . . . They could stop playing the game and return to where they had been the night after Father's wire had come to Hendaye. She had already rejected Woffles, and in this place which she called its soul she was ready to reject Rokesley too. He bent and kissed her closed eyes.

'I think we should go on playing the game,' he said.

Through the stiffness of the crimson cloth he could feel a tremor shake her body.

'Not if you don't want to,' he said quickly. 'Though it's been much more fun than I expected, and . . . well, I don't know about proposing to and being accepted by a girl on the rebound from a carrot.'

'Don't tease.'

'I'm not. It was only a way of putting it. When you brought me here you were pretty upset, weren't you? The row with Woffles, and having to tell your mother. But you don't have to— not yet, anyway. I think Bertie will manage things . . .'

'Kiss me.'

In the luxuriousness of her response he regretted his choice, but it was made.

'All right,' she said. 'I've had a row with Woffles and to rub it in I shall toy with the affections of another gentleman.'

'All six dances?'

'Yes. We'll go back by the nursery and tell them I'll drive you over, so they can go home when they want, poor things . . . Oh, Tom, I wish I wasn't used to being rich! I do love you, I do. But not if it means chicken farms.'

It was only when Tom was hanging up his uniform in the boxy little bedroom at Wiverham, with the dawn chorus racketing outside among the heavy-leaved limes, that the sustained ecstasy of those final dances slid abruptly away. He stood quite still for a while, his bare legs goose-pimpling below his shirt-tails, as he came to terms with the realisation that in persuading Judy that it would be unfair to her not to continue playing her rules for a while he had been behaving decidedly less honourably than he had at the time imagined.

11

Hull, 24th August, 1926

'Evening, Mrs. Barnes.'

'Good evening, Mr. Hankey. Mr. Barnes, he's out, but if you don't mind waiting. I've a pot on, not ten minutes.'

'Will he be . . .'

'Only up the Gangway Enders.'

As always when she spoke of her husband Mrs. Barnes's tone was of fretful patience, as if anything he was involved in was certain to be an act of wilful eccentricity, such as no wife could have foreseen or prevented but whose consequences she was now fated to endure. This attitude extended far beyond his politics and his gym and his atheism (she herself was a devotee of a splinter off a chip of a schismatic element of Primitive Methodism) to his ordinary work and his smallest comings and goings. The Gangway Enders was a club for retired dockers and seamen, an admirable and harmless institution in which Mr. Barnes, though not yet retired, had typically managed to involve himself as an unpaid helper. From it he brought Mrs. Barnes good gossip, as well as the occasional perk by way of a half loaf or a shin-bone to boil for broth, but Mrs. Barnes was certainly not going to approve of his being there—or anywhere, even at home. It seemed to be one of her axioms that whatever place he was in at a given moment was ipso facto the wrong one. Kate Barnes insisted that she loved him very much.

She was a very short woman, not four foot six, but without the impression of nippy humour which invested Mr. Barnes. Her build was more that of a Shetland pony, broad and stocky, almost but not quite stunted; moreover she had that animal's unhumorous and untrusting brown eye, and its air, even on fine days, of being forced to stand under its own private and invisible downpour. 'You'll make a fine widow when I'm gone, Tess,' Mr. Barnes used to say.

Tom followed her down the exiguous hallway of Number Five, Ulundi Close, past the foot of the stair and into the kitchen. By now he had seen three kitchens in the area and had found them very varied, despite being almost identically arranged and equipped. (Front rooms, into which strangers were normally shown, seemed much the same as each other, unused, airless, cramped with heavy furniture. 'Front parlours only come alive when you've a corpse laid out in them,' Kate had told him.) The spirit of Mrs. Barnes's kitchen was of obsessive precision. Every object not merely had its place, but looked as though it knew it. Indeed Tom happened to have been present when her sister, Mrs. Trawder—with whom Tom lodged when he was in Hull— had brought her a brass candlestick as a birthday gift. Mrs. Barnes had been delighted with it, and though it was already gleaming had at once given it a celebration polish, and then spent a good half hour arranging all the other movable objects in the room—pots and crockery as well as 'ornaments'—so that the candlestick should have its only and inevitable location towards the left of the shelf above the stove. When Mr. Barnes had come home that evening he had played a game which both of them clearly enjoyed, noticing first the change of place of his pickle jar, and then following the trail of clues back, greeting each with a nod and a grunt, until he reached the candlestick, but saying nothing in the end. They managed each other very well, Tom had come to realise; though they could hardly speak without instant disagreement, what they spoke about tended to be superficial; in glance and gesture they maintained a dialogue of deep and peaceful consensus.

Now Mrs. Barnes picked up her husband's chair and placed it to the left of the table. Ritual apparently decreed that though it was all right for a visitor to sit in it, he must not do so where Mr. Barnes sat. Tom folded his cap and put it in his jacket pocket, then put the parcel on the table. Mrs. Barnes looked at it and glanced away.

'Do you know anyone round here who drinks Ty-Phoo Tea,

Mrs. Barnes?'

'One or two perhaps, Mr. Hankey.'

'It's just that Father went and bought some and Mrs. Donkin felt he was accusing her of something. He found her putting it out for the bonfire and there was a terrific row and they each gave each other notice. I had to save the day by saying I knew someone who might like it.'

This was an almost true story, arising from one of Father's spasms of economy three or four years ago, and Tom felt no shame in updating it. At their very first meeting, the morning after he had slept on the front-room sofa following the riot on Marfleet Strand, he had mercifully guessed that it would not do to offer Mrs. Barnes any payment for the night's lodging. He now paid Mrs. Trawder for his room, and that was quite acceptable, but any help to Mrs. Barnes had to be accompanied by a face-saving pretext. He had found this tricky until one day he happened to mention some facet of the servants' life at Sillerby, and then it came out that Mrs. Barnes had herself been in service —scullery maid to a doctor's family in one of the gaunt laurel-surrounded mansions beyond the Willerby Road—and that a dream-life of domestic service in some great household still haunted her. It was possible to bait the trap of charity with tidbits about housekeepers and footmen—a story of Mrs. Bird's inquisitions or Stevens's bad temper making it necessary for Tom to sneak a torn jacket away for Mrs. Barnes to mend, and be paid for mending, or to bring a pair of loathed trousers for her to pawn—or just as likely give away to a needier neighbour. Now, for instance, she unwrapped the parcel of tea but stowed only one of the packets in her store-cupboard, putting the other three on the shelf by the door. Later she would distribute them round the Close. Next she poured Tom a pint of tea from the brown enamel kettle on the stove, and added a dollop of sweetened condensed milk. The resulting mixture was bright orange; the bitterness of the stewed leaves mingled with but did not overcome the caramel taste of the milk; it made Tom's ears ring, but he had found he could swallow it if he thought of it as boot soup rather than any sort of tea.

'How are things, Mrs. Barnes?'

'Well as can be expected, Mr. Hankey.'

She spoke as though the strike were a painful but not fatal ailment afflicting a near relative.

'It's a bad business,' he said.

'That it is. Baxter's they're rationing the bread.'

'Good Lord!'

'Language, *if* you please, Mr. Hankey.'

'I'm so sorry. Of course . . . but why should they need to ration anything? I can understand people not having the money to buy food during a strike, but the idea of the food not being there for them to buy—it's ridiculous.'

'Nineteen eleven it was the same, Mr. Hankey.'

'Yes, but that was a rail strike, wasn't it? And in any case isn't it only coal the railways aren't carrying? Besides, I thought the flour mills and the bakeries were here, in Hull, and there must be plenty of lorries and so on to get the bread to the shops.'

'It's not for me to understand,' said Mrs. Barnes rather stiffly, as though refusing to question the providence of her own severe version of the Deity. 'Now they're saying there's a train of food up at Selby, waiting to be given away for free as soon as the strike's done with.'

'Who's saying?'

'It's all over.'

'I'll try and find out. You think the owners have put it up there as a kind of bait?'

'The owners! You don't want to go believing all you hear about them. Mr. Barnes, he'll tell you it's the owners own the bakeries, and that's why there's no bread in the shops—but then, he'll tell you anything. You might think he'd gone to Russia, like our Kate did.'

'Did she? She never told me.'

'Aye.'

'Do you think it made much difference to her? I can't imagine anything or anybody persuading her to be anything other than what she is.'

'You've the right of it there, Mr. Hankey. Haven't you heard speak of our Kate's Prize-giving Day?'

'No. In fact she talks very little about what she's seen and done.'

'Head full of foreign nonsense. There's five decent men, to

my knowing, have asked Kate, and she's said No to the lot of them—*and* one of them a clerk in the Insurance, so it's no use her thinking she's too good for the likes of them.'

She muttered the history of Kate's unlucky suitors as if it were something mildly shaming to the whole family, but at the end she gave Tom a quick glance, to see how he had taken the news.

'What happened at the Prize-giving?' he said.

'That. You don't want to know about that.'

'Please, Mrs. Barnes.'

She frowned at him, thin lipped. It was clear that she was eager to tell the story, but needed a formula to demonstrate her own disapproval of something in it as yet unexplained.

'It's a warning,' she said at last. 'When you come to raise bairns of your own, Mr. Hankey, you remember what it did to Kate, Mr. Barnes putting his ideas into her head. Well, you know there's a Marfleet Boys' High and a Marfleet Girls' High? They're separate, but they have their Prize-giving Day together, and at the end of it all one of the bairns is put up to say thank you to the governors. Naturally it's mostly one of the boys, but seeing Kate had won every prize they were giving, *and* the Scripture, and was going off to London on a scholarship, they chose her. Mr. Barnes bought me a new hat, too. There all the governors were, up along the platform in their frock coats, Mr. Smythe and Sir Jack Wansdale and the Reverend Tarrant and Alderman Franks and the rest of them. Mr. Barnes and me we were right close facing them, all among the paying parents because of Kate's Mam and Dad being passed away. Every time Kate's name was called out I sat there all scammy with pride in my new hat and watched her climb up to the platform and give her bob to the Mayor and take her book and her certificate. My, I thought, how dainty she's conducting herself. If only I'd known! Not that she hasn't always had good manners—you have to say that for her. And at the end, the Mayor took her along the line of the Governors to shake hands with them all, and then he brought her to the front of the platform and told us what an example she was to the rest of them and sat down to listen to her saying thank you. Oh, Mr. Hankey, if only I'd known!'

'Go on.'

'Why, she stood there, so pink and white and innocent—she

should of been a cow-girl, my poor brother-in-law used to say—and I was wishing I'd had another go at that hair of hers to make it respectable, not that . . .'

She stopped and shook her head, apparently lost in the remembered impossibilities of Kate's coiffure.

'Do go on, Mrs. Barnes.'

'She didn't do it to shame me. She swore to me after she didn't. No, it was Satan put her up to it, him and Mr. Barnes. Never mind the Scripture Prize. She takes a deep breath, throws back her head as if she was going to sing, and yells at us. Not at *us*, you understand, sitting down there among the paying parents. No, at the back of the hall, where they'd put the parents to stand whose bairns got their schooling free like our Kate did. "Comrades!" she yells . . . My, Mr. Hankey, all round me I felt the whole hall go cold, where a minute before we'd been perspiring in our places. It was July, did I tell you? Kate paid no notice. She stood there and preached at us, like a minister preaching our sins, capitalism and oppression and the time coming for the workers to rise and inherit the earth. She hadn't been to Russia *then*, had she? Why, the war was hardly over.'

'How did the Governors take all this?'

'Sat there with faces like tombstones, all in a line. Only I saw the Reverend Tarrant smiling at his fingernails, that way of his. Then Mr. Claythorpe, he was Headmaster, came hustling from behind the Governors and snatched her by the elbow to stop her. They were shouting at the back for her to go on. I had to pull Mr. Barnes down, stop him shouting as well—I was wrong to say he'd put her up to it, Mr. Hankey. It was Satan did that, only Mr. Barnes was to blame in the first place, giving her the ideas for Satan to work with, and the Lord knows what He will say to Mr. Barnes at the day of judgment.'

'What happened next? Did the Headmaster manage to shut her up?'

'He did not, Mr. Hankey. She turned to him, quite calm, and whispered a word or two. Nobody's ever got it out of her what she said, though there's been plenty have asked. His face turned white as a china plate and he went stumbling back to his chair and sat there behind the Governors with his head between his hands and all the Governors looking the other way. Kate, she said her say out as if nothing had happened, and went back to her place like she was supposed to. Alderman Franks he stood up and smoothed it all over, talking about her fresh and vigorous approach, and how even scholarship children still have a lot to learn in the great school of life.'

'And that was all?'

'I sent my new hat to the jumble, to show Mr. Barnes what I thought of him and his notions. Mr. Claythorpe, he went and drowned himself in the Holderness Drain.'

'Good . . . I mean Great Scott! How did Kate . . .'

'Off to London by then, hunting for lodgings and such. Somebody, it wasn't Mr. Barnes or me, must of written and told her. She won't speak of that, nor of the Prize-giving. I tell you, Mr. Hankey, it's a sin, is Knowing Best. It is the Sin of Pride.'

She nodded vehemently, as if saying Amen to her own opinion and at the same time bringing the subject to a close. Tom was used by now to her apparently unlikely talent for long, coherent and often dramatic accounts of past events, but mostly these had been of things which she had not witnessed, and never in any case closely concerned with herself or her family. Now she rose from her stool, peered into the kettle, adjusted the position of a simmering pot and sat down again, but was clearly still restless for something more to expunge the memory of the recalled disaster.

'I never should of told you,' she said.

'I'm very glad to know. I won't tell anybody else.'

'It's the consequences they never think on, with their heads right up in the clouds.'

'Exactly.'

She seemed not to have heard him, but sat nodding ever more gently, as though the wavelets of Kate's long-ago splash were now at last reaching her shoreline. Tom, merely interested and amused by the account of Kate's outburst, had been ambushed by the sudden introduction of the schoolmaster's tragedy. He had argued with Kate many times about the effects of action, the difference between results and consequences, endeavouring to communicate some of his own feeling about the unmappable web of lives which hung trembling along its strands, sensitive to apparently remote events, and into which she proposed to plunge the clumsy fist of revolution. But as Kate said, too great a tenderness for the web made deliberate action of any kind impossible. And yet, eventually, one had to act.

'Mrs. Barnes, do you know a man who calls himself Ricardo.'

'I do not.'

'I'd like to meet him.'

'You won't do that, ever.'

'You know about him, then?'

'Why he can't go calling himself by his own name . . .'

'It's the fashion. None of these Russians—Lenin, Trotsky and so on—were christened by those names. I think I may have seen Ricardo. Tall, very thin, shaggy black hair. A friend of Mr. Barnes.'

'That's not him. That's Walter Dyke.'

'Is he a docker?'

'Ah, no, he's a seaman. On the timber ships, last I heard.'

'That would be in and out of the Baltic?'

'Aye.'

'How do you know he's not Ricardo?'

She pouted and frowned, as if trying to imply that Ricardo could not be Mr. Dyke or anyone remotely like him. Tom wondered how much she really knew. Dyke—Dick—Richard—Ricardo. That evening on Marfleet Strand Kate had had to argue with Dyke about Tom staying for the meeting. Hadn't the name been on Inspector Whitehorn's list, too? And the Baltic trade came very close to Russia . . . At any rate, it would be unfair to go on questioning Mrs. Barnes; if she knew the answer, her loyalties must be as divided as his own, and by now he was even further from certainty as to where those lay. Only the search for Ricardo still seemed to make clear sense, as something that could actually be achieved. The question of whom to betray could wait until he knew what there was to be betrayed. The enlistment of Doyle as a spy could almost be justified in this light; Doyle could serve his apprenticeship, perhaps, as Tom's spy. And yet . . . Although the purpose of his visit this evening was that circumstances had suddenly seemed to give him a chance to talk to Doyle alone, he was far from sure still what he would say, was reluctant even to think about it.

As much for his own relief as Mrs. Barnes's he made her

earlier mention of rationing an excuse to tell her about the episode with Dora and the butcher's boy at Diggleton. She thoroughly enjoyed it, appreciating all the nuances, and responded
with a wartime scandal about a Hull butcher who had scanted
his ordinary customers so that he could be lavish towards a few
citizens who were influential in some club to which he was hoping for election. Mr. Barnes came in as she was reaching the de-
nouement and waited grinning by the door so that she could
finish before the necessary relocation of chairs took place.

'Tess, I'm surprised at thee, telling Mr. Hankey that. It's a
parable of capitalism in action, if ever there was one.'

'Exactly the same goes on in your precious Russia,' snapped
Mrs. Barnes, putting his mug precisely on the ring it had made
in the chequered oil-cloth during a hundred similar meals and
arguments. 'Isn't that right, Mr. Hankey?'

'I expect so,' said Tom. 'I suppose they'd say that it's an im-
perfection they hadn't yet managed to get out of the system.'

'And never will,' said Mrs. Barnes. 'They've only got to read
their Bibles. Man is born to sin.'

'And woman is born to be sinned against,' said Mr. Barnes.
'You won't find our Kate here tonight, Mr. Hankey.'

Out of the corner of his eye Tom saw a minute movement of
skin on Mrs. Barnes's forehead, nothing that could be called a
frown, but quite enough of a warning in the unspoken language
in which she and her husband communicated. Mrs. Barnes had
very definite ideas about tact, as about everything else. Though
there might well be what she would have called an understanding between Kate and Tom, it was improper to draw attention to
it until they chose to announce the fact.

'I wasn't actually looking for her,' said Tom. 'I wanted to talk
to you about Ernie . . .'

'None of the lads'll be going down the gym tonight,' said Mr.
Barnes.

'Yes, I know. I came in on the spur of the moment because I
got the chance of a lift into Hull. I shan't be able to come on
Thursday. I hope you don't mind. I've been asked to a party for
York races, and it sounds rather fun, but . . .'

'Acourse you must go,' said Mr. Barnes. 'Why, you can put a
couple of bob on Bold Archer for the Gimcrack. Put it on for

Mrs. Barnes here.'

'You dare,' said Mrs. Barnes, visibly shivering with the wickedness of the suggestion. 'If I'd known you were a gambling man, Mr. Hankey . . .'

'I'm not. I'll bet the odd few bob because I'm expected to, but it's the people I want to go for, not the horses.'

Again he caught one of those typical flashes of understanding between the Barneses. He did not feel that he had said or done anything to encourage Mrs. Barnes in her belief that his interest in the gym was really only camouflage for his interest in Kate, but it had been difficult to discourage the notion, seeing how much time he and Kate spent together when he was in Hull.

'The only thing that bothers me is Doyle,' he said hurriedly. 'We've got to keep his momentum up. I wondered if I might take him off for a few rounds after his tea . . .'

'He'll be at his evening class,' said Mr. Barnes. 'Ambitious young fellow, Ernie. Book-keeping.'

'Would there be time after that?'

'You'll be getting late, Mr. Hankey. I doubt Minnie'll have your room ready.'

'It's all right. I don't have to catch a train. I'm being picked up outside the Alhambra at ten o'clock. Really, I only came on the off chance, because the lift was going.'

(Almost true. Judy had insisted on his coming, because the girl she had arranged to go to the cinema with had cried off, and she didn't dare let Mrs. Tarrant know that she was prepared to go on her own. It was not Tom's sort of film, some stifling weepie she had missed in London, and once clear of Brantingham she was happy to drop the pretence rather than inflict the nonsense on him.)

'Time enough, then, if Ernie's willing,' said Mr. Barnes. 'Give us our meat, Tess, and I'll nip round and have a word with him before he's off to his class.'

In the late evening calm the side-streets had an almost rustic feeling about them, a sense of day-time lives settling to rest and nocturnal creatures not yet stirring. Passing the corner shop Tom said 'Mrs. Barnes tells me they've started rationing the bread.'

'Aye.'

'That can't be necessary.'

'Acourse not. Why, go into any of the shops in Hull West, you won't find empty shelves, will you?'

'I'll look next time I'm that way.'

'Come a time like this there's always shortages, because of money being short. Mrs. Baxter won't go buying bread she can't sell, will she? She'll cut her order down.'

'Mrs. Barnes tells me a rumour that there's a train-load of food waiting up at Selby for free distribution as soon as the strike's over.'

'Women!'

'What do you mean?'

'Why, that's stores for when they bring the army in.'

'Who told you that?'

'I can't tell you. But it came from a chap that's ways of knowing.'

'Still, I don't think it can be true. I was talking to my father about the strike a couple of days ago. Anything to do with the army in Yorkshire, he hears about it. I'm sure he'd have told me if there were plans to bring them in.'

'I tell you, he's ways of knowing.'

'How can you be sure? The trouble about people who live by theory—I take it this chap's a communist—is that they're always expecting their theories to come true. If Marxist theory suggests that the government will eventually support the owners by force, then the army *must* be coming, so the food at Selby—if it's really there—must be for them.'

'He's been right before,' said Mr. Barnes obstinately. 'And I can prove it to you, Mr. Hankey. He knew there'd be trouble on Marfleet Strand. Why, he knew there'd be a man looking for me that week . . .'

'Did he, by Jove! How . . .?'

It was too late. The question should not have been begun, the surprise not shown, any more than Mr. Barnes should have been provoked into saying what he had. They had stumbled into one of the forbidden patches of their relationship, a mysteriously poisoned area that would not support the trust and mild admiration that grew readily elsewhere. Much earlier Tom had made a few carefully vague enquiries and had immediately discovered that the man called Ricardo inhabited such a patch. It was clear that they had now come to the same place from another direction

As if turning away from some unpleasant sight they wheeled round the corner into the Holderness Road and walked on in silence. A tram banged by. Tom swore at himself for allowing the conversation to take this course. He ought not even to have asked Mrs. Barnes about Ricardo. Would she tell her husband? Quite likely. Therefore this was not going to be the right moment to sound out Ernie Doyle—he could have gone with Judy to this idiot movie she was determined to see, sat beside her, enjoying at least her gasps and sighs, instead of which he'd be sparring with Doyle ... Mr. Barnes must now be persuaded to stay for that—time the rounds perhaps—yes ... at least it would mean that the decision whether to sound Doyle out had to be postponed ... that was a relief ...

As Tom settled the problem to one side he was snatched—as suddenly as if he had tripped the trigger of a gin-trap—by that mental process which answers a question which is not being thought about. What Mr. Barnes had told him about Ricardo's sources of information was very strange, but he had almost deliberately put it out of his mind for the moment. Now a lunatic solution leaped like a pantomime devil into his mind and stood there mouthing and gesticulating at him, shaped and recognisable, before any of the arguments that might make it marginally less lunatic crawled slowly onto the stage. Ricardo. Dick. Tom had for some time had a curious feeling that he would recognise Ricardo if he were to meet him, in the way that one seems to recognise certain strangers in one's dreams. Now there was a chain of dream-logic to go with this. Ricardo knew about him, therefore Ricardo knew him, therefore he knew Ricardo. Tom forced himself to think about the possibility with his waking mind. True, Dick was one of the very few people who knew what Tom was doing in Hull; then there had been that strange, sad-seeming argument at Bertie's champagne breakfast, about his sense of a need to test himself in the manner in which his elders had been tested in the trenches. He had said the comrades at Oxford hadn't taken his pretensions to communism seriously— could this not have driven him not out of the party, but further in? Would he then have been so ready to brandish his party card in that frivolous manner? Well, perhaps—a man who did that, who went to fancy-dress parties as a comic-cuts Bolshevik, couldn't really be one, could he? It was a disguise that suited Dick's temperament far better than any aristocratic lace and ruffles . . . and the rescue at Drewton Cutting! That tale of the innkeeper's son who had told his scoutmaster! That had come through Dick.

It had seemed an unlikely fluke from the first. Tom remembered the interview in his Oxford digs, Dick's unease and reluctance to explain how they had known. But if he'd made up the story of the boy scout for Bertie, when all along he'd known by surer means . . . but why should he tell Bertie at all? Because . . . because Ricardo needed Bertie almost as much as Bertie needed Ricardo. Just as Bertie wanted a genuine Bolshevik conspiracy so that his army could have an enemy to fight, so Ricardo would actually welcome a gang of rich young loafers, hooded, armed, lined along the cutting wall and cowing the workers in hooting, arrogant voices. What better bogey-man could an agitator ask for?

Tom shook his head. The idea remained absurd. Considering what trouble he himself had had making the smallest contact with Mr. Barnes . . . Hull was no more Dick's native ground than it was his own . . . but suppose Dick had been put in contact by Party Headquarters . . . with seamen such as Ned Dyke coming and going from the Baltic ports, there was likely to be a genuine Bolshevik organisation in Hull long before . . .

No. It would not do. The logic was still dream-logic, fantasising rational connections between images that come into the sleeping mind for reasons that have nothing to do with reason itself. Tom had only to wake and look around him to see that the dream could not possibly be true. There was no way in which Dick could have altered one footfall among the stream of men who had headed to Marfleet Strand. The bricks of the houses along the Holderness Road, the ribbons of slow smoke wavering up from the countless chimneys as the evening meal was cooked, the empty shelves behind the grimy shop windows, all declared their difference from any world in which Dick had power to act. Tom felt almost ashamed at having, even with a drowsing mind, believed in the possibility.

But still he was vaguely haunted, as one sometimes is by a dream. An image continued to nag, not of Dick, but of a far more shadowy figure. It was as though there had been something in the dream that he could not remember on waking—a glimpse, perhaps, of the man he had been looking for, head turned away, but . . . known? If that head had turned in the dream, what face. . . ? Was *that* absurd? Tom remembered his persecuted notion a few weeks back that the dockers would not speak to him because they knew why he was there. Only just now Mr. Barnes had let slip that the feeling had not been madness. Tom returned to that point. Ricardo knew about Tom. Was it not therefore possible that he actually knew Tom? And in that case Tom must indeed know Ricardo.

He was actually beginning to take the notion seriously, and applying his arguments to the not quite so impossible figure of Bertie Panhard, when Mr. Barnes gripped him by the elbow and drew him to a halt. Another tram was clattering away west-wards. The evening quiet closed in behind it like a calm sea smoothing out the wake of a liner. Tom stared at Mr. Barnes, startled. Had he muttered some secret thought aloud? But Mr. Barnes had his head cocked to listen to a far noise that had been drowned by the passing of the tram. A bell, two bells, in panicky, arhythmic bursts of ringing. Mr. Barnes stepped into the road and pointed. Tom followed. It had been a fine day, though hazed all afternoon with thin high cloud which now shone un-spectacularly with the diluted glow of sunset. Low above the roof-tops a nearer and darker cloud was rising, surging in the stillness with its own inward winds.

'Fire,' said Mr. Barnes.

'A big one, or is it a ship?'

'Timber docks. Best get along down. There'll be trouble.'

'What about Ernie?'

'He'll be coming.'

As they passed the next side-street Tom saw a man hurry from a house, jerking himself into his jacket as he did so and calling out to a neighbour. Further down three men emerged from one of the alleys between the back-to-backs. Ahead, a couple of boys wheeled into the main road at a scamper and raced away.

'What sort of trouble?' said Tom.

'Lads are very bitter. I'd like you there, Mr. Hankey.'

'Are you saying that somebody might have started the fire?'

'That's what the papers will tell us, whether or no.'

'Wouldn't it be better if everyone kept away?'

'If pigs could fly it would! There's Ernie now.'

Doyle, waiting as arranged on the corner of his own side-street, answered Mr. Barnes's wave and pointed towards the smoke-cloud. Mr. Barnes made a wiping-out gesture, clearly cancelling the training-session. Doyle waved agreement, turned and ran to catch up two of his friends, clapping them on the back when he reached them and saying something which had the effect of setting all three into a trot. Even the pace of the older men had a fidgetiness about it, as though they too were on the edge of running. Behind them, far down the road, came the clang of a bell. Tom looked over his shoulder and saw that a whole stream of men was moving down either pavement. Between them he could see the glint of the fire engine, and now hear the boom of the big engine nearing and nearing, punctuated by the shrilling of the bell. Another wave of sound came with it, a long rolling hoot of booing and catcalling from the men on the pavements, mixed with jeering whistles. The engine flashed between the walkers with its crew clinging to it, their helmets and equipment glittering like the accoutrements of a cavalry squadron, and was saluted as it went by with gestures of anger or derision. A second engine, following a hundred yards behind, had to run exactly the same gauntlet, and this time Tom saw a couple of missiles flying towards it from among the men. He turned to Mr. Barnes, who had not looked round.

'They're throwing things!' he said.

'I told you the lads were bitter. They must take it out on some-one.'

The crowd jostled to cross the narrow sidewalks of Drypool Bridge and turned south down High Street, a narrow cobbled way that ran first between respectable old brick offices and then became a canyon of brick warehouses. To their right, down another road, more fire engines clamoured towards the blaze. The men made no move to stop them, though several alleys joined the two streets. Instead they seemed to be drawn trance-like, as if by some outside will, to the event, not knowing what they were going to attempt or achieve by their presence but simply needing to be there. At the end of the canyon the smoke-cloud swirled. Tom could hear the fire now, a breathy roaring interspersed with crackles and louder explosions. Flakes like black snow, but edged at times with crinkling rims of ember, eddied down. The air stank of burning.

The street turned right and widened. In the corner of ground between the tributary River Hull and the dock that served the main Humber Ferry was a large timber-yard, which turned out to be the seat of the fire—or rather fires, for two separate columns of smoke, shot through with sparks, were roaring up among the arched shed roofs to join and compose the main cloud. It had seemed a windless evening, but here there were sudden gusts and roasting down-draughts created by the upward rush of the fires. A swirl of smoke brought by one of these was clearing from the area in front of the dock gates just as Tom and Mr. Barnes arrived on the scene. Having been already out on the road, on their way to meet Doyle, when they heard the alarms they were among earlier arrivals, but already a crowd three or four deep stretched from the dock wall right across the road. The newcomers, still drawn as if by a mass biological urge such as that empties an ants' nest for the flight of the queens, pressed forward to join them. Tom found himself being carried on by the current just as another fire engine swept past the front of the crowd. Boos and cat-calls rose. The crowd surged. He could see beyond them the dark outlines of the helmets of the line of policemen who were holding them back from the gateway. As the engine lurched between the gateposts the struggle relaxed, and in the general easing Tom came to his own senses. Seeing Mr. Barnes a pace or so ahead of him, he reached out and gripped him by the shoulder. The wrinkled old face turned. The eyes, usually bird-bright, seemed dazed.

'We shan't do any good here,' called Tom and gestured with his free hand away from the gates, then loosed his hold and nudged his way to his right. They had reached the line at the area of maximum density, the natural focus to which newcomers would press forward, so in a few yards the scrum thinned and Tom was able to wait for Mr. Barnes to catch up.

'Getting out, Mr. Hankey?'

'Find a better place—look—where those boys are.'

The space in front of the docks was twice as wide as a normal road, lined on its northern side with the usual jumble of offices and storage places built to serve the minor appetites of the river. Opposite the timber-yard gates was a small warehouse with barred ground-floor windows. Some boys had already climbed onto one sill and were perched clinging to the bars. Without waiting for Mr. Barnes's agreement Tom shoved his way across the current of men to a vacant window. For the moment nobody else seemed concerned with anything but to get as close as possible to the gates, or at least to the line of police who kept the entrance clear for the fire engines. They had not come to see but to take part. Even in Mr. Barnes's expression there was something that suggested that he had acted contrary to his nature in following Tom away from that magnetic centre.

'I'll give you a leg up,' said Tom.

The little man was heavier than he'd have guessed, the slight body muscled by a life of heaving loads from awkward corners. As soon as Mr. Barnes was on his perch Tom pulled himself up beside him. The four feet of extra height made an extraordinary difference, not so much in what there was to see but in the manner in which one saw it. The dockers were massed to Tom's left, restrained by a line of police with linked arms. Beyond the cleared space stood a much smaller and less homogeneous crowd of sightseers, with only a constable or two to control them. Over them all hung the broadening cloud, so dense and low as to turn the evening almost to nightfall. The ten-foot wall of the yard and the sheds and timber-stacks beyond it still hid the seat of the fires, though from time to time great flames would leap among the roofs and mingle with the black uprush. Around the two furnace-centres, elegant and apparently unhurried, curved the white water-jets from the fire hoses. But the roar of the fire and the steadier drumming of the pumps imposed the forward-driving rhythm of drama, like the long drum-roll at the climax of a circus act, declaring that at any moment some huge new event must burst into being.

The crowd at Tom's feet also seemed imbued with a sense of coming crisis. They were still gathering, still pressing forward,

with very few of the random swirls of men jostling for a better
viewpoint, but almost all in one blind but coherent mass, probing for a weakness where the restraining line of police might give
way. From his vantage-place Tom could see that the mass will
was not directing them with human intelligence. By arriving
almost all down High Street the men had allowed themselves to
be penned between the timber-yard wall and the warehouses,
leaving the other end of the street clear for the approach of the
fire engines. More police were even now gathering from that
direction, but a bell clamoured beyond them and they scattered
to let through not the expected fire engine but a couple of
ambulances. The crowd watched in sudden silence as these
swung through the gate, lurching to a seemingly impossible tilt
on their soft springs. Perhaps the police relaxed a little in the lull,
for as the ambulances vanished there was a surge from the crowd
that pushed the line almost to the gatepost of the yard. The
approaching policemen broke into a run and hurled themselves
against the wall of men. Two or three truncheons were out. Fists
struck back. Helmets rolled on the cobbles. By the gates the line
inched back, but at the same time it surged forward at Tom's
end until a wedge of men had forced their way along the pavement to his right. More police ran to this point. The pressures
stabilised in new positions.

It had been a near thing. Suppose forty or fifty men had
detached themselves from the back of the crowd, run back up
High Street, through one of the side alleys and down the road
taken by the fire engines. A quick charge out of the dusk, a
wavering of purpose by the police, a push from this side, and the
line would give. The men would be at the gates, pressing on
through to where the fires were raging ... Suddenly in his
mind's eye Tom saw a shadowy figure, lurking in a doorway,
seeing what he had seen, deciding in this very move. He tried to
put a face on the man but couldn't make it form. He turned to
Mr. Barnes.

'Is anyone telling the men what to do?'

Mr. Barnes shook his head.

'How did they come so quickly, then? Were they waiting for it
to happen?'

'Fire after fire in the timber-yards, nineteen eleven,' said Mr.

Barnes, almost yelling to be heard above a sudden clatter of explosions from beyond the wall. 'They know what's what, even
them that was bairns at the time.'

He turned, craning to be part of the crowd, and visibly
flinched when one of the down-draughts sent a fresh pother of
smoke sweeping across the men by the gates. Tom was aware of
the real gulf between the two of them. He also was more than a
mere spectator, but was unable to feel part of the mass below.
Instead he found himself shocked and distressed, not so much by
the outward manifestations of violence—the stoning of the fire
engines and the struggle against the forces of order—but by the
irrational mass will. Even this, he realised, was not something
wholly new to him. The whooping gangs of Oxford bully-boys
who had gathered to break up the rooms of their enemies the aesthetes—half-a-dozen purple-nosed squires growling fantasies of
feudalistic revenge against Lloyd George over Father's port—
both could be said in their small way to be animated by something of the same instincts as the men below. It was the sheer
mass of the collective will that shocked. It had the energy of
ocean, of storm-waves pounding a sea-front, while even at their
ugliest the violences of Tom's own class were little more than the
rufflings of inland waters.

How could anyone harness such a tide? At first Tom searched
the crowd for some eddy or movement that might indicate a presence there, a man who was not subject to the tide but was using
and directing it to his own ends. It was hopeless. The men's
heads, facing away from him and almost all covered with their
dark cloth caps, might have been a mass of rounded pebbles on a
beach. If the man Tom was looking for was among them he
would adopt that camouflage, lurking among the others like a
pebble-coloured crab, and careful to keep the stillness of a
pebble. But gradually, as the phenomenon of the tidal will
impressed itself more and more, Tom came to realise that nobody could hope to direct such a force. It would do what it would
do. Nobody could play Napoleon with it, using it as his army.
Even the cleverest revolutionary could achieve no more than
minor nudgings and coaxings, working towards an alteration in
the way the men thought and felt. If you wished to fight such a
revolutionary you had to do it in the end by the same means—

not, as it were, with restraining lines of police, let alone Bertie's private army, but with nudgings and coaxings in the opposite direction.

This fire, for instance. What mattered was not the burning of the timber, the success or failure of the fire-crews, but the presence of the strikers outside the gates. They had to be here, as Mr. Barnes had said. Their presence was symbolic but necessary. Whatever happened in the next half hour would become part of the way they thought and felt, and hence affect their future movements. In this light even the stoning of the fire engines could be understood, in a way. And therefore the important thing was to provide not a counterforce but opposing symbols, some event or action in which they took part and which moved their perceptions away from the direction Ricardo was working for.

This was of course sound Marxist theory, but Tom had arrived at the conclusion not through his recent reading but by what he felt as an intuitive relationship with the crowd beneath him. He was beginning to try and harness reason to his intuition, to work out what actual events might help the counter-movement he had imagined, when suddenly the long-threatened climax of the evening seemed to rush closer.

For twenty minutes there had seemed to be no real change. The hoses danced their slow rhythm, but the smoke grew neither more nor less. Then, without any warning, one whole roof which had seemed from where Tom stood to be clear of the fires collapsed with a tearing crash. Large objects, half aflame, cartwheeled skywards. All the jets wavered, some failed and when they renewed themselves they seemed fewer. The fire itself gasped, rumbled and continued with a louder roaring. The crowd's response was a cheer, long and mocking, which died only slowly away and then hushed completely as a bell clanged beyond the wall and an ambulance nosed out of the gates and accelerated away. At least they did not cheer or jeer that.

Tom had turned back to watch the fire when Mr. Barnes tapped at his shoulder and pointed along the road. He looked and saw nothing more interesting that a fresh reinforcement of police, including half a dozen on horseback. That was reassuring. He was about to make some kind of neutral comment to Mr.

Barnes when he realised that there was an unfamiliar expression on the pleasant old face, one of unmistakable hatred. Tom had never heard Mr. Barnes swear, but his present mutterings were clearly at least substitutes for foul language, broken off only to shout the name of one of the men below. A head turned. Mr. Barnes pointed. The man craned, raised a thumb in acknowledgment and nudged his neighbour. Awareness spread from that centre, a visible change in the nap of the crowd as heads turned and pressures shifted. It was possible to see the same change beginning and spreading from other points further off, until the whole crowd was looking not at the fire but at the approaching horsemen. Even the sound made by the strikers changed from inchoate mass noises to individual shouts and jeers arising from a general watchful silence.

'Now there'll be trouble,' said Mr. Barnes. 'Didn't I tell you?'

There was no hint of any irony, no apparent acknowledgment that what they had already seen would in most people's eyes count as trouble enough.

The leading horseman bent from his saddle to consult two senior policemen who had been directing operations from the middle of the road. One pointed almost at Tom as he answered. The horseman straightened and gestured to two of the others, who walked their horses forward until they reached the wedge of men who had pushed through along the warehouse wall.

'Move back there,' they called. 'Move back.'

Evidently their intention was to straighten and thus shorten the line across the street, but what they were asking was impossible. The men who composed the wedge were jammed between the warehouse wall and the line of police and held there by the crowd behind them, who were well out of range of any pressure the horsemen could exert. For all that the two men continued for a while riding their horses up and down the line and shouting their single monotonous command, like clockwork toys which having been wound up mindlessly perform one series of actions until their springs run down. The crowd, realising their impotence, began to jeer. The mounted men signalled to the restraining police to stand aside and breasted their horses into the crowd near the apex of the wedge, pushing the line back a few feet but effectively lengthening the wedge along the wall. The crowd yelled and hooted. One horseman drew and raised his riot stick, but at this point the leader of the mounted police rode over, studied the position for a moment and called the other two back. The men jeered and cat-called as the line resumed its shape.

Now the six horsemen formed up side by side, again at the base of the wedge but facing more towards the warehouse. They drew their sticks and laid them across their saddle-bows. Reined hard back but urged forward by their riders' heels the horses came in like tanks, slow and massive, with jerky tittupping steps. The policemen holding the line moved aside. Clearly the idea was to sever the wedge from its base, contain it while the men behind were forced to give ground, and then push the men who composed it back into the space thus gained. Two riders had their sticks half-raised, though the strikers before them were now doing their best to move out of their way. A howl of protest rose as the first stick beat down, though as far as Tom could see it had been the equivalent of a shot aimed into the air, a blow intended to do no worse than glance off a shoulder. The men directly in front of the horses were now struggling frantically to get clear, but at first were unable to do so as the horsemen had failed to make their intentions clear to the police at the apex of the wedge, who strained ever more fiercely to give not one inch to the increasing pressure. Tom glimpsed one of the senior officers hurrying across to take charge, but then, almost at his own feet, a man went down before the horses and wallowed, screaming with fright, among the hooves.

Tom yelled at him to lie still but his voice was lost in the clamour. The man continued to thresh. Tom was flexing to slither down and try and drag him out when the crowd to his left suddenly gave way, those at the back even starting to run off along the street. Two of the horsemen moved into the gap while the others backed their horses clear. The man on the ground got to his feet and stood shaking his head and swearing. Without any pressure from the police the thirty or forty men who had composed the wedge retreated along the pavement.

The skirmish was over. Indeed this episode on the flank seemed to be recognised by both sides as a turning point. Right across the road the line began to give. The policemen unlinked their arms, turned and started to make the kind of signal with which they would have controlled some peaceable gathering. Group by group the men at the back of the crowd broke off and walked away, frustration and despair speaking from every back.

Mysteriously Tom found he now shared some of their mood. Not that he had wanted the confrontation to become more violent, but still there was a sense that an expected climactic event was missing. The drums had rolled but the performance had not taken place. It ought to have been a relief, but it wasn't. He had no doubt that the retreating men felt the same, though much more personally and deeply.

He was gazing after them when a hard object rapped against his shin and he turned to see that one of the mounted policemen had ridden alongside the window and nudged him with his stick.

'Off there,' said the man. 'Move along now.'

For a moment Tom stared, astonished. He had felt so unable to join the men's participation in the events of the last half hour that it took him a blink of time to accept that others might not recognise the distinction. The policeman gave the slight frown of awareness of something not quite in order, but automatically hefted his stick for a firmer nudge.

'Hold it,' said Tom. 'I'm going. Give us a bit of room.'

This time he was aware of the man's reaction to the unexpected accent, but had no wish to try and pull social rank and be allowed to stay. He let the horse sidle clear and jumped to the pavement, then turned to help Mr. Barnes down. They moved off together, almost the last driblet of the retreating tide.

'Well,' said Mr. Barnes. 'What do you think of that, Mr. Hankey? What do you think of that?'

'It could have become very nasty.'

'Could have! Could have! Riding the lads down! Hitting at us with their sticks!'

'I got the impression they weren't hitting to hurt. That chap who fell got up all right, as far as I could see.'

'They'd no call to bring in the horses. No call at all.'

'I'm afraid I don't agree with you. I mean the foot police might have held the line, but the people in charge couldn't be sure. On the whole I thought they managed things pretty well.'

Mr. Barnes merely grunted in disgust.

'Why,' said Tom. 'Can't you just imagine what it would have been like if the men had got through the gates? They damn nearly did at one moment. Suppose your friends had been milling around inside there when that shed collapsed . . .'

Again Mr. Barnes merely grunted disagreement. Somehow the sound, refusing as it did the rationalities of human discourse, expressed a deeper and blinder intransigence than any words could have done. Exasperated beyond bearing Tom stopped, took Mr. Barnes by the shoulder and literally shook him.

'I can't understand you!' he cried. 'You're an intelligent man, but when it comes to seeing anyone else's point of view you simply close your mind. You make all the allowances in the world for your own side and you expect everyone else to do the same, even when it comes to throwing stones at firemen who are only doing their job. Can't you see, the policemen back there were in the right this time! In the right, I tell you! It was nothing like what happened at Marfleet Strand!'

Mr. Barnes looked up into his face with a calm and stony gaze, then turned his head with slow emphasis to stare at Tom's hand on his shoulder. Tom let go. Mr. Barnes brushed the place several times with his other hand, turned and walked on in silence up the street. Obstinately Tom fell in beside him, determined not to make the breach unmendable, but at the same time no longer to compromise with his true feelings.

'I'm sorry,' he said. 'I shouldn't have shouted at you like that. It's just . . . I wish you could see how it looks from the outside, Mr. Barnes.'

'Aye, that's it, Mr. Hankey. From the outside. You intend well, I've never a doubt. You go off to York races with your friends. Best forget about us.'

'No question of that.'

Mr. Barnes did not reply. The brief halt had dropped them still further behind the retreat, finally separating them from the feeling of belonging to the crowd as a definable entity. Indeed there were now a few small groups of men going in the other direction, presumably returning to watch the fire as sightseers for want of anything more amusing. Others, ahead, broke from the line of march and filtered away down the alleys that linked High Street with the road used by the fire engines. Even at a distance the attitude, pace and gestures of every man expressed frustration and defeat. Tom returned to his thoughts about Ricardo. His recent reading of Bolshevik tracts and pamphlets told him that this was exactly the state of affairs for which the revolutionaries aimed. The longer the equilibrium of the strike could be maintained, the worse the sepsis would become. In a sense the weird mass will which had gathered the men to the fire had been wise. It had known that they needed an event, a happening, not necessarily connected with their grievances, but somehow symbolic of them, sudden and dramatic, that would change the way they saw themselves and the world around them. What in fact had occurred was the worst possible result, or from Ricardo's point of view the best—an event promised and then withdrawn. Tom had no idea what that event might have been, or what could now take its place, but again the thought came to him that it might be possible to replace it with an alternative which would provide the strikers with what they wanted but at the same time symbolise something quite other than Ricardo and his kind would wish.

His thoughts were broken as they passed the first of the side-alleys by a hesitation in Mr. Barnes's stride, which drew his attention to a mysterious racket from the further end of the alley. It was mostly human voices, with occasional bangs and thuds. Add a few barks and horn-calls and it might have been the sound of a hunt at the kill. Mr. Barnes looked at him for the first time since the argument.

'Better take a look, Mr. Hankey,' he said, speaking with great formality. 'We don't want any arrests if we can help it.'

The alley itself was narrow, dark and featureless, but the scene at the end of it was sharp in the fading light. One man stood in a melodramatic pose of exhortation, arm raised, head and neck straining into a yell, as if contorted by a cartoonist to embody the anarchy of violence. Half screened by the wall other men heaved at some object out of sight. A silver missile flashed through the air, burst on the pavement with a splintering of glass and rolled out of view. Men whooped. A woman screamed. Tom broke into a run.

He had at the rational level no idea what he would find as he hurled round the corner, yet it was as if his body knew and was ready. The Lagonda stood slewed across the road, surrounded by a dozen men. One door lay on the cobbles. The near head-lamp was gone. Two of the men were wrenching at the other lamp. Tom let his rush slam him into the flank of the nearer man, knocking him and his companion sprawling. The driver's door hung open and a man was leaning through it, egged on by another. Tom charged down the flank of the car, stiff-armed the second man away as he turned, gripped the first by his collar and hoicked him violently out, not troubling to look and see how he fell. But even in the impetus of fury and fright he had realised that the man had merely been trying to wrench the gear-lever out. Judy was not in the car after all.

He turned, gasping, his back to the Lagonda, and saw her at once, cowering into the doorway of a shop, her knuckles to her mouth. His move towards her was blocked by the men who gathered to confront him.

'Why, 'tis the Honourable Hankeigh-Pankeigh,' said one.

'Bugger off, mate,' said another. 'We're not doing you any harm.'

'No,' said Tom.

The men growled and began to edge forward. Tom braced himself. If they closed in, he would try to break through to the right and go and look after Judy as best he could, leaving the car as a sacrifice; but he refused simply to slink away without any attempt to resist.

'Bugger off while you've the chance, mate,' said the man again.

Tom brought his hands up and balanced forward onto the balls of his feet. The men hesitated.

'Let me through, Mr. Hankey,' said Mr. Barnes from inside the car.

Tom edged to one side. Mr. Barnes climbed placidly out and stood on the running board.

'Let's have no fighting, lads,' he said. 'Let's have no arrests. We don't want them putting things in the papers against us. I'm surprised at you, smashing up motors. Our fight's with the owners, not the public.'

''Tis a Brantingham car, Ned.'

'Eh?'

194

'That Miss Julyan driving it. Ran down Frankie here. Show him thy leg, Frankie.'

A fattish young man, cringeing with shyness, was pushed forward to display a torn trouser and scraped calf, obviously sore but not serious. Mr. Barnes hesitated.

'No one along of her?' he asked.

'No.'

Tom looked over the men's heads. Judy had vanished. The crisis too was clearly over. The men, even if left to do so, would no longer have any relish in the destruction of the Lagonda. He felt an almost academic interest in Mr. Barnes's difficulty—if a fire engine is fair game, why should not a Brantingham car be? Moreover it had run down one of the strikers.

'I expect they came charging out of the alley and she couldn't stop,' he muttered.

Mr. Barnes nodded and faced the men.

'Still and all . . .' he began.

'Now then,' interrupted a voice of unmistakable type. 'What's up here, then?'

The men drew back. Several turned away, trying to compose themselves into convincing groups of bystanders who had had no connection with the destruction of the Lagonda. Three policemen moved stolidly up, but before they halted Judy darted from behind them, ran to Tom's side and buried her face in his jacket, gasping against sobs. Tom put his arm round her shoulders and turned to the policemen.

'There's been a bit of an accident,' he said. 'I think Miss Tarrant here must have been driving down the road when these men came rushing out of that alley. She hadn't time to stop and she knocked one of them down, but I don't think he's badly hurt. Are you, Frankie?'

Frankie's companions spoke for him in grunts and murmurs, confirming that his wound was negligible. The policemen studied the car, unamazed.

'She must have hit something when she skidded,' said Tom. 'That would account for the rest of the damage.'

'It's not what the lady told us, sir.'

'I don't think Miss Tarrant will want to press charges. Will you, Judy?'

She raised her head, amazed. He frowned warning. She pulled herself together and stood clear of him.

'Oh no,' she said brightly. 'Of course not. I was probably a bit hysterical after the accident. I expect I meant I was afraid they were so angry they *might* smash my car up, don't you see?'

The policemen looked at one another, looked again at the Lagonda and sighed a corporate official sigh.

'All right, then,' said one of them. 'Move along there now. Anyone hangs about we'll pull in for obstructing the highway.'

The strikers, mostly looking a little dazed after waking from the trance of violence, nodded and began to move away. One or two made tentative gestures at touching their caps to Judy, but despite that the old sullenness of frustration invested them all once more. The policemen stood back and watched as Judy climbed into the car, started the engine and backed along the far pavement. The catch of her door would not hold and the door swung to and fro as she manoeuvred. Tom picked up the loose door. Judy came across the road with a friendly smile.

'Thank you very much,' she said. 'I don't think it's as bad as it looks. It should get us home, provided no one stops me for driving with only one light.'

'Very good, miss,' said one of the policemen.

The three of them strolled off, also in Tom's eyes imbued with an air of expectation denied. Above them the smoke-cloud brooded, beginning to lose its distinction against the general darkening of the sky. Judy switched her smile to Mr. Barnes.

'Thank you so much,' she said. 'You were marvellous. Are you a friend of Tom's?'

'This is Mr. Barnes,' said Tom. 'Miss Tarrant.'

Judy held her hand out. Mr. Barnes took it only slowly.

'I hadn't known you were friends with Mr. Hankey,' he said.

'Oh yes,' said Judy. 'He's staying with us and coming to York Races.'

Mr. Barnes nodded, accepting the fact.

'Very well,' he said. 'Then I'll be saying goodbye to you, Mr. Hankey.'

He shook Tom's hand with deliberate formality, raised his cap to Judy and walked briskly away. Tom watched him go.

'Have I said something wrong?' whispered Judy.

Tom picked up his cap and dusted it against his knee.

'You couldn't have known,' he said.

'Oh dear.'

'I think he was through with me in any case.'

'Oh, I *am* sorry.'

He took her hands. She looked anxiously into his face.

'You're a remarkable little thing,' he said. 'You must have been absolutely scared out of your wits, and you still find time to worry about me and Mr. Barnes.'

'I'm all right. I wasn't, when I was just crouching there, watching them murder the Lagonda, but as soon as you came I seemed to get my wits back enough to go and find those policemen. Oh, Tom, when I saw you come dashing round the corner and start fighting all those men!'

'I thought you were still in the car.'

'Of course you did. But it is nice to see one's very own hero being heroic in front of one's eyes. Mostly they go and do it somewhere else, you know, and the girl only hears about it when it's all over.'

'Don't tease.'

'I must, or I'll burst into tears again. Oh, I wish there weren't so many people around. I need kissing like anything.'

'So do I.'

They found a place in one of the lanes that led up into the wolds before the Brantingham turn. Night had come heavy and slow, as though infected by the smoke cloud that hung and drifted above the glimmering lights of the estuary. Tom's arm ached with leaning beyond Judy to hold her door shut as she drove. He could feel that she was still far more shocked than she pretended; sudden uncontrollable tremors would ripple along her side where she pressed against him. She needed simply holding and comforting far more than she needed kissing.

'I was just driving along,' she said. 'I wasn't going fast, really I wasn't, but I *was* watching the fire, I suppose, what I could see of it. They shot out into the road from nowhere. I could have missed them if I hadn't skidded when I braked—I must have banged that boy with my back mudguard. Honestly I did the best I could. Of course I stopped and got out to see if he was all right, and he was. He picked himself up and I was telling him I was sorry. I was going to give him some money for new trousers, and then one of them said my name and it all changed. That was what was so awful. Tom, I didn't know they could *be* like that. Mummy keeps saying so, but I thought she was making it up.'

He sighed.

'Yes,' he said. 'But she could be like that too.'

'Oh, I know *that*. Only . . .'

'So could you and I and everybody we know, if we were pushed. We're lucky—privileged. I'm beginning to think that's what privilege really consists of. Not money or estates or servants—they're only mechanisms. The real thing is arranging our lives so that we don't get pushed.'

She answered with a questioning murmur, not so much disagreeing with what he had said as with the propriety of talking about that sort of subject at all.

'What were you doing down there in the first place?' he said. 'Wasn't the movie any good?'

'Oh!'

'What's the matter?'

'It was too awful. They stopped the projector and flashed it on the screen. I really didn't want to go on watching a silly old movie after that. I came out and just started to drive around until I saw the smoke. I was driving down to look.'

Tom frowned. His mind had slipped gears for a moment while she was talking. Out of nowhere, prompted perhaps by his talk of how far people could be pushed, a ridiculous notion had bubbled up, a far-fetched but possible answer to the problem of what event or change might release the tensions on which Ricardo and his colleagues relied. Instantly the idea began to ramify into violent growth, so that it was an effort to make sense of what Judy had been saying.

'Flashed what on the screen, darling? The fire?'

'No, no, of course not. How extraordinary to think we should be sitting here and I know and you don't. Not that I really thought he was marvellous—only the shop-girl side of me, I suppose, but even so . . .'

'What *are* you talking about?'

'Valentino's dead.'

12

Hull, 30th August, 1926

Each house in the wide road stood in its own grounds; each tried
to assert an individual personality by a flourish of architectural
quirks—a porch with crenellations, another scaled down from a
basilica, a corner-turret with a stunted spire—but somehow
these superficial differences only emphasised a complete inward
conformity. The houses had been built some fifty years ago to be
sold to respectable merchants and lawyers, the florid and frock-
coated money-makers who had then ruled Hull and had voted
solidly Liberal, construing the word to mean nothing wider than
freedom from interference in the process of money-making. In
accordance with their principles this road had been built, but a
public library had not; in accordance with their principles each
of them reared his children in a space that would contain three
whole closes of back-to-backs down behind the docks. Their in-
heritors lived here still, and though they no longer preached their
principles with the same outspoken fervour, the houses themselves seemed to imply that their thoughts still moved through
much the same channels. It struck Tom that this might be the
self-same road in which Mrs. Barnes had once been in service. It
seemed a truly extraordinary place for Kate to arrange a meeting.

'Summerlea' was typical, a weighty block of greyish brick,
corners and window-surrounds dressed with yellow stone, the
ground floor hidden from the road by a barrier of mottled aucuba.
Beyond the gate Tom found a gravel drive that curved round a
half-moon of lawn bedded out with grubby geraniums. The
house lacked the fantasy element of most of its neighbours, but

there was something about its stillness and slight decay that breathed a different kind of romance. The windows of the half-basement were grimy behind their bars. A rain-water pipe had cracked and streaked its paint with rust. The edges of the lawn had not been sheared and the grass was tangling into the gravel. These defects were nothing compared to the inadequacies in the upkeep of Sillerby (now at last being seriously catalogued and costed for Minnie Heusen to inspect) but seemed almost attractively eccentric in a road so dedicated to prosperity and conformity.

Kate answered the door herself, curtseying as she did so.

'I could have put on a lace cap and apron for you,' she said. 'I suppose you're used to a flunkey in knee-breeches.'

'Only one flunkey? I require a minimum of three before I will enter a doorway. One to take my hat. One to take my gloves. One to watch them do it.'

'My!'

Despite the banter she seemed to be in a brisk mood, not quite hustling him in before she closed the door. The hallway was clean, furnished with heavy old mahogany, but oddly bare of personal effects. He hung his hat on a completely empty hat-stand and put his gloves on a side-table which carried a small dinner-gong and nothing else.

'This way,' said Kate in bright unconspiratorial tones.

He followed her along the hall and into a square, large room with a handsome ceiling, elaborately moulded. Not one item of its cluttered furniture and ornaments seemed to have been bought since before the war, but at the same time nothing had that look of age which comes from regular use. The seats of chairs and sofas were straining bulges of upholstery, unmitigated by much sitting; the rugs seemed never to have experienced shoe-leather, nor the piano-keys the touch of fingers. All the room felt dead, except for two small areas of either end of the larger sofa, where two brass Benares tray-tables were laid for tea —scones, cakes and biscuits on one and on the other cups, a silver tea-pot and a silver tripod kettle, humming placidly over its mauve-flaming spirit-lamp. The large windows, though they faced out over a garden screened all round by evergreens, had the further privacy of lace curtains.

'Just like one of our front parlours, really,' said Kate. 'Except for being at the back.'

'Mrs. Barnes would like it.'

'Love it—no end to the different ways she could push the ornaments around.'

'How is she?'

'Bearing up. You've broken Uncle Ned's heart, though.'

She spoke the words without any variation from the tone she had used so far—in her socially neutral accent, but cheerful, almost excitedly pleased with the visit. It took Tom a moment to grasp their meaning.

'I'm very sorry about that,' he said.

'You sit at that end, by the cakes. It's very good of you to come at such short notice. I hope it wasn't a nuisance.'

'Not really. I wanted to talk to you in any case. You sounded a bit incoherent on the telephone.'

'I hate those things. And I'd had to ring Brantingham first, but you weren't there, only a butler kind of person who wouldn't tell me anything until I made him get Miss Julyan. She nearly fainted when I told her who I was, too.'

'Thrill. She thinks you're the bee's knees.'

'She wasn't so hot on telling me the number of Sillerby, though—oh, drat this thing!'

She was having trouble manipulating the kettle. When she tried to pour it into the tea-pot the tripod and lamp tilted with it.

'Hang on,' said Tom. 'There should be a little silver pin at the back, on a chain—at least there is on ours. If you pull that out it just hinges forward at the front. Mind out—it'll be hot.'

'Whew! Too late—and I knew I'd get something wrong. Now, Mr. Hankey, it's China tea, so do you fancy milk or lemon?'

'Oh, Kate!'

'Something else wrong?'

'Never mind.'

'I want to know.'

'That isn't what . . .'

'I mean it, Tom. Please tell me.'

'Oh well . . . something you said—what was it? Oh yes, "Fancy". But my dear Kate . . .'

'Thanks. I'll remember. Now, would you like milk or lemon?'

'Neither, actually. Yes, just like that. Thanks. If you want it stronger I should let it draw for a few minutes. China's said to be slower than Indian, I believe.'

'I should have brought my note-book.'

'What are you up to, Kate? I *have* come all the way from Sillerby and I've got to get back tonight. Do you want to spend the whole time talking about this sort of thing?'

'But it's fascinating. People who live their lives full of little silver pins that have to be pulled out or pushed in if they want a cup of tea . . . Won't you have a *scone*?'

She emphasised the short *o*, glancing at him in only semi-mockery for approval.

'I could send you a book on the subject,' he said. 'There must be hundreds of them, all utterly grim.'

'Exactly. That's another thing. The people who know about the silver pins keep shifting them round, so that if somebody does the sensible thing and writes a manual telling the rest of us where they're supposed to be, by the time we've learnt it up the books are all wrong.'

'I promise you, Kate, I—all the people I know—hardly ever even think about this sort of thing.'

'That makes it worse, you silly man! What you're saying is that there's just you and your crowd who got it all in your mother's milk—except I bet none of you ever tasted the milk of your own mother—and the rest of us, why, it's not worth our even trying! Do you believe that, Tom?'

'No, of course not.'

'Then there's hope even for Red Kate Barnes?'

'Of course there is. Oh, drat it, that's not what I mean. Why don't you ask me whether I've stopped beating my wife?'

'Much of that go on among the upper classes?'

'A bit, I believe.'

'Not the same problems we have down among the Closes, keeping the screams from the neighbours.'

Tom felt utterly exasperated. He had been nervous enough about this interview to find himself rehearsing snatches of possible conversations that might take place, but none of them had been anything like this. Originally he had planned to get in touch with Kate a day or two later, when his ideas were more fully worked out, and enlist her help. But her voice on the telephone, dry and urgent, had altered that. He must see her now, and before asking for anything he must do his best to repair the relationship. That, he had assumed, was what she had wanted too, but here they were, prattling about trivia, at the point where their worlds appeared to have minimum contact. For all her intelligence her view of the life lived by him and his acquaintances was almost irretrievably naïve—was it worth, for instance, trying to explain how the intricate village-like life lived among servants in a house such as Sillerby made secret wife-beating an activity just as difficult as it must have been down in dockland? And yet Kate seemed to have chosen this ground deliberately, as a means of avoiding any kind of explanations, or apologies, or justifications.

Upstairs somewhere a small bell clinked. Kate rose.

'Botheration,' she said. 'She's supposed to be asleep. You know, Monday after Monday I come here, give Millie and Doris their afternoon off, and she's never troubled me once. Now when I've got a visitor . . . She's always liked to interfere in other people's lives . . . Shan't be long, I hope.'

She picked her way out through the maze of furniture. Her stride went up the stairs two steps at a time. Tom, who had risen with her, was too restless to sit again. He wandered round the room, gazing at its strangely anonymous bric-a-brac. Twitching a lace curtain aside he saw that the garden behind the house was a dull rectangle of lawn with a pair of perfunctory, almost flowerless borders running down either side. A large holm-oak brooded near the far end. The hedges had been let grow twelve feet tall. It was more like a prison yard than a garden, but it did not look utterly untended—tidy, but never loved. That could be explained, as could Kate's choice of the place for a meeting, by the fact that the householder apparently lay bedridden upstairs; but gazing at the green, secretive rectangle Tom found that his own sense of mystery and unease was not allayed. He remembered the hall, so impossibly bare. Why was there not one hat, coat or brolly on the hat-stand? Where was the card-bowl which should have stood on the table with the gong? Why was there not one scrap of paper anywhere?

Quietly he put his cup down and left the room. Far off he heard a squeaking, querulous voice, answered by Kate's, mouthing her syllables strangely slow. Of course—the old woman was deaf. Both voices declared that, in their different ways. Yet another layer of secrecy. There were rooms on either side of the front door—the master's study most likely, and perhaps a smoking-room or 'library'. Both were locked, and Tom could not quite bring himself to stoop and peer through the keyholes, but hesitating at the left hand door he thought he detected an odour he understood. He had last smelt it, much more strongly, in the police station after the affair on Marfleet Strand, the dusty whiff of office papers.

At the back of the hall he found the dining-room. It had not the same unused look as the drawing-room, indeed the leather of the chair at the head of the table was worn almost through. A drawer of the ornate black side-table stood open, displaying a big service of florid silvery cutlery. Presumably Kate had got the teaspoons from here. Those were plain, but the handles of the dinner set were engraved with the letter H. Upstairs the voice of the old woman creaked on. Tom brooded. It was reasonable to lock the downstairs rooms in a building so little used, so that a housebreaker would not be able to roam freely through. On the other hand the dining-room with its silver was the housebreaker's dream. Kate might have unlocked it for the spoons, but in that case surely she would have left the key in the door, to lock up again when she was done. It wasn't there.

Under the stairs a smaller door opened into a little wash-room. On the shelf above the handbasin were a pair of ivory-backed hair-brushes, the sort young men got given around their sixteenth birthday. These carried the monogram ARH in lettering of exactly the same style as Cyril's brushes, which Tom himself had taken over. Another young man killed in the war? Very likely. They and the dining-room chair were the only signs that Tom had found of an individual human life ever having been lived here. He stared at them for a moment, moved by thoughts of Cyril, ashamed of his own prying and distrusts. A stair creaked above him. He flushed the lavatory, which ran with a monstrous roaring, and came out in time to hold the drawing-room door for Kate.

Her mood had changed. She smiled at him as she settled onto the sofa but he sensed an alteration of intent.

'Who does the house belong to?' he asked.

'Her,' she said, gesturing with a cock of the head towards the upper storeys, and contriving at the same time to refuse the topic. She drained her tepid tea and put her cup down.

'Now we'd better talk,' she said. 'You say you want something from me. Well, I want something from you, first. I want you to tell me straight why you came to Hull and struck up with Uncle Ned.'

'All right. That's one of the things I want to talk about too. But listen—this is important. All along I've never been sure what was the best thing to do, but almost as soon as I started I realised that I simply didn't know enough to make up my mind. So at least I've been able to tell myself that if I knew more I might come to the right decision. I started off, you see, trying to find something out—for reasons which I'm now not at all sure about and which you will think are downright bad. But however uncertain I've been about my original motives, I've always felt it was worth going on, simply in order to know. Do you understand?'

'Let's hear about your bad reasons.'

'I suppose that's the best place to start. You remember I was a blackleg during the General Strike, and fought a chap called Donovan in Drewton Cutting? On the same trip, while we were waiting to turn round, my guard became suspicious about some men who were loading boxes onto one of our trucks. He asked me to come and look at them. That's how I first saw Mr. Barnes —he wanted to talk to me about the fight, but another chap, the man you call Walter Dyke I think, stopped him. My guard opened one of the boxes when they'd gone and found a lot of Bolshevik pamphlets. Now, I happen to have a friend who's very interested in Bolshevik activities, and when I showed him the pamphlet . . .'

'Mr. Bertram Panhard, that would be?' she asked.

He stared at her.

'I heard about Mr. Panhard before ever we met,' she said. 'Putting a spy down into dockland to look for Uncle Ned. We'd spread it among the men not to talk to him. When you stood up from laying Harry Struther out and I got a chance to look at you the first time, I cottoned on you were Mr. Panhard's friend—fact, I nearly said so, straight out. Then it came to me you must also be the fellow Uncle Ned had been rabbiting on about, who'd fought Tinker Donovan, so I said that instead, to cover things up. Course, I knew Uncle Ned was longing to talk to you, but still . . . oh, it was sheer impudence me taking you to the meeting at all.'

Her expression was strange. Superficially she was enjoying the drama, the sheer outrageous tease of revelation, but underneath there was a note of sadness, almost of despair.

'What's the point of me telling you all this, then?' he said.

She smiled, deliberately relaxed.

'Because I only know the outside. You've mostly only shown me the outside so far, Tom. I've had to guess at everything else. Why, that first evening, when we were walking to Marfleet Strand and I realised how much I liked the look of you, I began to try and tell myself that couldn't be all there was. I've seen a lot of you since then, Tom. I've got to know what else there is to it before . . .'

'Before you spit in my face?'

She shook her head.

'Does Mr. Barnes know all this?'

'Course not. D'you think he wouldn't have shown it? That first evening, what with your boxing and then what you did for the men in the police station, he persuaded himself we'd been wrong about you. Only when he found you'd been staying at Brantingham . . . I told you, you've broken his heart. I'm just waiting for you to break mine.'

He was silent for while, staring at his knees and biting gently at his lower lip while he considered. She poured herself more tea. The cup shivered almost violently on the saucer as she picked them up.

'I'll start a bit further back then,' he said. 'The most important thing in my life is that I want to marry Judy Tarrant.'

He had not intended to look at her but her sudden release of breath startled his head round. She nodded encouragingly.

'That's better,' she said. 'Go on.'

'A couple of months ago it was the only thing in my life. I thought there wasn't anything I wouldn't do to bring it off. I suppose it's still more important than anything else, but now there seems to be a lot else which I can't actually sacrifice for that, without sacrificing part of it too. Even then I haven't been at all consistent. Everything that happens seems to change my viewpoint. Last week, for instance, when I saw the men stoning the fire engines and your uncle taking it for granted . . .'

'He's against that sort of thing, but . . .'

'Of course. He is a totally honourable and decent man, and I admire him as much as anyone I've ever met in my life, . . . look, that's the heart of it. Something to do with a blindness of the imagination. Everybody sees their own side, but they won't make the imaginative effort to see anything else. A fireman died, didn't he, in the fire last week when one of the timber-sheds collapsed? You wouldn't find a man in all that crowd who'd admit to wanting him to die, but all the same they cheered like a football crowd when the roof fell in. They won't make the connection! Nobody will!'

'You've got to the wrong end of the story, Tom. Go back to you and Miss Julyan.'

'In a moment. You said you wanted to know something about the inside. I suppose I've been trying to tell you you'll have to use your imagination as well as your intellect.'

'I'll do my best.'

It was strange how often during the past few weeks he had recounted the same events, and how different their elements had appeared each time. In the Collection Room at Sillerby there was a portable Remington which he and Father used to print labels for the specimens. It had no key for the figure 1; you were supposed to use the lower-case l. Father had not realised this, so had begun by using the capital I, which, even in the middle of a run of figures, remained intransigently a letter. It was different with the l. When you wrote 'Nymphalis polychloros, Helton Copse, July 111925' you pressed the l key eight times. Five times it produced a letter and three times a figure and the difference was absolute. It would need a gross effort of irrationality to read them wrong. So it seemed now with the events Tom described. The event was the same, but its meaning had become wholly different. The only fact he left out was that he had got as far as selecting Ernie Doyle as a traitor; the lad was still potentially innocent; it would be unfair to announce his potential guilt. Kate listened in silence. He seldom looked away from his own shoes as he was speaking, but when once or twice he glanced her way her face seemed to express an almost academic interest, without either irony or feeling.

'You must be thirsty after all that,' she said. 'Shall I pour you some more tea?'

'Yes, please.'

'You people do know how to look after yourselves. This kettle here, it looks just a frilly bit of expensive nonsense, but it makes a lovely pot of tea, and what's more keeps it going.'

'Are you going to spit in my face now?'

'No. It's my turn. I'm going to say my bit, and then we'll see what we shall see, if that's all right with you.'

'Of course.'

'Better had be, Tom.'

She drew a deep breath but did not speak. He looked enquiringly at her but she turned her head away.

'I'll start like you did,' she said at last. 'Something I hadn't meant to tell you, any more than you did me. Almost the same place, really, I suppose. Put your cup down so you don't spill on the carpet. You realise I love you, Tom.'

He felt the air on the back of his neck stand stiff like the hackle of a dog. His throat convulsed but made no noise.

'Some of it's the other way round, though,' she went on calmly. 'You said all that mattered to you used to be wanting Miss Julyan, but now it isn't that simple. All that mattered to me used to be working for the Party, but now it's not that simple for me either. If I had to choose between you and the Party I don't know what I'd do—so perhaps I'm lucky it looks as if I'm not going to be given the choice. . . . I want to tell you a bit about me. I'll start a long way back, when I was just leaving High School and you must have been a kid in knickerbockers still. I was the teachers' pride and joy those days. Plain as a boot and clever as a monkey. Of course they liked the plainness almost as much as they liked the cleverness . . .'

'Nobody with eyes in his head could ever have thought you plain.'

'Don't interrupt or I shall start saying things I don't intend.

Yes, now, there I was, plain and clever and angry, just ready to leave school with all my scholarships and prizes, put up in front of them all on Speech Day to tell the world how grateful I was for my schooling . . . I see someone's told you about this, Tom.'

'Mrs. Barnes.'

'I didn't know that was one of her party pieces . . . Still, I'm glad it came from her—she's a way of putting things, hasn't she? Funny she should bring it out—she was that ashamed at the time, I was almost sorry I'd done it. But I wasn't ashamed, and I'm still not, apart from what happened to silly Mr. Claythorpe . . . Yes, but for that, it was really something for a kid my age to bring off in front of them all.

'Next three years was London. Nothing I saw or learnt or heard changed my mind about how I thought of things. I started changing other folk's minds for them. I met people who thought the same way as I did. I got in with them, joined organisations, worked for the Party harder than I did at my books, got too busy with it to come home, even during vacations—why, I went to Russia. Aunt Tess tell you that?'

'Yes.'

'That was something. I'm going to put it in a book one day. But in the end the Party sent me back here, and I was glad. It wasn't because I belong here that I was glad—it was because I thought I could do more for the Party, by belonging. And that's true. The Party's had its ups and downs and a lot of them have come close to despairing, but the Hull Dock Nucleus has kept going through it all. We haven't a lot of members, but we've a lot of influence, one or two men on almost every committee that matters . . . Oh, I've worked hard. I was a teacher for a bit, but nobody'll employ me now unless I sign an undertaking to give up my work for the Party. I live on bits and bobs, and a little from the Party . . . But that's not what I want to tell you about. I came back here thinking, the way you do that age, that I knew everything. I'd been to Moscow, hadn't I? I was in for a surprise, because, going back to that Speech Day I'd almost forgotten, I found I'd started something I didn't know. It was a joint do, you see, between the Girls' High and the Boys' High, and sitting among the boys there'd been a young fellow, my own age to a month, but not like me at all that anyone could have guessed.

Not specially clever at his books, very quiet and polite in his shy way, but underneath bitter as alum. His father paid for his schooling of course, could have afforded to send him away to a proper public school like you went to, only . . . His father had come up from the docks, you see, started a little business, got an army contract in the Zulu War, made a pile of money all of a sudden, then married late and right out of his class, a solicitor's daughter. She was getting on too, so they had just that one boy and no more, and he became their battle-ground. Just because the mother was set on turning him into a gentleman the father wouldn't have it. The boy must earn his own living and have an education to fit him for it. She fought and fought, and long after the battle was over she went on fighting, dinning it into the boy's head that he should have been to a gentleman's school and become a gentleman, and one day walk round his own fields with his gun under his arm and his spaniel at his heels, instead of which, however much money he made, the people like that would always know he wasn't one of them. Think about him, Tom, sitting there among the other boys that day, all eaten up with hate of his father and his father's kind and knowing all the same that there was nothing else for him to do but become one of them. All round him is speech day going on, with the prize-winning boys and girls going up to the dais like kids going to their first communion, to show us all that they worship the same things as are worshipped by his father and his father's kind. Then, last of all, there's this wild girl, hair like a sweep's brush, face like a cow-girl, stands up and slings back her head and blas-phemes aloud against his father and his father's kind and all their sacred objects. He sat there quivering as if an electric current was running through him, bringing him alive like the monster in *Frankenstein*. He told me that when he looked me out after I'd come back from London and Russia. Nearly four years he'd waited, but he said it wasn't time wasted. His father had died and he could have given up work completely if he'd wanted to, but now he didn't any longer. He knew I'd come one day, and he'd spent the time perfecting his disguise. He had too. I'd never seen anyone look more like one of the enemy—shiny white collar, shiny black boots, shiny black hair, shiny black bottom to his trousers sitting at his desk all day being a little soldier in the great big army of oppression. And he wouldn't even tell me his name. It took six months for me even to begin to think he might be serious, but once I'd gone that far, my! He was a natural revolutionary. He didn't need anyone to tell him—he knew. When I was in Russia they talked a bit about fellows like him. Lenin invented a word for them. Moles. They burrow unseen and bring the system down from the inside. He'd worked that out for himself, and he's stuck to it. Even now there's only me and one other in the Nucleus know his real name . . . But the Party think no end of him. First off, I was using him to help with my work. Then we were working in harness. Now they've put him over me, and I do as he says. I don't mind. He's a genius. He was born to do what he's doing, and it's what I believe in, so why should I mind?'

She paused, as though searching for the answer to her own question. Tom was aware that she must be talking about the man they called Ricardo, but the discovery did not interest him, nor did the number of odd details she had told him which if sorted through and arranged might lead him to the truth. For the moment his whole attention was engaged in sympathy for Kate, the more so as he could see that she was doing her best not to ask for it, to keep her tone quiet and dispassionate and her features under control. All the same there was an element of wonder that she could not help expressing, as though like Tom himself she knew the facts of her own history but had not before ordered them into the pattern she was now gazing at.

'I've been his mistress these three years,' she said.

She glanced at him with a sharp little smile, inquisitive to see how he took the news, determined in spite of everything to enjoy the moment. In fact the emotional charge that had underlain her story had made him aware that she was telling him more than the origins of Ricardo's enmity to society; such shock as there was came only from the candour of the statement.

'Did you love him?' he asked.

'That's what matters, isn't it?'

'It must be one of the things that matters.'

'Oh, Tom! If the world was ending and fire and brimstone pouring from the skies, you'd be trying to hold them off from us with both your hands but you'd still be making distinctions

about the rights and wrongs of it! Don't laugh. It's one of the
reasons I love you. It's the reason I . . . Oh, you silly woman!
Stop it! . . . There, that's better. No, Tom, I can see now I never
loved him, and I don't think he's capable of loving anybody, not
even himself, not even the Party. He's in love with destruction.
He wanted me—he wants me—not because he particularly
needs a woman—born different he could have been a monk in a
cell. No, I opened the gates for him and showed him his road.
Having me around to see and touch and talk to he keeps that
moment fresh in his mind. It sanctifies his work, if you see what I
mean. And for me . . . Oh, Tom, if you knew how lonely and
despairing the work can be! All mankind is walled against you
except for your own small cell, and even them . . . It's a funny
thing about the English. They actually hate ideas. In Russia we
talked on and on about the ideas behind what we were going to
do. Here, if you move one inch beyond the practicalities they
look at you as if you were speaking a foreign language. Pretending to yourself you love someone is a substitute for a lot of other
things you miss . . . And in any case, Tom, I'm that kind of
woman. If I'd been the cow-girl I look like you'd have found me
rolling in the haycock once in a while, I shouldn't be surprised.
Not that I'm a loose woman. You mustn't think that, and
besides the Party doesn't like it . . . Oh, tell me what I've been
trying to say to you, Tom. Give me a hint you understand.'

'I understand, I think. For years you've been slogging away
in blinkers, hauling your load, seeing only the road in front of
you. Now something's crossed your path—it happens to be me,
but perhaps if I hadn't come along it would have been something
else—and you've stopped and looked round and seen there's
more in the world than the road and the load.'

'What do you think about *me*, Tom?'

'Do I love you, do you mean?'

'Bit much to hope for.'

'Oh, no, you're wrong. I think if . . . if I hadn't already
become so involved with Judy you'd have knocked me clean off
my feet, but . . . Look, when you were talking about this chap
and whether he loved you, I thought you were underestimating
yourself. None of us can really guess the effect we have on other
people. I can't believe any intelligent man wouldn't feel some-

thing. There's so much to you . . . if you can imagine, on a walking tour, coming over a pass and round a bend of the track and there it is, miles of intricate distance, taking your breath away, so your first thought is you wouldn't mind spending the rest of your life exploring it . . .'

'Only you never do.'

'No.'

'Your life's already spoken for.'

'I suppose so.'

'Miss Julyan. Oh, Tom, why . . .'

'Wait. There's something I want to try and explain. Everything connects with everything else, even something as secret and personal as who you chose to fall in love with. Did you understand what I felt when those miners outside Leeds chucked coal at us and smashed up most of the carriage windows? It was as though I was being made to become their enemy, an enemy of half the people in England. I have to prove, if only to myself, that I'm not an enemy. Nothing I say can prove it. It's got to be something I do. The action doesn't have to have any purpose—it can be entirely symbolic, like the refusal of the early Christians to pour a little scented water on a pagan altar. It wouldn't have made any difference to the world if they'd dribbled the water on the stone, but it made all the difference to them. I've been thinking about this a lot because it's connected with something I want to talk to you about later. But about you and me—it would be terribly easy for me to tell myself that the way to prove I was not an enemy was to let you represent them, and so loving you would be all I needed.'

'Distinctions, distinctions. Now will you tell me about Miss Julyan?'

'Only if you stop calling her that. Her name's Judy or Miss Tarrant.'

'Tom, I'm sitting here pouring tea for you out of this silver doodah and trying to behave as if we were just chatting about what happened at the Withernsee picnic, but it doesn't mean that I'm not seething with bloody jealousy all through, just as if I were one of the women down the Holderness Road flailing with her broomhandle at the bitch who's walked off with her man. It's not reasonable in you to ask me to be all sweetness and light! Tell

213

me about Miss Judy, then.'

'She isn't easy to explain. She keeps asking to meet you, you know, but at the same time she's certain you'd think her an empty-headed idiot.'

'And would I?'

'Yes and no. I mean, she wouldn't make head or tail of most of the things you and I usually talk about, but . . . well, she'd have understood everything we've talked about this afternoon. Really understood it, I mean, emotionally as well as intellectually.'

'And that's enough for you?'

'Oh, there's much more to her than that. She's unusually pretty, for a start, and it's no use pretending I don't . . .'

'Oh, I've *seen* her. You needn't go into details. How do you think of her, Tom? Just now you started talking about me as if I were a bit of landscape—I'm not sure I fancied that—lot of fellows staring down at me before making up their minds whether to tramp to and fro all over me . . . Do you think of her that kind of way?'

'That was only an image. I think of you as a very particular person—Kate Barnes.'

'Glad to hear it. Give me an image for Miss Judy, then.'

'Um . . . I don't think I've got one . . I often see one particular afternoon, only a couple of days after we met. She had a little sports car and we drove up into the foothills above the Bay of Biscay. We climbed a hill above a small town and watched the butterflies, and then there was a terrific sunset and we drove back to where we were staying . . . it doesn't sound much . . . it was magical . . .'

'Butterflies! That's how *I* think of her, anyway. Up there in the sunlight, above the rest of us, not a care in the world except to be beautiful! Don't you dare tell me that isn't fair!'

'Remember I've been brought up to like the creatures.'

'That you have! Oh, don't be spiteful, woman—you'll regret it after . . . 'Scuse my asking, Tom, but have you ever been to bed with her?'

'Yes.'

They were so far out into candour that it did not cross his mind not to tell her the truth, or to regret that he had done so. Kate sighed and was silent. When she spoke her tone did not match her words.

'Stainless Stephen. Another illusion gone.'

'When we got back to the villa there was a telegram from my father asking me to come home. We were head over heels in love, though we'd hardly known each other three days.'

'I bet it wasn't you went creeping along to her room though.'

'No. She came to mine.'

'Thought so. Oh, Tom, if you knew the nights I've lain at Aunt Kate's, thinking of you round at Aunt Minnie's and knowing there was no road past the two of them to reach you! Some people have all the luck. It isn't fair, really it isn't. Why should *she* be let go gadding round the continent without even one aunt to keep an eye on her?'

She managed to combine frustration and jealousy with comic self-mockery at herself for giving way to such things. He laughed, not out of embarrassment but because she wanted him to. Their mood was so close, their mental intimacy so perfect, that he felt as though he could see through the surface of the earth to the root-like network of meanings and impulses that flowered above that surface into speech. It was like dancing with Judy, except that it was two minds and not two bodies moving as one.

Kate fell silent, staring at the tea-tray. Her stillness filled the room until only one faint source of sound was left, the almost inaudible burr of the flame beneath the kettle mixed with the still softer tingling noise of water on the edge of boiling. Tom's thoughts would not order themselves, though he knew she was giving him time to think, to choose. As on the rockery at Brantingham, vistas of possible futures seemed to open and close, the scenery of the years heaving into place, strangely threatening in its sudden silent emergence and equally sudden vanishing. This room—dustless, cluttered, respectable—reeked of wasted lives and chances. A vision pranced before him of Judy in middle age, halfway to becoming an impossible old woman, still at times and in company brimming with frivolous energies, but at other times displaying like patches of a worsening disease a hardness and sourness—a sense, unmitigated by intellect, of steadily being cheated by the years. Already the enjoyable feud with a neighbour or two would be widening to become unforgiv- able quarrels with old friends, until her only driving force would seem to be an erratic malice towards all she had once loved.

He wiped the picture away. It was only a possibility, which care on his part might prevent. Still, a possibility it was, and no equivalent monster would form for Kate; though she too was capable of ferocious hatreds, her Furies would be creatures of the daylight, visible to Tom's eyes also. He thought of Judy in the shadowed dark of the old coach at Rokesley. 'I've got a witch mother.' Pure fantasy, but still embodying a truth—and the witch-blood was in her own veins also. Probably it would never manifest itself, and at worst he would merely solve the riddle (as many other men must have done since Jane Austen first posed it) of how Mr. Bennett had ever come to marry Mrs. Bennett.

But did he have to? Wasn't it inherent in the rules when Judy had first explained them that either player could renege? Without that, where was the excitement? Had she not explicitly freed him from the hurried commitment at Hendaye? Had he not, at Rokesley, reasserted that freedom, overtly for her sake, covertly —almost shamefacedly—for his own? Suppose, purely as an intellectual proposition, he were free to choose . . . Whom . . . ? But the intellect itself distorted the proposition, declaring for Kate. He and she were of one kind: serious, active, set to confront the world as rational beings. Not that the physical attraction was not, in all conscience, almost intolerably strong, even in this stiflingly furnished room and though Kate had flashed barely a glance at him during the whole interview. She had offered him more than Judy was prepared to, not just herself, body and mind, but her own past and future; all she had worked for, sacrificed herself to, she would betray for him. Whereas Judy had set limits. 'I do love you, but not if it means chicken-farming.'

Kate didn't even ask for marriage. She expected no commitment. She was offering Judy's game made real.

If he were free . . .

But the choice did not lie in the intellect. No argument could disprove his love for Judy. Time might, but the choice confronted him now, in this room, and his love and longing for her remained facts as definite as his love and admiration for Kate. They had little more in common than youth and an upbringing that allowed them to understand, without thought, what Kate would call the mechanics of silver kettles. From what Tom had seen in Hull, heard from Bertie, felt unconsciously at Sillerby, he guessed that another generation would make such knowledge valueless. If he were to marry Judy, he would stay the same man; if he were to marry Kate—the other alternative seemed unreal to him; somehow he knew himself to be the marrying kind, naturally monogamous—if he were to marry Kate, he must change.

And of course he was not free, game or no game. Chance might have loosed him from the burden of Sillerby and the duty to marry money to keep it standing, but another ancient edifice, spectral but just as compelling, still dictated his destiny. Honour, Father was fond of saying, was the devil's virtue . . .

Kate broke the silence with a sigh.

'You know,' she said, 'I've been trying to eat my cake and have it too. I'm asking you to give your Judy the chuck because I want you for myself, but one of the reasons I want you is because you're not the sort to do a thing like that.'

'You've been reading my thoughts.'

'Have I now?'

She rose, yawned, stretched and sat down beside him, sliding her arm round his shoulders.

'It's all right,' she said. 'I'm not going to try and come between you and your girl—I'm just going to wish you well with a good old working-class kiss. Come on, Tom. What was that you were saying about words not being enough? Show me you're not an enemy then.'

She was very gentle, neither devouring nor submissive. Her body, which he had unconsciously imagined to be sinewy and taut with its inner energies, was so soft that it seemed almost to be a liquid held in shape by her dark crackling dress. The energies transformed themselves to a generous glow. It was as natural to kiss her, to move against her, to respond to the motions of her mouth with his, as it is for a child to bury its face in the fur of a cat. When she leaned away from him, he leaned with her, as if in the movements of a dance. But there was an invisible frontier, which each recognised without a signal from the other. He straightened and she slithered away, laughing, to the far end of the sofa. She began to pat her impossible hair, as though any outward event could either arrange or disarrange it.

'Thank you,' he said, laughing with her.

'I don't get enough of that,' she said. 'With this fellow I was telling you about, there's always the complication of motive. Nothing's simple and straightforward. Talk about alienation of the worker! I think I'll find some young man down in the docks to set my cap at. Why, I might give Harry Struther what he wants for a bit.'

'But he's married!'

'Not married enough to my mind. I'm glad you enjoyed that, Tom. You haven't had all that practice, have you?'

'Not a lot.'

'You'll be all right though, with your Judy. She's got that look —you can see it in the eyelids, here . . . Tell me, are they all like that, up among the butterflies?'

'Butterflies don't have eyelids.'

'I'm not talking about that! The look, it's nothing to do with class—you see it down among the back-to-backs just as much. Not that there aren't plenty of frigid bitches there too—*and* the way some of the men go mad over them. No, Tom, it's fellows like you, kids who saw their Mums just an hour after tea if they were good, all they knew about women was a Nanny shaped like a bolster, then off to boarding school with a pack of other boys, swapping mucky little guesses about what happens under a skirt . . . why it's a wonder they can breed at all!'

'My Nanny was over sixty. She had a black moustache.'

'And still you knew what to do when Miss Judy . . .'

'Luckily I didn't have time to get steamed up about it.'

'I'm beginning to think she's cleverer than she looks.'

'I hadn't thought of that.'

She smiled, smugly knowing, and fell silent, apparently hypnotised by the glimmers of silver and brass on the tea-tray. With a sudden decisive shrug she leaned forward and slipped the little silver dome over the lamp of the kettle, extinguishing the flame. The vague, placid hum of simmering water died. With it died the complete openness and mutual understanding of the last half hour. The normal unknowability of other people, even of close friends, returned.

'Aren't you going to ask me his name?' she said.

'Ricardo.'

'Who told . . . But his real name, don't you want to know that?'

'Yes, but I'd rather it wasn't you who told me.'

'I would.'

'Then we would both be ashamed.'

She looked at him sidelong, pouting a little, uncertain. He guessed that she had asked for the meeting in order to make this betrayal. In a sense it was to have been the climax of the whole interview.

'You said you wanted something from me?'

'Yes.'

'Give up the Party?'

'No, nothing like that. I mean, if you decided to give it up because you really wanted to, or thought you ought to, I can't pretend I shouldn't be glad. But I'd hate you to do it for the mere sake of making an emotional sacrifice.'

'Nothing very mere about it. You aren't going to ask me to get the strike called off? I can't do that—I'm not in charge. No one is, in a thing like this. It's in charge of itself. It's got its own rules.'

'I know. But people can make those rules work in their favour. Tell me something about that—did you know what was going to happen on Marfleet Strand?'

'I knew there might be trouble, but I'd no idea what. You walked there with me, remember? D'you think if I'd known . . .'

'No. Who gave you the document you produced?'

'He did.'

'And after, when you realised how he'd been using you and the others?'

'We had a flaming row. At least I tried to have a flaming row but he wouldn't catch. He just kept saying he was acting on orders.'

'From Moscow?'

'Eventually. I can't do anything about that either, Tom.'

'No, of course not.'

'That all you want to know?'

She spoke briskly, as if to disguise even from herself the sense of emptiness and waste.

'It's not all I want. I need your help. You see I want to do something a bit like what your friend arranged on Marfleet

219

Strand, but on the other side. Nothing violent, I hope, but just making what you call the rules of the strike work in the opposite direction for once. I've been thinking about it since the fire. I've become obsessed—rationally obsessed, if you see what I mean—with the notion that something's got to happen, some event take place, before other things can change. It nearly happened at the fire itself, I felt, and if it had it would have been a disaster. Your friend Ricardo is waiting for the next chance for something like that. I feel it's up to me to make something different happen, something that will loose the jam, but in the opposite direction.'

'Just you alone?'

'That wouldn't do any good. The men have got to be part of it. That's why I need your help.'

She nodded but without assent, a mere indication that he should continue. Her eyes were unreadable.

'As far as I can make out,' he insisted, 'it's Party dogma that a situation like this should be exploited to the utmost. If an immediate gain can't be won for the workers, then things must be arranged so that the dispute becomes still more serious, feelings still more bitter, until the workers rally round the Party because it's the only place for them to go.'

'That's one of the lines,' she said drily.

'It seems to me utterly immoral.'

She looked steadily at him, waiting. He had refused to let her make one betrayal—why should he now expect her to make this only slightly different one? At least it was clear to him that not to have trusted her would be worse than having trusted her and been himself betrayed.

'What I want to do sounds quite mad and futile,' he said. 'Only if I bring it off I think it might do the trick. You know there are eight trucks of stores up at the Mills near Selby, waiting to be distributed when the strike ends? I want to borrow a locomotive and bring them down to the docks and distribute them now.'

'Tom!'

'You mustn't laugh. I'm serious.'

'I can see you are. But . . . oh, Tom!'

'It's *meant* to be a lark, I suppose. That's the point. Cheer everybody up.'

'It certainly would do that. Why, quite minor bits of mischief they pulled off in the General Strike, they're still telling each other. Can you really do it, Tom?'

'I think so. I shall have to go and look at a few things tomorrow —see exactly where the trucks are lying and so on. The junction at Eastrington may be a problem. But otherwise it's much easier than it sounds. With the docks on strike Mr. Tarrant is perfectly likely to be going for one of his night runs—he took me for one last week so I know the form. All I've got to do is make one tele- phone call using his voice—it's very easy to copy—borrow his engine, run it up to Selby, hitch onto the trucks, bring them back down to Eastrington—some of the signalmen may be a bit startled to see me going through with a load, but I'll be past before they can do much. At Eastrington I shall have to get them to let me switch onto the Wold Line—that's really the chief worry—and the Wold Line's not manned all night because of the strike. If all goes well I should be able to bring the trucks round to that bit of waste ground behind Belmont Street and leave them there for the men to unload while I get the engine back to its shed before the milk train.'

'Tom, they'll send you to prison!'

'I don't think so. With a bit of luck there's no reason why any- one should know I was involved. The Tarrants are away this week, staying with friends on the Tweed. Of course they'll learn it was Mr. Tarrant's engine, but if I wear the right clothes and speak a bit rough to the chap at Eastrington—he's the only one I'll have actually to talk to—I can make it look as if it was some- thing the men brought off by themselves. And as a matter of fact if they do find out I'll probably only have to pay for the cost of the stores. I think I know somebody I could borrow the money from.'

(Strange destiny for a driblet of the Heusen millions. Would the old shoemaker churn in his far-off grave?)

'This very week?' she said.

'Thursday night, if all goes well. Before anything worse happens. Are you on, Kate? Do you think it's worth a try?'

'Course it is. Even a try's worth it, show what we think about them keeping those trucks up there, dangling like a carrot in front of a donkey. The men have been really resenting that. Oh yes—they'll come and unload if I tell them the trucks will be

221

there.'

'Will you have to tell your friend?'

'You don't want me to?'

'I'd rather not.'

'I'll see ... after all, you're not telling Mrs. Tarrant ... what'll you say to her, Tom, if she cottons on it was you after all?'

'I don't think I'll mind—it might even be a good thing— provided Judy agrees, of course. I'm pretty sure she will, but I haven't had a chance to talk to her yet—she took her parents north last night and doesn't get back till this evening. I think she'll say yes. I hope so. She's got a funny relationship with her mother. If she doesn't, though, I'm afraid it's off.'

Tom had ten minutes to wait for his train at Paragon. Rather reluctantly, no longer strongly interested in the matter, he went to a telephone booth and leafed through the directory for the letter H. There was almost a column of the name he was looking for. Nothing under A.R. He ran his finger down the addresses and found it near the end. Hutton, Mrs. W.B., Summerlea, Danube Road. The old lady, now deaf and bed-ridden, who had fought and fought for her son to be allowed to become a gentle-man. Tom came out of the booth and stood under the wide vault of grimy glass, remembering the strange interview in the smoking-room at Brantingham, the soft voice and the pale, con-sidering gaze. He felt an extraordinary pang of sympathy for his enemy, knowing how he himself must symbolise all that birth-right of which the other man believed he had been defrauded. Ah, yes, and *that* was the chain by which Bertie had known what was happening in Drewton Cutting—the Bradford Bolsheviks had known, had told Hull, who had told Ricardo. Bertie had told Mrs. Tarrant his aims, and she had told her trusted wharf man-ager. The clash was deliberate, the further turning of the screw of class hatred, all manipulated, all foreseen, apart from the accident of the fight with Donovan, the absurd event which had caused the screw to slip and release the pressure ... But why should Hutton have taken the quite uncharacteristic risk of tell-ing Tom there was a man who called himself Ricardo? For quite different reasons, Tom guessed. Tom was the personal enemy,

222

and must be fully humiliated. How could Tom be made to grovel in the failure of his search if he did not know the name of his quarry? Poor fellow, a life for destruction. A.R.H. on the hair-brushes. No doubt his middle name was Richard.

13

Brantingham, Selby, Hull, 2nd, 3rd September, 1926

'Really, I do not know why I'm doing this,' said the Reverend Cyprian Tarrant.

Disembodied in a beam of orange light from a crack in the fire-box door, his spread hands caressed their fingertips gently against each other, as if he were about to embark on a refinement of the concept of the homoousian.

'I'm very glad you are, sir,' said Tom warmly. 'We've got a much better chance with you helping.'

This was a mild exaggeration but it seemed to satisfy Mr. Tarrant. 'Don't forget,' Judy had said, 'he isn't used to being admired. Butter him up, Tom.' Tom was doing his best, within the bounds of honour.

Half in the moonshadow of the sandpit shed they waited for the midnight mail to pass up the main line. Apart from the quiet hiss and creak of the old engine the level meadows imposed a quietness that seemed deeper than mere night-time. Though still a mile from the estuary the shed stood only a few feet above high-water mark. Moonlight and flatness gave the illusion that vast distances, right to the Lincolnshire shoreline, were visible, though in fact it would have been hard to pick out a man stand-ing fifty yards away. Mr. Tarrant turned and craned out over the step, listening, as if he might change his mind if the signal was not given soon.

Tom still had no real grasp of how Judy had persuaded her father to join the adventure. The only help he had planned for had been to bring Pennycuick's son Derek down to stoke for him. Apart from that, all circumstances seemed to have conspired together to make the absurd enterprise possible, as though the immaterial world was determined that it should be done. But then the luck-god, ironic to the last, had set Judy in his path.

'No, you can't possibly . . .'

'Darling . . .'

'You don't understand. It's something he's always been longing to do, take his engine over the Wold Line. Ever since I was tiny. Honestly. I simply can't let you do it without him.'

'In that case the whole thing's . . .'

'You'll need his help anyway.'

'I don't think so, really. Besides, he wouldn't dream . . .'

'Yes he will.'

'And it's got to be now or never. He's in . . .'

'I'll take the Morris up and fetch him.'

'But . . .'

'No, Tom. Listen. This is important. You remember what I told you in the old coach at Rokesley, about me having a witch-mother?'

'Judy, this isn't . . .'

'I'm going to break her power.'

'I don't . . .'

'It really is important, Tom. More important than anything since . . . since I met you, I suppose. I've been waiting for a chance like this for years. If I can make him do something Mummy is dead against, and he knows it, and still he does it because I want him to . . . Darling, I don't expect you to understand. It's between me and her. You'll just have to believe me. But I promise you, if I don't do it now I'll never get free, not even when she dies. Do you want that?'

'No, of course not, But . . .'

'Oh, I can make him. I think. He wants to get free too, you know. Before he's too old. He's been simmering up to it—even this food train. It's perfect. You see, he's not at all happy about it. Did you realise that the food actually belongs to our churches?'

'No. How . . .'

'I heard them rowing about it. They have horrid kinds of rows. Daddy bleats and Mummy whispers. She always wins. As far as I could gather, the food is supposed to have been bought by *all* the churches for them to dish out as soon as the strike's over. But really quite a lot of them wanted to dish it out now, and anyway the others haven't got any money, but our churches have got The Fund which Grandfather set up. Mummy can do what she likes with that so she simply went ahead and bought the food without telling anyone. Daddy was furious. He's serious about his religion, you see. He couldn't stand having it used as a weapon in something like this. Of course Mummy had no idea what he was bothering about. Everything's so simple for her. The strikers are wicked for striking, so God would want them to be punished until they change their minds and repent, and *then* it's all right to reward them. She actually quoted the Bible at him —the bit about the fatted calf. He was bleating so loud that the dogs had started yapping and I'd come down to see what the row was. I'm a great listener at doors, Tom. You'll have to get used to that.'

'Do you really think . . .'

'I don't think, I know. Don't ask me how, but I do. I realised when I was listening to his bleats that he was absolutely ripe, and what I needed now was something I could make him stick in his toes about. I was thinking of getting him to marry us with Mummy still saying no, but that was going to be messy. We'd be married, you see—there for Mummy to nag on at. I really wanted something that would be over and done with. This is perfect.'

'Well . . .'

'It'll be pie, darling. If I start at four tomorrow morning I can be there at ten. Mummy will be out fishing by then. Daddy'll be all alone in the Library, working on his book. I can park behind the stables and creep round through the knot garden and in at the french windows. Suppose I take an hour to persuade him, I can get him back here by supper. He always sleeps in the car, so he'll be quite fresh for the night. You can have the Lagonda if you don't mind driving with its door roped up, but you won't need to fetch Derek. You could use it to go and look at level crossings and things. Honestly, darling.'

'I feel like bleating.'

It was true that Judy, sitting on the hearthrug in the morning-room at Brantingham with her legs folded beneath her, had dropped her voice to a whisper, monotonous but emphatic. Now she shrank back and stared at him as though he had spoken obscenities.

'Never say anything like that again!' she croaked. 'Never!'

There were neat rounds of scarlet on her cheeks that were not make-up. Her neck was tense and quivering.

'I'm terribly sorry . . .'

She shook her head violently, then struggled into a smile.

'I suppose everybody has their sore places,' she said. 'I think you might have guessed that was one of mine. I *am* like her in some ways. But I'm not her. I'm not going to become her. That's what she wants, and you've got to help me stop it happening.'

'I'll do my best.'

'Then I'll go and kidnap Daddy, and you look after everything else.'

Mr. Tarrant held up a hand, fine and silvery where it caught the moonlight. Tom pricked his ears. The intrusion on the silence was far and faint, but unmistakable. It faded.

'The line curves round Redcliff Sand, you see,' said Mr. Tarrant at his most scholarly. 'It points directly towards us for about five hundred yards and then curves away again. I have no idea of the scientific explanation, but the sound of a locomotive seems to carry further in the direct line of its motion. She will pass the spur points in four and a quarter minutes.'

'Shall I fire now?'

'Hm. Let me see.'

Mr. Tarrant took the shovel from Tom, flicked the fire-door open and reached with it into the back of the box, holding it upside down and moving it from side to side so that he could see the surface of the coals reflected in its metal. Tom craned beside him, screwing his eyes up. It was hard to recognise any differentiation in the wavering glare.

'There, you see,' said Mr. Tarrant. 'A slight darkening, hm? That's the trouble spot. It would do like that for twenty minutes or so, but after that you would begin to burn the floor through. It is always the same place, so an extra half-shovel of coal from time to time . . . Yes, she could certainly do with a feed now, if you please.'

It was not that Mr. Tarrant became a different person when he was driving an engine, indeed the process seemed to exaggerate his characteristics; his voice and tone remained precise but timid-sounding, and he had peered into the fire-box with the same rabbit-like tremor as that with which he studied the big Bible on his lectern before starting to read the lessons. Despite this he clearly knew what he was doing. Even a rabbit, presumably, is confident in its rabbithood. Tom wondered whether a different history might have made Mr. Tarrant a different man. There were strong emotional powers there, leashed tight. The discovery that Judy not only understood but loved her father had altered Tom's view of him. As Father had implied, he was something more than a holy worm, and perhaps no less interesting than Judy's remarkable mother.

Tom straightened from his shovelling and booted the fire-door shut. At once he was aware of the approach of the mail-train, driving with a breathy regularity into the eighteen-mile straight across the Humber meadows. Mr. Tarrant was listening with his head cocked slightly to one side, as if appreciating a subtle passage in a string quartet. The rhythm faltered as the train took the points at Brough. Soon. Now . . . All Tom saw of the train itself, six hundred yards away to his left, was a hummocked band of glittering silver erupting westward where the smoke was thrust into the still air and hung there in the moonlight.

Mr. Tarrant took the old engine gently forward. Tom poised on the step, jumped as the wheels slowed, and ran to the points lever.

'Jacta est alea,' said Mr. Tarrant as Tom climbed back after closing the points behind them.

'Much less than an empire for us to conquer, sir.'

'Yes, thank goodness.'

The first Broomfleet crossing was normally left open between the passing of the midnight mail and the milk train. The second would have been closed but for Mr. Tarrant's telephone call. As they flashed through Tom saw the keeper leaning on the gate in his shirt-sleeves, and giving a perfunctory wave as if to acknowledge a perfectly common routine. There was little for Tom to do, apart from occasional bouts of firing. He spent most of the twenty-five minutes to Selby peering ahead along the glimmering track. Mr. Tarrant drove with professional calm, not ceaselessly fiddling with the controls as Tom would have done, fretting for some imagined perfect setting. Still, his manner was slightly different from Harry Hackby's; though Harry loved his engine it was still the tool of his trade, a device for getting a dead weight from one place to another; to Mr. Tarrant it was an instrument in the sense that a piano is one, rather than in the sense that a hammer is.

At first he did not speak at all. The noise of the locomotive—lighter but also louder than those Tom had driven during May—would have made his normal tones inaudible, and it was difficult to imagine how he could raise that particular voice to a shout. Only when they approached the Eastrington junction he eased the regulator down, reducing the clatter and rush to a milder rumble. As the lit turret that was the signal-box slipped past he leaned from the cab to peer backwards along the other line, then turned and cupped his hands to Tom's ear.

'I have never driven the Wold Line,' he hooted. 'It will be interesting to see how she takes the gradients.'

Without waiting for an answer he opened the regulator and steamed for Selby. Tom was amused. Mr. Tarrant's voice, though utterly different in quality, had held exactly the same excitement as that with which Woffles used to announce the latest speed trial for his Bentley along the Bicester Road. That men so apparently dissimilar could have at least one element in common was, if you thought about it, an encouraging phenomenon.

Nothing else happened all the way to Selby. The line ran endlessly straight and level, all the gates were open, all the signals were up to show that the mail-train had cleared the section. They flicked through the cutting at Cliffe. A minute later Mr. Tarrant closed the regulator decisively. The urgency of onward movement changed to a sliding drift, with the loudest noise the bang of the rail-joints. By the time they reached the points of the Beverley branch line they had slowed to a walking-pace. Mr. Tarrant barely needed to brake to let Tom jump down and open the points of the mill spur a hundred yards further on.

He closed them as soon as the engine was past, ran to it, reached into the cab and took the lamp, boltcutters, chain and padlock from where he had laid them ready on the floor. The chain on the gate was a poor rusty thing and sheared with little pressure. He slipped the new chain ready through the bars, swung the gates open and waved the white lamp. The trucks were still lined up where he had seen them two days back. He ran to the sidings points, heaved both levers over and waved the lamp again. With dream slowness Mr. Tarrant brought the engine up against the buffers of the first truck so gently that the clank of touching might not have been heard twenty yards away. As the buffers compressed Tom slipped under, hooked and locked the couplings, ducked out and ran down the line of trucks. Only the last one had its handbrake set. Tom loosed it, hung the red lamp at its tail and waved for the final time. The first noise that could have told the old nightwatchman, dozing in his shed at the far side of the mill, that anything was up was the bang and bang and bang of the couplings as the eight trucks jerked into movement. Tom trotted behind them to the gates, closed and fastened them with the new chain and padlock, tossed the keys over for someone to find in the morning, and scampered along to open the points onto the main line.

'Four minutes twenty seconds,' said Mr. Tarrant as Tom climbed panting back into the cab. 'We appear to have gained eight minutes already. I wish I could study the faces of the signalmen as they watch us go through with eight trucks behind us.'

'It's the fellow at Eastrington I'm worried about.'

'I shall speak to him firmly and that will suffice.'

He sounded so confident that he roused an obstinate element in Tom, as though this was no way to treat the luck-god.

'Almost too easy so far, Sir?' he answered.

'Indeed we should by no means count our chickens, hm hm. Now fire her well up, my boy, for those gradients.'

As they moved off Tom discovered that the nature of the adventure had changed. Perhaps it was partly that they were now moving backwards, peering along the line across the coal-tender; perhaps partly that with the addition of trucks the old locomotive seemed to have altered her nature. Coming up the line she had almost bounced along, as though it would be no problem for her to forsake the rails and steam lightly across the mist-banded levels. Now she moved seriously, ponderously, hauling the kind of load she was built for, eight full trucks, not carrying material of real mass such as coals, but still inertia enough to mean that they had barely accelerated to a decent speed before they passed the crossing at Cliffe. Tom, straightening from the fire-box, saw the crossing-keeper's goodnight wave falter and his whole body straighten as he became aware of the trucks. Then he was gone. Mr. Tarrant nodded happily. Tom guessed that but for the racket of the engine he would have heard him actually chortling.

For the next six miles the line crossed only lanes and tracks; many of the crossings had no gates, and those that had were left open for the milk train, due in four hours time. They steamed quietly along at about thirty miles an hour, a perfectly safe speed on such a clear night and that far-reaching track. Travelling backwards, though a quite normal procedure, was greatly enjoyable, with the night air streaming into their faces unmixed with the reek of their own smoke. The world was full of natural odours, cattle and the dried mud of the dykes and autumn grass and fainter river smells. Tom worked at his fire, banking it up bit by bit to a glowing mass, ready for the climbs ahead. He was bending to this task when he heard the note of the cylinders soften, then the brakes suck and sigh. He swung the fire-door shut, rose, and turned, steadying himself against the deceleration. Some way down the line a red lamp was swinging slowly from side to side. The signal lamp beyond it was red too. Mr. Tarrant brought the train to a halt between the platforms of Howden. Tom heard him muttering as the noise of movement stilled.

'Come what may . . . come what may . . .'

'What's up?' said Tom.

'Samuel Paddick, I imagine, the crossing-keeper at Cliffe—he has always been a fusser. No doubt he has telephoned through to the stationmaster here. New man. I wish I knew him better.'

Mr. Tarrant leaned from the exiguous cab. The lamp was moving towards them through the darkened station. Quick steps ran before it. A hand-torch blazed in his face.

'Daddy? Tom?'

'Judy!'

'Miss Barnes is here. I drove her out and asked the station-master to stop you. It was the only thing I could think of. He's been sweet about it.'

Tom managed to push through past Mr. Tarrant and down onto the platform.

'Turn that light off,' he said. 'I can't see a thing.'

It was dark again, pitch after the glare.

'Kate?' he said.

'I've let you down,' she said. 'I told him.'

'Oh. What's he going to do?'

She went on as if she hadn't heard the question.

'He must have smelt something was up—he's like that. He didn't ask direct, but . . . I promise you I couldn't have got the men down to Belmont Street without his knowing, and he could have stopped them whatever I said. I was very careful. I only told him bit by bit. He seemed quite pleased with the whole thing —I thought he was going to try and make out it was something the Party had planned . . . Only this evening he told me he'd changed his mind.'

'The men aren't going to be there.'

'Oh yes, they'll be there, waiting. Only you won't come.'

'How . . .'

'He telephoned Mr. Panhard yesterday and told him there was a rumour of the strikers trying to steal the train tonight. You see?'

Tom grunted. He could see her now, and Judy, and a man— presumably the stationmaster, beyond them. Yes, he thought, that would be Ricardo's style—to promise relief, excitement, a victorious skirmish, and then to see that it never came, pre-vented by the sinister forces of oppression. What had begun as a lark, which could fail without disaster, was now something more serious. Mr. Tarrant's voice spoke above his head.

'Come what may I am going to take this train along the Wold Line.'

'Of course you are, Daddy,' said Judy. 'Tom will think of something.'

The stationmaster coughed, anxious but diffident.

'Kate,' said Tom. 'Do you know where they're going to try and stop us.'

'No . . . but I think he does. There was something, almost a joke . . . before he went out tonight. He was excited . . . Yes, he knew something.'

'Then it will be Drewton Cutting again,' said Tom.

'Oh, yes, of course,' said Judy.

'How can you be sure?' protested Mr. Tarrant.

'It's the only place they know,' said Tom. 'They aren't railwaymen. They've seen a train stopped there before—it's absolutely isolated. Bertie . . .'

'Young Panhard!' exclaimed Mr. Tarrant. Evidently he had not caught the name when Kate had said it. For the first time there was a real note of doubt in his voice.

'I think we could talk him out of it,' said Tom slowly. 'If we explained what we're up to.'

He could sense the other's disbelief in the silence.

'I know something Bertie doesn't,' he said. 'I can offer him a bargain, because he really wants to know. I think he'd take it.'

'It will be no use if we are de-railed already,' said Mr. Tarrant. 'We have not the time to go so slowly that we can spot every obstacle.'

'No,' said Tom. 'I've got to get there first.'

'I've got the Lagonda,' said Judy.

'And Judy could fire the engine,' said Mr. Tarrant. 'She has done it before, have you not, my dear?'

There was a wistful note, recalling old days and a different level of companionship.

'No, let me do that,' said Kate.

'Miss Barnes?' exclaimed Mr. Tarrant. 'Er, *the* Miss Barnes, hm hm?'

'That's right, *and* a docker's daughter. I ought to be able to stoke a boiler—I'm as strong as an ox. Let Miss Judy go with Tom. If he's going to talk them out of it, and he's got her there . . . but if it's me, you see?'

Yes, thought Tom, Judy's presence would make a difference, alter the balance quite perceptibly. Did Kate guess—did she know —that Tom's bargain-piece was the real name of Ricardo? A web of other questions tried to ramify in his mind. No time for that now . . .

'Right,' he said. 'Give us as much time as you can, sir. The tunnel before the cutting's about three hundred yards long, with a gap in the middle. Try to come out of it at a walking-pace. If the line's clear I'll wave a white lamp or a torch from side to side, if I can find one. Otherwise it'll have to be a white cloth. It must be about fifteen miles by road—can you do that in twenty-five minutes, Judy?'

'Twenty,' she said.

'So if you're at the cutting in half an hour, sir . . .'

'I will be there.'

The stationmaster coughed again.

'One moment, if you please . . .' he began.

'Ah, yes,' said Mr. Tarrant, beginning to climb down from the cab. 'Smith, isn't it? I'm very pleased to meet you. Now I want you to arrange something for me. The signalman at East-rington . . . drive carefully, my dear.'

'You too,' said Judy.

The voices faded behind them as she and Tom hurried along the platform.

The Lagonda had still only one light working. The single beam cut a narrow tunnel through the night, far-lit but with no side-vision at all. The Brantingham chauffeur had made an adequate job of mending the latch on the driver's door but had merely lashed the near-side front door into place, so Tom sat in the back, staring ahead over Judy's shoulder as they rushed down to Howden, squealed round the sharp corner into the main Hull road and accelerated east. The battered bodywork squeaked and rattled and the exhaust-noise echoed back from the walls of the little town as Judy worked ruthlessly up through the gears. The car seemed to Tom to be making barely less racket than a locomotive. Once clear of the buildings Judy treated the road like a racing-track, taking the sharpest line through the curves and exploiting the camber on the wrong side of the road as she did so. She drove very erect, prim in her concentration. Her ear was only an inch from his cheek and he was strongly aware of her closeness, not as a sensual joy but as an expression of partner-ship in the task in hand. He felt her relaxation as they reached top speed down the first long straight.

'That's a stunning girl,' she said suddenly.

'Yes.'

'I'd no idea. This man, I don't know his name, he was playing with her like a cat with a bird, keeping her there till it was too late for her to do anything. He pulled the telephone out of the wall before he left and there wasn't another one for miles. But she knew a boy who had a motor-bike near there and she got him to bring her out. They missed you by five minutes. Howden was the first place I could think of stopping you.'

'You did marvellously. I think this is going to be all right after all.'

'She's desperate about this man, Tom.'

'I know.'

(What did that mean? How could he imagine what Kate might feel? When she had first told him about Ricardo her attitude had been deliberately ironic but once or twice the thrust of passion had almost cracked the surface—not the simple passion of love for a lover, but the tangled frustrations of love for a cause, of toiling years, of being betrayed and of betraying. It was good, at least, that Judy realised. Good but typical.)

'I'm not sure that she actually had to tell him,' he said. 'She may have thought she did, but I suspect it was more of a way of making her mind up. If he let her down, you see . . .'

'Yes.'

The first signpost to Eastrington flashed past. After driving for two days round this network of roads he knew that turn well —had in fact parked the Lagonda a mile or so up it in order to walk back along the line and chat, pretending to be a journalist, with the signalman who controlled the crucial junction. He craned north, hoping to see the silvery smoke of the old engine pulling away along the Wold line but the hedge blocked his view. They should be just about there by now, and through the junction without any trouble if Mr. Tarrant had managed things as smoothly as he had shown every sign of doing. Mentally Tom compared times. The roads were much less direct, but at the speed Judy was driving she might be almost as good as her word and make it to the lane above the cutting in twenty minutes . . . say five minutes down across the rabbit-nibbled slope of the

Warrens, five to talk to Bertie . . . the train had the gradients to cope with, and two gated crossings to stop at, open the gates, stop again to close them, move on . . .

The second Eastrington signpost glimmered ahead, still shining as if with its own light when the beam of the Lagonda's single lamp had passed it by. Tom's mind registered the oddity a moment before he realised that there must be another car coming down that side-road. As they whipped past the turn the interior of the Lagonda glowed for a moment in the beam of far headlights. The road was fast but tricky, a series of longish straights ending in variable curves, some gentle enough for Judy to take flat out, others forcing her to change down, keeping the revs close to the limit and roaring away into the next straight. She seemed to know the road perfectly until she misjudged a corner and had to brake sharply near the crown. Tom felt the back wheels beginning to slew and clutched at the safety-bracket on the door-pillar. Judy twitched the wheel, caught the skid, straightened and accelerated out of the bend.

'Sorry,' she said. 'I thought it was the next one.'

'Don't worry. You're doing marvellously. I don't believe Segrave could drive this road faster.'

'Somebody is,' she said.

Tom twisted to look through the rear window. He saw the hedge of the previous curve whiten, and then, just as the Lagonda reached the end of the straight, the darkness glowed with a strong slant beam. The next straight was shorter, but the following car was again almost in sight before the bend hid it. They boomed up a straggling one-streeted village. The brick houses stood suddenly sharp-shadowed on either side of them and their own single beam seemed lost in the glare of the huge headlights behind.

'Pull the blind down, darling,' said Judy quietly.

Tom tugged the canvas from its roller and clipped it fast, cutting out the blaze through the back window. Now they were driving in a pocket of dark along a floodlit street. Judy had her foot right down. The surface was cobbles, and the car bounced and leaped as she swung to the right of the road and took a blind corner almost on the pavement.

'You don't have to . . .' muttered Tom.

'The camber's wrong the other side,' she said. 'You can come off there at forty. Gosh, I think he may have! No.'

The lights of the following car wavered in their smooth swing across the left-hand houses, and when they caught the Lagonda again they seemed to have fallen back. That village became the next one with hardly a gap between the buildings and the road was cobbled all the way, with great dips and potholes near the kerbs. Judy hogged the crown, bouncing through the night at over sixty, but the lights of the car behind closed and closed. Tom could hear the beat of a far larger engine before a twin horn started to blare.

'Might as well let him through,' he said.

'The road gets better in a minute. Tell him to get off my tail.'

Tom wound his window down and gesticulated to the other driver to fall back. The only answer was a renewed blaring of the horns and a sense of the headlights closing to swallow the Lagonda up until the monster could not have been a yard from their back bumper. His arm-waving became more a gesture of fury than advice to be patient.

'Not impressed,' he called. 'Do let him through, darling.'

'In a moment. He must be bonkers. Now . . .'

The houses were gone. Without slowing she pulled to the left as the tyres hummed onto the tarmac. Tom beckoned the pursuer through with generous waves. At once a long bonnet nosed into the gap, an open tourer, details invisible, a roaring dark mass behind its headlights. Tall at its wheel the driver came into view. He had no human head, just an indeterminate mass protruding above the shoulders.

'Look out!' yelled Judy. Tom was flung against the back of her seat as she braked. 'Idiot!' came her voice. He glimpsed the road ahead, but it wasn't there, only an angled slice of grass between the hedge and the other car. His grip was torn from the safety-bracket as the near wheel leaped from the bank. Something slammed at his head. He was aware of Judy, still fighting with the wheel and still yelling but being whirled away from him as the dark universe swung round making no noise, with him in a trance of pain at its centre. He was floating in the dark, flying, aware next of the groaning grunt of air being squeezed from his lungs as a huge mass shoved into his back.

He tried to get to his feet but slithered on sloping earth and fell onto hardness. His ears rang and he could taste blood in his mouth. He pushed himself onto his hands and knees, conscious of the feel of metalled road but having no notion why it should be there. Heavy footsteps sounded to his left, running. He staggered to his feet and turned to face them. There was a car standing fifty yards off, with its tail-lights glowing red and its headlamps whitening the distance. Silhouetted, a creature came pounding towards him, a human body with a log instead of a head. Drearily Tom drew breath and brought his leaden hands up to fight.

'You all right?' said the creature in a strange gruff voice.

'I suppose so. What . . .'

'Serve you right. I'll be toddling along then.'

'You utter pig!'

That wasn't him or the monster. It was Judy! Yes, driving . . . Where . . . Oh, Judy!

'Judy!'

That *was* the monster, but in a quite different voice.

'I didn't know,' it went on. 'I say, I thought it was only Tom. We'd seen him driving around in your bus . . .'

'Woffles, come here at once and help me out.'

'Right oh. I say, I'm terribly sorry. I thought . . .'

Tom turned, his head still ringing but his memory leaping back. The Lagonda was on its side in the ditch. Judy's head and shoulders were protruding through the window of the strapped-up door. The monster—Woffles, gripped her beneath the arms and lifted her clear, right over his masked head, and down.

'Where's Tom?' she said. 'Oh, darling, are you all right?'

'Are you?'

'Not a scratch, I think. You sound a bit groggy. Is that blood?'

'I'm all right, just stunned and winded. I suppose I must have been thrown out before you went over. I landed on the bank, I think.'

'Well, if you're both all right,' said Woffles.

'We're coming with you,' said Judy. 'We've got to see Bertie.'

'I don't know . . .'

'Woffles!'

'Oh, all right.'

She sat on his lap, cuddling against him and picking the glass out of his hair by touch. He could feel, as after the strikers' attack on her car, the tremors of shock quivering through her body, and this time he shared them. The whip of the night air seemed to have cleared his mind completely. The Bentley's engine snarled and drummed as Woffles pushed it through the tortuous corners of North Cave. Tom felt Judy's fingers caress a tender patch above his left ear.

'You're going to have a terrific lump there tomorrow,' she said.

'If that's all . . .'

'And the Lagonda. Oh! I think you're still bleeding! Tom, oughtn't we to get you to a doctor?'

'Got to see Bertie first. It's become much more important. Kate's friend . . . Woffles, I take it Bertie's at Drewton Cutting.'

'How did you know?'

'Guessed. How many with him?'

'Half a dozen. Some of the chaps have lost interest, and some . . .'

'You late?'

'Course not. I mean, dash it. I was out at Eastrington seeing which way the train went. I thought you'd be on it, but . . . If it went through the Wolds, you see, that was fine and I could beaver up and tell them at the cutting, but if it went the other way I had to hare into Hull with a letter from Bertie for the top bobby. You see?'

'Why did you push us off the road?' said Judy.

'I didn't know it was you, I tell you. I knew it was your bus, but Tom's been driving around in it. I mean, I was shirty enough already at whoever it was for not letting me through, and then when he started to wave his arm around like that and I recognised his jacket . . . I mean, I couldn't have known he was in the *back* seat, dash it . . . I'm afraid I lost my rag . . .'

'Poor Woffles,' said Judy. 'What bad luck.'

'Really? That's jolly decent of you.'

'Provided Tom's all right and you get us to the cutting in time.'

'Right oh. Just you watch. Nearly there.'

They were silent for a minute or two, but as they climbed rowdily between the hedges of a narrow unfamiliar lane beyond

North Cave, he spoke again. His normal eager burble was muted and strained.

'I'm getting a bit fed up with all this,' he said. 'It's not nearly the fun I'd imagined. Nothing much happens, and when it does it goes wrong. I mean, I might have killed you both, I suppose. I admit I'm pretty sick with Tom, but dash it . . . And Bertie spends all his time writing letters and reading drearie Bolshie pamphlets. He's getting pretty difficult to argue with, you know? Sometimes I think he's going off his nut, and next thing he'll have us marching about in coloured shirts and giving fancy salutes . . . I think I'm going to pack it in. Do you know anything about Kenya? I met a chap, you see. You can buy whole mountains there for a few thousand quid, and there's masses to shoot.'

'Woffles, that's an awfully good idea,' said Judy, wholly earnest and sympathetic, as though they had been discussing his future strolling on the lawns at Rokesley.

'Mother doesn't think so,' he said.

'Tom and I have formed a conspiracy to break the power of parents. Why don't you join?'

Woffles grunted and concentrated on his driving. The lane twisted through a series of corners, climbing all the way. They reached a larger road and plunged across, up what seemed to be a cart-track. The big car lurched and slithered. Its engine roared in erratic bursts as Woffles, in low gear and with a lot of clutch-slipping, picked his way among the ruts or careered at a freakish tilt with his near wheels up on the bank and his off wheels on the smoother ridge between the ruts. They climbed almost a mile, past woodland and over the brow of a hill where for a moment Tom saw all the uplands lying dark under the stars, with a black cleft almost straight ahead that must be Drewton Cutting. Then steep down and sharp left, steeper still along the edge of rough pasture. Tall hedges made a sudden tunnel. The headlights swept across two cars standing in an open patch. Woffles drew in beside them and switched off lights and engine.

'Noisy kind of secret,' said a man's voice out of the dark. 'Two? Hello! Passengers?'

'Where's Ber . . . One, I mean?'

'Down the line putting out the lamps. We saw your headlights so we decided to go ahead.'

Tom opened his door.

'Try and borrow a torch,' he whispered as Judy eased herself free. 'I should think Woffles must carry one.'

He climbed out and stretched, wincing with unsuspected aches; but his head now seemed perfectly clear, indeed full of an almost visionary stillness and certainty, as if he had reached that stage in a logic problem where, though the solution is not yet known, the belief that a solution exists and is ready to be discovered transforms itself into a certainty, a fact along with all the other facts in the problem. Without waiting for permission he picked his way on down the path. It dipped still more steeply to run slantwise down the cutting wall. The moon, westering now with the wear of night, shone almost directly along the cleft, so that the long curve of the rails glimmered into the distance. Far down them red lamps glowed, some still, some moving. Tom adjusted his pace to the distance between the sleepers and broke into a trot. Footsteps crunched on ballast. A dark figure, hooded, emerged from the illusory clarity of moonlight and strode towards him.

'Two?' it said.

'No. Where's Bertie?'

'Halt.'

'I've got to see Bertie. Something vital to tell him.'

'I said "Halt." '

Tom had already done so. He thought he recognised the voice from one of the Rokesley shoots, but couldn't put a name to it.

'Woffles brought me,' he said.

'Oh. Oh, well, I suppose in that case . . . Right oh. One's at the signal-box. But I say, be a good chap and don't call people by their names. You're looking for One and Two brought you.'

'I'll remember.'

'Aren't you Hankey? I thought you were driving this train that's supposed to be coming. Is that all off? What a bore!'

'No it's coming. Not long. Don't do anything till you hear from One.'

Tom trotted on. He could see almost a dozen lamps now, some arranged in pairs on either track and others still being carried towards him. The shapes of men solidified.

'Heard it coming?' said a new voice, deliberately languid as if

241

to mask excitement—Dick.

'Few minutes more,' said Tom. 'Where's One?'

'Tom! What's up?'

'I've got to see him.'

'If you must. I say, One!'

'Here. They coming?'

'No. It's Tom. On foot.'

'Is it, by Jove? All right, you fellows. Carry on. One more set of lamps twenty paces on, Five and Nine hide theirs under their jackets but get ready to wave them. Rest of you well up the banks and lying flat. Don't move till you hear Three's whistle. Tom, back here.'

As Tom passed the others he saw by the glow of the lamps that two of them were wearing cloth caps and collarless shirts and had their faces streaked with grease. He found one more masked figure waiting by the line a few paces further on. So strong was the personality that despite the darkness and the hood Tom found himself almost seeing the carefully amiable smile and saurian gaze.

'Keep your voice down,' said Bertie. 'Don't want to alarm the troops. Well?'

'I want you to let this train through.'

'Not on your life.'

'Listen . . .'

'No, hang on a tick. This way.'

They crunched towards the dark block of the signal-box. Bertie led the way behind it.

'Stand against the wall there,' he ordered.

'There's not much time.'

'Enough. Fire away.'

There was a click and light from a hand-torch glared into Tom's eyes. Beyond that white centre everything—a moment before dark but distinguishable shapes in the moonlit cleft—was now pure black.

'Great Scott!' said Bertie. 'Been in a scrap?'

'Woffles ran us off the road. Listen, do you know who's driving this train?'

'One of your Bolshie pals?'

'Mr. Tarrant.'

'Bosh.'

'No, it's true. He's doing it of his own free will, and what's more the stuff in the trucks is his to dispose of. Judy's here. She'll tell you if you don't believe me.'

'I don't see it makes any difference. Tarrant's an ass. The fact he may have the law on his side doesn't matter a blind bean. If this train goes through it'll encourage the strikers to carry on, and that's that. We've got to break their will.'

'You're wrong. Listen, I've been living down in the docks. The mood's awful, and the worse it gets the longer the strike will last and the bitterer it will become. That's exactly what the men you're fighting against want.'

'My sources of information are as good as yours. They don't agree.'

'Hutton?'

For the first time Bertie hesitated. Footsteps sounded on the track. The beam swung away and illuminated a tall man in a hood with Judy looking tiny beside him.

'Two?' said Bertie.

'Here,' said Woffles, as though answering Call-over in School Yard.

'May I have a number?' said Judy. 'Something-and-a-half?'

The beam swung back and seemed to hold Tom against the signal-box by mere pressure of light.

'It won't wash,' said Bertie. 'We've got to stick to our plan—break the men's will. The train will go through all right, but there won't be anything in it except a message from me.'

'Can't you see that's exactly what the Reds want?' said Tom. 'Where they'd only got twenty real members in the docks yesterday, they'll have two hundred tomorrow—and next week there'll be rioting and looting, and the troops called in, and men dead in their own streets!'

'Do you know,' said Woffles, with that tone of amazement typical of him when he found himself actually following an argument, 'I'm not sure Tom isn't right. I know how I'd feel if I was in those laddies' shoes.'

'Shut up,' snapped Bertie. 'This is my pigeon.'

'Mine too,' said Woffles. 'Whose idea was all this in the first place, I'd like to know?'

'Do shut up,' said Bertie.

He was answered by a rustling sound, and the flop of an object hitting the ground near his feet. The beam dropped, picked out a loose black cloth and swung to Woffles, now bare-headed and even in anger looking startled by the energy of the emotion.

'We'll talk about this later,' said Bertie.

'No,' said Woffles. 'Now.'

Judy, close beside him, squeezed his elbow. Tom heard a faint noise further up the bank, glanced that way, and saw a hooded man near the top of the line of rough steps that ran up from the signal-box to the woods. If all the gang were to gather now . . . Not much time to debate and vote . . .

'Tom's right,' said Woffles.

'Of course he is,' said Judy.

'If you let the train through I'll tell you Ricardo's real name,' said Tom.

'Whose name?' said Bertie, swinging the torch back to him.

'Ricardo. The chap at the centre of all the trouble. He's a real Communist. You remember you told me to look for the main Communist cell? Well, I've found it. The men themselves don't know how they're being used. I promise you, if you expose Ricardo, that'll have more effect than stopping twenty trains.'

'And if I don't agree?'

'I'll write to the Home Secretary and put it through the official channels. This is your last chance, Bertie, to bring off something big.'

Beyond the glare of light Tom could sense Bertie's will begin to waver. The night was very quiet, its stillness suddenly emphasised by one far sound—the whistle of a locomotive—Mr. Tarrant nearing the other end of the tunnel. Bertie drew a deep breath to speak, and let it go with a snort. Silence closed round again. Up the bank, metal slithered against metal, a faint but familiar sound, the movement of a safety-catch. Bertie's torchbeam swung.

The man had come down the steps and was only ten feet away. The hooded head was cuddled to the stock of the shot-gun, which wavered as the blaze of the torch caught the night-blinded eyes.

'Down!' yelled Tom, flinging himself sideways. The gun roared in the same instant. Glass tinkled round him, and seemed still to be falling as footsteps hurtled past and up the bank. Hugging the ground Tom twisted his head to see.

The beam of Bertie's torch held the man, now scrambling up the steps. His gun caught between his legs, half-tripping him. He slithered, scrabbled, dropped the gun, started to climb again. Woffles rushed into the circle of light taking the steps two at a time, flung himself upwards, caught an ankle. The man fell, slithered back, tumbled into Woffles, who fell too, loosing his hold. The man started to scrabble up the bank again. There was something almost clownish about his silent, desperate, hopeless flight.

'That's your man,' said Tom as he rose. 'You'd better help collar him. You're in for a shock. Come on Judy. Got the torch?'

'Here.'

'Got to get well beyond the lamps. Quick as you can.'

He started to run down the track, two sleepers at a time, a stretching ungainly lope which almost spilt him headlong as he missed his footing. He shortened his pace to a rapid trot. Two men were coming up in his direction.

'It's all right,' he called. 'Go and give them a hand.'

'What's up? Who fired?'

'Tried to shoot me. Woffles has got him.'

He was past them, past the first lamps. More voices called from up the banks. 'Hold on,' he shouted. 'Stay here. Bertie's got the chap he was after. I'll deal with the train.'

He snatched up one of the second row of lamps and ran on. Now he could hear the breath of the coming locomotive. He slowed, swinging the torch from side to side as he ran. Ahead, a black slab of shadow, loomed the tunnel face. A faint light glowed at its centre, becoming a bronze-gold glow. Above the shadow silver smoke streamed up into the moonlight. He stood to the side of the track, holding the red lamp behind his back and waving the hand-torch to either side. Judy came panting up behind him.

'I think the others are coming,' she gasped.

The train was in the open now. The gold glow vanished as the fire-door closed. He brought the red light into view and shone the torch on himself. The pulse of the cylinders eased as the regulator closed. He put the lamp down and ran forward, waving his arm in the torch-beam. Mr. Tarrant's silver hair craned from the cab.

'Keep her moving!' Tom yelled. 'Judy!'

'Here.'

She seemed to weigh nothing as he heaved her bodily into the cab. He grabbed at the moving handrail, hopped, scrabbled for the step, hauled himself up.

'There appear to be warning lamps,' hooted Mr. Tarrant.

'Nothing there. Full power, sir.'

He heard the renewed effort of steam, but still they seemed to be trundling desperately slowly up the gradient. The comparative lightness of the old engine meant that any sudden increase of power would merely spin the wheels. Mr. Tarrant, shadowed orange and black, stood by the regulator rapt in communion with his machine, feeding fresh steam with gradual touches. Yes, perceptibly they were moving faster.

Tom leaned from the cab and peered forward along the side of the tender. Dark figures emerged from the moonlight, running.

'Kate,' he called. 'Get down out of sight. Give Judy the shovel. Judy. Other side. Anyone who tries to board, hit him. With the flat, not the edge.'

He picked a lump of coal from the tender and crouched at the cab entrance. They must have been doing about ten miles an hour when the first man appeared, yelling 'Stop! Danger! Stop.' He was one of the cloth-cap johnnies, but had forgotten to make his voice match.

'Carry on, sir,' yelled Tom.

The man was running alongside now, reaching for the rail, and the step. He made a valiant try and for a moment his face appeared level with Tom's. With open palm Tom stiff-armed him away, thrusting him out clear of the following wheels. He heard a shout of 'No you don't' from Judy, the slap of metal and a yell. A hooded man was running beside the tender, another was tumbling down the bank. Metal and glass rattled as the lamps went over beneath the wheels. The man was beside the step now, eyeing the distance perhaps but also seeing the impossibility of grabbing a moving handhold in the dark with all those wheels behind to fall into. Everybody was shouting. Now there was the signal-box, and beyond it a sudden patch of clarity and stillness among the rushing, clamouring shadows. Bertie's torch shone down on a patch of ground. Mr. Hutton lay flat on his back, with Woffles kneeling on his chest. Mr. Hutton's hood was gone and he was looking not at Woffles, not at Bertie's black shape beyond the torch-beam, but straight up into the sky, his face pale and completely calm, a martyr blessed with ecstatic vision in the mid-agony of the flame. Tom leaned from the cab to watch. Some of the pursuers stopped running and went over, obscuring his view. Back down the line small flames glimmered where the spilt oil from some of the lamps had caught, and outlined against that erratic light one of Bertie's army continued to run, a mad and shambling figure behind the last truck, a hooded absurdity, waving his arms in hopeless gestures, the last wisp of a nightmare.

The whistle blew, deafeningly close. Tom withdrew into the cab, took the shovel from Judy and gestured to her to tuck herself into the corner, out of the way. He flicked the fire-door open with the tip of the shovel and bent to inspect the coals. The tunnel closed round them, but they were doing some twenty miles an hour now, moving fast enough to clear their own smoke. When he turned to shovel coal from the tender he saw the two girls sitting in the opposite corners of the floor. Judy might have been on her own hearthrug, gazing dreamily into the embers after a long day, then lifting her eyes to smile at Tom; but Kate sat motionless, eyes closed, the muscles of her face taut, like an initiate undergoing her trial before some ferocious altar.

For more than a mile they thumped up through the close-echoing dark, bathed in the gold warmth from the fire. Then with the usual shocking suddenness they were out into another moonlit cutting, this time at the top of the Wolds. At the same moment, between one stroke of the cylinders and the next, the pulse of the engine changed. The beat of the wheels against the rail-ends took up a sharper rhythm on the level, and sharper still as the gradient tilted in their favour and they began to rattle through a series of long curves, steep down all the way to Hull.

After the dash and striving, the almost trance-like impetus of action, ordinariness closed round. There was cheering as the train steamed into the darkened wasteland behind Belmont

Street, changing to cries of amazement and distrust at the sight of Mr. Tarrant. Fierce disputes broke out among the men. Kate roused herself and spoke to them from the step of the locomotive, but in a strained and hesitant manner, lacking any of her usual fire. Only her talismanic presence was enough to tip the balance and persuade most of the men to start work. Then that took far longer than Tom had allowed for, and was barely begun when a night-patrolling policeman turned up. There were more arguments, until Mr. Tarrant left with the man to thrash the matter out with his superiors at the police station. Soon it became apparent that there was no prospect of returning the locomotive to Brantingham before the main lines were busy again. The first glimmerings of dawn lightened the sky. Tom felt quite unable to force his tired brain to calculate further consequences. It was as though the intricate network of tensions had for a few hours spun itself into a single strand so that he could draw it through the one possible opening—in a dream-like way he found himself thinking of this as the actual cuttings and tunnels of the Wold Line—and now beyond those narrows it was spreading out again into its normal unknowable intricacies. He longed to sense the mood of the men. Their early hostility had been a shock, but as they stacked the crates and cartons onto barrows and wheeled them away he began to persuade himself that there was an alteration in their stances, in the tone of their voices, an element of interest and even amusement, very different from anything he had heard or felt in dockland for many weeks.

Two pleasing things happened. A small group of men held what seemed to be a conference a few yards from the track, then came up and asked to speak to Miss Tarrant. They turned out to be some of those who had attacked the Lagonda, and wanted to absolve their guilt in ritual handshakes. Judy was absolutely delighted, clearly still feeling something of the same need. Chaste, film-starish kissing supplanted the handshakes. Tom wished he had a camera.

A little later he heard a disturbance at one of the entrances where the barrows were being wheeled away. Wearily he began to climb down to see what the trouble might be, but Judy called 'Oh, look!' in a voice that made him go back and stand beside her in the cab. The men by the entrance were a dark mass against a wooden fence, made harder yet to distinguish by the contrast with a single pale streetlight beyond. Into the glow of this lamp, silhouetted above the fence, rose a shape, Mr. Tarrant teetering on the shoulders of the men. Erratic cheers broke out, admittedly mixed with the odd cat-call and boo. Mr. Tarrant raised a hand, waved, lost his balance and was lowered in an undignified manner to the ground.

'I bet they never do that for Mummy,' said Judy.

'Perhaps you'll get them to do it for you one day.'

Tom drowsed, resting his head on his arms on the rim of the cab wall. He was conscious that on the whole he had done right, but that this was really through no virtue of his own. Exactly as, very occasionally in history, a just war gets itself fought and almost by accident one set of bishops can really tell the men going off to be slaughtered that they will die in a good cause—though neither bishops nor soldiers can at the time distinguish this from the innumerable other wars in which all such blessings have been meaningless—so Tom felt that however blunderingly he had been doing things that later on he might be able to remember without a sour taste in the mouth. Not all, of course, was bliss. Even a just war has its rapes and ruins. He was distressed for Kate, disturbed about what Bertie might do next, and certainly in no mood to believe that he had by more than a hairsbreadth diminished the ignorance and intransigence of either of the two forces he had been caught between. There was even an area of guilt, made no more comfortable by it not being concerned with anything he could have altered. His thoughts kept returning to Mr. Hutton. It was clear to him what had happened. Hutton had left Kate in order to be present at the ambush. He could make his way down through the woods and join Bertie's party, hooded like them, lurk on the fringes waiting for any opportunity for trouble. He might have intended from the first that somebody should be hurt, or even killed, thus jerking the screw round another turn, increasing the bitterness and anger on both sides. Perhaps, consciously or unconsciously, he intended the victim to be Tom, the symbolic adversary who had added to all the crimes of luck—birth, education, ease, esteem—by stealing Kate's love. Had Kate told him? He would have guessed, sensed . . . At any rate, when he heard Tom make his offer to Bertie, to name

Ricardo, the logic of killing Tom would have clicked all into place, as smoothly as the sections of a fresh-cleaned shot-gun slot into their catches . . .

'What do you think she's telling them?' whispered Judy, leaning against his side, a light area of warmth.

Tom looked up. Almost all the men were gone now, and it was more light than dark, though still an hour or so before plain day. Well away from the track a dozen men were gathered round Kate. She was talking. Their attitudes were wary, tense, absorbed. One of them tried to break in, impatient and angry. Two others supported him, but were hushed with fierce gestures by the rest. Kate went on, talking quietly and calmly, but looking twenty years older than Tom had ever seen her. He guessed that this must be some inner and trusted group, the Hull Dock Nucleus, perhaps, to whom she was explaining why she had disobeyed orders given her by her Party superior, and who that superior actually was, and why he had done what he had.

'She looks as if she was telling them about the end of the world,' said Judy.

'Yes,' he answered.

14

Biarritz, 6th June, 1929

They ate langoustes and peaches in what had been Bertie Panhard's favourite quayside restaurant. Two of the old waiters were
still there, and the fat woman with the wooden leg appeared with
the old regularity at the kitchen door, stared at the customers
with the same look of mad malice, and clumped away; but of
course nobody remembered them. Judy wrote a postcard to
Nanny and passed it across for Tom to add a few words to.

'What do you mean, "This is our very ship!"'?' he asked.

'Well, it might have been, Nanny won't know, and Tots
won't even understand when she shows it to him.'

He turned the card over. Sure enough a perfectly plausible
cruise-ship bulked among the yachts and fishing-boats. The
already slightly faded sepias of the photograph—unsold from
last season, probably, and so having endured more than its share
of sunlight—did no kind of justice to the blaze and glitter of the
harbour. He turned the card back and wrote his message. She
took and read it.

'What do *you* mean, "Kiss Tots on the soles of his feet for
me."? Tom! What'll Mrs. Billows think? You know she reads
all the postcards and tells the whole village.'

'It's a perfectly respectable place to kiss a baby. They appreciate it.'

'You mean you would appreciate it if Nanny were to kiss you
on the soles of *your* feet. I knew we should have got somebody
three times as old.'

'My Nanny was. She had a moustache and smelt of boiled
cabbage. That's why I think it can do Tots nothing but good to

251

have a Nanny who's roughly the same shape as a normal woman
—especially when you aren't there to put the right ideas into his
mind.'

'I don't feel quite normal yet,' she said.

'You've had two helpings of langoustes.'

'Don't be a pig. What shall we do this afternoon?'

'Um. Take a taxi up into the hills and watch the sunset?'

'Do you want to?'

Her tone was flat. The brooch he had given her when Tots was
born caught a quick dapple of sunlight where the vine above them
shifted a leaf in the breeze off the harbour. At first he had been
irked by not being able to find one which represented a particular
species, but by now he was used to this product of the jeweller's
fantasy, actually liked it and thought of it as a species all on its
own, *Vanessa Judiana*, the ultimate rarity.

'I'm not sure,' he said slowly. 'I feel very yes and no . . .'

'Have we got any spare money?'

(By the marriage settlement her allowance from her parents
exactly matched his Treasury salary, but she always insisted on
paying it straight into his account.)

'A bit,' he said.

'Let's lose it.'

'Right oh.'

The Casino had so far modernised itself in the past three years
that it now boasted a set of tables for Blackjack, which Judy
chose to play. Tom, in no mood even for that level of decision-
making, stuck to Chemmy. After a couple of hours they met to
drink the Casino's version of tea—a lukewarm yellow wash tast-
ing faintly of lemon—and compare luck. Tom had won two
hundred francs and Judy was eighty down. Despite his mild
good fortune Tom was bored, but tried to keep his voice neutral
when he asked whether she wanted to go on. She tilted her head
sideways and simply nodded, but her eyes were glistening. He
recognised the symptoms of one of those violent gusts of impulse
which occasionally blew through her, and which she never tried
to resist, but gave way to with complete and almost mystical
trust. He was glad now that she would need to come to him for
fresh funds, though it would be tragic to spoil this longed-for and

so far blissful holiday with a row over money.

Tom lost his winnings quite quickly, won a bit, lost that, and went on down till he reached his modest limit. He strolled off to see whether Judy was ready to leave. Spectators had begun to gather round her table. She had a fair-sized pile of chips in front of her. She looked up, as if sensing his presence, smiled, and signalled with her head for him to come round and watch. He went and stood behind her. She seemed not to notice him any more, but played on, taking strange risks, completely ignoring the odds, drawing a card when there was barely a chance of making her number or refusing chances which anyone else would have taken. Usually she bet to the limit, but when the dealer suggested she might like to move to the high-stake table she shook her head. Three times she hit a losing streak, and Tom ached to drag her away, but the bad luck didn't last and she began to win again. Then, in the middle of an apparently invincible run she stood up, tipped the dealer with a five hundred franc note, gathered up her chips and left the table. She had won twelve thousand three hundred francs.

They walked along the quay towards the ship, he still tingling with the vicarious drama, but she quiet with that almost shocked sobriety that comes when you know that the luck-god has inhabited your body for a while and then left you without his parting curse.

'You could buy yourself a new Lagonda,' he said.

'No . . . I don't think so. You realise it happened because we didn't go up into the hills?'

'In a negative sort of way, I suppose so.'

'In a positive way, darling. I've never told you . . . I'm not sure I really ought to now . . . but you gave me this, didn't you, so I think you probably know . . .'

Her hand rose to her neck-line, bright pink fingernails long and oval on the blue of the brooch.

'That afternoon,' she said. 'The butterflies on the hill . . . whenever things are bad, f'rinstance when Tots was being born and it hurt so much . . . I take that afternoon out and look at it. I've still got it. I'll never let it go.'

She dropped her hand and felt for his. They walked on, slowly, through the dusk that smelt of motors, and sea-weed, and fresh-cooked food.

'Say it,' she said. 'It's all right?'

'And the night?'

'It's part of the afternoon, somehow. And so's the next day, even, when you were gone and I had to be bright as a beastly begonia because I wasn't going to let Bertie guess how much I minded—that's part of it too.'

'I spent that day in trains, going further and further away.'

'I felt you going, every single kilometre. What I'm trying to say is . . . I wish I could talk like your friend Kate . . . Look, nothing's ever the same. If we'd gone up there we couldn't have helped wanting it to be the same, and it would be changed. And that's right. I want things to change. I want to be part of the change, to accept it, to swim in it. That's what's so marvellous about being alive now!'

'Not stunning?'

She remembered the reference at once and laughed.

'That was *that* year's word,' she said.

She began to run, still holding his hand, pulling him towards the boat.

Peter Dickinson, the son of English parents, was born in Zambia. He returned to England at age seven, and attended Eton and Cambridge. After serving for seventeen years as assistant editor of *Punch,* he turned to writing books at age forty. Since that time he has written eleven detective stories and thirteen children's books. Several of both kinds have won prestigious prizes, including the Crime Writer's Association Gold Dagger and the Carnegie Medal for children's books. Among his more recent books are *Tefuga, Death of a Unicorn, Hindsight,* and *The Last Houseparty.*